Is it WRONG to TRY to PICK UP GIRLS IN A DUNGEON?

VOLUME 10

FUJINO OMORI

ILLUSTRATION BY SUZUHITO YASUDA

NEW YORK

IS IT WRONG TO TRY TO PICK UP GIRLS IN A DUNGEON?, Volume 10
FUJINO OMORI

Translation by Andrew Gaippe
Cover art by Suzuhito Yasuda

Original Japanese edition published in 2016 by SB Creative Corp.
This English edition is published by arrangement with SB Creative Corp., Tokyo, in care of Tuttle-Mori Agency, Inc., Tokyo.

Yen On
1290 Avenue of the Americas
New York, NY 10104

Visit us at yenpress.com
facebook.com/yenpress
twitter.com/yenpress
yenpress.tumblr.com
instagram.com/yenpress

First Yen On Edition: December 2017

Yen On is an imprint of Yen Press, LLC.
The Yen On name and logo are trademarks of Yen Press, LLC.

Library of Congress Cataloging-in-Publication Data
Names: Ōmori, Fujino, author. | Yasuda, Suzuhito, illustrator.
Title: Is it wrong to try to pick up girls in a dungeon? / Fujino Omori ; illustrated by Suzuhito Yasuda.
Other titles: Danjon ni deai o motomeru nowa machigatte iru darōka. English.
Description: New York : Yen ON, 2015– | Series: Is it wrong to try to pick up girls in a dungeon? ; 10
Identifiers: LCCN 2015029144 | ISBN 9780316339155 (v. 1 : pbk.) |
ISBN 9780316340144 (v. 2 : pbk.) | ISBN 9780316340151 (v. 3 : pbk.) |
ISBN 9780316340168 (v. 4 : pbk.) | ISBN 9780316314794 (v. 5 : pbk.) |
ISBN 9780316394161 (v. 6 : pbk.) | ISBN 9780316394178 (v. 7 : pbk.) |
ISBN 9780316394185 (v. 8 : pbk.) | ISBN 9780316562645 (v. 9 : pbk.) |
ISBN 9780316442459 (v. 10 : pbk.)
Subjects: | CYAC: Fantasy. | BISAC: FICTION / Fantasy / General. | FICTION / Science Fiction / Adventure.
Classification: LCC PZ7.1.O54 Du 2015 | DDC [Fic]—dc23
LC record available at http://lccn.loc.gov/2015029144

ISBNs: 978-0-316-44245-9 (paperback)
978-0-316-44246-6 (ebook)

1 3 5 7 9 10 8 6 4 2

LSC-C

Printed in the United States of America

VOLUME 10

FUJINO OMORI
ILLUSTRATION BY SUZUHITO YASUDA

BELL CRANELL

The hero of the story, who came to Orario (dreaming of meeting a beautiful heroine in the Dungeon) on the advice of his grandfather. He belongs to *Hestia Familia* and is still getting used to his job as an adventurer.

HESTIA

A being from the heavens, she is far beyond all the inhabitants of the mortal plane. The head of Bell's *Hestia Familia*, she is absolutely head over heels in love with him!

AIZ WALLENSTEIN

Known as the Sword Princess, her combination of feminine beauty and incredible strength makes her Orario's best-known female adventurer. Bell idolizes her. Currently Level 6, she belongs to *Loki Familia*.

LILLILUKA ERDE

A girl belonging to a race of pygmy humans known as prums, she plays the role of supporter in Bell's battle party. A member of *Hestia Familia*, she's much more powerful than she looks.

WELF CROZZO

A smith who fights alongside Bell as a member of his party, he forged Bell's light armor (Pyonkichi MK-V). Belongs to *Hestia Familia*.

MIKOTO YAMATO

A girl from the Far East. She feels indebted to Bell after receiving his forgiveness. Former member of *Takemikazuchi Familia* who now belongs to *Hestia Familia*.

HARUHIME SANJOUNO

A fox person (renart) from the Far East who met Bell in Orario's Pleasure Quarter. Belongs to *Hestia Familia*.

EINA TULLE

A Dungeon adviser and a receptionist for the organization in charge of regulating the Dungeon, the Guild. She has bought armor for Bell in the past, and she looks after him even now.

CHARACTER & STORY

The Labyrinth City Orario——A large metropolis that sits over an expansive network of underground tunnels and caverns known as the "Dungeon." Bell Cranell came in hopes of realizing his dreams, joining *Hestia Familia* in the process. After being saved by the Sword Princess Aiz Wallenstein, he became infatuated with her and vowed to grow stronger. As he ventured into the Dungeon, he fought fierce battles beside the supporter Lilly, the smith Welf, the girl from the Far East named Mikoto, and the renart Haruhime as a member of *Hestia Familia*. Only now he has encountered a dragon girl named Wiene, a monster who can speak using human words, as well as a group of monsters called "Xenos" just like her. However, mysterious "hunters" have Wiene in their sights…

TSUBAKI COLLBRANDE

A half-dwarf smith belonging to *Hephaistos Familia*. Currently at Level 5, Tsubaki is a terror on the battlefield.

BETE LOGA

A member of a race of animal people known as werewolves. He laughed at Bell's inexperience one night at The Benevolent Mistress. However, he recognized the boy's potential after witnessing Bell's battle with a minotaur.

FINN DEIMNE

Known for his cool head, he is the captain of *Loki Familia*.

OTTAR

An extremely powerful member of *Freya Familia*.

LYU LEON

An elf and former adventurer of extraordinary skill, she currently works as a bartender and waitress at The Benevolent Mistress.

ASFI AL ANDROMEDA

A very gifted creator of magical items. She is the captain of *Hermes Familia*.

OUKA KASHIMA

The captain of *Takemikazuchi Familia*.

WIENE

A vouivre girl Bell meets in the Colossal Tree Labyrinth of the Dungeon. Can speak.

REI

A beautiful siren, she's the Xenos's third in command.

FELS

A mage shrouded in mystery who answers to Ouranos directly.

DIX PERDIX

Captain of *Ikelos Familia* and ill-tempered hunter of rare monsters.

HEPHAISTOS

Deity of Orario's most well-known and respected familia of smiths, *Hephaistos Familia*. She has loose ties with Hestia dating back to their time in the heavens.

LOKI

Deity of Orario's most powerful familia and has a mysterious western accent. Loki is particularly fond of Aiz.

RIVERIA LJOS ALF

High elf and vice commander of the most prominent familia in Orario, *Loki Familia*.

FREYA

Goddess at the head of *Freya Familia*. Her stunning allure is strong enough to enchant the gods themselves. She is a true "Goddess of Beauty."

SYR FLOVER

A waitress at The Benevolent Mistress. She established a friendly relationship with Bell after an unexpected meeting.

HERMES

The deity of *Hermes Familia*. A charming god who excels at toeing the line on all sides of an argument, he is always in the know. Is he keeping tabs on Bell for someone......?

TAKEMIKAZUCHI

The deity of *Takemikazuchi Familia*.

CHIGUSA HITACHI

Another member of *Takemikazuchi Familia*.

LIDO

A friendly lizardman, he leads the Xenos.

OURANOS

The god in charge of the Guild, he also manages the Dungeon.

IKELOS

God of *Ikelos Familia*. Desperate for entertainment, his moral scale is based on whether something is interesting or not.

INTERLUDE
NOTES OF
OBSESSION

There once was a man consumed by obsession.

He was wise, accomplished, and a renowned artisan.

His achievements ranged from crafts of every kind to the creation of whole structures. Even after making countless contributions to culture and society, his fixation on receiving praise from the gods and goddesses drove him to complete a massive white tower. Beautiful yet solemn, it reached closer to the heavens than any other building. A monument most befitting the deities, it was conferred the name "Tower of the Gods."

Indeed, the designer was an undeniable prodigy. No one before or after has ever approached his level of brilliance.

There was nothing he could not build.

The man had no doubt that he was unparalleled.

However, at the far edge of the world, *he became entranced by something.*

It was the entrance to a massive void found in a corner of the continent. A gateway to another world that opened up under his feet.

He found an underground labyrinth filled with fantastical phosphorescent light, overflowing with flowers and minerals that had never been seen before. Divided into many strata, the various floors changed in appearance the deeper he traveled. It was also an abyss that constantly spawned monsters and seemed to extend downward with no apparent end—this was the Dungeon.

The man beheld this world completely isolated from the surface and perceived it as a "work of art."

Only a will that surpassed mortal bounds could have crafted this creation. Not long after, the man trained his body and improved his Blessing in order to journey deeper and deeper into the labyrinth.

The more he learned, the more obvious it became.

Its composition, its shape—everything was far too complex for human intelligence to comprehend.

The mystical Dungeon.

It broke him.

He was overwhelmed by the beauty, that ultimate chaos, that seemed to encompass all of existence.

From the broken man's throat arose a howl, the sound of a monster that had thrown away its humanity.

The man devoted himself exclusively to his craft thereafter.

Although he continued to fulfill the tasks given to him, the man began to stray from rational thought and walk down the wrong path. With every passing day, more and more people found that they could no longer grasp the concepts driving his creations. Once heralded as a genius, he soon became known as a madman. He disappeared between the pages of history soon after.

His own exceptional skill and the strength granted to him by his unique but flawed conviction inspired him to create a world even more magnificent than the underground labyrinth.

—Limits to what man can accomplish? As if I care.

—I'll create something better, you'll see.

—If gods are irrelevant to this domain, they must first be outdone.

No matter how much blood he shed, though his skin tore to reveal the flesh beneath, the shovel and pickax in his grasp never lay idle. No one knew that the man persisted on this new path alone.

However, his body gave out long before his ambition could be realized.

One man could live for only so long.

He cursed his mortal flesh and fell into despair as his limbs refused to obey his commands. He lamented his faltering, flickering life. Then he left behind a curse—words that would allow him to overcome these limitations—in a notebook.

Along with the "blueprints" that filled his mind.

The man left everything to those yet to be born, his successors who would carry his name and legacy into the future.

* * *

Build, you will build!

Build a creation to outdo it, build your desire!!

This is your purpose!! You are my descendant, though I know not your name or face!

Should your eyes pass over this notebook, there shall be no escape from the blood filling your veins!

The mad hunger and insatiable thirst will never fade! The fire burning in your belly can only heed my call!!

Carry out my desire!

Obey your blood, remain loyal to the yearning.

Stay true to what we long for!

Ambition, ambition, ambition!!

Fulfill the aims of our cursed existence!!

It was all written in the notebook.

The man's persistence was clearly spelled out.

"……"

Dix leaned against the back of a sofa as he held the tattered old notes in one hand, reading silently to himself.

He turned a page, the ink upon it faded and smudged to the point of illegibility in places, beneath the magic-stone lamplight as a voice called out to him from behind:

"Dix, everything's ready."

A large man appeared as Dix lowered the goggles strapped over his forehead. The smoky-quartz lenses covered his eyes as his lips curled into a sneer.

"Great, let's get to it."

Rising to his feet, Dix tossed the old notebook onto the sofa without a second thought. He grabbed an ominous spear propped up against the wall before following his hulking companion down a hallway shrouded in darkness.

The air smelled of stone and felt chilly, as though it had never known the warmth of the sun's rays. Dix smiled to himself as black iron bars and cages came into view before whispering under his breath.

"'Stay true to what we long for'...Well said."

Rattle, rattle. Chains shook fearfully from every direction.

The vile hunter listened with glee, laughing from deep in his throat.

CHAPTER 6
BEFORE THE STORM

A bright light rouses me out of my light sleep, drawing my consciousness awake.

Feeling the morning sunlight, I open my eyes.

Familiar sights fill my blurry field of view: crystals that I couldn't bring myself to sell and a jar of fruit seeds, a desk and chair adorned with various things taken from the Dungeon, a few books and an exhausted grimoire on a wooden shelf, a half-open remodeled closet storing weapons and armor.

This is my room.

My personal space inside *Hestia Familia*'s home.

"......"

Not only did I skip my usual morning training, but according to the clock on the wall it's almost time for breakfast.

As I begin to rise, the rest of the bed comes into view. I look at the spot beside me.

Nothing. No one is there.

Just a hollow, empty feeling and wrinkled white sheets.

I'm looking for a girl who's no longer here. I turn away and get up.

After changing out of my sleepwear, I head out the door. The hallway is jarringly silent. No matter how many times I look out the windows over the central garden, I don't hear that playful voice. Has our home always been this quiet?

The warm sunlight slanting in through the windows leaves no doubt in my mind that summer has arrived as I make my way from the third floor down to the first.

"Morning..."

The rest of the familia is there to greet me in the dining room.

"Yo."

"Good morning."

Welf and Lilly smile as I make my late entrance. I have a feeling they're trying to be cheerful for my sake.

Mikoto and Haruhime in her maid outfit notice me as well. "Good morning," they say with heavy smiles.

A fragrant aroma is wafting in from the kitchen. Mikoto probably made her Far East–style fried eggs this morning.

I think to myself that they probably taste sweet as a feeling of déjà vu hits me.

"It's unusual for you to sleep in."

"Sorry…"

"Mr. Welf isn't blaming you. Breakfast is almost ready, so please wait a few moments, Mr. Bell."

"Okay…Um, where's our goddess?"

"Lady Hestia said she had an errand to attend to before going to her part-time job, so she left early this morning, Sir Bell."

"Yes, and she was stuffing Jyaga Maru Kun into her mouth as fast as she could…"

Welf, Lilly, Mikoto, and Haruhime are all talking like nothing's changed…but something is different. Like gears that aren't lining up right…as though one part is missing, leaving the rest spinning around uselessly.

Everyone's a bit off.

Hardly any conversation is going on. It's bright and sunny outside, but the mood doesn't match that at all.

Everyone looks lost, or maybe just absentminded as they prepare for breakfast.

Haruhime has it the worst.

Instead of her usual radiance and cheer, she's filled with gloom, and her fox ears and thick tail hang limply.

Her eyes twinge with worry as she works her way around the table, setting out plates.

"…Lady Haruhime."

"Ah…What is it, Miss Mikoto?"

"There's, just, one too many plates…"

Mikoto grimaces as she points it out. Haruhime's shoulders jump when she notices.

"M-my apologies!" She quickly clears the extra set.

She had absentmindedly put it where a girl had always sat until just a little while ago.

A girl who always wore an innocent, pure smile…a vouivre girl.

Lilly, Welf, and I saw it happen but couldn't say a word.

"Let's eat…"

Everyone takes a seat at the table.

Once the meal begins, only the sounds of forks on plates and quiet chewing fill the air.

Two days have passed since the Guild issued a secret mission for us.

The events that took place in an unexplored frontier region on the twentieth floor of the Dungeon—in a Xenos Hidden Village—left a dark cloud over *Hestia Familia*.

Xenos. Monsters who can talk.

They possess a great deal of intelligence and self-awareness, despite being beasts, and are shunned by both people and the average monster.

A black-robed mage called Fels—who claims to be the shadow of the Sage—said that the Xenos all share a desire to walk on the surface and interact with people. This incredibly difficult goal uniting them originates from their dreams of their own past lives, dreams they all have.

Shocking was not enough to describe this string of revelations.

There were so many that it almost seemed better to give up on thinking at all.

But right now, the real reason that we're brooding so much is… much simpler.

Our parting from Wiene.

For a time we sheltered and protected the young vouivre girl, but in the end we entrusted her to her fellow Xenos. Despite their wishes, there's currently no place for monsters on the surface. In the past, the people had claimed this realm for themselves by seizing land from monsters. The two could never coexist.

Before we lost everything, there was no choice but to go our separate ways, for Wiene's own safety.

In fact, Fels also said that there are hunters lurking in Orario who will stop at nothing to capture a Xenos. I already told Fels about the god Ikelos and how he sought me out to ask about a talking vouivre. Apparently there's nothing we can do about it now.

We feel powerless, so lost and lonely it's like a part of us is missing. Those emotions are refusing to let go.

"……"

I'm not really surprised that conversation never picked up. Welf and Lilly did their best to find a topic, but nothing really stuck.

It's been like this ever since we finished the mission and returned from the Dungeon early yesterday morning.

My heart cringes every time I remember the look on her face at the end, tears running down her cheeks.

Looking up, I notice that Welf and the others are staring at the open spot next to me…where Wiene once sat.

It's empty.

It feels like a dream that someone so full of life was there not long ago.

Everyone's looking for her, not just me.

It's hard to believe that the absence of one girl could leave all of us so downtrodden—Haruhime, Mikoto, Welf, and even Lilly.

Though amid the sadness…there is a silver lining. We know the moments where we felt like a family weren't a lie.

Even if that girl was a monster, different from people like us.

"…Bell?"

I'm on my way out of the dining room after breakfast when Welf calls my name.

"I think I'll…go to the Dungeon for a bit." I pause for a moment to answer.

Glancing over my shoulder, not only Welf but Lilly, Mikoto, and Haruhime all look at me with concern.

I put on my most reassuring smile. "It'll be fine. I'm planning on coming back right away."

There's something I need to know.

If I'm going to continue being an adventurer in Orario...I can't keep on without confirming something.

"You sure you're okay?"

"Yes..."

I answer as calmly as I can before opening the door and exiting the dining room. I make a quick stop at my room to grab equipment before I leave our home in Hearthstone Manor.

"......"

There isn't a single cloud in the sunny blue sky.

The perfectly aligned paving stones of the street sparkle in the sun's rays. The warm path is the only thing I see as I trudge through the street, head downcast. I don't notice the rest for a while.

Sounds of horse-drawn taxis. Townspeople going about their business. The noises that fill the city every day are still here, unchanged.

Yet I make no sound as muscle memory leads me along the route to the white tower stretching toward the heavens: Babel.

"Bell."

"Oh...Syr."

A voice breaks through the din as I travel down West Main Street.

Tap, tap. Seeing me pass by, Syr comes down the steps from The Benevolent Mistress's front entrance and approaches.

"Good morning. I made a lunch for you again today, so if you'd like...Bell?"

Syr holds up a basket full of food with a big smile on her face, but her words trail off as she leans in for a closer look at my face.

Her eyebrows arch in concern; her silver hair swishes around her shoulders.

"Did...something happen? You look really pale..."

"...!"

Either Syr is amazing at reading people, or my thoughts have made themselves too obvious on my face.

Whichever it is, I have to reassure her right away so she doesn't worry.

"No, I'm fine. Just overslept a little this morning..."

"...I...see."

"And, well, I won't be spending much time in the Dungeon today. So, about the lunch...Um, sorry."

I can't accept this basket. Doing something else pathetic would only make her worry more. Thinking this, I promptly refuse today's offer of lunch.

I quickly force a rather unconvincing smile, and as I start to string together a genuine apology...she stares intently at me and then takes a step closer.

"Huh?"

Now she's right in front of me, leaving barely any space between us.

I can detect a pleasant whiff of her soap, which brings a blush to my face as Syr points her finger directly between my eyes.

"Bell will cheer uuup, Bell will cheer uuuuup."

"......"

...She starts twirling her little finger around and around.

"Bell will smiiiile."

"...Um, Syr?"

"Yay!"

"Wha—!"

She finishes with a tap on the tip of my nose, and I let a yelp slip.

I blink several times in surprise as Syr beams with joy.

"Magic words to make you feel better...I do it all the time for the kids at the orphanage, too, you know?"

She leans in close enough to whisper into my ear as though sharing a secret. That was the last thing I was expecting to hear...but even more surprising, my faces relaxes and I start smiling a bit, too.

It's a natural expression, probably one that I've forgotten how to make during the last few days.

And I do feel a little better, I think, thanks to this cheerful girl.

"...Thank you, Syr. I'll be on my way."

"Of course. Take care."

Grateful that she didn't press any further, I leave Syr behind, feeling bad that I couldn't say more.

"Chalky-hair blockhead! If you don't eat Syr's lunch, we're the ones who have to take care of it, meow...!"

"As troubling as it is...the little adventurer didn't look himself today."

"I've never seen him so down in the dumps before, meow."

Ahnya, Runoa, and Chloe watched the conversation on the street from one of The Benevolent Mistress's windows and chatted among themselves after the boy left.

Sob...! The human Runoa turned to look over her shoulder as Ahnya, standing next to her, did her best to hold back tears.

"Are you worried, too, Lyu?"

"No, I..."

Lyu, who had also spied on Syr and Bell with her coworkers, was about to dismiss their concern when she stopped herself.

"...Actually, yes. This does worry me."

She and the Amazon Aisha had accompanied the boy down to the eighteenth floor five days prior. Lyu gave an honest answer as memories of his strange behavior came to mind.

Just like Syr outside, she watched the boy's retreating form.

Sunlight filled the city streets.

Summer had arrived on the mainland, each day warmer than the last. Orario was no exception, meaning that most people out and about were wearing short sleeves and other light clothing to stay cool.

As for the adventurers on their way to the Dungeon, they were fully equipped with battle cloth and plate armor as always. The metal adorning their bodies glinted as they moved about the city. Animal people and dwarves wearing thick body armor had to squint to keep sweat out of their eyes. It would be no laughing matter if one of them wound up dying because the heat outside drove them to wear less armor. Adventurers walked a little faster than normal as they entered Central Park, knowing that they would be safe from the fiery sun inside the Dungeon.

As Bell was joining their ranks on the way to the Dungeon…

"Hello. I hate to do this, but is there any chance I could speak with Ganesha?"

Hestia, faint traces of sweat on her skin, reached a giant statue depicting a man wearing an elephant mask that stood outside another familia's home.

"I don't have an appointment or anything, so I know this is asking a lot, but…"

At this request from a goddess even smaller than themselves, the animal person and dwarf standing guard at the front gate exchanged glances.

The location was in the southwest section of Orario, close to the city's flea market. The spacious property was separated from the rest of the city by a tall white fence. In the center was an incredibly bizarre statue of a giant man wearing an elephant mask sitting with his arms and legs crossed.

This was *Ganesha Familia*'s home, Iam Ganesha.

The towering statue, or rather building, was so oversized that taking in the whole thing hurt people's necks. The awe-inspiring structure was famous for the story that the slightly eccentric god residing there spent his familia's entire savings to pay for its construction. It ranked alongside Babel and Orario's shopping district as a must-see location for tourists visiting the city.

Sticking out like a sore thumb, as always, Hestia thought as she beheld the unusual building that served as *Ganesha Familia*'s home.

"Please wait here," the animal person guard said before heading to the compound. Hestia was grateful for his polite reception even though she, the deity of another familia, had personally come to visit. She watched Ganesha's follower disappear into the statue's groin—the building's main entrance.

"If Lord Ganesha could just do something about those incomprehensible whims of his, then we could...Arrgh!"

"Ahh, I'm sure you guys have it rough."

Hestia lent a compassionate ear to the dwarf's complaints, but it wasn't long before the young animal person returned to the front gate.

"Lord Ganesha is currently in the backyard. He says he doesn't mind if you come on your own."

"Oh, thanks."

The goddess offered a quick thanks to the guards as they opened the gate and she passed through.

She thought the elephant-faced god was being a little too careless at first, but then decided that Ganesha must trust her enough to allow it. Feeling a little more positive about her visit, she made her way around the giant statue's base toward the backyard.

The grounds of Iam Ganesha were grassy fields—or maybe a large open pasture. If it weren't for the merchants' loud cries calling from the nearby flea market, Hestia could have forgotten she was in the middle of a sprawling metropolis. She noticed from the corner of her eye several stone stables the size of small factories as she approached the rear courtyard.

"Whoa!"

The goddess flinched as soon as she rounded the statue's knee.

The calm, rolling plains were interrupted by a metal fence, the bars glinting in the direct sunlight. Each shaft was thicker than Hestia's torso and possibly made from mythril or perhaps Damascus steel, a foreign material used to forge weapons, or even adamantite. At any rate, each thick rod had been driven straight into the ground and stood up like a post. Fully armed adventurers stood at attention on both sides, continuously monitoring the grounds. The air was thick with tension.

Several adventurers, most likely tamers, were on the other side of the fence with monsters—some in the process of being tamed—issuing their commands.

"D-don't see this every day..."

An aquatic horse known as a kelpie was on a rampage, its beautiful blue mane whipping in the air. Three almalosaurs swung their bludgeoning tails back and forth and attacked with the spikes protruding from their hide. The awe-inspiring tamers looked equally impressive as they faced terrifying monsters from below the lower levels of the Dungeon with whips, bending the beasts to their will by force.

Hestia had heard somewhere that *Ganesha Familia* alone had legal permission to not only keep live monsters for the Monsterphilia but to also extract monsters from the Dungeon and house them in the city proper.

If the Guild's information was accurate, it was also Orario's largest familia in terms of membership.

With its many first-tier adventurers and high average Level, it was safe to say that *Ganesha Familia* was among Orario's best. They possessed an S Rank and were worthy of being mentioned alongside *Loki Familia* and *Freya Familia.*

Also known as "Orario's Peacekeepers," the sheer size and strength of the familia was probably the main reason why the Guild allowed them to keep monsters in the first place.

God of the Masses, eh…?

Ganesha Familia maintained close ties with the Guild and had members stationed at all of Orario's gates to help preserve the peace. Average citizens held them in high esteem.

Due to this great level of trust, the people of Orario still felt safe despite the monsters housed inside the city. Everything was possible because it was *Ganesha Familia*, renowned for its accomplishments.

For several minutes, Hestia was transfixed by the sight of the tamers engaging the monsters one-on-one before she remembered why she had come in the first place. She began scanning her surroundings.

Her first thought was to ask one of the adventurers keeping watch near the fence, but then she heard a shout.

"I am Ganesha!! Ergo, do not snap your teeth at me, monster!"

Found him.

The ridiculously loud masculine voice led her right to the deity.

He wore an elephant mask and stood inside the fence, staring down a monster as he cautiously approached it. The infant dragon before him had been fitted with a magic item, a plate at the base of its neck—evidently it had been tamed. Seeing a tamer at the god's side, the dragon didn't lash out at once but instead eyed Ganesha, watching his every move.

"Nothing to be scared of. Nothing at all!"

"......"

"It's not scary, not scary—that's a good dragon! Who's a good dragon?"

Ganesha wrapped his arms around the towering dragon's chest the moment he was within reach and started scratching the creature's neck and shoulders as though he were playing with a dog.

"RROOOOAAARRRR!"

Without warning, the infant dragon's fangs flashed in the sunlight as its open jaws sped toward the elephant mask.

"Whoooa!"

"What do you think you're doing?!"

"How many times have I told you not to do anything stupid?!"

Roll, roll, roll! Ganesha managed to jump away in the nick of time, but he lost his balance in the process and tumbled through the pasture. At the same time, his followers shouted all kinds of reprimands as they rushed in to help. The tamers immediately stepped in to calm the raging infant dragon.

Hestia watched the scene unfold, dumbstruck.

"Ganesha, avoiding disaster by a hair!!...Whew, thought I was a goner."

"So tell me, does that happen a lot, Ganesha?"

"Oh? If it isn't Hestia! You were here?!"

Ganesha had rolled all the way to the fence. Sounds of battle ringing in her ears, a slightly perturbed Hestia looked down at the elephant-masked god at her feet. Ganesha, fit and muscular, sprang to his feet the moment he saw her. With an "alley-oop," he grabbed hold of the metallic fence and vaulted over the top.

Landing right next to Hestia, he immediately struck one of his strange poses.

"Welcome to my abode! And to answer your question, I'm out here whenever I have a spare moment!"

"Putting your life at risk to play with monsters?"

"To find the meaning of true friendship!"

Ganesha flashed a needlessly pleasant smile, displaying his shining white teeth. Hestia could only sigh.

Without any further small talk, she got right to the point of her visit.

"So, I hear you know about the Xenos?"

"……"

As Hestia broached the topic, Ganesha's comical demeanor instantly disappeared, and his mouth snapped shut.

The expression beneath his mask—most likely—became gravely serious. "We need privacy," he said, turning his back to her.

Ordering his guards to stay behind, Ganesha led Hestia to a wooded area close to the white fence at the edge of the compound. Alone, the two gods started talking.

"You know about the monsters who possess intelligence?"

"That's right. Straight from Ouranos's mouth, to boot."

Ouranos. Hearing that name connected all the dots for Ganesha. He had no further questions.

Just as Bell and the rest of the familia had discovered the Xenos on their secret mission, Hestia had learned about Wiene and her kind from the deity in charge of the Guild, Ouranos.

Not only that, but the majestic deity had informed her of his actions and that Ganesha was in the fold.

"It was a shock. Not just the fact that you're working with Ouranos but the truth behind the Monsterphilia, too."

"When I was first approached…When Ouranos first told me, I didn't believe my ears."

Ganesha then proceeded to explain how he came to understand Ouranos's will, as well as how he had been placed in charge of the Monsterphilia—a festival with the purpose of not just simply putting monsters on display but promoting friendship with them and encouraging the birth of monsterphiles.

Hestia marveled at the completely unfamiliar gravitas in Ganesha's eyes as he brought her up to speed.

"Did you believe him? What Ouranos told you?"

"Well, I had a chance to meet one of them on a separate occasion. It was a goblin, wearing a red hat… I couldn't turn a blind eye to one with such a fluent command of language."

Apparently, Ganesha had been at a loss as to how to react when Fels smuggled the small-bodied Xenos out of the Dungeon to meet him in person. Hestia and the others had had much the same reaction to Wiene.

After that, Ganesha went along with everything.

With a Xenos present, he accepted what he'd seen firsthand and decided to cooperate with Ouranos's proposal—to organize the Monsterphilia.

"…Have you told your children?"

"Only a very select few. You may think it laughable that I would hide something from the children, but…my familia is very much in the dark."

The circumstances called for it. Preventing the worst possible outcome required staunching the flow of information as much as possible. The masses would, no doubt, become incredibly apprehensive or even violent if they learned the truth.

Even now, the truth hurt.

Ganesha gazed at the tamers and adventurers on the other side of the fence.

"We have permission to keep approved monsters in captivity…We do it under the pretext that our main purpose is to study their habits and tendencies as well as collect information to assist adventurers in the Dungeon."

"That's what your children think they're doing as well, isn't it…?"

In truth, they were carrying out that goal, too.

The Guild had received from them detailed and valuable information about the weaknesses and characteristics of specific monsters, which they archived and currently used to aid adventurers putting their lives on the line in the Dungeon. Even Royman Mardeel, the most powerful person in the Guild, recognized the value of their work and continued to support them.

The true objective of eventually establishing a friendly relationship with monsters was still a secret. What's more, no one had any reason to suspect it.

"What about yours, Hestia?"

"They're the reason I know in the first place...Bell and everyone knows."

Hestia explained how everything began with Wiene's arrival and her familia's decision to protect the young monster girl, sharing information with one of the few others who knew the truth.

She also told her familia about her conversation with Ouranos while they were away on their mission. She was aware of everything they had learned at one of the Xenos's Hidden Villages.

The only thing she left out was Ouranos's will—his belief that Bell and her familia had the potential to become the bridge between monsters and people.

"What do you plan to do, Hestia?"

"...My children are more important to me than anything."

Protect Bell and the others. Be with them. That was Hestia's sincerest will.

That, and—.

"—If my children have decided on something, then I'll cheer them on and do everything I can to help. If they want to save the Xenos, then I'll lend them a hand."

"I see..."

"I won't give orders as a goddess or force anything on them."

Hestia's decision hadn't changed since the moment she engraved her Blessing into Bell's back—it was here that she revealed her own will.

"This is their story, their path."

She would let them decide, assist them when she could, and watch over them.

Hestia continued, "...I'd be lying if I said I wasn't worried, though."

Confronted with Ganesha's questioning gaze from beneath his mask, Hestia averted her eyes and let her honest concerns surface.

What would the Xenos's presence bring to Orario, to the world as a whole?

Hestia knew it was risky to attempt to realize the absurd vision of making peace with monsters, and yet she could still see a fleeting image of the vouivre girl's teary eyes in the back of her mind. Caught in a quandary, Hestia gazed out over the pasture.

Wounded tamers affixed chains to newly tamed monsters beneath a bright blue sky.

"...Ganesha, how do you feel about all this? What do you think is going to happen?"

"To be blunt, I don't know."

"I figured as much..."

Ganesha gave an honest answer as he followed Hestia's gaze out over the grounds.

The goddess sighed as the two of them watched a tamer instruct a monster to walk by hitting its hide.

"However."

"?"

"If these Xenos—no, monsters in general—truly desire peace and not bloodshed..."

Ganesha turned to face Hestia.

"Then I will cease to be the 'God of the Masses'—and become 'Neo Ganesha, God of All Beings' for people and monsters!!" he declared, as if to drive away the gloom threatening to settle in.

Flashing a smile, the deity confidently looked to the sky and puffed out his chest as Hestia watched in amazement...until her lips started to curl upward.

"...This is the first time I've ever thought you were cool, Ganesha."

"That's because...I am Ganesha!"

Hestia let herself laugh at his confident boast.

A wide array of maps covered every speck of open space on each wall.

In addition to being completely wallpapered with diagrams of terrestrial and marine topography, the room was filled with interesting trinkets and unusual items, many of which were rarely seen in Orario. Several plants more suited for an arid desert, as well as an impressive collection of shells and pearls, decorated the furniture and tables. A stand of well-worn traveler's hats, each decorated with a feather, stood out among the clutter.

A man and a woman sat facing each other over a desk in a room fit for a true world traveler.

"Failure, huh…That's not good."

The god Hermes sat on a chair with his elbows planted on the desk, fiddling with a sand dial as he spoke.

The gorgeous woman, who sat stiff as a board on the other side of the desk, was Asfi.

She had come to her god's private quarters in *Hermes Familia*'s home to report the results of her most recent assignment.

"I have no excuse. After our targets retreated, my subordinates and I remained in the area until earlier today in hopes of finding new leads, but…it's entirely my fault that we allowed them to escape."

"Come now, I'm not blaming you."

Asfi's face had steadily lost color during her report and subsequent apology, but Hermes waved it off, indicating that she shouldn't worry about it.

The two of them were discussing the failed plan to track *Ikelos Familia*.

The Guild—or rather Ouranos—had issued Bell and *Hestia Familia* a mission: to journey to a Xenos Hidden Village. The true purpose was to use them as bait to draw out *Ikelos Familia*'s hunters, then it was up to a group of *Hermes Familia* adventurers under Asfi's command to trail them. Their goal was to locate the hunters' undiscovered home base, where they held captured Xenos until they could be smuggled and sold on the black market.

However, *Ikelos Familia* had realized they were being followed in the Dungeon and broke off their pursuit of Bell's party to make their own escape. Asfi's mission ended in failure.

"But they prevented you, Perseus herself, from completing your task...Tell me, what did you think of them? The targets."

"...Rumored connections to the Evils notwithstanding, the entire group seems to be a congregation of brutes and thugs. Especially their leader, a man wearing goggles..."

Ikelos Familia was a Dungeon-prowling familia with a history shrouded in darkness.

Residing in Orario for well over twenty years, their familia ranking was B. Its members had reportedly made several trips into the Dungeon's deep levels. However, the group itself remained in the shadows; perhaps due to the inordinate amount of time they spent underground, hardly any of their members had gained any notoriety or fame on the surface.

"The man is sharp and cunning. Even as he gathered enough forces to overwhelm our party, the moment he discerned our identities, he immediately decided to withdraw."

The leader of *Ikelos Familia* had been cautious of Asfi, a brilliant item maker whose extraordinary talent was known worldwide.

Known as Perseus, she invented a number of phenomenal and mysterious magic items like Hades Head, a helmet of invisibility.

Since they didn't know what Asfi's side had hidden up their sleeves and their home base might be discovered, the leader of *Ikelos Familia* ordered all his subordinates to retreat without leaving a single person behind to avoid the risk of capture.

"A man who wears goggles...Would that be Dix Perdix?"

"The same. Not only is he *Ikelos Familia*'s leader...He became a second-tier, Level Four adventurer nearly ten years ago."

He had been given the title "Hazer."

At the time he received it, the man was already famous for massacring monsters at a pace that bordered on insanity.

"Assuming he's only been growing stronger and more experienced since then...it's possible that he's as powerful as a *first-tier adventurer.*" Asfi's eyes became grave, her voice taking on a severe tone. Hermes lightly sighed to himself.

"First things first, we'll need to apologize to Ouranos…With that out of the way, we should assume that the enemy has a good idea where the 'nest' is located. I assume they've been able to work out that much information based on our actions alone." Hermes's orange eyes narrowed as he voiced his train of thought.

"What about the monsters in question…?"

"They were told to relocate to a different nest no matter how our plan turned out. Most likely, they're on the move as we speak."

Hermes explained that Ouranos wanted to account for as many variables as possible and had instructed the Xenos to leave the Hidden Village on the twentieth floor and travel deeper into the Dungeon.

Even so, Asfi could hear a hint of concern as the deity explained, almost as if he were talking to himself.

"There's nothing more we can do from here, so I know it's pointless to be worried, but…"

"……"

"Aaagghhh, I got a bad feeling about this."

Hermes didn't waste any time after whispering those words.

Looking up, he barked a new set of orders.

"Keep an eye out for any movement on the middle levels, Asfi. Use Rivira as your base and stay on guard."

"Affirmative."

As though his divine intuition had told him, he said:

"It won't be long now—they're going to make their move."

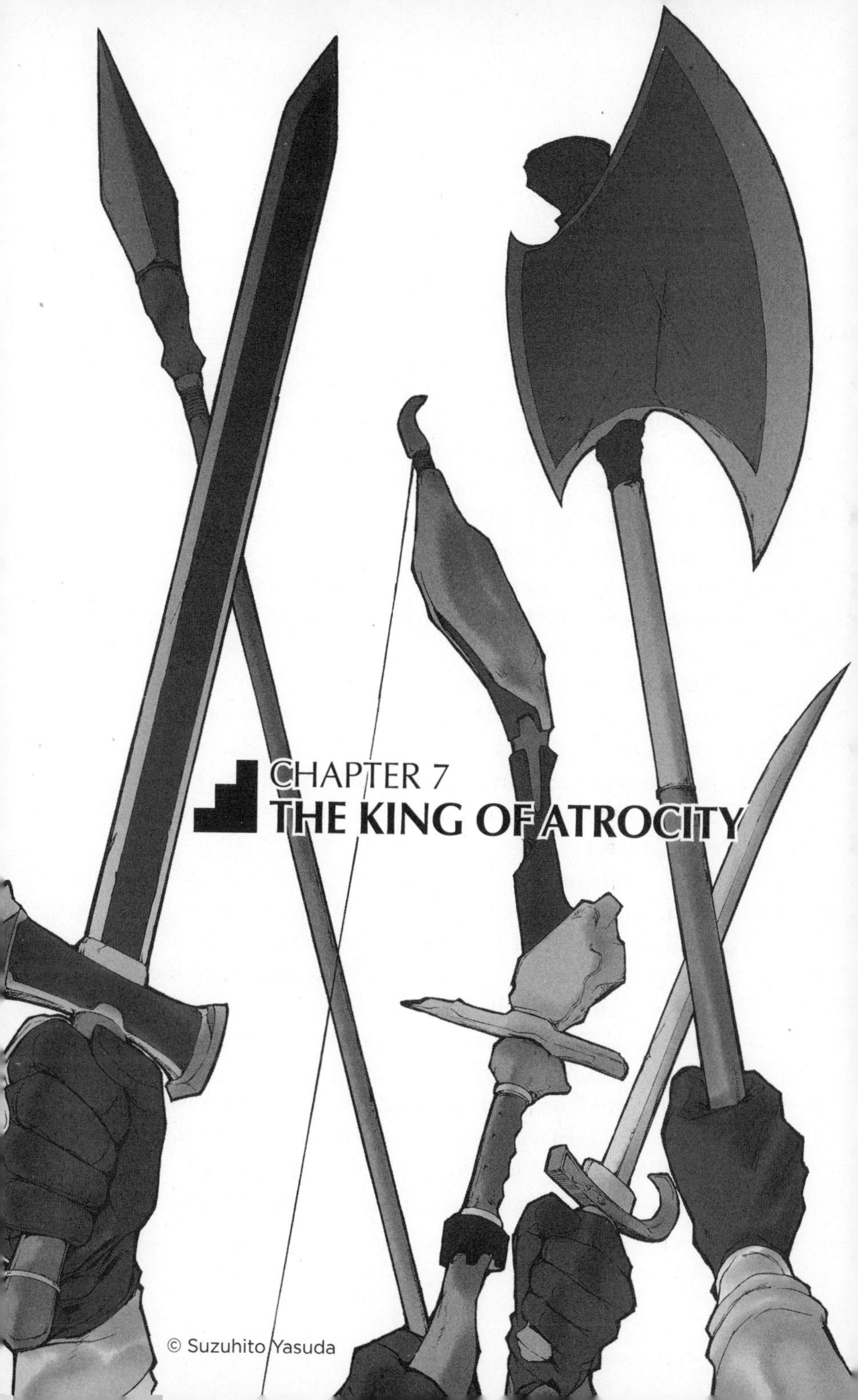

CHAPTER 7
THE KING OF ATROCITY

Luminescent moss clinging to the ceiling twinkled like stars dotting the night sky.

The moist air smelled of a primeval forest after a heavy rainfall. Grasses and wildflowers grew along the floor. In one corner, beads of moisture dripped from the roots of a massive tree into one of the puddles here and there, creating soft *plips* and tiny ripples.

The tree bark covering the passage walls marked the Dungeon's Colossal Tree Labyrinth.

A dragon girl stood alone.

Her silver-blue hair glowed in the light. Her amber eyes, streaked with tears, gazed high overhead, toward the ceiling hidden by wood and illuminating moss.

The girl knew the real stars.

She had gazed upon the night sky of the world above with a boy, standing inside a small garden.

It was beautiful. So much that she had felt her chest tighten.

She had held onto the boy, enjoying his awkward smile, and always watched him.

All the trees and plant life illuminated by the specks of blue light couldn't hold a candle to the constellations in her memory. This dreamlike realm had stolen the hearts and minds of countless adventurers. However—it looked dull and subdued to the girl who had seen starlight with her own eyes.

After all, she had never stopped yearning for the real thing.

For the view on the surface.

For the people who had taken her in as one of their own, as family.

For the smile of a certain boy, who was always startled and flustered at her behavior before eventually indulging her.

The girl, Wiene, thought about what lay far, far overhead, beyond the many floors that separated the Colossal Tree Labyrinth from the surface, and clasped her hands together by her chest.

"Bell..."

Her lips quivered as they formed his name.

A sharp pain ran through her chest, so intense that her amber eyes started glistening with a fresh wave of tears.

"Wiene, we're leaving."

Wiene heard the harpy girl's voice behind her but didn't acknowledge it right away. She gave a small nod after a few moments passed.

Tearing her gaze away from the ceiling, Wiene turned, her silver-blue hair fluttering.

She stepped forward to join her comrades, and together they left the room where they had been waiting.

The twenty-fourth floor of the Dungeon.

Wiene's group advanced through the passageways.

The young vouivre girl, still unable to fight, walked in the center of a small squad of Xenos.

The group consisted of an arachne, a harpy, a formoire, a hippogriff, a war shadow, and the vouivre herself, Wiene. A party of six monsters.

The other Xenos had split off into groups ranging from five to seven members for the journey to their destination, much like adventurers would do on an expedition.

Even without armor, a group of unrelated monsters from various floors traveling through the Dungeon in a group would stick out like a sore thumb. In fact, the sight of an arachne and a harpy clad in robes and walking in single file would have the same effect as a circus parade through the center of town.

There were currently more than forty-four Xenos. If all of them moved together as a group, adventurers would surely spot them, and rumors would spread like wildfire. One of them being discovered was bad enough, but if a large group of armed monsters traveling together became public knowledge, it would cause many problems.

Not only would the sighting spread fear and panic among adventurers, it would also invite unwanted attention.

Hence why they always split up into smaller groups when proceeding en masse to avoid being noticed by passing adventurers. This was especially true in the middle levels, which were relatively cramped compared to the vast passages found in the deep levels.

Xenos leaders like the lizardman, Lido, and the siren, Rei, were part of the first two groups to set out. It was their job to secure a route for the comparatively weaker Xenos to follow by making sure no adventurers were in their path. They also eliminated other monsters and dealt with Irregulars along the way. Their role was the most dangerous in that they were often drawn into combat and forced to adjust to ever-changing circumstances.

Wiene was assigned a safe position toward the back.

Her protectors included a formoire from the deep levels along with seasoned veterans from the Xenos's ranks.

Wiene wore a long black robe with a hood hiding the glimmering garnet embedded in her forehead. Unable to distance herself from thoughts of Bell and the others, she walked with her head down and constantly on the verge of tears.

"Wiene, you have cried enough."

"S-sorry, Ranieh..."

The arachne at the head of the party scolded her harshly, causing Wiene to flinch and shrink a little.

Her name was Ranieh.

She possessed the shapely upper body of a human female but walked with the many legs of a spider—an arachne Xenos. Their group had been placed in her care. Ranieh's upper body was well protected by adventurer's armor, and her helmet's visor hid most of her face.

"This is no Hidden Village. Our wild brethren could attack at any time. A mind distracted by thoughts of humans will get you killed."

Ranieh's sharp rebuke was laced with irritation, and her flowing white hair shifted as she glared at Wiene from behind her visor. Her humanoid red eyes—arachnes typically had compound eyes—were proud and willful.

Her skin was white as the frozen tundra, the same color as her hair. A human would assume from her pallor that she was deathly ill. However, that did nothing to detract from her stunning beauty.

If an adventurer caught a glimpse of her, her arachnid legs would immediately inspire fear and dread, only for her alluring feminine figure to draw their attention. She possessed beauty that would make goddesses jealous.

Despite that, Ranieh was extremely wary of both people and monsters. In fact, she refused to remove her helmet in the presence of anyone other than fellow Xenos, hiding her loveliness from view.

"Wiene, are you still sad?"

"...Yes."

"The surface dwellers...Bell and his friends. You'll see them again, I know it."

The harpy named Fia, dressed in a robe similar to the vouivre girl's, noticed that Wiene was struggling to cope with Ranieh's reprimand and came to walk beside her to reassure her. Fia seemed about the same age as their new companion, with deep-red hair flowing past her shoulders and a smile on her face.

The vouivre girl used her arm to wipe away her drying tears as well as the fresh ones building up in her eyes, then managed to give the slightest of nods...when a giant, fur-covered finger reached down and gently wiped the last of the tears from her cheek.

"Uooh..."

"...Thank you, Foh."

Wiene's smile grew as she looked up at the hulking formoire named Foh. Despite his massive and intimidating frame, Foh had a kind heart.

Unable to use language like Wiene and the others, he communicated through various howls and grunts. However, his expressive body language and tone were more than enough to convey his warm personality. In battle, that body became a shield thanks to the gigantic breastplate across his chest, transforming him into a living wall. Foh would then use his large mace to either crush enemies or launch them high into the air to protect his comrades.

Although it was difficult to interpret his thoughts just by looking at his round pitch-black eyes, he was always watching over the group.

As did the others.

The harpy Fia was much more interested in the surface and its inhabitants than anyone else. Bubbling with curiosity, she always had a question to ask.

Cliff the hippogriff preferred to be airborne, and the sound of his flapping wings was always close by. The lighthearted and cheerful monster also enjoyed teasing those around him.

The war shadow Orde, though unable to produce any sounds, was always the first into combat and willing to do anything to support the group.

Ranieh might have been scary, but only out of concern for the safety of those like her.

Everyone was kind.

They welcomed Wiene with open arms from the moment they met. Very little time had passed, and yet she was treated like a long-time friend and ally.

Wiene belonged here. It was the one place she could be among those like her, ones who accepted her.

But still...

Even though Wiene understood all that, she couldn't expunge that twinge of loneliness from her heart no matter how hard she tried.

All because of those people who had found her when she was crying alone, held her, and smiled together with her.

The vouivre girl still longed for their warmth.

It didn't matter that they were people, unlike her.

"...Wiene, forget them. They'll never bring you anything but pain."

The arachne Ranieh appeared to take issue with Wiene's conversation and issued an irritated, contemptuous warning.

Unlike Lido and Rei, Ranieh was part of the group of Xenos that detested the people who lived on the surface.

The senior gargoyle, Gros, was the leader of this faction. While those who shared their beliefs were in the minority, they still made up about one third of the Xenos, united by their mutual hostility toward the surface races.

Wiene had no idea of what had happened to them in the past.

But it made her sad.

"Ranieh, why do you hate Bell and his friends so much…?"

"……"

"Bell, Haruhime, and the goddess are all very nice. They gave me lots of hugs!"

"That's only because they felt like it at the time…"

"That's not true!"

Ranieh's refusal to acknowledge the bond that Wiene had shared upset the vouivre girl, bringing tears to her angry eyes again.

The arachne's face contorted bitterly as she watched her new companion.

Ranieh had been this way since they met. She had better command of the language spoken by people than most Xenos, but her feelings concerning the surface dwellers were far from longing or admiration.

Her words were always infused with anger, hatred, or perhaps something bordering on grief.

"Such ignorance."

"Huh?"

"You know nothing of the people. Nothing of their cruelty, their cunning."

Other members of the group remained silent as Wiene glared at Ranieh with burning intensity. The arachne's response was short.

One day, they'll come for you, too.

Just as those words began to leave her mouth, something happened.

Wiene's curved, tapered ears picked up a desperate scream in the distance.

"!!"

Wiene's shoulders gave a huge twitch.

Ranieh and the other Xenos turned toward the voivre girl, confused as to why she'd suddenly stopped walking.

"Wiene?"

"Hey, what's the matter?"

"A-a voice......"

The arachne watched with concern as Wiene's ears flicked back and forth.

Dragons were known as the strongest of all monsters for a reason, as their potential strength and abilities were much greater than other species'. Vouivres, a type of dragon, had particularly acute senses, such as hearing.

The very faint sound was coming from somewhere far away on this floor—a scream inaudible to the other Xenos, though the dragon girl's ears could pick it up.

"She's crying...'Save me'..."

Wiene knew right away.

The scream didn't belong to an adventurer or monster but to a Xenos like themselves. A monster capable of thoughts and feelings, one of their own kind.

At the same time, the shrieking was so desperate that Wiene almost felt like she was the one being torn apart.

Wiene hadn't been alive very long, but this was her first time hearing such an agonized scream.

Shuddering, she wrapped her thin, branch-like arms around her body.

"'Save me'...Is it one of our comrades calling for help?!"

"Y-yes...She's hurt, really bad...We have to save her!"

A wide-eyed Fia inquired about what she had heard, and Wiene nodded.

It took all the courage the vouivre girl had in her small frame to reply as she tightly hugged her body. Memories flooded her mind, reminding her of how that boy had responded to her cries, as she looked around at her companions again and again.

"What should we do, Ranieh?"

"......"

The harpy, hippogriff, war shadow, and formoire all looked to the arachne.

Judging by Wiene's words, the screaming didn't belong to a

member of their group. Chances were that it was a Xenos they had never met before.

Ranieh paused for a moment with all her companions' eyes focused on her. Taking one last look at the tears forming in Wiene's eyes, she broke the silence.

"...We will investigate. Wiene, lead the way."

The arachne, in charge of the group, could tell from the dragon girl's eyes that something was seriously wrong.

In the vast Dungeon, ignoring a comrade desperately calling for help while in mortal danger was something that the Xenos could not do.

As Ranieh donned her metal helm, the atmosphere became tense. The formoire's fur stood on end, the war shadow audibly tensed, while the hippogriff flapped its wings vigorously.

As they postponed their plans to rendezvous with Lido in the deep levels, the arachne led the party in a different direction.

"Orde, go."

"———."

The war shadow took off quickly at Ranieh's order. The rest of the party followed him a few moments later.

The war shadow wore full-plate body armor.

Since his human-shaped shadow form was hidden from head to toe beneath the armor, it was impossible for adventurers to know there was a monster beneath it at first glance. Therefore, he took the point position to make sure their path was clear of adventurers and other dangers before the party advanced.

Orde raced through the dark hallways, seeming to the unwary observer like no more than a solo adventurer on the prowl in clinking heavy armor. He checked around corners and scouted intersections before informing them it was safe and guiding the group to a clear path. Whenever a monster barred their way, he pulled back his gauntlets to reveal five sharp fingers—a war shadow's deadly armament—and easily sliced through enemies on his own.

"—Gros, we may have found another like us. Going to take a look."

Ranieh held a red crystal and spoke into it while rushing ahead on four legs.

The crystal glowed for a moment before producing a response.

"What?—Wait, Ranieh. Do nothing until we arrive."

"No, I must insist."

Ranieh firmly vetoed the reply from the crystal.

"Listen, Ranieh. Something isn't right. It could be a trap—."

"Even so, it cannot wait, Gros."

She interrupted the escalating plea and tightened her grasp on the crystal.

"Now that I've heard the cry, nothing can stop me."

The group was close enough that the others could hear it as well.

It was a sharp cry, like metal scraping against metal, that made them want to cover their ears. The sound grew louder with each step and agitated them. Their feet thudded a little harder, and their wings flapped a little stronger as the Xenos accelerated.

Ranieh clenched her fangs together to endure the tormented wails piercing her ears.

"If humans are behind this, all the more reason we cannot ignore it."

Her face devoid of emotion beneath her visor, she ended the conversation.

The arachne ignored the voice attempting to stop her and shoved the crystal back into a pouch beneath her armor.

"There…!"

"Orde, the room up ahead!"

Wiene had guided the party this far, but her directions were no longer necessary. Ranieh shouted orders at the top of her lungs.

She was looking at a tall gap in the bark-covered Dungeon wall. It led to a room that branched off from the main path. Orde, in his full-plate armor, charged through the opening.

As soon as Ranieh, Wiene, and the rest of the party made it inside a moment later—a horrifying scene greeted their eyes.

"Wha—?"

The ground was flecked with feathers and red droplets.

Luminescent moss lit the center of the room. A single, lone tree stood there with blood pooling at its roots.

And chained to its thick trunk was a thin body.

It was as though a shrike had caught and impaled her.

Her body was covered in wounds from head to toe, and she had lost so much blood that her garments appeared glistening red—evidence of the torture she'd been subjected to. Her winged arms, spread wide, and bloodstained lower body formed the shape of a cross as her head hung limply.

It was a lone siren, both her wings nailed in place with steel stakes.

"Eep…?!"

Wiene had no words for the horrid scene. Only a gasp of shock escaped her lips.

The crucifixion of a monster.

A grotesque sight that was unthinkable in the Dungeon.

A swarm of giant black insects buzzed in the air, circling around the top of the tree like vultures. More than likely, the deadly hornets were drawn here just like Wiene and the Xenos. Their unfeeling eyes were trained on the dying siren as they darted about, moments away from digging their pincerlike jaws into her flesh.

"…!! Fia, Cliff!" Ranieh shouted an instant later.

The harpy flung the robe from her shoulders before their leader finished calling her name and leaped with the mightily howling hippogriff. The swarm of giant insects immediately moved to intercept, but they were no match for feathery projectiles and a razor-sharp beak. Soon, the skies were clear.

Then they rushed to the siren, shattering the chains and stakes with their talons.

Suddenly free, the siren's limp body toppled forward as the formoire dashed to her side with huge strides and caught her.

"What happened?! Answer me!"

Ranieh rushed to the siren lying in Foh's massive arms. Wiene and the rest were close behind.

The siren's feathers were naturally brown. Even covered in blood, she had a shapely form and a beautiful countenance. Most important, the moment they saw other monsters attack her, they knew she was one of their brethren.

The girl was a different race of siren from Rei's, and she must have lost the ability to speak. Glassy-eyed, she barely moved her lips as she tried to tell them something.

Damn...!

It was impossible for monsters to do something like this. It was clearly *people.*

Ranieh's rage at what one of her kind had been subjected to reached a boiling point. But one memory still lingered in the back of her mind, a voice she had heard on the way here cautioning her this could be a trap.

The arachne looked up, determined to warn her allies, when—

"—Run...away."

Eyes open, the blood-soaked siren pleaded in a wavering voice.

And then—

"Wow, so monsters really can cry, huh?"

A man's thin, wispy laughter reached them.

"You guys care for one another way more than us adventurers do."

Discarding their tree-bark-patterned camouflage, some twenty adventurers revealed themselves, forming a ring around them.

Tossing aside the fragrant pouches that masked their scent, the adventurers surrounded the tree, trapping Wiene and her companions.

The Xenos looked toward the room's only exit and found a man in goggles tapping the shaft of a red spear against his shoulder and blocking their escape.

"Agh, seriously, that was too easy."

The man's lips curled like a crescent moon.

"Adventurers...!"

All questions had been answered—Ranieh snarled at the people who had ambushed them.

More accurately, at the band of hunters.

It was a mix of humans, animal people, dwarves, and Amazons. All of them wore the same cruel smile as the apparent, goggled leader while tightening their grips on an assortment of weapons. Several blades and spear points dripped with fresh blood, almost certainly having torn into the siren's body over and over.

"You're the ones who...!"

"Do you even have to ask, spider lady?"

Their tortured companion had been bait.

The adventurers had chained her to a tree and nailed her down to prevent her from escaping, then tormented her to make her scream.

The hunters had used the siren's exceptionally loud voice to cut through the din of the Dungeon and lure in the Xenos.

Ensuring that Wiene, whose sensitive ears could hear the screams, would come.

Behind the smoky-quartz lenses, Dix seemed amused by the stunned girl.

"We set up here to make sure you didn't get into the deep levels but...damn, I didn't think it'd work this well!"

With five hunters at his side, their backs to the room's only exit, Dix had sealed the Xenos's escape route.

The man's ominous laughter echoed in the deserted corner of the Dungeon.

"!!"

It happened in an instant.

While most of the group was still trying to grasp the situation, the ever-silent Orde shattered the silence and rushed at Dix head-on.

He tore through the air with speed worthy of a mid-level, second-tier adventurer. His heavy jet-black armor was a blur as the seething war shadow channeled his rage into the tips of his claws and descended on his target like a vengeful spirit.

However, the man wearing goggles didn't even bother raising his spear in defense. Just as Orde's outstretched arm was about to strike him right between the eyes...

"————!!"

A greatsword appeared from behind Dix's shadow and cut Orde in half.

"Eh?"

Another sound slipped from Wiene's lips.

As if in slow motion, she watched the war shadow's body split in two and collapse to the floor.

The massive blade had cleaved through the plate armor—Orde's torso fell away from his lower body and rolled to a stop.

"Gran, you idiot. What if we could have sold the monster inside?"

"M-my bad, Dix..."

Orde had been slain by a tall, muscular man.

A black tattoo covered most of the bald hunter's face. It was unmistakably that of a criminal.

Despite his towering frame, Gran had swiftly jumped out from behind his leader and eliminated the threat with one flash of his greatsword. But even with his jaw-dropping strength and speed, one angry quip from Dix was enough to make him cower in fear.

"O-Orde...?" whispered Wiene in disbelief as she drifted listlessly toward the dying war shadow.

As Orde lay facedown, his armor clattered as he extended a shaking arm toward the dragon girl—*Stomp!*

Dix drove his foot straight through the helmet, crushing Orde's head.

A pool of blood grew from beneath his boot, the dark liquid seeping out in every direction.

A moment of silence passed among the Xenos. But the man didn't care. Dix took a few steps forward without even glancing at the fallen monster.

"Less than I expected...Guess there's no need to use that, then." The man in goggles mumbled, "What a letdown," in disappointment. However...

The corners of his lips peeled back as his gaze fell on Wiene once again, frozen in place.

"All right—the hunt's on."

The hunters howled their approval of their leader's order.

"Damn you all!!"

As Ranieh yelled, the Xenos let loose their howls.

In the blink of an eye, the grinning hunters had collided with Ranieh and the others in battle.

"Ah...ahh...!"

Wiene couldn't move.

The mixture of ferocious howls, clashing blades, and unbridled desire to kill was too much for her. Her comrades, who had been so kind and warm to her, suddenly became savage beasts that only heeded their instincts. They brought talons, claws, and fangs down upon their enemies without hesitation.

Blood spurted through the air, followed by shrieks of pain.

The arachne ensnared several hunters with her spider webbing, the harpy's feathery missiles ricocheted off armor, and the hippogriff dived at the hunters over and over from high above.

Any human or animal person who came too close was instantly caught up in the onslaught.

"?!"

"Ha-haa—!!"

However, the hunters weren't fazed.

One adventurer would seem to fall as another leaped over him from behind; the shielded body blow that followed would become a swipe at the legs to knock a monster to the ground before it knew what had happened. They struck out with their blades, using even their own allies as bait, and worst of all was the light of magic bringing supernatural healing and arrows of flame.

The hunters were strong. Moreover, they had a solid strategy.

None of them was foolish enough to single-handedly take on any of the Xenos, who were much stronger than average monsters. Instead, they overwhelmed weak points with sheer numbers, attacking in quick succession like a vicious pack of wolves. It might have been humanity's most rudimentary strategy for hunting monsters, but it was efficient and effective. What's more, the hunters forced Ranieh and her allies out of formation by targeting the vouivre girl.

The four Xenos fought valiantly to protect Wiene, who was unable to join the battle. However, they drifted farther and farther apart as time dragged on.

"Agh!"

One Amazon snuck past her badly injured allies and managed to get in range, slamming the harpy girl to the ground with a high roundhouse kick. At the same time, a magic spell hit home and sent the hippogriff hurtling to the floor. As soon as he reached the ground, several spears mercilessly skewered him at once. Ranieh was so focused on protecting Wiene from volleys of arrows and thrown hand axes that she didn't see Gran's greatsword in time, her lapse luckily only costing her her helmet.

With such a wide array of weapons and magic at their disposal, it appeared the hunters would overwhelm the Xenos in a matter of moments.

"ORRRHHHHHHHHHHHHHHHHHHHHHHHHHHHHHH!!"

"Wha—GEHHH!"

Suddenly, the formoire unleashed an earsplitting roar and swung his mace in a sweeping arc that sent several hunters flying.

Foh stood alone, his two-meder-tall frame staying upright no matter how many hunters tried to cut him down. Their clever teamwork and strategy weren't enough. Unlike typical monsters, Foh could read their movements, giving him the chance to protect himself from the waves of arrows and magic raining down on him with minimal injuries. The formoire knocked the hunters away, one by one.

A dwarf attempted to block the incoming mace with a shield but wound up facedown on the floor from the sheer impact.

"It's no good, Dix!! This thing's insanely powerful!"

One of the hunters raised a desperate cry. Even with five ganging up on the formoire, they couldn't suppress him.

"Oh, come on. It's just one beast."

Dix watched the battle from his spot at the entrance, responding with exasperation. He lifted the twisted spearhead as he hoisted his red weapon.

The man in goggles, nothing more than a spectator up to this point, began to move.

"ORHOHH!!"

The formoire Foh noticed the man casually advancing.

Seeing the badly injured hunters take several steps back, he narrowed his eyes at the newcomer. Shoulder muscles bulging, the Xenos took aim at the man's head and swept the mace to the side with all the strength he could muster.

It traced a straight horizontal line.

The air howled from the powerful force.

The attack could instantly turn him into a mangled lump of meat, and Dix—smoothly deflected it with the shaft of his spear.

"———."

Sparks flew as the loud clash of weapons rang out.

A single spear turned aside the massive mace, delivering the blow to empty air.

Though the formoire's arms were three times larger than Dix's, the hunter successfully neutralized the attack.

Skill and technique. It was a demonstration of the strength and ability the ruthless hunter had cultivated.

In the moment before the next attack, the man's evil sneer reflected in the formoire's black eyes.

Dix used his momentum to slip past his opponent and position himself in a blind spot.

"One time I got busted up pretty bad capturing a big one."

Still at the end of his swing, Foh's back was completely exposed.

Dix's eyes locked onto his solid, muscular target, and he thrust his spear straight forward.

"You ain't what I need."

Shing! A sharp, metallic sound echoed through the room.

The rubellite spearhead pierced the heavy breastplate before plunging into the formoire's thick torso.

Foh was completely run through, and blood spurted from his mouth.

"Foh?!"

Ranieh screamed, still fighting on her own farther away.

Wiene could only stand and watch.

"Gurh, oorh……!"

The mace slipped from his weakened grasp.

Looking down at the sinister spearhead protruding from the middle of his chest, the formoire took hold of it with trembling fingers.

As he tried to pull it out—Dix laughed cruelly behind him.

"Die."

He yanked upward with all his might, and the spearhead sliced through the rest of his torso.

The formoire, chest split apart from the sternum, dropped to his knees before collapsing to the ground.

"———."

Just before hitting the floor, Foh looked slightly to the side, his lifeless gaze meeting Wiene's eyes.

Blood pouring from his body, he still managed to reach out slightly with his right hand—the same large, furry hand that had once dried her tears. The world lost all color for the dragon girl.

"...Foh?"

There was no answer to her faint call.

Wiene could hear the arachne fighting against more hunters as tears began blurring her vision.

"Orde, Cliff, Fia......?"

The cloven war shadow lay in a pool of his own blood, several spear shafts protruded from the deceased hippogriff's body, and the limp harpy lay facedown on the floor, possibly dead as well.

The siren had been laid to rest on the floor, the light already gone from her eyes.

Wiene called out her friends' names, her spirit breaking.

"N-no......No!"

Tears spilled from her amber eyes, streaking her light-blue cheeks.

Her building emotions burst free, tearing through her as she screamed.

"NOOO!!"

Yelling at the top of her lungs, she rushed to the slain formoire's side.

She kneeled next to him, paying no attention to the blood before embracing his large right hand against her chest. Never again would it wipe away her tears.

She didn't know how to stop the gushing from her eyes and simply kneeled there, wailing.

"No, no, noo...!!"

With gasping sobs, she dampened the formoire's corpse with tears.

This can't be happening.

This has to be a dream. Someone, please wake me up!

Wiene pleaded as emotion rent her heart in two. But the silent Dungeon didn't grant her wish, only showed her the cold reality of the corpses in her midst.

She clung to the formoire, her sobs showing no signs of stopping. Then.

A dark shadow fell over Wiene.

"Don't fret, monster."

"——."

Dix looked down at the sobbing dragon girl and grinned.

He laughed, as if nothing could give him more pleasure than the pain in her eyes.

"You're not gonna be left out."

Wiene's tearful eyes opened wide.

Her hood had started to slip off. He caught a glimpse of the beautiful jewel glinting underneath and swung his red spear with one hand.

Her vision flashed red. Jarring pain coursed through her entire body.

Wiene lost consciousness soon after.

"Gah, raaawh…!"

Both arms and all spider legs broken, Ranieh fought to the last but reached her limit.

A deep silence fell over the room. It was so quiet, the battle that had just transpired seemed like a distant dream. However, the badly gouged floor and walls told the story of the fierce struggle that had only just ended. Apart from the hunters, the room was eerily still.

Ranieh was dragged up to where Dix stood near the harpy girl.

"Just had to do it the hard way—didn'cha!"

"GAH!"

"Damn, that hurts…"

The large man, Gran, kicked her with the tip of his boot before unceremoniously throwing her to the floor.

Pressing the wound he had suffered from fighting Ranieh, the man scowled at her. Many around him tended to their own injuries with a combination of magic and potions.

......!

Ranieh had lost her helmet, leaving her beautiful white hair and snowy skin in plain sight. Lying on her stomach, she scanned the surroundings.

Wiene lay motionless at her side. The dragon girl's eyes were hidden by her hair, so it was impossible to make out her expression. Ranieh could, however, see several bruises and lumps all over her body. The hunters must have administered a beating to ensure the defenseless girl remained unconscious. Her robe was damaged and torn in many places; even her tough scales were cracked and broken.

"When did these things get so strong...? Damn."

"That formoire, I tell ya. These guys must've been the cream of the crop."

Foh was dead. Orde and Cliff had been killed as well. All three of them were nothing more than piles of ash now.

The harpy lying on the other side of the dragon girl was still breathing. Eyes closed and face slack, she was only unconscious like Wiene.

Only monsters with human features had been left alive.

Ranieh immediately understood what that meant.

These were the hunters the Guild messenger Fels had told them about. These people captured monsters like Wiene and sold them on the black market to satisfy their own greed. The arachne knew they intended to sell off the Xenos to some unknown buyer.

Ranieh gritted her fangs as she listened to an Amazon and animal person chat nearby and drowned in her own anger and feelings of powerlessness.

"Hey, all of you. Get your asses moving and carry the vouivre out of here. There could be more of these things on the way, so keep your eyes open."

Dix issued orders while tapping the spear against his shoulder.

The other hunters shuddered and obeyed at once. They split into two groups, one to take care of the monsters emerging from the Dungeon walls and the other set to work on the Xenos.

...!

As Wiene was lifted from her line of sight, Ranieh focused what strength she had left into the tip of her finger.

Pointing at the vouivre, she launched a single thread of silk. It was normally used to ensnare prey—a spiderweb.

However—*slice!*

"......?!"

"What do you think you're doing?"

The warped, rubellite spearhead severed Ranieh's web.

Somehow, Dix was able to spot the nearly invisible thread. The arachne forgot to breathe as he stared down at her.

"Spiderweb...Trying to leave a trail? That ain't happening."

The goggled man smirked as Ranieh scowled and trembled with rage.

This man was clever, cunning, and sly.

Those very traits inspired fear in his allies. He was always calm and prudent, leaving nothing to chance. Ranieh was certain that the reason her Xenos comrades, Fels, and the others on the surface were still unable to locate the hunter base of operations was because this man was in charge.

She glared at him with enough hatred to kill. But Dix just stood there, red spear over his shoulder.

"Aww...This one's no good. We can't relax around it. Pocketing this one would just set your jacket on fire."

He grabbed a fistful of Ranieh's white hair and hauled her up so that her eyes were level with his sneer.

Dix's smile only deepened as the arachne's face, contorting in pain and anger, reflected off his goggles.

"This one dies here."

"......!!"

He sentenced her to death, merciless judge, jury, and executioner.

Other hunters gathered around Dix as he let go of her hair and stood up.

Ranieh broke out in a cold sweat as she watched the humans unsheathing their weapons and drawing near.

"H-hey, Dix, can we?"

"Can we what?"

Just then, three men took a step toward Dix to get his attention.

Their intentions were evident from the grotesque smiles on their faces.

"We're gonna kill it anyway, so before that...can't we have a little fun?"

"......"

"We don't got much time, I know that...J-just look at it. It'd be a waste."

Ranieh didn't know what they were talking about at first.

However, a wave of nausea and revulsion coursed through her the instant she understood.

"...Do as you like."

Dix glanced between the arachne and the men before sneering.

He jerked his chin in Ranieh's direction, and the three men couldn't have been more excited, dark smiles twisting their faces.

"H-heh-heh...Be good now, you hear?"

Rough breaths, perverted grins.

Gazes that practically licked her body. She understood.

These men had a monster fetish.

It was a perverse attraction that some people felt toward monsters, more specifically humanoid ones like lamia or monsters that possessed human characteristics.

Most people shunned and despised them for it.

And they were going to violate her.

Not only had they robbed her of her friends, they intended to trample her dignity as well.

Dix and the other hunters watched with anticipation as the clearly excited men descended upon her.

Ranieh's fists clenched beneath her broken forearms, shaking with rage.

"S-stop this...! Don't touch me!!"

"Don't be feisty, now. You there, hold it down."

The men ignored Ranieh's threats and feeble thrashing and reached for her.

Badly injured and outnumbered three to one, she could do little to defend herself. Her arachnid lower body was pinned in their strong grasp, and goose bumps rose on her skin. Her armor was ripped away, exposing her substantial chest, and a single layer of adventurer's battle cloth was her last line of defense from the hunters' prying eyes.

The first signs of fear passed over her face as their hands crept closer and closer.

The men noticed her expression, and their hearts skipped a beat in sadistic excitement. Licking their lips, the three of them dove for her.

"——."

In that moment.

Ranieh's expression changed from fear of abuse to her body and soul to something much more vicious.

Her fangs bared, and her pupils narrowed to slits to form the face of a truly ferocious monster.

She opened her jaws wide and spat some *fluid* onto the three men in the blink of an eye.

"Geh—GAHHHHHHHHHHHHHHHHHHHHHHHHHHH!"

A chorus of bloodcurdling screams ensued.

"I-it burns…!!"

"It's melting!"

"Ha-ha-ha-ha-ha-ha-ha! The hell are you guys doing?"

Lured in by Ranieh's acting skills, the three men staggered back in excruciating pain. The other hunters chuckled at the spectacle as the three men clutched their eyes or collapsed to the floor.

Insectoid monsters were known for their poison-based attacks.

While many of them were paralyzing agents designed to prevent prey from escaping their webs, Ranieh's was highly acidic and powerful enough to liquefy targets.

Indeed, the onlookers recoiled from the clouds of putrid smoke rising from the three men.

"G-GODDAMN MONSTERRRRR!"

Enraged, the trio who had fallen for the arachne's unexpected trap drew their weapons.

Ranieh saw the metallic blades flash—and smiled.

"—Ghh!"

Three swords pierced her torso all the way through.

The blade tips struck the Dungeon floor, protruding from her back.

Blood gushed from the three wounds and burst from her mouth.

The liquid splattering across the floor was red, no different from a human's.

"Agh, gh, ha…ha-ha! Aha-ha-ha-ha-ha-ha—AHHHHHHHHH-HHHHH!!"

Cries of pain and suffering became one ferocious howl.

Ranieh, her lips dyed red and slick with blood, swung her broken arms around with the last of her strength. Though fatally wounded, she managed to strike the three men who stabbed her. They tumbled backward, screaming.

Dix whistled at the spectacle as the other hunters called out to one another, arming themselves once again.

"*Hah! Haa…!* I won't allow any of you bastards to shame this body!!"

Forcing herself upright despite her broken limbs, Ranieh breathed heavily, then shouted as loud as she could.

The hunters watched, taken aback by her overwhelming fortitude.

"Even…if I die—I'd never let you have it!!"

Then, using her hand, Ranieh *gored* herself in the chest.

Dix and the hunters watched in amazement as Ranieh took hold of the "core" buried deep inside her flesh and flashed a bloody smile.

"Gro…s—I leave the rest to—."

Those words trickling from her mouth became her last.

She tightened her grip, and *crack!* Everyone heard it—the magic stone shattered.

The bloody yet still alluringly beautiful arachne disintegrated into a large pile of ash right before their eyes. A moment later, it vanished.

"……I-it freaking offed itself."

The hunters shrank back after witnessing the monster choose her own escape.

A pile on the floor was all that remained of her. She hadn't even left a drop item behind.

The hunters watched with quivering eyes, her brave yet tragic death burned into their memories.

"Ho-ho…Now that's what I call cool. That's my kind of style."

Dix was the only one among them unaffected by what had just transpired.

Seeing their leader completely unmoved by the spectacle, the subordinate hunters began to recover, their calm smiles returning one by one.

The man in goggles smiled at the heap of ash—the monster's remains on the floor.

"She was on to something there. The only one allowed to do something to me is me. I take orders from no one. Turns out we were pretty compatible," Dix declared self-centeredly, even though he was the offender.

The male hunters jeered, "Are you really one to talk?" inviting laughter and guffaws.

The man adjusted his goggles with one hand and turned to face them with a slight grin.

"We could use this as bait to draw out more of the ones that might be around but…no need to get greedy. We're leaving," Dix flatly stated as he turned on his heel.

The three men with patches of melted flesh staggered to their feet, and the rest of the hunters followed the leader toward the exit.

"We got us a vouivre to show off. Best to get it back to base first."

Turning their backs on the ash that was once an arachne, the hunters left the room for good.

As the group of criminals advanced through the Dungeon halls, the harpy's and vouivre girl's limp bodies swayed under a hunter's arms.

A single, round tear dropped from a closed amber eye as the

dragon girl was taken farther and farther away from what was left of her comrades.

Several hours later.

"......ou."

A gargoyle landed in the middle of a room absolutely littered with ash.

The monster's gaze traveled from end to end as a unicorn and a silverback came up beside him.

A familiar breastplate with a gaping hole in the middle. An oversize mace. A shredded robe and a complete set of heavy plate armor sliced in half. The monster's stone body trembled and clattered at the sight of the scattered equipment among the ashes.

From there, the gargoyle walked to the other side of the room and reached into an uprooted flower bed.

His quivering fingers grasped a red crystal that had been thrown there while the marauders were distracted.

The gargoyle held another crystal just like it in his other hand. Gros flung his head back and gazed toward the ceiling.

"OOOOOOOOOOOOOOOOOOOOOOOOOOORRRHHH!!"

He unleashed a monstrous roar of burning indignation that echoed throughout the labyrinth.

"———?"

I turn around and look behind me.

All I see is the bluish Dungeon walls and ceiling. Randomly located light sources illuminate the intersections and labyrinthine halls that seem to stretch on forever. A party of adventurers must be close by because I can hear their restless voices coming from around a nearby corner.

I'm standing in the middle of a passageway, staring at the ground that so many of my fellow adventurers have walked.

I could've sworn I heard something……that the Dungeon just shook.

"BGYAA!"

"!"

As I look over my shoulder, a sudden cry rushing toward me gets my attention.

A goblin is charging. I spin away from the low-level monster's swipe at my chest and raise the Hestia Knife in my right hand.

I'm in the Dungeon, third floor.

It's been so long since I spent time on the Dungeon's upper floors that this area looks new to me. Back when I first joined my goddess's familia, when I was just Level 1, I came through here all the time. This is where my adventures started.

I've been on this territory for lower-class adventurers since morning.

"GIII!"

The monster swipes at me with both arms in a frenzy, but I dodge by leaning slightly left and right.

The goblin's movements are slow and lethargic, or at least that's how it seems to me now. I could bury my knife in its chest, breaking the magic stone inside right now if I feel like it.

But I can't bring myself to follow through on a counterattack.

"UggAHH!!"

"……!"

The goblin yells at me, frustrated that none of its attacks are connecting.

Its rage-filled eyes lock on to me—its urge to kill sends a jolt down my spine, making my hand twitch.

My fight-or-flight instinct kicks in as a natural urge to challenge monsters pushes me forward. The Hestia Knife traces an arc through the air.

"—GIAA!!"

The violet blade carves a chunk out of the monster's chest.

Just like I wanted, it pierces the magic stone.

The goblin freezes in place, as if it knows its core crystal has broken, before fading into ash with a soft *swish*.

I slew the monster with a technique that has become second nature.

"..."

I look down at the gray pile at my feet.

There's a sharp tooth in the middle of it.

It's a drop item like any other...I stare at the goblin fang for far too long, unable to bring myself to pick it up.

I came into the Dungeon today because there's something I need to know:

Can I still kill monsters?

Can I still hunt monsters and stay as an adventurer in Orario?

...I...can do it.

I've slain several of them since entering the Dungeon this morning.

All by breaking their magic stones, reducing them to ash like just now.

Yes, but—I haven't been able to look away from the truth that complicates everything, that nothing can sugarcoat.

Not since I met Wiene.

I know the monsters called Xenos can feel emotions and think for themselves.

Now, when it comes to murdering monsters...I hesitate.

Even though I can still fight...it's nothing like how it was before.

I wonder if I'll ever go back to how I was, prowling the Dungeon like the adventurer I used to be.

It's impossible to get the question out of my head.

A single second is the difference between life and death when facing monsters. It's only a matter of time before I die if this keeps up. And to a monster's claws or fangs, no less.

"GRUAHH!"

"OOO!"

Several kobolds and a dungeon lizard climbing on the wall appear as I meander through the Dungeon halls. I grit my teeth and engage them in combat.

The small group comes at me at once, and my body responds on its own. While I evade their deadly attacks, their dying breaths reach my ears as my knife destroys the dark-purple stones inside them.

"Don't waver. Don't hold back for our sake."

A certain lizardman's voice rings in my ears every time I come face-to-face with a monster.

It was the last thing he said to me at the Xenos hideaway before we went our separate ways.

"Don't you ever die. I want to see you again."

I'm pretty sure I'd be practically useless right now if he hadn't said that.

Don't die—I can still hold a weapon thanks to that admonition.

Because he…a monster hopes I stay alive so we can meet again one day.

"……"

I turn away from the piles of ash that were once the monsters I defeated and walk on. In the end, no clear answer has presented itself, even after all my contemplation. My heart still troubled, I set a course for the exit.

I should hurry up and reach a decisive conclusion.

That would be the logical thing to do.

Regular monsters are completely different from Xenos like Wiene and Lido. Even if I hesitate, monsters will keep trying to kill me. People and monsters are bound to fight.

But for the purpose of earning money…and catching up to my idol…is it really okay to kill them? Am I allowed to fight and kill for personal gain?

I realize that I don't really have a reason why I need to kill monsters.

If I'm having thoughts like this in my line of work…I won't last long.

"Bell Cranell…"

"It's the Little Rookie."

A party consisting of animal people, prums, and other demi-humans glance at me as I silently trudge by, whispering among themselves. I'm sure I heard my title at some point.

The Dungeon layout is circular.

It gets wider with each successively lower floor.

The fifth floor, part of the upper levels, is said to be about as wide as Central Park on the surface. I wonder if it's because there's less space up here compared to the middle levels, but it feels as though I keep finding adventurers around every turn. Then again, there are a lot more lower-class adventurers in the first place, so it only makes sense people run into one another more.

I guess *Hestia Familia*'s fame from the War Game against *Apollo Familia* is still alive and well. People recognize me fairly often.

It's true that I'm hanging around a floor that people officially recorded at my level don't usually stick around—and all by myself, too—so I'm sure it's a sight to see. Every time I meet their eyes, they seem puzzled.

But I can't do much more than stare back.

Oh, I'm already here...?

Having arrived at the Beginning Road on the first floor, I make my way up into the yawning opening that connects the Dungeon to the surface.

There's a spiraling staircase beneath Babel Tower, and the ceiling overhead is decorated with a sky-blue mural. There's hardly anyone else here, since the morning rush is over, and it's too early—right before lunchtime—for most adventurers to head home. My eyes are fixed on the silvery steps as I ascend one at a time.

Just one foot in front of the other until...someone stops in front of me.

"Ah..."

When I look up, I see a single adventurer.

A silver breastplate and a single sword hanging from the waist.

Long blond hair sparkles in the magic-stone lamplight like radiant sand in the desert.

And two eyes the same golden color as her hair look back at me.

"Aiz..."

My idol's name slips from my mouth before I realize it.

"......"

The blond-haired, golden-eyed girl and white-haired boy exchanged a few words before returning to the surface together.

A black-robed mage silently watched the scene unfold *through a blue crystal* set atop a pedestal.

"Has something happened, Fels?"

"...No."

Fels responded curtly to the deep voice's question from beneath the robe's black hood.

This was the Chamber of Prayers beneath Guild Headquarters.

The four burning torches in the middle of the room were all that kept darkness at bay in the stony space. Directly in the center of this seemingly ancient temple was a towering, majestic altar with an equally majestic deity seated on it like it was a throne—Ouranos.

"So then, there has been no movement beneath Babel."

"Unfortunately not. These hunters...There has not been a single sign that *Ikelos Familia* has passed through the tower."

Fels nodded, confirming Ouranos's thoughts.

Fels had an "eye" set in place over the pit leading to the Dungeon beneath Babel in the form of a spherical blue crystal hidden in the artwork adorning the tower's basement ceiling.

It was an oculus, one of a set of twin crystals created by "Fels the Fool," once known as the Sage.

Each crystal could display what its twin was seeing and hearing. It was the only magic item in existence capable of long-distance communication. They were extremely difficult to make; Fels had struggled from lacking the correct materials on hand, and the task had required a level of mastery that even Perseus had yet to achieve. The mage had also supplied the owl familiar that had been rescued from death with one of these magic items to replace its missing eye.

Fels used the power of this mobile oculus to keep a literal eye on outlaws and blacklisted adventurers—similar to how Wiene had been monitored while she was on the surface.

These activities were such a well-kept secret that Ouranos's subordinates—in other words, the Guild employees themselves—didn't even know Fels existed. Ignoring minor transgressions or isolated incidents, the black-robed mage had kept watch over the Labyrinth City for many years to make sure Orario and the Dungeon did not take a turn for the worse.

"There have been no new developments, Ouranos. Despite learning our enemies' true identity, tracking them has proven impossible."

Thanks entirely to *Hermes Familia*'s efforts, they were almost certain that the hunters responsible for selling monsters on the black market belonged to *Ikelos Familia.*

Fels had used an oculus to observe the Dungeon's entrance during the recent journey to the Xenos Hidden Village two days ago. Despite the constant surveillance since then, there were no sightings of any adventurers registered with *Ikelos Familia* passing through.

The movements of the hunters remained in the dark, as if they were laughing at Fels's efforts.

"Since they haven't returned to Babel, they're either still in the depths of the Dungeon or hiding in Rivira...But then again, that seems unlikely."

The heart of the problem was how they were able to avoid Fels's eyes while still bringing captured Xenos *to the surface* and smuggling them outside Orario's walls.

Only one possibility came to mind.

The black-robed mage turned away from the blue crystal on the pedestal and peered up to make eye contact with the deity on his seat at the altar.

Making the best attempt to speak in a calm, concise voice, Fels laid it out plainly.

"It must be what we've suspected for some time...There is *another Dungeon entrance*, separate from Babel."

"..."

"As we thought, our enemies who abduct monsters are not operating from a base located *on the surface—.*"

Crackle. Sparks scattered from the torches.

Motes of light fell to the stone floor as silence descended on the Chamber of Prayers.

In the dim light, Fels and Ouranos exchanged eye contact but no words.

"What is the Xenos situation?"

At long last, Ouranos spoke again.

Fels's intricately patterned black glove disappeared inside folds of dark fabric.

"I believe they're en route to a separate Hidden Village as planned…However, I have yet to receive word from Lido confirming their arrival."

Another crystal the same shape as the one on the pedestal appeared from Fels's robes.

Being on the surface didn't prevent the mage from maintaining regular contact with the Xenos, thanks to another set of oculi. The magic item served as an important link that enabled Fels to maintain communications wherever they happened to be in the Dungeon, as well as rapidly issue quests to investigate and/or eliminate Irregulars.

However, the oculus did have one drawback, in that it could interact only with its paired twin. In other words, Fels needed a separate crystal pair for each location that required surveillance and each person who required a line of communication. It was cumbersome at best. Indeed, Fels's full-body robe was bulky with crystals.

The Xenos had been given several sets of oculi to use, but their leader, Lido, carried the only one that connected to the surface.

Fels grasped a yellow crystal, attempting to peer inside—and abruptly froze.

"What is the matter?" Ouranos inquired, sensing something was amiss.

After a long pause, the black-robed mage finally spoke in a shaky voice.

"Lido's crystal has gone dark…"

A violent sound cut through the air.

The yellow crystal slammed into the floor and shattered.

"—What're you doing, Gros?!"

A lizardman's surprised and angry voice echoed in the Colossal Tree Labyrinth.

It happened inside a room deep within the Dungeon's twenty-fourth floor. Sundry monster species had gathered in a dark room devoid of Lamp Moss. They were equipped with armor and weapons: Xenos.

The lizardman Lido and the gargoyle Gros were in the middle of the group, staring each other down.

"Why'd you break the crystal?! Now we have no way to reach Fels and…!"

"We have no reason to listen to Fels's words!! No reason to follow his commands!! We know what must be done!!"

Now that the only oculus capable of communicating with the surface was broken, Lido demanded an explanation from Gros.

It started with a message from Gros's group.

—Ranieh's band has been slaughtered; Wiene and Fia, captured.

Hearing the news, Lido had used all the oculi in his possession to summon each Xenos troupe. The siren Rei and other leaders immediately led their units to the current room to receive details and share information. Then, just as Lido was about to inform Fels—Gros's stone claw ripped the crystal from his grasp and destroyed it.

"Fels will say the same thing he always does! 'Endure. Stay your hand for now.' Enough!! We've tolerated far more than we can take!"

The ash-colored gargoyle shouted back, overpowering Lido's voice.

Fels and those who sided with the mage were concerned only with keeping the Xenos a secret. Gros no longer cared about the concerns of those on the surface.

He had dammed up his rage every time another of their comrades was abducted, but now he howled furiously.

Several pieces of broken armor and weapons lay at the feet of the Xenos assembly.

Gros had retrieved what was left of their slain allies and brought them here.

"I saw everything; I heard everything!! I saw what the people did; I saw Ranieh's death!!"

"……!"

He shared a set of twin crystals with Ranieh.

In an ironic twist, it was the oculus Fels had given him that pushed Gros over the edge, igniting the black flames in his heart. After witnessing firsthand the hunters massacre his friends, nothing could soothe his seething hatred.

Gros wasn't alone.

Both Xenos factions, Lido's and Gros's, were up in arms.

Gros's side viewed people in a negative light to begin with—but the Xenos who allied themselves with Lido were also boiling.

A griffin's eyes smoldered with anger that the hippogriff had been murdered.

A lamia whipped her hair about as she wailed, swearing revenge.

A troll pounded the ground, fists clenched so tightly that blood dripped from between his fingers as debris filled the air.

A unicorn, a silverback, a crimson eagle, a metal gazelle…Most of the Xenos gave in to the fury coursing through them.

Other than Lido, the only Xenos capable of rational thought were the depressed, downtrodden red-cap goblin, the tight-lipped siren Rei, and an al-miraj with her front paws clamped tightly over her eyes, fighting back tears.

"We don't need Fels's help! Nor will we allow anyone to stop us!! This is our problem and we will solve it!!"

Shaking with rage, Gros widened his red stone eyes, incapable of tears, as he howled a truly monstrous declaration:

"Revenge!! Revenge for Ranieh, Orde, Cliff, and Foh!! Rescue our brethren!! The surface dwellers shall regret this day!!"

The gargoyle roared.

The surrounding Xenos joined in, howling in agreement.

—Revenge!! Revenge!! Revenge!!

The room shook as more voices joined, rife with intensity.

Amid his comrades howling with no regard for nearby adventurers or monsters, Lido winced.

His scaly red hands clenched into trembling fists.

"Kill them all!! Murder anything and anyone that stands in our way! Wipe them out!!"

"If we—if we do that…we'll be no better than the ones who kidnapped Wiene and Fia…!"

Lido bellowed through clenched fangs. On the verge of tears, the lizardman forced the words from his throat.

The flames in his heart blazed as strongly as Gros's faction's. There was only one thing allowing him to stay calm enough to see reason—his yearning.

"After everything we've done, everything we've been through—are you going to throw it all away?! Will you abandon the dreams of our fallen comrades, to one day see the light on the surface…?!"

It was his dearest wish to walk aboveground, to coexist peacefully with humanity.

Lido couldn't let go of this powerful desire in his heart. This ideal gave him a sense of purpose and a reason to live. He pleaded with the other Xenos to see how they were about to step over a line that shouldn't be crossed.

"There are people like Bellucchi!! Have you already forgotten?!"

Lido shouted the name of the boy who had shaken his hand.

"Not all adventurers, not all people are bad!"

Lido poured his heart and soul into every word, but it was no use. His comrades were too far gone.

Without faltering, Gros immediately countered.

"How many times do you need to be betrayed to understand?!"

"!!"

"Where are all the people who showed us kindness now?!"

Many Xenos had been fortunate enough to encounter merciful

adventurers before meeting Bell. Lido and his group felt hope for the future every time that happened.

However, when push came to shove, they all sided with the surface races.

They abandoned the Xenos to their fates.

"The truth is that that boy will turn his back on us!! He will forsake us one day! People and monsters cannot live together in peace!!"

"......!"

"Open your eyes, Lido!"

The gargoyle pulled no punches as he urged the lizardman to give up on his absurd dream.

Lido had no response, offering little resistance as Gros pushed him aside and called the Xenos to action.

"We'll take back our friends, no matter the cost!! Ranieh's last wish shall not be in vain!"

Gros spread his ash-colored wings and flew out of the room.

Answering the gargoyle's thunderous roar, other Xenos followed him.

Thirty-some monsters had come together to accomplish a singular goal as one.

"It's no use, Lido...Nothing can stop them now."

As Lido slumped, tormented that he couldn't stop his allies in time, Rei approached and spoke to him.

She had tucked both winged arms against her chest as if hugging herself, and it was all she could do to keep her shoulders from quivering.

"Damn it all..."

He glanced at the siren resisting her anger as his face contorted.

Then he looked straight up, gazing toward the surface landscape he had never seen.

"I'm sorry, Fels...Bellucchi."

His feeble apology faded into the darkness.

The die had been cast. The only option left was to move forward.

Even if things could never return to how they once were—his comrades could be freed at the very least.

Lido's mind was set. At the same time, he released his dam of anger and rage and let them wash over his heart. The raw emotion he kept sealed away instantly consumed him.

The lizardman took on a vicious aura as he jerked the vertical longsword and scimitar at his feet out of the ground.

"Rei, Lett. Come with me. We follow Gros."

"...Yes."

"Understood..."

"Aruru, go find that person."

The al-miraj gazed up at Lido's emotionless face with round red eyes from next to the siren and red-cap goblin.

"They should have arrived at the Hidden Village by now. Explain the situation and bring them along."

The rabbit monster stayed quiet but nodded, long ears flicking forward.

With a short high-pitched squeak, the al-miraj jumped onto the hellhound waiting beside her. She straddled its back like a horse's, and the hellhound bounded away. The rabbit's blue battle jacket fluttered in the wind behind her.

"Let's go."

Lido and his allies raced to catch up with Gros.

The lizardman's thick, snakelike tail whipped back and forth as he picked up speed.

The bloodshot yellow eyes in his profile—were already those of a monster.

"Falgar, they're here—Ikelos's crew."

Hiding their emblems, which depicted winged traveler's hats and sandals, a small group of people started to follow three men.

Trailing the new arrivals, they blended into the flow of adventurers in Rivira. As always, crystals shone overhead.

Light shone down from the rock formations shaped like mums in bloom, indicating it was afternoon on the eighteenth floor. Upper-class adventurers walked in and out of the small town built atop an island in the center of a large lake. Many used this amalgam of hotels, shops, and bars as a base for trips deeper into the Dungeon or as a rest point on their way to the surface. Thanks to the town's various businesses, heated negotiations between greedy merchants and residents were not uncommon.

Angry shouts formed a cacophony with hearty laughter as members of two rival familias stared each other down on the streets. A fight broke out soon after, but no one batted an eye at such a familiar sight in the town of rogues.

"Boris!"

"Yeah? What's buggin' you?"

It didn't take long for the residents of this town surrounded by jagged rocks and crystals to realize that something out of the ordinary was happening.

"The monsters seem restless...Something isn't right."

The fully equipped adventurers gathered on a cliff for a better view.

Every set of eyes was drawn to a single location amid the forest and plains of the safe point.

At the center of the floor, where the roots of the Central Tree led below...

"Those are..."

Now that I'm out of the Dungeon, the sky is bright and blue like always.

The sun is right overhead, so it must be close to noon already.

I'm a good distance away from a main street. Shops of all kinds line the road. There's a crowd of people around a flower shop manned by several young demi-human women who don't have connections to any familia. Several neighborhood kids are with them, bright smiles on their faces as they look at the colorful plants. I watch them for a few moments before I realize that I'm staring.

For a moment, surrounded by lively, peaceful sounds of the city, I feel like I've gotten lost wandering down some unfamiliar street.

Erasing those thoughts from my mind, I walk past all the shops before coming to a stop.

"...Um, sorry. For, you know, taking up your time."

"It's all right."

We face each other in a vacant lot surrounded by houses. It's just Aiz and me.

During our chance meeting on Babel's spiral stairway, I stopped her knowing full well she was on her way into the Dungeon.

As for why, I wasn't sure. But I've been chasing after her for so long as my idol, and I felt like there's something that I needed to ask her.

My mind wouldn't settle down. Aiz must've noticed my internal struggle and suggested that we go someplace else. Leaving Babel, we started looking for a sparsely populated corner of town. Now here we are, face-to-face.

"..."

"..."

Our eyes meet.

How long has it been since the two of us have been alone like this?

Her beauty could give any elf or goddess a run for their money, and looking at her is enough to make you forget time is moving. Her face doesn't show much emotion, and I can't tell what she's thinking, but it's like her eyes keep pulling me in.

I forget almost everything, and I even start to think, *If only that golden luster could keep me under its spell...*

"...What's wrong?"

Aiz asks slowly.

Her words are heavy with meaning. It's like her golden eyes see right through me. As though she's asking, *What happened? Why do you seem so confused?*

My lungs feel tight. My heart is pounding obnoxiously loud in my ears.

My mouth is drying...Finally, I manage to spit it out.

"Aiz..."

"..."

"If monsters had a reason for living...had feelings just like you or me, what would you do?"

And now I've said it.

If you met monsters who could smile like people, worry about things, shed tears just like people—could you still draw your sword against them? I ask the swordswoman who I adore.

"..."

Aiz closes her delicate lips.

Even though she almost certainly doesn't understand why I'd ask such a question, she's still thinking of a sincere answer rather than responding casually or analyzing the question.

Time passes.

A warm summer breeze passes between us.

Never once taking her eyes off me, Aiz finally opens her mouth to speak.

"If monsters hurt someone...No, that's not it."

She stops in midsentence, shakes her head—then she gives me her answer.

"If anyone cries because of a monster—I'll *kill* that monster."

"!!"

My shoulders jump after hearing those words. I'm not breathing.

Aiz declared her intentions without any hesitation whatsoever.

Even if the monster had a soul like a human, she would strike it down right then and there.

My idol's reply is blunt and brutal. I freeze up.

Aiz's saber mercilessly tearing into Wiene and the other Xenos... The image flashes through the back of my mind.

Dumbstruck, I stare at her focused, unchanging expression.

In fact, her eyes are asking me:

—*Would you not?*

"......!!"

That's right. I've lost someone important, too.

Gramps, an irreplaceable person in my life, was killed by a monster.

And I remember how I cried when it happened.

The reason I didn't become consumed by hatred and a desire to avenge his death is because I never actually saw his body and that I felt so lonely at the time that the anger never had a chance to set in.

I'm paralyzed, straddling the threshold between ideals and reality, between people and monsters.

My heart drums a furious rhythm under Aiz's stare.

"I—"

Then.

As I break out into a sweat and muster the courage to speak—at that very instant…

Clang! Clang!!

A shrill ringing echoes through the sky.

"""?!"""

Aiz and I turn and look up.

The bells that go off every day at noon? No.

Those always ring from the east end, but this sound is clearly from the north. What's more, the intensity of the ringing definitely isn't normal.

It's like the messenger is distressed.

"That direction, probably Guild Headquarters…The city's warning bells?"

Aiz's mumbling sends a jolt down my spine.

Yes, now I remember. I heard these bells go off not too long ago.

When the Rakian army—when *Ares Familia* launched an attack on Orario, they rang the same huge bell above Guild Headquarters.

An alarm only used to announce a *state of emergency.* This is for sure Orario's alert system.

I hold my breath as that earsplitting tone assaults my eardrums.

"—Emergency! Emergency!! Attention all familias residing in Orario! The Guild will soon issue a mission!!"

As if confirming my fears, magic-stone amplifiers carry a voice from Guild Headquarters.

A familiar half-elf's voice echoes throughout the city streets.

"*Monsters equipped with armor and weapons* have destroyed Rivira on the eighteenth floor!! Large numbers of them on the move have been confirmed!!"

—Then comes the knockout blow, emptying my lungs of air.

"The Guild is ordering the immediate deployment of all adventurers to exterminate—What? A-are you certain?...U-understood."

As the world comes crashing down around me, the announcer pauses in utter bewilderment before continuing.

"All citizens, including adventurers, are hereby forbidden to enter the Dungeon!! The Guild will contact familias directly. Please stand by at your respective homes!! Once again..."

The urgency is palpable.

Aiz's intense gaze looks up at the sky. I can't say a thing.

Rivira, destroyed?

Armed monsters? Large numbers on the move?

Lido and the others...Wiene?

It can't be. What could've...?

A wave of heat rushes through me as my thoughts spin wildly, to no avail. Confusion and turmoil flood every corner of my being, and sweat pours from me.

The warning bells echo endlessly through the city, while my vision blurs.

Our everyday lives have been turned upside down. The ominous news drops like a stone and sends ripples out into the city.

Trouble is about to fall on Orario.

CHAPTER 8
CITY PANIC
© Suzuhito Yasuda

"Listen to what I'm telling ya! Monsters carryin' weapons attacked us!! Rivira is gone, wiped out!!"

A man bellowed, wounded all over.

He slammed his bloody fists onto the countertop, flinging red droplets. The receptionists and Guild employees paled as they listened to Boris, acting head of Rivira, who looked as though he had barely escaped with his life.

Pandemonium had descended upon Guild Headquarters.

Rivira's residents pushed and shoved their way through the white marble lobby to the reception counter after their near brush with death on the eighteenth floor. Most of the sweaty adventurers had plopped to the floor with exhaustion, and many had suffered severe injuries.

The reason why they had pushed themselves so hard and pressed their way through the Guild lobby was obvious.

They needed to warn people on the surface of the Irregular attack that just occurred in the Dungeon.

"They came up from farther down the Central Tree! All sorts of species were there, and the only thing they had in common was that they're all damn strong!"

Mysterious armed monsters from lower floors. These creatures, most likely a special subspecies, had the potential to go toe to toe with upper-class adventurers. They made a beeline for the island in the middle of the lake, for Rivira, howling the whole way.

Rivira's residents were used to dealing with Irregulars, but this assault struck faster than anyone could react. Once its outer walls were broken, the Dungeon's outpost town was overrun in a matter of moments. Unable to put up much of a fight against the monsters' onslaught, the residents joined the adventurers who happened to be in town and raced back to the surface.

The 334th incarnation of Rivira lay in ruins.

"What species? How many were there?!"

"Were you pursued?! How far up have they come?!"

Healers walked among the adventurers at the behest of Guild employees, casting curative magic, distributing recovery items, and wrapping wounds with bandages as receptionists tried to collect as much detailed information as possible. As they continued their interrogations and analysis, they began to grasp the situation—an Irregular of epic proportions.

"P-please hold on a moment! Wh-what are the adventurer casualties…?!"

"Most of us got out somehow but… some didn't make it. By now, they're…"

Boris wrinkled his brow as he spelled out the sad truth. Misha, a pink-haired receptionist, listened with tears brimming in her eyes.

"This is really bad…!"

The hectic situation was worsening by the moment when Eina returned from making the emergency announcement.

The half-elf looked around the Guild lobby, face twisting with sadness.

"Oh, Tulle, you're back. We need more people; get to work immediately."

"Of course, Chief!…But if I may?"

Her chienthrope supervisor rushed up to meet her, but Eina had her own question.

"Why was the announcement changed…?!"

The Dungeon was now off-limits to all adventurers. They had been ordered to stand by at their homes and wait for further instructions.

Time was a luxury they didn't have.

The town of Rivira had fallen to a party of monsters that forced their way up from deeper floors. The safety point was their last line of defense. Without it, the Guild—no, all the people who lived on the surface—had to consider the possibility of monsters breaking through and reaching aboveground.

If that happened, and the gods and goddesses who protected

the Labyrinth City lost ground here, then the whole world was in danger.

Just like when the two strongest familias failed to slay the Black Dragon—when they failed to complete the Three Great Quests in the past—the world, as they knew it, was on the verge of being plunged into chaos.

Eina was unable to blindly accept the sudden change in orders.

"...It was upper management's decision."

"Upper management?!"

"Yes. They forced us to alter the announcement...Then again, the boss didn't look too happy about it. If I had to guess, I'd say this decision didn't simply come from upstairs..."

The slim animal person trailed off as if his point was clear enough already.

Eina's emerald-green eyes widened behind her glasses.

It can't be! her heart cried.

"Lord Ouranos...?"

"God Ouranos! Why would you issue such an order...?!"

The rotund elf shouted in desperation, sweat pouring down his face.

In the Chamber of Prayers, below Guild Headquarters...

Ouranos listened to the dire appeal of the highest-ranking person in the Guild, Royman Mardeel, and responded with equal vigor.

"Calm yourself, Royman."

"Be calm?! Emergencies don't get any worse than this! If we don't stop the monsters' advance now, there will be nothing to stand in their way up here! If they break through, all the Guild's power, o-o-our prestige will crumble...!"

Royman's piglike body shivered, his high-pitched voice trembling with fear.

The elderly deity remained stoic as he responded to the head of the Guild, who was more concerned about losing his political influence should the city's governing body fall.

"If these monsters were intent on breaching the surface, they would have followed the adventurers from Rivira and would be at Babel's doorstep by now."

"Th-that's...a valid point."

"There is no doubt that this is an Irregular. However, it is too soon to declare the city is in danger."

Ouranos watched relief wash over the pudgy elf's face before officially putting his fears to rest.

"Above all, my Prayers have not been broken."

"Ohhh...!"

Royman's face lit up at that pronouncement.

As the deity known as the "Father of Orario," Ouranos kept the Dungeon in check with "Prayers" from this very chamber. His unfathomably strong divine will allowed adventurers to make a living in the Dungeon because it prevented monsters from migrating to the surface en masse.

Ouranos wielded so much authority that his assurances were far more convincing than thousands of logical explanations could ever be. With all doubts cleared from his mind, Royman finally regained a sense of calm.

"Sending many familias into battle at once will only cause confusion. *Ganesha Familia* will form the subjugation team. Their duties will include rescuing adventurers still in the Dungeon and investigating floors beneath the middle levels. Relay the orders."

"Yes, right away!"

"More instructions will follow. Go."

"Y-yes!"

Royman's heavy form kneeled before the deity, then he rose to his feet and turned away.

He quickly ascended the long stairwell that connected to the first floor, his stout belly shaking from the effort.

Then, almost as if taking his place—

"This isn't good..."

"Indeed."

—a shadow emerged from the darkness at the end of the chamber, coalescing into Fels.

Ouranos donned a more serious expression as the mage's form and emotions revealed themselves.

"Royman acted before we could collect information."

"I would have preferred making sense of the situation and drawing up a plan before stirring up a panic...!"

Armed monsters believed to be of various subspecies had launched an attack on the eighteenth floor. Believing this to be a sign of an imminent surface breach, Royman and the other members of the Guild's upper management had declared a state of emergency.

It was a natural reaction for someone unaware of the circumstances surrounding the events. The appearance of monsters hailing from not only the middle levels but the deep levels—monsters usually only ranged from their predetermined areas one to two floors at most—was more than enough to inspire terror.

Ouranos, who understood the whole picture, had been too late to react.

Despite the late start, they took the next best option and tried to quell the rising tide of panic by altering the announcement and the mission.

"If our information is accurate, the Xenos are no doubt behind this. Their reasons have yet to be determined, but they attacked Rivira...!"

Fels's black robe trembled. He did not want to believe those words.

The mage, who preferred to be called the Fool, struggled against an inner turmoil.

"What do you think happened, Fels?"

"It's very likely this incident and the loss of contact with Lido are connected. This is only a guess but...an attack by the hunters? And then *something* caused them to advance on Rivira..."

Ouranos posed the question to Fels almost as if asking himself. "The wrath of the monsters, is it...?" The deity seated on the altar quietly closed his eyes. "...My orders are ready. Prepare your familiar."

"So then..."

"Yes. First, as I said to Royman, direct *Ganesha Familia* to the eighteenth floor. Their defensive posts throughout the city and at the gates will need replacements. The mission participants will be handpicked from our closest allies."

Sending *Ganesha Familia* into the Dungeon was a front to reassure the public that the vaunted elites would keep any damage from the monsters to a minimum.

The true reason, however, was to ensure the Xenos weren't killed in the fighting. It was also to prevent them from carrying out their vengeful massacre of adventurers.

Everything was already in motion. As the governing body of Orario, the Guild had no choice but to act.

On the other hand, the Guild's upper management had no knowledge of these intelligent monsters. Ouranos directed his trusted ally, Ganesha, to handle the situation quickly and with the utmost secrecy in order to keep it that way.

"What of *Hermes Familia*?"

"Have them continue their investigation into Ikelos and his followers. Once all the pieces are in place, Fels, accompany *Ganesha Familia*."

The elderly god added that he would issue orders to Royman directly. Fels acknowledged the instructions.

Then, just as the black-robed mage was turning to leave...

Ouranos opened his mouth with a hint of concern in his eyes.

"Fels—include Bell Cranell in the mission."

"...Ouranos, that would be—"

"We will have our answer. We will test that boy...the one and only adventurer to ever take the hand of a Xenos..."

Ouranos brought up the events at the Xenos's Hidden Village as he narrowed his blue eyes.

"Is he a child who gets swept up in circumstance, a human who dances in the palms of gods, or perhaps...?"

The deity's words echoed into the dark recesses of the chamber.

Fels nodded after a few moments, black robe illuminated by the torch's dancing flames.

"I understand...and I shall obey your divine will."

The mage turned once again and retreated from the altar.

The god remained still, watching intently as the situation unfolded at an ever-increasing pace.

A crowd of demi-humans has already assembled on the front lawn, hiding the building from view, by the time I arrive.

The Pantheon—the Guild Headquarters—grows larger with every step as Aiz and I accelerate toward it.

"!"

The heat and noise in here hit me like a slap in the face.

Bleeding adventurers are sprawled out on the floor, others are angrily ranting at the receptionists at the counter, and Guild employees are rushing this way and that.

Aiz and I didn't listen to the instructions of the emergency announcement. Instead, we made a beeline for Guild Headquarters.

Aiz is here to gather as much information as she can; as for me, I couldn't just meekly wait at home. I had to know why they issued those orders, and I ran all the way here even though the shock hasn't worn off.

"All these people …!"

"Yes, they're from Rivira…"

I look around the lobby, panting for air. Aiz stands beside me: calm, cool, and collected. Breathing normally, she nods.

Information is coming in from everywhere. The residents of Rivira, having escaped death by the skin of their teeth, are sheltering here and making enough noise to turn this place on its head. Also, Aiz and I aren't the only adventurers in here. Quite a few people from other familias, including a few gods and goddesses, have arrived to hear the news firsthand and are pulling Guild employees aside whenever one happens to pass by.

"We won't get a chance to find out anything like this…"

Aiz is right. Finding someone in this chaos is going to be…!

My impatience is rising, and I grit my teeth against the urge to just do *something*. Shaking my head, I'm not sure what to do—and I see bloody, battered, and bruised adventurers no matter where I look.

A werewolf, hunched over and leaning against the wall. A dwarf with a hand to a head wound, blood rushing down his face as he receives treatment. An elf, desperately trying to keep her badly injured party conscious.

Did Lido and the others really do all this…?

I can't look at the truth.

I don't want to believe it.

As if to escape, I turn away.

"Oh—Miss Eina!"

Just as I look away, I spot a half-elf out of the corner of my eye and call out to her.

Aiz turns to look in the same direction. Sure enough, Eina whirls around in surprise.

"Bell! And Ms. Wallenstein!"

"Please, tell me what happened!"

There's no time for pleasantries. I get right to the point.

She apparently wants to say something, but she gives up after seeing the serious look on my face, I think. After a quick glance in Aiz's direction, she starts talking.

"Exactly what I said in the announcement. Rivira has been destroyed."

"And what about the monsters that did it…?!"

"According to the adventurers, they were equipped with armor and carrying weapons. A particularly violent gargoyle was leading the charge, but many species were involved…Like a unicorn, a lizardman—"

As the list expands, the blood drains from my face.

There's no denying it now. The truth hits hard, like a nail through the chest.

"From what I understand, the Guild has asked *Ganesha Familia* to dispatch a subjugation team. The elites will settle this…Bell, Ms. Wallenstein, our messengers will inform you the moment other familias are needed. Please stand by at your homes."

That's her way of saying we're only getting in the way here.

Somehow managing to collect my thoughts, I bristle my eyebrows as I frown. I beat down the part of me that wants to accept the situation and go along with it, and I tell myself that if there's time to hang around doing nothing, there's time to do something useful.

I glance up at Aiz beside me. We make eye contact and nod.

"I'll be on my way...See you."

Assuming the expression of an adventurer, Aiz makes a quick exit from Guild Headquarters.

I try to sound as believable as possible when I tell Eina I'm going back to my familia and turn to follow suit.

"—What?!"

But just as I'm about to take the first step...

A sudden outburst catches my attention, and I glance over my shoulder.

Misha is whispering something in Eina's ear, but she looks very uneasy. Whatever she's saying, Eina is absolutely floored.

She raises her head, eyes quivering—and stops me.

"...Wait, Bell."

The city was rattled.

"What's this about a mission...? They wouldn't ask us to do anything, right?"

"No, no. We wouldn't make much difference..."

"D-don't forget, all three of us are upper class..."

In a run-down building located at the end of a backstreet was the Blue Pharmacy.

Daphne, Nahza, and Cassandra had gathered in the item shop that doubled as *Miach Familia*'s home. Daphne said it was pointless to worry about it, while the chienthrope completely ignored Cassandra's words and busied herself with stocking the shelves.

"B-but Daph, I just had a dream about a big black monster...!" "Yeah, yeah, good for you." "You two, help me finish so we can go gather information..." Their deity, Miach, strolled past the building's metal shutters, face rigid as he listened to his followers' conversation.

"Armed monsters...Then there's little doubt that vouivre is at the heart of this, huh?"

"Weren't those creatures supposed to be friendly, Hestia...?"

At *Takemikazuchi Familia*'s home, the Sojourn Townhouse...

Takemikazuchi whispered in a hollow voice within the antiquated communal housing.

"Lord Takemikazuchi!"

"Ouka, you've returned!"

The tall, broad-shouldered human who headed his familia rushed in to greet him, closely followed by the rest of the party. Takemikazuchi breathed a sigh of relief. His followers, still equipped with an assortment of axes, spears, bows, and backpacks from their trip into the labyrinth that day, began speaking in turn.

"We heard the gist of what's going on in the Dungeon. *Ganesha Familia* is instructing adventurers to return to the surface."

"They told us to tell any remaining parties to do the same...The Dungeon is in an uproar..."

Their physically imposing leader, Ouka, began, and Chigusa finished.

"Is that so..." mulled Takemikazuchi with a nod after several heavy, silent moments. Then he turned to face his followers. "I realize you've only just returned, but we are going out into the city. There are citizens much less informed than we. Whether you simply calm them or give them courage, go and alleviate their distress."

"Sir!" The humans shouted in unison and obeyed their deity's command.

Takemikazuchi roughly scratched at his hair, styled with loops on either side of his head, and muttered, "All right," before following his familia out the door.

"So what's it gonna be, goddess almighty?"

At *Hephaistos Familia*'s branch shop located on Northwest Main Street, also known as Adventurers Way...

Hephaistos looked away from her office window when one of her followers, a woman wearing an eye patch like hers, approached her with a question.

"...Do as the Guild says, for now." There were too many risks should a familia as big as hers start acting independently, the goddess explained to the familia's leader, Tsubaki.

"All right, then," she replied with a nod. "Should I round everyone up? Don't think there'll be much call for smiths like us, though."

"Yes...Summon them back home, just to be safe. I'll be heading over there shortly."

Hephaistos watched Tsubaki leave before returning her gaze to the main thoroughfare below.

Adventurers were loitering around the streets. More than a few were shifting restlessly, as if bobbing in the waves of an oncoming storm.

Reflecting on the information she'd received from a divine friend, just as Miach and Takemikazuchi had, the Goddess of the Forge narrowed her unpatched left eye as thoughts of the Xenos filled her mind.

"Move! Move it!!"

"We have orders to leave the gate and other posts to replacements! Call everyone back in from the city!"

"Babel is under lockdown!! Unless they're an adventurer coming back out, don't let anyone get by you!"

Countless adventurers rushed from place to place, carrying out their duties.

Orario was in an unparalleled uproar, but it was nothing compared to the chaos unfolding inside *Ganesha Familia*'s home. A Guild messenger had delivered their mission, informing every member that regaining control of the Dungeon was now entirely their responsibility.

It was time for Orario's largest familia to demonstrate the full extent of its power.

"......"

Ganesha was out on the front lawn, watching his followers race about, when a single owl fluttered down from the sky.

The familiar landed on the deity's outstretched arm and extended a roll of paper clutched in its talons.

After the owl took flight again, Ganesha silently looked through his elephant mask at the unrolled paper in his hands.

"—This must be important, if I'm being called out at this early afternoon hour."

Ker-tap. Ker-tap. High heels echoed off the floor as locks of gorgeous silver hair flowed down the woman's back.

"Your presence is appreciated."

A goddess possessing unparalleled beauty strolled down a long hallway closely followed by her boaz attendant. The solemn inner garden of her palace lay just beside her line of sight as she stepped through a set of imposing double doors.

"So, what is happening outside?"

Freya's voice reverberated through Folkvangr's massive gathering hall. Her followers and their captains had already assembled for her arrival.

The prum quadruplets were there, along with a graceful elf and dark elf and other demi-humans. A cat person with black-and-ash-colored fur, Allen Fromel, appeared from the throng and came to the goddess's side.

He began to explain the situation with his body bent in a bow.

"Entrust everything to Ganesha and take their position at the gates, you say…?"

"Yes. Those were indeed the Guild's orders."

Freya's silver eyebrows arched while she considered the instructions they had received from the Guild messenger.

This was a bizarre move on the Guild's part. Her suspicion was obvious.

But she was also smiling.

"We're being told to protect the city at a time like this…Are we so untrustworthy?"

"Even if that were the case, this decision seems unnatural."

Her attendant Ottar expressed his opinion that such a large relocation would take time, a luxury they didn't have in this state of emergency.

Freya's followers watched as the goddess's smile broadened.

"The Guild—no, Ouranos has something he wants to keep hidden."

"……"

"They want us *as far away as possible* from the eye of the storm."

The Goddess of Beauty saw through Ouranos's train of thought. "Very well, then," she said with a smile that could charm any mortal or god.

"Maybe I can finally get rid of the penalty for destroying the Pleasure Quarter. If we follow the orders as stated, as protectors of the city…Yes."

"Then…"

"Yes. Stand in for Ganesha's children at the gates. We shall protect Orario for a day."

She gave the order to divide their forces into eight groups, one for each of the city gates. Lower-ranking members made a quick bow and then exited the hall before their captains.

"I shall return to my chamber in Babel."

"*Ganesha Familia*'s blockade is already in place…"

"I'm sure someone will let me sneak past, if I ask the right way."

"Shall I escort you?"

"It's fine, Allen."

She smiled at the first-tier adventurer known as "Vana Freya" on her way out of the gathering hall, leaving Folkvangr soon after.

"Stand by? What kind of bullshit is that?!"

A werewolf howled angrily from a room adjacent to a hallway.

"It'd be faster to send us in to clean up the mess!! Why leave it to Ganesha's guys at all?!"

"Bete, shut up, would you!!…But do we really have to wait around? That emergency announcement broadcast was a bit confusing, too."

Loki Familia's home, the Twilight Manor.

The leaders of the city's most powerful familia had gathered inside the reception room of the compound famous for its long, tall spires.

Aiz had returned from the Guild and joined the group. Their goddess, Loki, sat in an unladylike fashion on top of a nearby table and watched over the first-tier adventurers discussing the latest news.

"What's bugging me is that Rivira has been destroyed how many times now? Why's everyone freaking out now?"

"I agree, this is an overreaction, issuing a mission to the entire city like that. Monsters with weapons and armor—is that really such a big deal?"

"I've seen that on the Guild's bulletin board, about monsters wearing armor..."

The Amazonian twins Tiona and Tione continued to speak, with Aiz chiming in.

The high elf Riveria glanced in their direction from her spot off to the side.

"These are not nature weapons but armaments used by adventurers in the hands of unusual monsters. There is a high possibility these beasts are enhanced species, and organized besides."

"All the more reason we should be down there!"

"Tone it down, Bete. These ain't yer regular ol' Irregulars, strange as it sounds...Seems fishy, don't it?"

The dwarf Gareth scolded the fuming werewolf even as his own brow furrowed.

Loki Familia still had many questions, but the Guild had been less than forthcoming with information.

"Well, whatever's going on—" Another voice cut in to the conversation.

Everyone in the room turned to face their commander, the prum Finn, who remained seated in a chair as he continued.

"—it's not going to end like this, for sure...That's just my hunch, though."

He stated this with a fair amount of confidence after running his tongue along the base of his thumb.

Lastly…

They asked their goddess to reveal her will.

"Eh. I hate bein' outta the loop, but…I gotta agree with ya, Finn."

Her narrow eyes opened slightly wider as the corners of her lips angled upward.

"This'll continue. Orario is gonna be rumblin' for a while."

Trembling. Trembling.

The city was trembling.

"Hee-hee-hee-hee-hee-hee…!! Failed, now did you, Dix…?"

Far above the city streets, on top of a building with a great view…

"Now this is what I call interesting…!"

Ikelos chuckled as he looked out over Orario, watching the tension build as all the thoughts and expectations converged into a maelstrom of chaos.

"What the hell is going on?!"

Welf yelled in a hoarse voice.

Hestia Familia's home, Hearthstone Manor's living room.

The young smith's short red hair and long black jacket trembled as he shouted with anxiety.

"The hell are they saying? Armed monsters flattened Rivira?! That means…the mavericks are the ones who did it?!"

"Lilly doesn't know!! All information is coming from second or third sources, there's no way to confirm…!" Lilly shouted back, just as tense.

Haruhime, as pale as a ghost, was also in the room along with a visibly shocked Mikoto. Hestia had just returned to the manor and joined them in the living room.

After hearing the emergency announcement, Welf and Lilly left Mikoto and Haruhime right before noon to gather information in the city. It went without saying that they ran to Guild Headquarters first, but the place was so inundated with adventurers and civilians trying to do the same thing that they were crowded out of the front lawn. They never even set foot inside the building.

With nowhere else to go, they returned home.

"*Haa, hah*...No point...in going, directly anymore...Babel is off-limits, along with the Dungeon...They kicked us all out...! *Kughf!*"

Hestia, who had done a great deal of running herself, made no attempt to hide her fatigue as she gasped for breath between words, shoulders heaving as she coughed.

After paying Ganesha a visit, she'd been working at her part-time job for one of Babel Tower's tenants. She was forced to leave along with every other employee. Currently, only authorized personnel remained within the nearly empty white tower.

"What about the city? What are other people doing...?"

"Well, they're not exactly rioting in the streets..."

"Same as us. No one saw this coming, so they're not really sure what to do."

Lilly and Welf described the general mood to Mikoto, who had remained at home.

Welf, Lilly, and Hestia agreed on one word: *unrest.*

While chaos had yet to erupt, the emergency announcement had sent waves of anxiety through all Orario's citizens. They remembered hearing the warning bells when Rakia's army tried to invade, but no one knew how to react during such an unprecedented situation. Many people stuck their heads out of top-floor windows or went into the city to gaze at the white tower. Gods were no different. Some smiled and watched everything unfold with their beady eyes filled with glee, while others observed with varying degrees of deep contemplation.

Particularly sharp citizens and opportunistic merchants theorized that monsters would soon breach the surface. Several pockets within the city walls were on the verge of panic, but the quick response of Ouranos and the Guild kept them under control. They sent several teams to canvass the city and maintain calm, however uneasy it might be. Dispatches from well-meaning gods also helped a great deal.

Many humans and demi-humans lined the streets and alleys,

exchanging anxious looks and taking guesses as to what was really happening.

"Even if it was them, why would they? That 'dream' of theirs must have been more like an afterthought."

"Well..."

"...Perhaps those shady people or whatever who go around capturing Xenos have something to do with it?"

After no one had an answer for Welf's question, Hestia brought up the hunters she'd heard about.

Something had happened to the Xenos—something that had provoked a counterattack.

Lilly, Welf, and the rest exchanged tense glances as all sorts of images ran through their minds.

"If...if...those nice Xenos really were the victims of an attack..."

"Lady Haruhime..."

"What will become of them?...What will happen to Lady Wiene?" asked Haruhime, her voice shaking just as much as her ears and tail.

Silence fell. Lilly forced herself to stay calm and said in a flat voice:

"If the information is accurate...and monsters have destroyed Rivira, then Orario has no choice but to exterminate them...At the very least, there needs to be some sort of *conclusion*," Lilly said, and Haruhime's cheeks paled as the strength left her body.

Mikoto quickly grabbed hold of the weak renart to support her.

A silent lull engulfed the room as Hestia and her followers contemplated the end result. It would be only a matter of time.

"...Has anyone seen Bell?"

"Mr. Bell went into the Dungeon. He did say he would return right away..."

Hestia scanned the room as she spoke, and Lilly answered in a perplexed voice.

While everyone was wondering why he had yet to come home considering the circumstances—Mikoto whipped around to look behind her. Then, as if in response, the doorbell announced a visitor.

She went to the front door and returned with a rolled-up piece of parchment.

"Who was it?"

"A Guild messenger! Lady Hestia, please!"

Mikoto thrust the parchment toward the goddess after answering Welf's question.

Hestia cracked it open and hurriedly skimmed it. Lilly and Welf, closely followed by Mikoto and Haruhime, peeked over her shoulders to see for themselves.

"State of emergency declared, stand by in reserve…So then, basically…"

"We are to wait for further orders. Just stay aboveground and keep our mouths shut…!"

Only the bare minimum of information had been provided for their new mission. As her followers voiced their agitation, Hestia's reaction was quite different.

Her blue eyes opened wide as they interpreted the designs inscribed on the parchment—the hieroglyphs concealed in plain sight—and she read them aloud with a shout.

"Bell has been assigned to journey with the subjugation team to the eighteenth floor?!"

""""He what?!""""

"Eh?!"

Lilly's, Welf's, and Mikoto's voices united in disbelief. Haruhime was a moment behind, her shoulders flinching in shock.

It was the same type of parchment that Bell had received the other day, the one that had sent the familia on their secret mission. Ouranos had inscribed the message so that no one, not even Guild employees, could read it before Hestia.

"Ouranos, what are you thinking…?"

That settled it—the Xenos must be at the center of this incident. After reading the message laying out her duty now that he was "borrowing" her follower, Hestia was convinced.

I can't let this happen! She raced out of the living room.

To reach Bell. To get to Central Park before the subjugation team set out.

Startled by Hestia's sudden departure, Lilly, Welf, Mikoto, and

Haruhime fumbled around for a moment before following her with just as much determination.

Hestia Familia burst out onto the city street, forgetting to close the door behind them.

"I'll bring you up to speed on the situation, Bell Cranell. Please listen well."

"Y-yes!"

In a dim, underground stone passageway…

Bell followed Fels through the hidden tunnel that connected to a trapdoor in Guild Headquarters.

After Eina called him aside, she had instructed him to immediately go to a certain room—alone. Unable to bring her along, he found the black-robed mage waiting for him when he reached the room in question. Fels had ignored the boy's surprise at the trapdoor leading to the passage the mage had built as an escape route for Ouranos—not even Guild employees knew it existed.

Bell's nerves were starting to get the best of him as the mage, apparently pressed for time, hastily explained what had happened while guiding him through the tunnel with a magic-stone lamp.

"Our information is spotty at best. As of now, we cannot determine what triggered the event. The only thing we know with absolute certainty is that it involves monsters carrying weapons—the Xenos took over Rivira by force."

"……!"

"No matter our course of action, we must regain control of the situation."

Fels continued by saying that the best-case scenario would be to restore order and keep the Xenos safe, but Bell's mind was spinning too fast to register the words.

Thoughts of Lido, Rei, the other Xenos, and Wiene flashed across his mind.

"One more thing: The Xenos haven't moved from the eighteenth floor."

"Huh…?"

"We know this because no returning adventurers have confirmed their presence on higher floors after Rivira's fall. The stories of the adventurers from the middle levels are consistent, so I believe we can take their word."

Fels glanced down at the blue crystal in the palm of his other hand.

"Therefore, I believe there's a reason the Xenos haven't moved from Rivira."

"...And that is?"

"I have a theory, but that's all it is at the moment. First off, we must see with our own eyes what happened."

With those words, Fels came to a stop and turned to face Bell.

"We plan to include you in *Ganesha Familia*'s forward team."

"...!"

"I realize we have not known each other long...but please lend us your strength," Fels requested from the dark space beneath the robe's black hood.

Bell could feel the Fool's gaze, despite knowing there were no eyes—or skin or muscles for that matter. He shook his head.

"I should be the one to ask. Please let me do this. I want to go."

"...You have my thanks, Bell Cranell."

He wanted to see for himself. It didn't matter what was down there waiting for him.

With Fels's words of gratitude in his ears, Bell clenched his fists and attempted to calm his beating heart.

"No stopping things now..."

Hermes fiddled with the wide brim of his feathered hat as he sighed.

He was seated in his room at *Hermes Familia*'s home. The restless commotion of his followers sounded from beyond the closed doors as their severe leader, Asfi, stood before him with a grave expression.

"How are Falgar and his team?"

"They have received medical attention, and it seems they will survive…but have yet to regain consciousness."

Just like Rivira's residents, members of *Hermes Familia* who had been caught up in the attack on the town sustained serious injuries during their escape. A small team had been dispatched to Rivira to keep an eye on the middle levels. "Ikelos's adventurers appeared in Rivira, and that's when the monsters attacked…" was all the leader managed to say before passing out.

With another sigh, Hermes instructed Asfi to ensure that the wounded were comfortable and in good hands, then narrowed his orange eyes and continued on to other business.

"But dragging Bell into all this…You've done it now, Ouranos."

Fels's familiar had delivered a message detailing the mission. A list of members for the subjugation team was also included.

Hermes gave a bitter, almost ironic chuckle.

It was an extremely unusual expression for the normally energetic dandy deity.

"…This is unexpected. I thought you would have been overjoyed to push Bell Cranell into this challenge and see how he performs, or something similar."

"I would've preferred that Bell stay out of this one."

His and Ouranos's stances were different, he added.

Asfi raised a suspicious eyebrow as Hermes continued mumbling to himself.

"Adversity makes the man…or something like that? I think that's how Takemikazuchi put it."

"……"

"True, overcoming adversity is required to become a hero, there's no doubt…but this goes far beyond any test I would put together."

It didn't abide with his will, Hermes stated.

Then, with a little fear in his voice, he said:

"One wrong move and it's all over."

With that, he pulled the brim of his hat over his eyes.

The deity stood up from his chair at long last and issued orders to Asfi.

"Go to the eighteenth floor, just not with Ganesha's group. Gather as much firsthand information as you can. Don't bother with needless engagements."

"What about you, Lord Hermes...?"

"I have somewhere to be. Someone I have to meet to sort some things out."

Once Hermes fell silent, a chienthrope girl waiting outside opened the door as if she had sensed it was the right time. The dandy god acknowledged his follower, who possessed the information he'd been waiting for, smiled, and jokingly said, "I've got to get to work, too."

"Take it from here...Oh, yes."

Then, just as he was about to leave...

Hermes turned around as though he had almost forgotten to say something.

"I'm worried about Bell. Take Aisha with you."

"Lyu, you have a visitor."

Summoned by the human Runoa, Lyu the elf turned to face her.

Along West Main Street, at The Benevolent Mistress...

"Holy crap, meow!" "What happened, meow?!" Two cat people made a ruckus once they spotted the beautiful, long-legged Amazonian courtesan standing in front of the café bar.

Lyu eyed Aisha Belka with a skeptical glare as she stepped inside.

"Do you have some business with me?"

"You busy now?"

"The customers have left, given the current situation..."

"Then let's take this outside."

Lyu stood silently under the Amazon's forceful gaze, glancing at The Benevolent Mistress over her shoulder behind her.

With nothing better to do, the waitresses inside were busy chattering noisily. Lyu decided they would be fine on their own, and when Aisha jerked her chin in the direction of an alley behind the bar, the waitress followed.

Lyu glanced up at a small window overlooking their hidden meeting spot, but she didn't care and returned her gaze to the Amazon.

The elf and the Amazon stared at each other, shielded from the sun's rays in the alleyway.

"All this fuss is happening because some angry monsters decided to act up. But they apparently stayed put on the eighteenth after dismantling Rivira. *Ganesha Familia*'s heading a subjugation team that's about to set out."

"...?"

Aisha didn't bother with a greeting or small talk and started sharing information. Lyu's eyebrows furrowed as she grew warier.

The elf gazed back at her and leaned against the building while the courtesan folded her arms in front of her generous cleavage.

"Why are you telling me this?"

"Just poking my nose into your business...You seem to have a thing for Bell Cranell, so I thought you ought to know."

Aisha waited a beat, then kicked off the wall and leaned toward Lyu.

"That boy's been added to the subjugation team. He's about to cross into some rough territory—at least that's what my god says, anyway."

"!"

"How do I know so much? It's because I converted into *Hermes Familia*."

The name of the fairly distinguished familia, known for their information gathering, gave some weight to her claim.

However, Lyu found it strange that the Amazon would choose to join that group and couldn't stop herself from asking.

"Why that faction specifically...?"

"They got their reasons, I got mine. They needed someone with more combat potential, and I wanted to make sure to be the first to hear if a certain stone made its way here."

Hermes Familia operated a "delivery service" that took packages in and out of the city. Therefore, not only did they have a firm handle on the flow of information, but they were naturally aware of black-market dealings. Aisha now had easy access to what she wanted to know.

The former *Ishtar Familia* member explained that both sides got what they wanted.

"I already knew this, but that deity of mine's seriously crafty. I only belong to the new familia in name, and he never lets me off the leash. He tricked the Guild into thinking I don't belong to him so he can stay neutral."

"......"

"But yeah...He's kept up his end of the deal real nice. So I got no problem keeping up mine, doing what he asks. This time it just happens to be checking out the eighteenth floor and covering Bell Cranell's back."

Aisha finished explaining how she came to be a member of *Hermes Familia* and her current situation.

"...You and I accompanied Mr. Cranell to the eighteenth floor but a few days ago. The boy has been acting strange ever since. Is there a connection to the current arrangement?"

"Beats me. I just converted in, so I'm at the bottom of the pack... I'm nothing more than convenient muscle. I only just found out about this myself, and I have no clue how Bell Cranell got involved. Haven't been told much of anything."

Aisha shrugged, fed up with her position.

Lyu paused for a moment. The anxiety she'd felt watching the boy disappear into the crowd this morning returned, and the gears of her mind turned a little faster.

When the elf didn't speak, Aisha pressed a bit further.

"You're Gale Wind, right? You fought in the War Game."

"...What are you implying?"

"I'm not gonna start digging up your past," she said. "Just keep your ears open. *Ikelos Familia* seems to be at the center of this incident. You might've already heard but...they were rumored to be in league with the Evils back in the day."

Lyu's aura changed in the blink of an eye.

Her expression was the same, but a roaring flame—emotions that she'd kept under lock and key—flared to life in her sky-blue eyes.

"Evils..."

It was a name Lyu could never ignore.

She had once been known as Leon, when she belonged to a now-deceased familia that stood for justice and equality. Her connection to the Evils ran deep.

Lyu's delicate hands curled into fists, tight enough to turn her fingers white.

"Bell Cranell might be in a tough spot with those guys."

"……"

"So, what do you say?"

Silence fell for a moment.

Until at last, Lyu opened her mouth to speak.

"Very well. I shall join you."

Her answer brought a smile to Aisha's lips.

"Wouldn't have it any other way."

Lyu could see the female warrior's excitement at the prospect of fighting alongside a strong ally. Dressed in her waitress uniform, the elf anxiously rubbed her chest and attempted to suppress the emotions coursing through her.

The ex-adventurer had decided to intervene.

"I hear that Babel's entrances have been sealed. How do you propose we enter the Dungeon?"

"Ever heard of Perseus? Now, I only just teamed up with her myself, but she's got a bag of toys you've gotta see to believe."

Rather than giving a straight answer, Aisha discussed the famous item maker.

Lyu sighed, disappointed in herself for asking such a foolish question, as Aisha grinned at her own flippant remarks.

"Now then, let's get to it."

With that, Lyu started to make preparations.

She turned to face the Amazonian warrior just before leaving.

"Antianeira."

"Yeah?"

"Why are you going to such lengths to assist Mr. Cranell?"

"I owe him."

"Is that really all?"

Lyu's question brought a fearless and yet slightly alluring smile to the face of Aisha, whose long black hair swished behind her.

"Who knows?"

Their conversation ended.

The pair left soon after. Lyu disappeared from the café bar, most likely to prepare her equipment, as Aisha went off in the other direction with plans to meet her at a different location soon.

As soon as their footsteps had faded, Syr's hands uncovered her mouth. She had held them there the entire time as she eavesdropped from behind the wall.

"And there you have it."

Turning away from the wall, Syr faced the dwarf owner of the establishment, Mia, who had her arms crossed in front of her.

They were inside the bar's stockroom. A small window close to the ceiling of the wooden structure was slightly open.

It allowed the two of them to eavesdrop on Lyu's conversation in the alleyway behind the bar.

"Seriously, how many times has it been now...?"

The two second-tier adventurers had of course noticed Syr's presence, but the dwarf ex-adventurer hid herself so well neither sensed her—although the noisy cat people in the dining room helped as well. Her patience waning, the stout dwarf sighed with her entire body.

"I knew it from the start, but that girl ain't cut out for this kinda work. She can't cook, she's the opposite of friendly, and above all, she's too soft. Might be 'cause of that sense of justice she holds on to, but she doesn't have it in her to sit still in the same spot too long."

Mia kept muttering to herself, thinking that Lyu had shown improvement recently, and then set her gaze on Syr.

"Now you tell her this: If there's some other place she wants to be, she should get the hell outta my bar and go. The way she's always on the fence like this is just a pain in the neck."

"...Okay. I'll tell her."

Syr paused briefly and then agreed with a nod.

"So...are you willing to overlook this time, too?"

Mia's face darkened with anger as Syr made her request with soft, upturned eyes.

Then she let out another long sigh.

"I doubt we're gettin' more customers today, and it'll be a trickle at best. Not like there'd be anything for her to do."

"Yes."

"And that lad's been a regular for some time...If he stopped coming, it would mean another regular we can't feed good food to anymore."

"So then?"

"I'll look the other way."

The bar owner's expression soured as Syr's lit up with an ear-to-ear smile.

"Thank you so much!" Syr said with glee and was halfway into a bow when—

"Don't forget, there's still work to be done, even without any customers. Lyu ain't here, so I expect ya to work three times as hard."

Mia grumbled as she tottered out of the stockroom.

Once Syr was by herself, the smile on her face stiffened a little.

Clatter, clatter.

As though resonating with the turmoil occurring in a place far away, the sounds of rocking cages and rattling chains rang out endlessly.

"Dix!"

"Yeah, what? You're in the way, Gran. I'm about to teach these things the meaning of pain."

Dix stood up in the dark stone chamber, holding his wickedly curved spear at the ready as he turned to face his subordinate. But the large man rambled on, cutting off part of his boss's irritated reply.

"A-armed monsters showed up in Rivira and annihilated it...It's a real mess out there!"

"...Got any details?"

Dix's red eyes focused on the trembling mountain of a man from behind his goggles.

Gran explained as requested. He told him everything about the group of monsters that swept through the eighteenth floor. He also told him that Orario had declared a state of emergency as a result.

"Armed monsters…Hey, hey, you kidding? If that's true, our prey came right to us," Dix said.

Gran turned to look down the hallway.

A long series of iron cages was lined up like a prison on top of a cold stone floor. Their size varied from small to extremely large but continued for as far as the eye could see.

The figures inside said cages, too many to count, squirmed around.

"They lose their cool? Pissed off at us for hunting?"

"I-I don't know for sure, but…"

"But why would they move on Rivira?……Aha, so that's it."

Well played, monsters.

A twinge of hatred was evident in Dix's sneer.

He had a pretty good idea of what was happening outside their home base.

"What's Rivira look like now?"

"…Rubble. So bad that the Guild had to issue a mission, I hear," said Gran in a low, quiet voice. If he listened closely, he could hear among the monster howls signs that the other hunters were upset at the sudden turn of events.

"We hit the bushes too hard? Looks like the beasties are stronger than we thought."

His words might have been serious, but the smile never left his face.

Dix chuckled with excitement despite the news that these monsters were strong enough to destroy Rivira. Gran was relieved at the familiar sight of the leader's usual calm, fearless demeanor and dark, evil gleam in his eyes. A smile returned to his face, though his skin broke out in a different kind of cold sweat.

"That lord of ours still hasn't come back. Figures…Now, what to do…"

Thumping the shaft of his spear against his shoulder, Dix turned around.

A dragon girl appeared in his line of sight, chained up like a living sacrifice, still unconscious with fresh tears streaking down her cheeks.

"—Tame them?! We have to tame the targets of our mission?!"

A youthful woman's voice traveled far into the blue sky.

The city, still engulfed by shaking, nervous energy, had shifted its attention to Central Park.

Adventurers and citizens, gods and goddesses. A ring of bystanders had formed around the park's edge, all focused on the strong adventurers gathered inside—*Ganesha Familia*.

At the center of it all, one announcement had the subjugation team up in arms.

"What's up with that?! We're in a state of emergency, are we not?!"

"I-it was written on a document the Guild sent Lord Ganesha and he passed it to me...b-but forbade me to show anyone."

"So what? That doesn't tell me nothing! Give me details! Details!! Umm—whatever your name is!"

"You know I can't do that, Ilta! Also, my name is Modaka!!"

A young man cried at the top of his lungs, correcting the wheat-skinned Amazon with fiery red hair in front of him.

Just before *Ganesha Familia* set off on its mission, last-minute instructions from the Guild had sent the group into chaos. Without giving any explanation, the Guild had ordered the subjugation team to tame the monsters, a far more difficult task than simply slaying them. Especially considering these monsters were powerful enough to destroy Rivira.

First-tier adventurer Ilta Faana was now the center of an argument triggered by the Guild's outrageous and downright incomprehensible order.

"Get a hold of yourself, Ilta! It's not that hard to figure out! These monsters are using weapons, right? The Guild's got valis signs in their eyes, thinking that these rare subspecies will draw in large crowds for the Monsterphilia, and they want us to bring them back alive—there's no other explanation!! Damn those greedy pricks! It's not the time for that!! Send me down there and I'll incinerate them in one of my fire tornadoes! Burn, baby, BUUUUUUUUUUUUURN!!"

"Shut up, Ibly! You're on the surface team!!"

"WHAAAAAAAAAAAAAAAT?! NO ONE TOLD ME ANYTHING!! GO MY FRIENDS, WIIIIIIIIIIIIIIIIIIIIIIIIIIIIIINNNN!!"

"Please, everyone, settle down! And Ibly, enough already!!"

Ganesha Familia's self-proclaimed "chattering fireball" went through his own casting motions in the middle of the park, stoking Ilta's rage. Other leaders, including Modaka, knew this wasn't the time or the place to let emotions get out of hand—although it would be much worse if their god were here—and called for rational thinking as they looked out over the ranks.

A wave of anxiety and nervous whispers started to spread through the crowd of citizens watching from outside the park.

"Ilta, relax. That goes for the rest of you, too."

"But, sister…!"

"C-Commander Shakti…My apologies."

The head of *Ganesha Familia*, Shakti Varma, spoke up as she stepped into the chaos.

With bluish hair cut precisely at the nape of her neck, she possessed an intelligent poise. She was surprisingly tall at 170 celch, and her reputation as a ravishing beauty was well deserved. Her long legs were equipped with metal boots, and oversize brass knuckles protected her hands, ensuring she was more than ready for close-quarters combat. Bearing the title "Ganesha's Cane, Ankusha," she ranked right alongside the Sword Princess as a first-tier human adventurer.

The Amazon Ilta referred to her as a sister, recognizing her strength (by force), and fell silent in the larger-than-life warrior's presence. Other elite adventurers bowed their heads as Shakti cast her gaze on Modaka.

"What are our lord Ganesha's thoughts on the matter?"

"F-follow the Guild's orders…"

"I see," she responded, the only calm in the storm swirling through the familia. She closed her eyes.

Opening them a heartbeat later, Shakti turned to face her subordinates and declared:

"We will tame these monsters. Bring them back here, alive."

"Sister, are you sure?!"

"We serve the Lord of the Masses, Ganesha. Our faith lies with him, and we follow. Am I wrong, Ilta?"

A jolt ran down the Amazon's spine at Shakti's sharp, unclouded gaze. Her eyes opened wide before she nodded.

In awe of their leader's rock-solid faith and devotion to their god, other members of *Ganesha Familia* assumed calmer expressions. "We leave on my mark. Be ready!" Shakti's cool voice snapped through the air like a whip.

"W-wow..."

Amid all the jittery voices swirling through Central Park, Bell quickly slapped a hand over his mouth to stop a whisper in its tracks.

He was wearing a long rope over his armor and had a backpack over his shoulders—similar to Lilly's usual equipment—to make him look like a supporter.

He was away from the anxious citizens waiting to see the departure and closer to *Ganesha Familia*'s internal spat, already mingling with the subjugation team.

"Lord Ganesha said that you'll be useful in determining why this happened, so we don't have much choice, but...keep your head down, Little Rookie. I'll explain that you're just a supporter to anyone who notices, but don't stand out. It'll be a real pain if Ilta finds out you're here."

"U-understood...Sorry."

Modaka paused to whisper in Bell's ear on his way by. Bell fearfully apologized out of reflex.

His point made, the hardworking *Ganesha Familia* member went on his way. A quiet voice sounded from Bell's side just as the young man left.

"Taming, just as we asked. God Ganesha has really come through."

"Fels..."

"The subjugation team will keep your presence a secret. Stay with them to the eighteenth floor."

The voice reached Bell's ears from a seemingly empty space.

It belonged to Fels. The mage was wearing a veil that granted invisibility, like the helmet Asfi had made and Bell had already encountered. Therefore, no one could see the black-robed figure.

Bell had received his equipment soon after emerging from the hidden passage from Guild Headquarters to blend in with the supporters. The mage, looking very out of place and suspicious as they approached Central Park, disappeared into thin air beneath the veil before joining the subjugation team.

"It's time to go. I'll enter the tower first."

"Okay."

The mage moved toward Babel to avoid bumping into others during their journey. Bell could vaguely make out Fels's presence, and he was watching the faint ripple disappear when suddenly...

"Bell!!"

"Bell!" "Mr. Bell!"

"!"

Someone called his name, and he felt a hand on his shoulder.

He whirled around and immediately spotted Hestia, Welf, Lilly, Mikoto, and Haruhime working their way through the crowd.

Members of *Ganesha Familia* who were staying behind stood in a ring around Babel Tower for crowd control. Several had to hold back the group as they desperately called out to the boy.

Why would you be—? Bell's surprise lasted only a moment.

Noticing the concern in his friends' eyes, he poured every bit of his will and determination into his gaze.

I'm going in. Please let me do this.

Lilly and Welf looked annoyed, clearly hell-bent on having their say. Mikoto and Haruhime were much the same. They couldn't join him in the Dungeon or stop him altogether.

Hestia made eye contact with Bell amid the yells of encouragement coming from the crowd.

—Be careful, got that?

—I will!

Their exchange required no words.

The goddess managed to push all her fears aside and offer her support. The boy responded with a strong nod.

"Advance!!"

The citizens erupted with cheers the moment Shakti issued the order.

Hestia and her familia watched Bell go through Babel's gate with the rest of the subjugation team.

"Aisha! You mentioned nothing about Leon joining us!"

"What's the big deal about one more person? You know how strong she is, so don't be so uptight."

"So tell me, what was your plan if I didn't have a spare Hades Head on hand...?"

"Andromeda, *Ganesha Familia* is on the move. We must make haste."

"~~~~~~!!"

Beneath a wide-leafed tree in Central Park, away from the cheering masses, a human, an Amazon, and an elf exchanged words.

With a groan unbefitting a young woman like herself, Asfi thrust the magic items toward Aisha, who was carrying a massive wooden sword, and toward Lyu in her hooded robe. The three disappeared, dissolving into thin air the moment their items were in place, and then made their way past the crowd control with *Ganesha Familia*'s members none the wiser.

All the Xenos... Wiene.

The subjugation team following orders, the black-robed mage, the uninvited intruders, and the boy went through the gate with varying thoughts.

They pressed ahead into the Dungeon, under a beautiful blue sky and the gazes of the citizens supporting them.

CHAPTER 9 DREAMS OF BEASTS

A cracked and broken blue crystal pillar gave way and crashed to the floor.

Piles of scattered debris were the only remnants of tents and wooden buildings, while broken magic-stone products burned amid the rubble. The town of outlaws had fallen silent amid swelling dust clouds and pillars of smoke.

The Dungeon, eighteenth floor. The Under Resort.

On top of a large island in the middle of the lake on the western side lay the ruins of what once was the town of Rivira.

The walls of stone and crystal that encompassed the town were badly damaged and crumbling from the north gate—a gruesome record of the attackers' overwhelming onslaught. Blue and white crystal stubs stuck out of the wreckage; the ground was strewn with broken sword blades and shattered ax heads and splashes of blood. The wreckage spoke to the residents' and adventurers' desperate attempt to fight back.

Smoke was still rising in small columns throughout the Dungeon's outpost town, now a mere shell of its former self.

"What have you done with my kind?! Out with it, human!!"

A deep, monstrous voice speaking in the language of the surface echoed through the rubble.

An ash-colored stone gargoyle stood with its massive wings spread wide over a male adventurer, who lay on his back with both legs broken, at the end of a now abandoned street.

"Wha—huh…?! What're you talking about, freak…? I don't understand…!"

The man was one of the few adventurers who hadn't reacted to the monsters' attack in time. He gasped at the pain while blood gushed from his legs. With tears building in his eyes, the man madly yelled at the ominous monster, insisting that the beast's claims made no sense.

Fresh blood dripped from the goliath's stone claws—and Gros bared his menacing fangs.

"Do not take me for a fool!! You reek of arachne acid!!"

"......?!"

"The will of my comrade says you're filth!!"

The human's face contorted as Gros bellowed each syllable with burning rage.

It wasn't that the man had failed to escape in time. Unlike the other adventurers, Gros and the other Xenos *hadn't let him escape.*

He belonged to *Ikelos Familia* as one of the hunters who had attacked Ranieh's group. The man left the group to receive medical attention for the venomous burns and entered Rivira after the hunt concluded, mingling with those who had a reason to hide from the law.

The arachne poison's acidic fumes guided the Xenos to Rivira just like a string of webbing would have. That was her goal all along.

Monsters possessing an extremely acute sense of smell had no trouble leading the others directly to the source.

Not only was destroying Rivira a way to weed out Ikelos's followers, it also symbolized just how deep the Xenos's anger ran.

"Answer the question!! Where did you take my kind?!"

The gargoyle's grating yells continued as other Xenos with Gros formed a threatening ring around the two of them. Terror and despair flooded the man's face at the dozens of deafening, beastly howls.

The other two hunters who accompanied him had been discovered and slain soon after the attack on Rivira began.

The claws and fangs of the enraged Xenos had torn them apart. Their shredded, bloody remains were sprawled out in front of the monster ring.

With no way to talk his way out and no hope of escape, the deathly pale man shivered as his trembling lips formed a smile.

"HAH! HA-HA-HA!...It'd be pointless to tell you, 'cause you'd never make it...!"

He forced a brave face and tried to toy with his captors—but when Gros plunged a merciless claw straight into his shoulder, the man's laugh turned into a high-pitched scream. "KYAHHHHHHHHHHHHHHHHHHHHHHHHH!!" he yelled as blood sprayed from his wound like a geyser.

"Speak!! Spit it out!!"

The gargoyle leaned in, his fangs close enough to sink into the man at any moment.

Gros's terrifying interrogation was too much to handle, and the man quickly gave in.

But rather than speaking, he lifted the only appendage still under his control, his right arm, and pointed.

That trembling finger was aimed away from the island town—toward the forest that dominated the east.

"The forest...? Where in the forest?! Tell me what is there!"

"E-east edge...There's a door...!"

Gros glared down menacingly at the man whose face was a mess, covered in rivers of tears and snot.

The Xenos were familiar with many Frontiers, like their Hidden Villages, as well as many shortcuts that adventurers didn't know existed, but none of them had ever heard of the door on the eighteenth floor.

Gros reared back with a howl, hoping to extract more information out of him, but...

"Like I said, you don't *have one of those*, so you'll never make it inside...!"

"Explain!!"

"It's pointless...! Just give up...!!"

The man's answer made one thing clear: they were wasting time on a pointless interrogation.

The gargoyle's stone-cold expression shifted into a fierce scowl, glaring with fire in his eyes at the *Ikelos Familia* hunter who had outlived his usefulness. His claws swiped down.

Ignoring the severed hand rolling across the floor, Gros turned to face his fellow Xenos and spoke.

"To the east! The surface dwellers have our comrades in a base on the forest's eastern edge!! Find it!!"

The monsters' instantaneous howl of approval rumbled down the flattened street once the order was given.

They took the shortest route, a straight line leading east. The Xenos who couldn't fly bounded down the sheer cliffs around Rivira while winged monsters took to the air, their eyes locked on their target.

"—Gros!"

The gargoyle was just about to join them when another Xenos called out to him.

He turned to look where his comrade was pointing—the eighteenth floor's southern edge.

"Those are...!!"

A group of adventurers emerged from the tunnel that connected to the seventeenth floor.

"Rivira...!"

Bell spotted pillars of smoke rising from the west the moment he emerged from the dim, rocky tunnel.

The subjugation team tore through the Dungeon at a breakneck speed and arrived on the eighteenth floor in record time. *Ganesha Familia*'s elites single-handedly eliminated the monsters in their way without breaking stride on the trip down, while Bell was the only one gasping for breath and struggling to keep up in his supporter garb.

The thirty-member subjugation team arrived at the scene and wasted no time jumping into action.

"Commander, your orders...!"

"Wait, sister—look there!"

The Amazon Ilta interrupted Modaka and pointed high above their heads.

Several dark shadows were flapping along in unison just beneath the ceiling's bright crystal lights.

"Winged monsters...wearing armor."

Shakti had difficulty believing what she could still clearly see.

Monsters equipped with protected plates and other armor.

According to their information, these were the monsters that had attacked Rivira, and what they had been sent to tame.

Ganesha Familia's strongest adventurers narrowed their eyes, making Bell even more nervous, and stepped out of the tunnel. The group marched directly through the thin forest in their path and dashed into the vast plains beyond.

"…! There's other monsters, in the plains…!"

"Moving eastward…to the forest? Why would they be going there?"

Coming from where Rivira stood on the western side of the floor, they dashed across the plains and passed the Central Tree entirely, going into the lush forest to the east.

Ganesha Familia watched the group of monsters, who outnumbered their winged companions, travel across the landscape.

As for why the monsters that had destroyed Rivira would go into the large forest, the subjugation team could only guess.

"Sister, what say you?"

"…We'll split in two. Momonga, take a small team to Rivira! See if there are any survivors!"

"Yes, ma'am! Also, my name is Modaka!!"

"The rest of you, with me! We follow the monsters into the forest!"

The young man, his name mistaken yet again, swiftly assembled a team of five adventurers to join him before separating from Shakti's main force. Bell paused for a moment at the back of the formation as both groups took off in opposite directions, wondering which way he should proceed, when…

"Let's make for the forest."

"Fels!"

"Rivira is likely little more than a ghost town. Lido was among the group that went east."

Fels, practically invisible at Bell's side, conveyed the information.

It was true; Bell had seen them as well.

He had seen a siren and gargoyle among the winged monsters in the air. And the ground procession included a lamia, a troll, a unicorn…and a lizardman racing across the plain.

The truth was starting to set in for Bell, his heart pounding harder than ever before. The boy was relieved not to see the dragon girl among their ranks at first, but then it made him uneasy.

With a deep breath to calm the surge of complicated emotions, Bell gave Fels a nod and turned to follow the larger group. He pumped his arms and ran so fast that his robe flapped behind him like a flag in the middle of a storm.

The dense, thick forest that stretched from the southern edge all the way to the eastern perimeter of the eighteenth floor was shaped like a massive gulf, the perfect spot for a port if the safe point in the Dungeon were connected to an ocean. It was enormous, covering more than one fifth of the Under Resort. Compared to the southern region of the floor, the foliage of the eastern and southeastern areas was a deeper green, and the trees were noticeably bigger.

Moss grew on the exposed tree roots. Tall trees formed a thick green canopy far overhead. Pristine blue rivers snaked along the ground. The trickling sound of water filled the air. White and blue crystals so large they could have been mistaken for shortswords sparkled. All this dreamy, beautiful landscape was nothing but a blur. Bell was so focused on keeping up with the subjugation team that he didn't have time to wonder if the invisible Fels was still with him.

Then Shakti, who had kept a consistent eye on the winged monsters far overhead through the branches and leaves at the head of the formation, raised her arm. It was a signal to her subordinates. They were on course to intercept their targets. The long-awaited encounter was upon them.

Bell braced himself for the moment. But before he got close enough to see the monsters himself, snarling howls drew his attention elsewhere.

"Huh...?"

"What the hell is...!"

Ganesha Familia accelerated toward the ferocious roars coming from just ahead and saw—monsters locked in an all-out brawl to the death.

"They're fighting each other...!"

The leader Shakti, the Amazon Ilta, and the other members squinted and tilted their heads, struggling to comprehend what was going on.

In fact, the only ones who understood what they were seeing were Fels and Bell.

The Xenos, targeted by both humans and monsters like themselves, were under attack.

At first glance, Bell didn't realize that the monsters hell-bent on tearing their opponents apart were the ones he'd shaken hands with only a few days ago. Their aura was so different. It was almost as though bloodthirsty savages were hacking and slicing their way through obstacles—bugbears and mad beetles—in their way.

Bell stared from beneath his hood, eyes trembling, when one of the Xenos realized they had company.

Suddenly—the Xenos let out a roar and charged without a second thought.

"?!"

Battle broke out before Bell and Fels could process their shock.

Seeing humans reignited the Xenos's rage, and their bloodshot eyes pulsed as they descended upon the newcomers with beastly vengeance.

"Forward, my warriors!!"

Shakti spoke with calm determination, the rest of *Ganesha Familia* howling their own war cries behind her.

The clashing of swords echoed through the forest.

"Sister! Do we have to tame each one of these things?"

"Only the subspecies! Focus on the ones wearing armor!"

Without warning, all the monsters that had been fighting among themselves suddenly turned to attack the adventurers in a mad rush. Supporters hastily drew taming whips, passing them to Shakti as she issued orders to Ilta.

Their targets were easily distinguishable. Monsters fighting with nothing more than the claws and skin they were born with stood out from the ones equipped with blades and steel. There was no question their focus was on the latter.

But above all—they were strong. Even if their targets weren't wearing armor, the adventurers could tell the difference immediately on contact.

The bugbears and mad beetles fell easily, but they were at a loss as to how to handle the armed monsters. *Ganesha Familia* members scrunched up their faces in frustration as their weapons were effortlessly knocked away time and again.

"Fels—!"

"ORHOOOOOOOOOOOOOOOO!"

"—Gah!"

Bell became separated from Fels in the surge of enemies. It took all he had just to keep his feet. With no time to draw his knife, he dove, jumped, and evaded incoming claws and fangs until he was forced to defend with the gauntlets beneath his robe.

The battle inside the lush forest had become a three-sided free-for-all.

"Those *Ganesha Familia* guys are losing ground."

—A few sets of eyes watched from a high vantage point not too far behind.

Aisha, Lyu, and Asfi lurked behind a thick bush as they observed the tide of battle.

The three women had followed Bell and the rest of the subjugation team all the way here, staying far enough behind to avoid detection. The unexpected battle was well under way when they arrived.

"The armed monsters…they're strong. Some more so than others, but all are combat veterans."

"Yeah, and their blood's boiling by the look of them. Good luck trying to tame that. So it looks like 'Ankusha' and the other leaders are holding their own…"

"Well, that's assuming they can even be tamed at all."

Asfi remarked in a quiet voice next to Lyu as the elf removed her helmet, appearing out of thin air.

Ganesha Familia had more first-tier adventurers than any other familia in Orario, eleven in total. All of them might only have been at Level 5, but they could safely travel well into the deep levels on expeditions, making the group one of the Labyrinth City's prominent familias.

Now, the subjugation team was composed of thirty adventurers all at Level 3 and above. There was no shortage of first-tier adventurers in their ranks.

However, being straddled with the unfortunate obligation to tame these monsters meant *Ganesha Familia* couldn't fight at full strength. This unorganized scuffle of a battle only made matters worse.

But their biggest fear was the armored monsters' power.

At the very least, three of them—a gargoyle, a siren, and a lizardman—had demonstrated the potential to go toe to toe with the subjugation team's first-tier adventurers and come out on top. Stone wings went from being a shield one moment to a blunt weapon the next; powerful sound waves blasted from overhead; a longsword and scimitar moved with a skill belied by the wielder's wild techniques. Other than Shakti, the adventurers were forced to defend lest the vicious counterattacks finish them off.

With access to a plethora of information, Asfi had been aware of the Xenos's existence beforehand. She stayed calm, carefully observing the situation from afar.

"Asfi, Leon. Please avoid unnecessary engagements. Explaining ourselves if we're seen will cause more trouble than it's worth. Our purpose here is only to collect information and to serve as Bell Cranell's—"

Whoosh. Lyu suddenly stood up in the middle of Asfi's directions.

"I shall assist."

"Huh, wai—Leon!"

The elf warrior's sense of justice wouldn't allow her to sit on the sidelines and watch *Ganesha Familia* suffer.

"Moreover, we have lost sight of Mr. Cranell. I shall fight and search at the same time."

"Aren't you being a bit overprotective there? That kid can fend for himself when he has to."

"You are the one who brought me here for the sole purpose of protecting him…or am I to believe that you will stay behind?"

"Oh, you know I'm going."

Ignoring Asfi's gaping mouth, the Amazon Aisha lifted her thick wooden sword and placed it on her shoulder with excitement.

"A-at least wear the helmets! It's much easier to move when unseen, and convenient besides…!"

"I have a natural aversion to hiding my form in battle. Cowardly tactics don't suit me."

"I don't need it, either. All helmets and armor do is get in the way, am I right?"

Asfi reached out, glasses sliding down her nose. "Wait…!!" she cried out in vain as Lyu and Aisha discarded their Hades Head items on the ground. Battle cloth shifting as they turned, the two women raced into battle.

Perseus custom-made rare magic items, worth hundreds of thousands of valis each, lay abandoned on the floor.

"I swear…!!"

Asfi quickly moved to collect them. The item maker, whose life work had been rejected, left her Hades Head right where it was and stayed invisible.

The fierce battle between surface people and monsters continued to escalate.

With the need to tame their adversaries holding them back, the adventurers fought hard as the monsters unleashed their rage.

The armed monsters—even the humanoid Xenos—were doused in fresh blood.

It hid their normally tidy appearances and formed an outward sign of their inner fury, transforming them into hideous beasts. Pupils narrowed to vertical slits, dripping in the blood of their victims, they overwhelmed the adventurers.

"————————————————!!"

"Guh…!"

The Amazon Ilta fell to one knee after taking the brunt of one of the golden-winged siren's malicious sound blasts.

The two had been fighting at a blistering pace, zipping from tree to tree. The Amazon's punches and kicks tore through the air, but her opponent's ranged attack also damaged her nearby allies. With no answer for the siren's troublesome technique, it was only a matter of time before the first-tier adventurer took a hit.

The siren flapped its wings, launching a volley of feather bullets directly at Ilta—but...

"Careful there!"

"!"

A large wooden blade swung in from out of nowhere, deflecting every bullet in one swoop.

"You're just full of surprises, aren't you?!"

"?!"

Aisha kicked off a nearby tree into the air and forced the siren to jerk out of the way of her oncoming heel.

Ilta, arms still raised to protect herself, watched in shock.

"Antianeira?! Why are you here?!"

"Don't get hung up on small details, Amazoness. Let me get in on this."

Aisha looked over her shoulder with a grin the moment she landed.

"Besides, you could use some help, right?"

"...Enough sass. Defend us while we tame!"

Ilta shouted and slammed the whip in her right hand into the ground hard enough to send a plume of dirt into the air as she and Aisha raced back into the fray.

"Their strength is undeniable—but their rage blinds them."

"GAH!" a monster shrieked.

"While they are a force to be reckoned with head-on, they are vulnerable to sneak attacks."

While the Amazonian warrior went her own way, delivering blow after powerful blow, Lyu dropped into battle from a tree overhead with her wooden sword ready to strike. She locked on to an armored silverback's head and knocked it out with one blow.

Lyu appeared just in time to save a male adventurer from certain death. Dumbfounded, he stared at her while she readjusted her hood to keep her face hidden.

"Y-you! Who are you? What are you?!"

"...Just a traveler passing through."

"You can't be serious!!"

Ganesha's antics had made his followers familiar with the art of responding to nonsense. The unknown hooded adventurer joined the battle in support while others chimed in.

"Reinforcements...? Must be adventurers who came up from the deep levels. Then again, that elf..."

Shakti took notice of Lyu and Aisha almost immediately. She realized that having two warriors not restricted to taming in battle could be advantageous. After sending a charging troll flying backward with a single punch, she whirled away from a unicorn trying to skewer her and knocked it off balance with her whip. The monster spun to the ground.

Her battle cloth probably would have been more appropriate at a festival rather than the battlefield. The long slits in the fabric allowed her freedom of movement and whipped around as the other members of *Ganesha Familia* regrouped around her.

"SHAAA!!"

"Wh...?!"

Elsewhere, Bell was struggling to defend himself just beyond the newcomers' range.

A lamia's long, sharp blades flashed out of his line of sight. Its green hair, splattered with just as much blood as its face, billowed behind it. A putrid smell assaulted Bell's senses as the creature attempted to slice him apart.

A combination of fear and sorrow prevented the boy from calling out to the Xenos who had once shaken his hand. Bell's throat tightened, his eyes filled with anguish.

"!"

He tried to jump past the lamia to dodge a swipe, but it drove its bladelike claws straight through his robe.

Bell lost his disguise along with his backpack and revealed himself to the battlefield.

The Xenos fighting the forest monsters were on the verge of regrouping despite the adventurers surrounding them, when suddenly—

"GRAAAAAAAAHH!!"

A single lizardman burst through, appearing from between an adventurer locked in combat with monsters.

—Lido!!

The lizardman charged headlong toward the momentarily frozen Bell.

Rather than using the longsword and scimitar strapped to its sides, it grabbed hold of both of Bell's shoulders and drove him to the ground instead.

"—Why have you come, Bellucchi?!"

"?!"

The lizardman was several times heavier than Bell and overpowered him as they rolled across the forest floor, but he spoke like a sentient being. The two became entangled, moving away from the battle as Bell got an eyeful of Lido's monstrous face.

Next, Lido used the centrifugal force to throw Bell farther into the forest.

When the lizardman jumped back to his feet in pursuit, Bell understood what he was trying to do. So rather than fight his momentum, he let it carry him even farther away from the battle.

"Newcomers...More surface dwellers have come!"

A fair distance away from Lido and Bell's scuffle at almost the same time...

The gargoyle Gros studied the tide of battle from behind the Xenos's line.

His eyes narrowed at Lyu and Aisha, glaring with hatred as his kind fell into disarray.

"—Gros!"

"Fels?!"

Gros turned to the side at the sound of his name.

Out of the adventurers' sight, the black-robed mage appeared in a crystal pillar's shadow.

Casting the veil aside to disable the invisibility, Fels called out to the airborne gargoyle.

"Bring an end to this battle at once!! There is no point to our conflict!"

"No!! Should we stand down now, those adventurers will slaughter us!"

"I promise you, I will not allow that to happen! Please listen—!"

Clashing metal and the roars of battle drowned out the conversation.

Fels pleaded with the Xenos leader, desperate to convince him to see reason within the chaos, but…

"Then make the adventurers retreat!! We will rescue our comrades!"

"?!"

"You promise with words, show me action!"

Fels had no immediate response for Gros's demand from overhead.

The goliath looked down at the mage, then howled with an explosion of anger as if he already knew the answer.

"That's impossible, right, Fels?! Because at the heart of it, you are on *their side*!!"

"……!"

"You must put humans first, not us! You could never understand our rage!!"

Nearly fifteen years had passed since Fels first made contact with the Xenos.

It had taken many conversations over those longs years to establish trust.

However, the gargoyle was so consumed with rage that he had forgotten the bond they shared.

"I will not be swayed by your sweet words!"

"Gros, I'm…!"

"It's far too late now!!"

Gros turned his back on Fels as if to signify the end of the conversation and chase away the last of his doubts.

He took off deeper into the forest, ash-gray throat wide open and pulsating.

"——————————————————————OOo!!"

It was a howl directed to his fellow Xenos.

He called to his companions fighting in the forest with a sound human ears couldn't distinguish.

It was an order to search for their kind, and to follow him.

—Rei, keep the humans distracted!

—Understood.

The gargoyle made eye contact with another airborne Xenos, the golden-feathered siren, just before leaving the battlefield.

Rei, whose face was just as bloody and filled with rage as the other Xenos's, led a group of their comrades into the fray out of the corner of his eye, and Gros turned his attention to the eastern edge of the forest, his destination.

"Lido...!"

In a small clearing a great distance away from the tree-lined battlefield...

Bell and Lido stood face-to-face in a clearing surrounded by thick tree trunks and tall blue-and-white crystals.

"Why...Why did you come here, Bellucchi...?!"

Roars of battle were off in the distance.

Nothing stood between them in this place Lido had chosen for their discussion.

In any case, he didn't want their reunion to be like this.

Clutching a scimitar and longsword, the lizardman narrowed his reptilian yellow eyes as though trying to bear great pain.

"I heard...I heard that Rivira, the adventurers' town, was destroyed by monsters armed with weapons...! Was it...was it really the Xenos? Did you guys do it?"

"...Yes. We attacked it."

At those words, Bell remembered the face of a brokenhearted girl.

"But why?!"

"My comrades were murdered...by adventurers in that town. No, by hunters."

His rubellite eyes opened wide.

Lido continued, strengthening the verbal assault on the motionless boy.

"Those humans also took Wiene and Fia...!"

Bell's blood turned to ice.

Hunters had captured Wiene—*Ikelos Familia*?

The god Ikelos's unnerving smile appeared in the back of Bell's mind.

The possibility had been eating away at him since the beginning, and now he knew it was true. Buckets of cold sweat poured from his skin.

"Sorry, Bellucchi...Turns out we're just as the surface races say: monsters."

"Huh...?"

"I tried to stop them, all of them. But it was no use!"

He couldn't stop Wiene from being taken and couldn't stop his kind.

Lido offered an apology, stewing in his own uselessness. A powerful resolve soon took its place, however.

"But it's not only them. I'm just as furious!! Can't control...the rage...!"

Bell gasped as he saw the lizardman's irises split in two, the whites of his eyes turn bloodshot and become their natural form.

"I thirst for revenge, to kill the ones who killed my...!!"

Bell could see every muscle in the monster's body twitch, as if preparing to charge and exact revenge right now.

Lido's eyes pulsed, and Bell knew his monster instincts were taking over.

He lost himself for a moment and took an involuntary step back. Bell desperately tried to force his muscles to stay in place.

—But that's...

The same as humans.

Humans also burned with indignation should anything happen to their friends and allies.

All the emotions coursing through Lido and the other Xenos right now were not monstrous.

Bell opened his mouth to put his thoughts into words, but nothing came out. Those thoughts remained silent, buried in his heart.

"Our comrades are here, in the eastern forest."

"...! How did—?"

"Forced it out of a hunter in the town; he said there's a door around here. We're going to rescue Wiene and Fia."

Bell was stunned, but it made sense. All the Xenos's seemingly bizarre actions now made sense.

There was so much he had to think about.

However, right now, Wiene being in captivity came first.

"—Lido, I'm coming, too."

No sooner had the words left his mouth than—

"Stay back!!"

Lido swung the longsword, slicing into the ground at his feet.

Bell immediately shielded his face with his arms from the oncoming wave of rocks and dust.

"......!"

Bell had to swallow his surprise as soon as his vision recovered.

A long, deep crack had appeared in the ground between him and Lido, separating the two.

A visual barrier keeping their worlds apart.

"Bellucchi, do not cross. Go back."

"Lido...?"

"We're finished. There's no taking back what's done. Our dreams will never come true," the lizardman stated, tightening his grip on both swords. All hope was lost.

"But even so, we will stop at nothing to free our comrades...!!"

However, the fighting spirit in his eyes was still burning bright.

"We will take Wiene and Fia back...So Bellucchi, stay out of it."

"......!"

"If you're seen with us, you're finished, too. All of this is our fault. I don't want you involved."

Please don't cross that line.

Lido was pushing him away.

He was trying to keep him off the path to ruin.

He was trying to keep his burning hatred for surface people at bay.

He was afraid of being betrayed.

Bell couldn't move under the gaze of those beady reptilian yellow eyes, contorted with pain.

No, he didn't move.

He couldn't bring himself to agree with what the "monster" was saying.

"...What are you hanging around for, Bellucchi? What if you're seen?! Go back to the surface, back to Lillicchi and the rest!!"

Bell bit his lip, trying to gain control of his trembling body with Lido's fuming voice in his ears.

His knees shook, his gaze was locked with Lido's, and he wouldn't tear his eyes away.

Crystal light flashed off the lizardman's two blades, burning his eyes.

As far-off echoes overtook them—the gargoyle had left the battle.

"You are human, Bellucchi! Don't waste time worrying about monsters!!"

"Lido..."

"Go!"

"Lido...!"

"Get out of here!!"

"Still, I—!"

Bell took one step closer, over the crack in the ground. Lido didn't let him finish.

"OOOOOOOOOOOOOOOOOOOOOOOOOOOOOOOOO!!"

A shiver of fear traveled down his spine at the monstrous roar.

The boy's face contorted, his spirit broken as the lizardman howled his flat-out refusal.

"—Mr. Cranell!"

"「!」"

A sharp voice sounded; a thin wooden sword flashed between the two of them immediately afterward.

Lido deftly dodged the attack aimed in his direction, jumping back as a hooded adventurer wearing a torn cape landed in front of Bell.

The lizardman took one look at the elf protecting the boy before spinning around and racing off in the other direction.

Bell was left behind, watching that thick tail disappear into the trees.

"Are you injured, Mr. Cranell?"

"...Miss...Lyu? Why...?"

"I shall provide details at a later time. For now, it is dangerous to proceed on your own. Rendezvous with *Ganesha Familia* for the time being."

Lyu, who had followed the lizardman's howl to the clearing, turned to leave.

Although Bell saw her cape flowing from her back, he stood firm, as if his feet were nailed to the spot...and looked down.

"Mr. Cranell?"

Realizing the boy hadn't followed, the elf turned to face him.

"I'm sorry, Miss Lyu..."

Then Bell looked up to meet her gaze.

"That monster...I'm going after that lizardman."

"!"

Lyu recoiled in surprise beneath her hood as he shouted what was in his heart.

"I...have to follow that lizardman...!"

The boy might have been on the verge of tears, but there was no wavering in Bell's eyes.

Lyu fell silent before him.

"May I know your reasoning?"

"......"

Bell responded with only silence when she finally spoke up. Lyu studied him, unblinking.

Her sky-blue eyes probed his rubellite ones.

"Have you not been drawn into the Evils's...*Ikelos Familia's* foul plot? I have heard as much."

"!"

"You have not been yourself as of late. Syr is worried......As am I."

"......"

"Your reasoning for chasing after that monster is a mystery to me. However, I...I do not want you involved with that familia."

With eyes full of unrestrained emotion, Lyu extended her right hand to the boy as though sensing danger, as though afraid of what was to come.

Just as on that day when they shook hands on this very floor.

"Will you not return to the surface?"

Bell didn't look away.

He stepped away from the hand trying to stop him.

That step took him across the crack in the floor, bringing back the painful memories of how it got there—and thus Bell retreated from Lyu, just as Lido had done to him moments ago.

"I see..."

A second silence fell. Lyu looked away from the fiercely determined boy.

It pained Bell to turn a cold shoulder to one so kind, but he knew he needed to endure. Suddenly, an incredibly powerful noise from the battlefield blew through the trees.

A siren's song of destruction was protecting the Xenos's rear flank.

Lyu narrowed her eyes at the rush of sound that was far more powerful and damaging than those thus far.

Then she made eye contact with Bell once again.

"You have become a full-fledged adventurer."

"Miss Lyu..."

"Any attempt to stop you would be futile. Follow it."

Lyu pulled a small pouch from her waist as she spoke.

She then proceeded to pull out an assortment of high potions and other healing items.

"However, I will be following right behind you…Once the subjugation team is out of danger," she added.

Bell couldn't turn her down.

He had no choice but to accept.

"Thank you very much…and sorry."

Bell took off at a sprint.

He sensed Lyu run off in the opposite direction behind him as he tightened the pouch's drawstring and raced forward.

"Dix, word is that the monsters are closin' in on our base."

Dix looked up at the stone-slab ceiling once he heard Gran's report.

"Baroy or somebody couldn't keep their mouth shut…I'd love to drive my fist through their faces, but they're probably already dead anyway."

Sitting on top of a small, empty cage, the man in goggles started laughing in joyous anticipation.

He then looked back toward his subordinate and lobbed something over to him.

The large man caught the piece of processed metal, an ingot that fit in the palm of his hand.

"Gran. Open the door, would you?"

"D-Dix? Are you sure? If monsters get in here…"

"Ganesha's followers can't be far behind 'em. It'd be real annoying if they got suspicious, seeing a whole bunch of monsters hanging around outside."

The man grinned below his goggles.

"I say we give the monsters a little invitation."

A dark, evil chuckle came from his throat.

"We hunt on our home turf."

"Gros!"

"You're late, Lido!"

The lizardman caught up with the gargoyle leading the Xenos's advance.

They had arrived at the forest's eastern rim. The end of the floor. A steep rock face rose all the way to the ceiling in front of them.

There was no way forward. The ground didn't go any farther than this.

Many Xenos were scouring the vegetation and crystal pillars for clues, combing the area for any minor detail they might have missed, leaving no stone unturned.

"What of the door? Have you found it?"

"No, there's nothing here!! Our comrades won't answer, no matter how much we call!"

Gros was getting anxious. Lido joined the search, his field of vision obscured by trees or stone in every direction. Nothing seemed out of place in the repetitive scenery.

Perhaps they had been deceived after all. Gros, Lido, and the other Xenos fought to remain calm as a certain hunter's last words—*You don't* have one of those, *so you'll never get inside!*—rang in their ears.

"—Lido!"

That's when it happened.

A red-cap goblin cried out in shock as it pointed.

Lido's gaze followed the goblin's extended finger.

"That's..."

Bell was dashing through the trees, jumping over roots that crisscrossed the ground like giant tentacles, when suddenly a black shadow came into view.

"Fels!"

"Bell Cranell! You've come!"

Long robe flapping, Fels joined Bell to run by his side.

"Are you all right?" asked the mage with a sigh of relief once they were shoulder to shoulder.

"Yes!" Bell answered.

"I made contact with Gros, but it was no use. He mentioned something about taking back his kind...The only conclusion I can draw is that the hunters sparked their attack. Nothing can stop the Xenos now."

"I spoke with Lido!"

Bell recounted his conversation with the lizardman. He told Fels that several Xenos were killed, that Wiene and Fia had been captured, everything.

A painful groan escaped from beneath Fels's hood.

"While I do not want to admit it, the hunters were a step ahead...I believe it is safe to assume that they belong to *Ikelos Familia*."

"...!"

"But this door you mentioned...Does it lead to the enemy's home base?"

Fels and Bell exchanged words as they advanced, matching each other stride for stride.

"Fels, what about...the Xenos fighting Lyu and the subjugation team? What about them...?"

"Not an issue. *Ganesha Familia* has been ordered to tame them. I doubt any of the Xenos will die. I'm more concerned about the tamers, to tell the truth. The Xenos are not themselves at the moment... although, now that Gros and Lido have left the battle and divided their forces in half, I'm sure those fears are unnecessary."

Fels explained that now was *Ganesha Familia*'s chance.

"We might have failed to convince them to retreat, but we are able to move about unimpeded. Now, we must find and infiltrate this hidden base."

"I'm right behind you...!"

At last, a clue to find the hunters was in their grasp. The memory of Wiene's tears when they parted ways spurred Bell onward, and he picked up speed alongside Fels.

The dome of branches overhead thinned, and the trees in their path parted to reveal a stone wall. A cluster of blue crystal pillars stood in an oddly circular formation nearby. But the two figures didn't bother taking in the view, instead rushing at top speed to reach their destination.

"Is this it...?"

"Yes, the eastern edge of the forest and our destination. However..."

Fels's voice trembled slightly next to a startled Bell, who surveyed the area after coming to a stop.

"The Xenos are nowhere to be found...Disappeared? Inconceivable."

They had followed the path of destruction the Xenos made on their way through the forest, and there were uprooted plants and broken crystals scattered everywhere. The Xenos were here, of that they were certain.

But they were nowhere to be seen. Bell and Fels listened closely to their surroundings, but there was nothing.

The Xenos had vanished. All those monsters were gone, in the blink of an eye.

"What exactly is the door? Did they find it...?"

The two stood back to back, scanning the area with increasing urgency.

But they couldn't find any spot, any clue that would signal the existence of a "door." Between the eerily tranquil forest air and the demolished floor surface, their uneasiness only continued to grow.

As the sound of his own heartbeat was starting to mess with Bell's head—something caught his eye.

Fragments of a large crystal destroyed by the Xenos were scattered across the ground.

While it was the sparkle that caught his attention, the crystal's rapid regeneration kept it there. It was re-forming right before his eyes.

A certain sound reached his ears as the crystal began to take its former shape, a sound that he had heard once before.

I've seen this before, but where...?

"...The Xenos Hidden Village?"

A wall of quartz had kept the Frontier entrance well hidden. That quartz repaired itself in no time at all.

Bell's eyes opened a bit wider when he realized the patch of crystals on the wall was the same type of quartz, and that they were recovering just as fast.

Then Bell felt something hot under his armor as he took one determined step in that direction.

"Huh?"

"Bell Cranell?"

Feeling Fels's inquisitive gaze on his back, Bell reached for the hot spot, equally confused.

His hand wrapped around the pouch that Lyu had given him.

Reaching inside, his fingers worked past the high potions and antidotes until—he pulled out a piece of metal, an ingot that fit in the palm of his hand.

"Bell Cranell, what might that be…?"

"A magic item…?"

Streaks covered the edges, as though the metal had once been so hot it almost melted. But yes, it was a magic item for sure.

The roundish silver object was probably made from mythril.

A red orb was embedded deep within the metal—like an eye staring out from the core.

A very simple character that wasn't written in Koine or hieroglyphs had been inscribed on the item's surface: a *D*.

"Wh-what is this…?"

The circular magic item kept producing heat, giving the two no time to acknowledge the dread growing in the back of their minds.

What's more, the heat and intensity varied based on location as though it were responding to something nearby.

Bell's mouth hung open as he let it guide their path.

The magic item brought them to a protruding segment of the rock wall.

"Nothing looks unusual about this…"

"Fels, this area…it's the same as the room that led to the Xenos Hidden Village."

There was nothing different about this piece of the wall from any of the other jagged formations that spread out in either direction as far as they could see. As the magic item reached a fever pitch in the palm of his hand, Bell told Fels about his earlier observation.

The black-robed mage paused, gazing at the wall with the utmost intensity.

"Stand back, Bell Cranell."

A right arm appeared from the swishing black robe to point at the wall.

The intricate patterns on Fels's glove flared to life.

Suddenly, a colorless shock wave burst forth from the palm.

"...!!"

"Well, that's unexpected..."

Not only had the thundering wave caught Bell off guard, but what lay beyond the wall after the explosion left him speechless.

A single tunnel entrance yawned before them as the last bits of quartz fell to the ground.

It was large enough to allow large-category monsters to easily pass through, and the passage was made of *numerous types of rocks and minerals.*

"This is not a natural Dungeon formation but something...*artificial,*" said Fels in a stunned whisper, taking a step inside.

After they crossed the regenerating threshold, Bell forgot to breathe as the two made their way farther into the tunnel.

Their path was suddenly blocked by a towering metallic gate not even five meders in.

The two froze in front of the gigantic doors. Two demonic statues looked down from either side of the gate in front of them.

"Orichalcum—a masterpiece ingot that can be forged into unbreakable Durandal-class items. It surpasses even adamantite."

It was the densest rare metal in the world, the end result of blending various materials together with human and demi-human techniques. Even Bell, still on the outer edges of the adventurer hierarchy, had heard the name.

"It is physically impossible to destroy...But."

Fels glanced over and beckoned the boy forward. Bell stepped closer.

He held out the magic item with trembling hands—the crimson jewel buried deep within the item flashed in response.

The tunnel rumbled around them as the door rose.

"Unbelievable...Something like this, inside the Dungeon?"

A dim tunnel was waiting for them on the other side, barely illuminated by flickering magic-lamp light.

Bell cleared his throat, staring down at the round item in his hand as Fels whispered quietly at his side.

The magic item was the "key" that opened the door.

Did Lyu know about this when she gave me her pouch? Or is it just a coincidence?

Ikelos Familia—the Evils—was an organization said to have infested the Dungeon a mere five years ago but was much more prominent than today, and a vile group.

Lyu said that she had fought to the last with *Astrea Familia*—their emblem depicted a winged sword of justice—to protect Orario from them.

Bell thought back to the day when the elf ex-adventurer told him that story on this very floor, in a hidden spot where her comrades had been laid to rest.

She might have seized this magic item from one of her foes during her quest to avenge her fallen allies.

Many thoughts crossed through Bell's mind as his hypothesis came together. Then he looked up.

The stone tunnel in front of him had clearly been designed and constructed by human hands.

The statues weren't the only indication.

Since it was hidden behind a regenerating Dungeon wall in a safe point where monsters were never born, construction could have gone unnoticed.

But that triggered so many more questions, like who built it? When? How? The list went on.

Fels walked past Bell, who didn't even notice the cold sweat covering his skin, and approached a piece of the wall beyond the door.

The stone surface was silent but for a single shabby sign in Koine.

"...Daedalus."

Fels read a single name in a hollow voice.

A cold chill completely unrelated to the Dungeon swept through Bell. The boy stared into the dark abyss that seemed to stretch out endlessly before him.

The bright sun of the surface started to sink from the center of the sky.

Babel Tower stood tall in Central Park, which was still crowded even though the subjugation team had long since departed.

Ganesha Familia was still hard at work maintaining a no-entry zone around the tower. Other adventurers approached them for information, but most of the crowd was anxiously waiting for a triumphant return. As time passed, however, the tension waned to an easy lull.

"Dammit, are we really stuck waiting on the sidelines...?"

"With this heavy surveillance, sneaking inside is out of the question...Every adventurer and deity who tried got caught."

"Waiting is hard, isn't it...? I do this every day, Welf."

"Master Bell..."

Welf, Mikoto, Hestia, and Haruhime had gathered in a corner of Central Park. They exchanged words while gazing at the white tower from afar. With no way to assist Bell's return or find out the Xenos's fate, all of *Hestia Familia* was on edge.

"Back to what we were talking about before...If it's true that those hunters started this whole mess by kidnapping one of the Xenos, why don't we try to find their base? If they're working the black market and selling to collectors or whoever, they gotta keep their stock somewhere in the city, right?"

"That must be true...but if the honorable Fels and the Guild have been unable to locate their hiding place, what point is there in us trying...?"

"Hermes is good at this kind of thing, but...then again, capturing monsters and selling them for profit? Only someone with no fear of the gods or the Dungeon would even try."

Hestia voiced her displeasure as she listened in on Welf and Mikoto's conversation.

That was also the moment when Lilly, the brains of the group, had an epiphany after hearing Hestia's words.

"Sell monsters for profit..."

She tilted her small head to the side as though memories were flooding through her mind.

"Lure out monsters, capture them, and *sell them for profit...*"

"...Li'l E?"

"A-are you feeling unwell?"

Welf and Haruhime glanced at the prum with concern as Lilly continued muttering to herself.

Suddenly, the small girl's head snapped up as the rest of her familia eyed her.

"Let's go."

"Supporter?"

"Lilly might have a lead."

Lilly turned her back on Babel and strode away with those words. Hestia and the others made brief eye contact before taking off after her.

"Go? Where to?"

Lilly turned around to answer Welf's question.

"Lilly's former deity—to Lord Soma."

Soma Familia's home and "wine cellar" stood between East Main Street and Southeast Main Street in Orario's third district.

Lilly led the group to the former first.

"Lilliluka Erde...How is your health?"

They met the god Soma in his private quarters.

His long hair kept his eyes and the vast depths behind them practically hidden. He looked more like a hermit than a being from a higher plane, but he was also none other than Lilly's former god, the head of *Soma Familia*.

"It has been a long time, Lord Soma. Lilly is very well, thank you."

"Hey, Soma, what'd you mean by that? Does it look like I've been that rough on Supporter to you?"

Lilly bowed to the deity she had not seen in nearly two months as Hestia jumped out from beside her. "Sorry..." said the god in a feeble voice as Hestia scowled at him with puffed cheeks.

Soma Familia's strange behavior had become all but nonexistent after Lilly's transfer and the War Game. It was because Soma had stopped using the divine wine soma as a reward to manage his followers.

Lilly knew just how little Soma cared for the people of this world, so his slightly friendlier appearance made a deep impression on her—and made her happy as well.

She briefly summarized their situation. "All right..." Soma nodded without any resistance. "I'll summon Chandra..."

He motioned to one of his nearby followers. A rugged dwarf appeared at the door a few moments later.

"It has been a long time, Mr. Chandra. Lilly heard you became the leader. Congratulations."

"Enough of that. I ain't cut out to lead a damn thing...Can't drink soma like I used to, either. Just adding insult to injury."

Chandra Ihit's surly response was somewhat fatigued. The short-haired, short-bearded dwarf who had joined *Soma Familia* for the sole purpose of drinking the world's finest wine had assisted Lilly in her time of need and now sat at the head of the struggling organization.

He led Lilly and the rest of the group to the wine cellar, taking a swig from the gourd hanging at his waist as they moved along.

While *Soma Familia*'s home was relatively close to the city center, their wine cellar was located only a few blocks from the city wall.

The deity had all but given up on producing soma, a wine potent enough to entrance any person on Earth. The familia was now focused on developing delicious wines essentially for the purpose of earning small profits, and the wine cellar had been renovated to support this research. However, only one place remained unchanged:

The holding cell, where the familia used to keep unruly members under control.

"You there...Food! Where's the food? Hurry it up, I'm starving!"

A gruff man's voice, not much different from a stray dog's bark, came from deep within the stone hallway.

As unreliable magic-stone lamps flickered and the damp air cooled on their skin, Soma and Chandra led the way with *Hestia Familia* close. Lilly tensed.

"Pipe down, Zanis. Quit your yappin'."

"Ehh? Chandra, what're you doing here...? Oh, if it isn't our lord and...You lot..."

A familia member serving as a guard pointed them to a certain cell containing a human man.

The prisoner with sunken cheeks gazed at his visitors one by one until he reached Lilly at the end. His lips curled into a sneer almost at once.

"Ha-ha-ha-ha-ha......! Never thought I'd be seeing you here."

It took everything Lilly had to keep her expression steady under his unblinking stare.

The man's name was Zanis Rustra. He was a Level 2 upper-class adventurer like Chandra, and he had been in charge of *Soma Familia* until recently.

He was a shadow of his former self. There was no trace of intelligence in his visage, and his glasses were nowhere to be seen. Given his ragged and torn clothes, the word *shabby* summed him up nicely.

Zanis had been stripped of his position after the events that led to Lilly's departure from *Soma Familia*.

In addition to the many victims of the familia's violent, rowdy behavior, the deciding factor for his dismissal was how he used and sold Soma's divine wine to manipulate others for his own personal gain.

His Status sealed by Soma as punishment, the man now spent his days confined in the holding cell.

Welf was visibly angry, and the man cast a hostile glare in his direction as he walked up to the black iron bars and addressed Lilly at the front of the group.

"Come to laugh at poor Zanis, have you, Erde?"

"……"

"My, my, how things have changed. We were on opposite sides last time…" said the unshaven former leader, peering at her with a dark grin.

Lilly looked up into Zanis's tortured, hate-filled eyes.

"…Lilly has…a question for you."

"For me? What could the one who robbed me of everything possibly want to ask?"

She ignored Zanis's sarcasm and asked in a calm voice:

"About talking monsters…Would you happen to know where the 'business venture' you mentioned is based?"

The man froze, completely silent after hearing her words.

But it was only for a heartbeat. His sneering chuckle swelled into delighted laughter.

"Now I get it…Ha-ha-ha-ha! Did you see one? Did you meet one of those talking monsters, Erde?"

The man's laughter resounded in the hallway.

So it's true, Lilly thought upon seeing his reaction. Chandra cocked an eyebrow, Soma silent at his side.

It had all happened just before the War Game, when Zanis locked Lilly in this very cell during negotiations with *Apollo Familia*. The man came to Lilly in her weakened state and asked for her assistance.

His plan was to use Lilly's transformation magic, Cinder Ella, to capture monsters.

"There's a project in which I would love your participation. Nothing much, just a new business venture. Luring out monsters, capturing them, and selling them for profit…Isn't that simple?"

Lilly had laughed it off at the time. Monsters profitable? She told him as much, and the man laughed right back at her with greedy eyes.

But now she knew. She knew which monsters would fetch a high price.

Because now she knew of the beautiful and sentient Xenos.

Zanis had known about them that day, possibly even well before then.

Judging by the way he spoke, it was highly likely Zanis was involved in the black-market dealings, selling the talking monsters to depraved collectors. Therefore, he was much more involved with these secret transactions and the hidden base where the Xenos were kept than any of *Hestia Familia*.

Hestia and her followers watched with trembling eyes as Lilly frowned and demanded an answer.

"Fwa-ha-ha-ha-ha...! Well then, you might find something interesting on Daedalus Street, should you be going that way."

The man twisted around with a sneer on his face, and his sunken eyes fell on Lilly as he provided a tantalizing clue.

Lilly's nerves tightened as she pressed for more information.

"Where exactly would that be?"

"Go find it yourselves. I'm not saying another word."

Zanis's laughter once again echoed through the stone halls; he clearly enjoyed the position Lilly was now in. "Wanna convince him with a little force to talk?" offered Chandra, but Lilly shook her head, declining the violent suggestion.

Zanis would never break. At the very least, not until this incident was resolved.

"Our best lead lies somewhere on Daedalus Street...Let's go."

Lilly turned her back on the holding cell and addressed her allies. Once they gave her a nod, she asked Soma and Chandra to keep what they heard to themselves before leading the group back down the hallway.

"Best of luck to you, Erde...Hah! Ha-ha-ha-ha-ha-ha-ha-ha-ha!"

With the man's sinister laughter echoing behind them, *Hestia Familia* set a course for Daedalus Street.

"This place...connects to Daedalus Street...?!"

Bell made his way through the stone hallway, unable to hide the surprise in his voice.

"Yes, I have no doubt. A route to the surface that circumvents our surveillance and allows illicit sales outside Orario...Should this structure go aboveground, it would be the last logical piece of the puzzle. It's safe to assume there's an underground passage leading outside the city wall as well, enabling them to avoid inspection at the gates."

Fels explained his train of thought as the two ran deeper into the hallway.

The intertwining network of stone hallways was complex. Each fork and intersection had been painstakingly measured to create perfect angles that didn't exist in the Dungeon, signifying this was a man-made labyrinth. If it weren't for the trail of blood left by the monsters wounded from battle, the two would have gotten lost in no time. Although no monster would be born into the darkness from these walls and ceiling, eerie sculptures and statues depicting the beasts stood throughout the halls.

The feeble lights embedded in the walls illuminated Fels's vague, floating outline.

"The assumption that this connects to Daedalus Street is based on that sign carved into the wall..." groaned Fels. "Mad Daedalus... A famous architect who lived at the turning point in history when gods came to this world, the one who built Babel Tower and several other structures that became the very foundation of Orario..."

Fels explained that this human lived nearly one thousand years ago, long before the Sage's birth.

The black-robed mage delved deeper into the story of one of history's greats.

"Legend has it he was among the followers of Ouranos, the first deity to grant Falna on Earth."

"!"

"He made many contributions to Orario, following Ouranos's will...However, it is said that the man's speech and actions grew more outlandish with each passing day once he entered the Dungeon. Hence, the epithet 'mad'...Then at some point, he disappeared from Ouranos's sight and Orario itself."

Fels explained what he knew, bringing the situation to light.

"Apart from Daedalus Street, his citywide sewer system and other creations have been a thorn in the Guild's side for some time. Do you not remember, Bell Cranell? The bizarre network of passages that exist beneath the city."

"Now that you mention it..."

Fels's words triggered a few memories, specifically ones involving Haruhime and Syr.

The hidden tunnels beneath the Pleasure Quarter. Phryne and Haruhime said that it was because Daedalus Street was so close. In the same vein, Bell recalled the stairwell behind the orphanage that he had used along with Syr and the children. That confirmed it for Bell—Daedalus's legacy was ingrained into Orario's very core.

Back then, people had shuddered to think that one man could build so much on his own, but Fels explained that might be the reason Daedalus the Artisan lived on as one of history's greats—and as a madman.

Bell swallowed, completely awestruck by the prodigy who had surpassed the physical limits of the human body thanks to a Blessing. He didn't know the man's face or if Daedalus was even his real name.

"We have considered for some time the possibility of a second entrance into the Dungeon separate from Babel. Of course we investigated Daedalus Street, but...Damn it."

"Fels...?"

"...To be blunt, this far exceeds anything we ever imagined."

Their thoughts dwelled on the legendary architect as the two arrived at another metallic gate.

Fels withdrew Bell's key from the sleeve of the black robe and pressed it against the gate. The tightly closed door swung open.

Once inside, Fels reached toward a nearby wall. Light traced through the glove's intricate designs, and another colorless shock wave burst from the palm. Bell looked over his shoulder in surprise to see a completely intact metal plate beneath the crumbling stone surface.

"What's that...?"

"Adamantite. I noticed a metallic gleam coming from behind a deteriorating rock face on the way here. These hallways were first lined with adamantite before a layer of stone was adhered to the surface."

Although its purity varied by level of origin, adamantite was an extremely rare, dense metal that could be mined in the Dungeon.

It went without saying that the expensive substance was not easy to acquire.

Another shock ran down Bell's spine.

"A main entrance protected by orichalcum, hallways constructed with adamantite…Without this magical key, it would have been next to impossible to infiltrate, even if we did manage to locate this structure."

Crick! The glove on Fels's outstretched hand creaked as it clenched into a fist.

"A series of artificial passageways connecting to the Dungeon… As difficult as it is to believe, only history's most famous madman could have accomplished this feat."

But unanswered questions still remained.

Was it physically possible for one man to create a structure from the surface to the Dungeon's eighteenth floor, and possibly farther? There was also the orichalcum-and-adamantite issue to contend with.

Fels spoke up as if reading Bell's mind.

"We have yet to comprehend the scale of this structure. Daedalus might have been in a league of his own, but it would be next to impossible to do this alone. However…"

Fels let that word hang as he peered farther down the dark hallway.

"The answers we are looking for surely lie ahead."

Another entrance to the Dungeon, one created by human hands.

They had discovered *Ikelos Familia*'s hidden base.

Years of hard work and suffering finally had borne fruit. The mage's voice trembled with swirling emotions.

"We finally found it, Ouranos…!"

"I've found you—Ikelos."

A voice drifted out across the sky.

On the surface, far above the underground labyrinth…

Hermes addressed a certain god from behind as he stood on the roof of a tall brick tower.

"…Hee-hee-hee! So you have."

The god Ikelos slowly turned around on the deserted rooftop.

It was part of a series of residential buildings designed with no rhyme or reason, inconsistent in height and breadth, making the area difficult to navigate.

Hermes and Ikelos stood on top of a brick tower directly in the middle of Daedalus Street, Orario's "dungeon town."

"How did you ever find this place, Hermes? Truth be told, I never thought anyone would catch up after coming this far."

"Sure wasn't easy...finding a god who's hiding his trail with his power. It might not be much, but using your ability for your own gain while here on Earth borders on blasphemy...You broke the rules."

"Hee-hee! What's wrong with showing off a little bit? Not like it would do anything to stop those high-level brats...Besides, how boring would it be if I got caught before all the fun started?"

Ikelos stood at the railing-less tower's edge.

All of Daedalus Street was visible from this spot beneath the sky over Orario.

Alleyways weaved in all directions, surrounding the tower like a web. Stairways led up and down amid a jumble of multistoried buildings. Only those close to its creator could understand the source of his inspiration, the chaos he was trying to emulate.

Hermes ran his fingers along the wide brim of his feathered hat, glaring intensely at his quarry through narrowed orange eyes.

As for Ikelos, the god was laughing as if enjoying a game.

"You've won this round of hide-and-seek, Hermes."

"......"

"It won't stop the show, but...I think I'll answer any and all questions as your reward."

The navy-blue-haired, wheat-skinned god opened his arms as if teasing the other deity.

A faint grin on his lips, he narrowed his eyes at Hermes.

"So then, what would you like to know?"

Several shadows passed over the stone floor under the magic-stone lamps.

Footsteps in sets of two and four echoed through the man-made, stone-enforced hallway, closely followed by the sound of dragging tails and flapping wings.

More than twenty monsters marched onward.

"Our comrades' scent guides us closer—advance!!"

The airborne gargoyle shouted as the battle boar's acute sense of smell led the way. The faint scents lingering in the air guided the procession of monsters, the Xenos, through the stone passageways. At every fork in the road, the Xenos always chose the direction with the strongest traces of their companions and picked up speed every time.

"Lido, every door in our path has been open…We're being lured in!"

"I know that, Lett! But we have to go…!!"

Lido squeezed the hilts of his swords as he responded to the red-cap goblin just behind him.

Once the group broke through the wall of rock on the eastern edge of the forest, they immediately saw an open door at the end of the tunnel.

Fully aware that this was the enemy base, and most likely a trap, the Xenos charged headlong into this man-made realm.

Driven by insatiable anger and a singular purpose—rescuing their captured friends—the Xenos found themselves at their ultimate destination.

"What is this place…?!"

When they reached the top of a stone stairwell, a vast chamber unlike any of the tunnels appeared in front of their eyes.

It was perfectly rectangular, over one hundred meders wide and several times that in length. The whole area, including the high ceiling, was constructed from stone and shrouded in darkness. The incredibly massive space shared many characteristics with the Great Wall of Sorrows at the end of the seventeenth floor.

But Lido, Gros, and the rest of the Xenos were focused in one direction.

"Everyone…!"

Countless lines of black cages.

And inside this hellish prison were lamia, Scylla, and mermaids, along with many other dazzling monsters with human characteristics as well as extremely rare monsters like a carbuncle. Every one of them was scarred from torture and locked in a cage with heavy chains.

The harpy Fia was in the first cage in the row, clinging to the bars.

"———!!"

Lido, Gros, and the other Xenos could hear the rage seething inside themselves.

Whoosh! As their fur and feathers stood on end, they rushed forward en masse.

"Break the cages!! Set our comrades free!!"

Gros howled as he tore the nearest cage to pieces.

Lido and the other armed monsters hacked and slashed their way through the iron bars while others bent and twisted the metal with brute force. Free of the chains on their limbs, the prisoners were finally released from the cages.

Gros led the Xenos farther back, leaving broken cages in their wake. While some of the freed monsters were indeed once part of the Xenos, there were others they had never seen before. They had two things in common: a sparkle of intelligence in their eyes and an inability to break free themselves due to weakness and injury.

Time passed. The number of cages never seemed to decrease no matter how many they destroyed; the calls for help never ceased. Catching their kin on the verge of collapse, embracing them one after another, the Xenos destroyed cage after cage amid the echoes in the vast chamber.

"Fia, where's Wiene?"

"I don't know. They dragged her away, unconscious, toward the back…!"

After Lido set her free, the badly injured harpy willed her muscles to move, pointing a feathered wing into the darkness.

Narrowing his reptilian eyes, Lido left Fia in Lett's care and took off at a sprint.

"—Such a touching reunion."

Then, right there…

A hollow clap echoed through the air, as if its maker had been waiting for the right moment.

"…?!"

"Welcome to our humble abode, monsters. Do make yourselves at home."

A man wearing goggles appeared from deep in the darkness.

Lido came to a screeching halt, and Gros turned away from a broken cage. Every set of Xenos eyes zeroed in on him.

They stood face-to-face with the dreaded hunter at last.

"Are you the hunter selling off our kind…?"

"Oh? You knew about that? Yeah, I'm the one who snatched your buddies and turned them into cash—once I taught them some manners so they'd obey the customers, that is."

"Bastard…!!"

A grin formed on the man's—Dix's—face as he tapped the shaft of his wickedly curved red spear against his shoulder. He didn't bat an eye under the waves of hostility rolling off Lido, Gros, and the rest of the Xenos.

"Well, I shouldn't really say 'I.' More like 'us,'" he said, and hunters appeared all over the chamber.

A few stepped out from behind Dix, others from the walls on the left and right, and some even materialized from the entrance the Xenos came through.

Lett and Fia jumped in surprise from their spot behind the Xenos line, watching a variety of humans and demi-humans move to surround and trap the group.

The Xenos and the broken cages at their feet were encircled by hunters.

"…!"

"You might have the edge in numbers, but…can you protect all of your precious cargo at the same time?"

It was just as Dix said. The newly released monsters could barely stand.

The healthy Xenos could never fight at full strength if they had to worry about protecting their allies. Luring Lido and the rest into this chamber and waiting for the Xenos to free the other monsters was all part of the plan.

Lido and Gros bared their fangs at their crafty, grinning foe and menacingly clacked them together.

"—Lido!"

"Wha...Bellucchi?!"

That moment, Bell and Fels burst into the chamber from the stone stairwell.

Lido was the first to whirl around in surprise. Gros and the other Xenos quickly followed suit. As for the hunters, they were absolutely stunned.

"You're that boy from...You, why have you come?!"

"Now's not the time, Gros!"

Gros's reaction turned to anger at the fact that Bell had followed them here, but Lido held out his arm to hold him back.

The lizardman looked up, his reptilian irises meeting Bell's rubellite ones.

Why, how, turn back already—so many urgent words and questions appeared in Lido's gaze before disappearing.

"Oh come on...Gran, you idiot! The hell's going on? Why do we have guests in our 'secret' base? Did you seriously forget to close the doors?"

"I c-closed them all! I ain't lying to you, Dix! Once the monsters were through, I closed them all, I swear...!"

Sweat poured down the towering bald-headed man at Dix's cold voice, and he desperately pleaded his case.

Gran had arrived with the second group of hunters behind the Xenos, and Bell and Fels had a clear view of the item in his possession.

"Isn't that...?"

Bell whispered in disbelief as Fels looked down at the similar magic item in his grasp.

"A key...?!" A wave of disbelief passed through the hunters once they saw it, too.

"Ohh, so that's how it is...So, what bumbling idiot did you take it from? Guess we shouldn't pass those things out left and right after all."

One look at the magic item in the newcomer's hand and Dix seemed to connect the dots. His mood worsening by the moment, he smacked the red shaft of his spear against his shoulder and berated himself.

Gran and the other hunters were not keen on facing enemies on two fronts. They moved out of the way to rejoin their allies, allowing Bell and Fels to approach the Xenos.

"Signor Bell..."

"Surface dwellers...Have you come...to help us?"

"......!"

The harpy, sitting up with the red-cap goblin's support, spoke from her spot on the floor.

Painful cuts and bruises covered her body. The chain might have been severed, but a pair of shackles far too big for her little legs was still firmly in place. A wave of nausea overtook the newcomers at the depraved sight.

Bell couldn't speak as Fia looked weakly up at him.

Where's Wiene?!

Bell couldn't help imagining the dragon girl in a similar state and immediately started searching for her. However, despite all the people and monsters in the chamber, she was nowhere to be seen.

"I can't believe it—a chamber this size..."

While Bell was growing more and more anxious, Fels studied their immediate surroundings with a groan.

The Sage's hood shifted and turned toward Dix, and the mage called in a voice loud enough to be heard across the great distance between them:

"Hazer, Dix Perdix...So you're the mastermind."

"Who are you, mage? Gotta say, that's a shady getup you got there...How about telling me what you are to these monsters? You, too, Little Rookie."

Fels and Dix exchanged words as the hunters and Xenos glared at each other in the chamber. Uneasy boot steps echoed off the walls as the tension between the two groups became severe enough to explode at any moment.

"I'll cut right to the point. This is a Daedalus creation, is it not?"

"Ha-ha! Noticed, have you? It's probably exactly what you think."

"...How long has it been in use? No, when did you learn of its existence?"

"How should I know? The ancestors dumped it on me. As a descendant, it shouldn't matter when or how I use it, yeah?"

Dix's words not only caught Fels by surprise but stopped Bell in his tracks.

"Ancestors...Descendant...?!"

"Do you claim to be part of Daedalus's family tree?!"

Both the boy's and the mage's voices shook with surprise and confusion. A satisfied smile appeared on Dix's face as the Xenos lent their ears to the conversation, doubting his claim.

"I ain't bluffing. Look—I'll prove it right now."

With that, the man raised his goggles.

"———."

His fearless red eyes were exposed for all to see.

There was a *D* marking his left iris.

"There, proof of my Daedalus heritage. Anyone with even a drop of that lunatic's blood in their veins is born with this mark in their eye."

A cursed bloodline.

He confronted them all with proof.

Whether it was authentic or not, they couldn't be sure. There wasn't enough information to make a decision either way. However—Bell stopped breathing when he looked at Fels's hand.

The sphere inside the magic item bore the same mark.

The thing embedded inside the ingot *didn't merely resemble an eye—*

"The doors in here only respond to our eyes. They were made that way so that descendants could go where they pleased and get to 'work'...But nowadays we carve the eyes out of their dead bodies and use them as keys to take advantage of it."

Fels, Bell, and the Xenos stood like statues as Dix declared its name.

"The man-made labyrinth Knossos—a ridiculous piece Daedalus left for all his descendants to work on."

* * *

"Knossos?"

Hermes repeated what he had just heard.

Ikelos responded with a grin and a quick "Yeah." He was answering the other god's questions as part of his "prize." "That's what's written in the notebook, anyway."

"Notebook? You can't mean..."

"That's right, Daedalus's Notebook."

The breeze atop the tower rustled the deity's cheap black clothing and carried his voice to Hermes.

"Daedalus...Dix's forefather went a bit off the deep end after seeing the Dungeon. He just had to create with his own hands a piece that outdid the labyrinth in every way...How stupid is that? Hee-hee! There used to be so many crazy children back in those days. Now they're all just stuck-up brats."

The god sneered as if nothing were more entertaining than the notebook of a man's regrets and burning desires.

"Of course, one man could never finish something like that. I doubt it could ever be done at all. But at any rate, Daedalus died when the project was still in the beginning stages, and he willed it and the notebook to his offspring."

"......"

"Along with a nice blueprint to go with it. And those descendants have been following it ever since."

Hermes let a few moments pass before responding.

"Ikelos, if what you're saying is true, then...those descendants have..."

"That's right, Hermes. Those descendants have been working on Knossos for nearly—"

"—*One thousand years,*" Dix said as he pulled his goggles back down over his eyes. "That's how long the ancestors were building this thing without the Guild finding out."

Bell, Fels, and even the Xenos had difficulty believing the man's incredible claim.

"Impossible! All those years and not a soul caught on...?!"

"Okay then, mage, how would you explain how the labyrinth you're standing in got here? Do you think this piece of 'artwork' running along the Dungeon's edges was seriously built overnight?"

The Dungeon layout was *circular.*

It expanded outward with each floor wider than the last.

And—Knossos was *concave* around it.

Bell used his knowledge and Dix's claim to arrive at that conclusion.

Daedalus's blueprints called for a structure that sat in the negative space around the Dungeon's circular edges, transforming it into a pillar of sorts beneath the city. This man-made labyrinth wrapped around the Dungeon's circular floors.

The underground network of sewer systems that Fels had mentioned, the secret tunnel that Bell had found, all of it was built as part of the plan to create this one grand piece.

Bell's face turned pale as he struggled to comprehend Knossos's full scale.

"My old man, granddad, and other ancestors expanded Knossos all the way down to the middle levels, and I don't even know their faces."

A thousand years had passed since Mad Daedalus's death.

Knossos was the result of one thousand years of insane, blood-driven obsession.

Bell could almost see Daedalus's flawed vision taking shape, as hands crawling out from beneath his feet.

"But on the other hand…one thousand years and still only the middle levels."

Only 30 percent of the blueprint had been completed, he told them in a spray of spit.

"…I never would've believed this was the truth behind the suspected link between *Ikelos Familia* and the Evils…" Fels whispered to himself, certain he was on to something.

Dix sneered at him.

"I ain't got a clue when the ancestors first started working with the ones you call Evils. But by the time I was born in this shady labyrinth, they were practically joined at the hip."

* * *

"—And all to finish that project of theirs."

Ikelos went on.

"Daedalus's piece cost time, labor, and way too much money."

Orichalcum and adamantite.

Not to mention an abundance of rocks and other building materials.

Knossos didn't have the Dungeon's regenerative ability—it was imperative that this piece be nearly impossible to break in order to realize Daedalus's vision. That was because the madman's intention was to create something that surpassed the Dungeon itself.

And of course, the materials required to build Knossos were extremely difficult to acquire.

"So that's why Daedalus's descendants got involved with the Evils and other shady groups…"

Consequently, those descendants from Daedalus had connections with a wide array of underground and black-market organizations. They sought out organizations that had an abundant supply of orichalcum, building materials, or gold on hand. They didn't care if it took unlawful business dealings or downright theft.

As a second entrance into the Dungeon, one far away from the watchful eyes of the Guild, Knossos became their bargaining chip.

The man-made dungeon expanded deeper over time. Some organizations doubted its usefulness in the beginning, but they eventually discovered Knossos's value and made contributions of their own. The evil groups worked together to conceal its existence from the Guild.

Everything fell into place in Hermes's mind as he ran his fingers along the brim of his hat.

Knossos itself became a hotbed for evil—the darkness had threatened to consume the city for centuries.

"Word has it these descendants did whatever it took to complete their dungeon. Becoming obsessed with acquiring Enigma, kidnapping women to make sure there would always be someone working on their piece…"

Ikelos went on to say that Dix was born from one such abductee.

Half siblings and incest were common.

"While it might be Daedalus's legacy, I find it hard to believe that these descendants would devote their lives to such an absurd work..."

"What can I say? Must be something in their blood."

Ikelos shrugged off Hermes's comment. "Cursed blood...as Dix puts it."

A smile spread on the deity's lips as he gazed down over the Labyrinth City.

"Daedalus's descendants were all dancing to the tune of a single notebook, building this thing."

His red eyes were just barely visible behind the translucent lenses of the goggles.

With those words, Dix lifted his spear, the same shade of red as his eyes, into position and drove his point home.

"...In other words, selling captured Xenos is a way for you to acquire funds."

As to when Dix and the hunters had become aware of the Xenos, that was yet unclear.

However, Dix needed a great deal of money to contribute to Knossos's completion. After joining a familia to gain a Blessing, he gradually took control of the group, guiding them toward Orario's black markets.

Dix snorted at Fels's hypothesis.

"Yeah, at first."

Those words sent an uneasy chill down Bell's spine, and then—*BANG!*

"Enough talk!!"

He looked over in time to see Gros's claws tear through a nearby cage, destroying it.

The gargoyle's eyes flashed, and the ash-colored wings on his back spread wide.

"Your cruelty to our kind and your murder of Ranieh remains unchanged!—You will feel our wrath!!"

The gargoyle took flight, launching himself toward Dix in one swift motion.

The man in goggles quickly grabbed a nearby subordinate by the collar, throwing him directly into the gargoyle's path. "Huh?" The man's confusion quickly turned into a blood-chilling scream the moment Gros's stone claws made contact.

That first splash of blood ignited the battle.

"Gros and I will lead the charge! Dole, have your team protect the injured!"

"Wha—GYAH!"

The lizardman shouted orders to his allies while inflicting a deep gash into the nearest animal person. Other Xenos moved to protect their newly liberated comrades, crossing blades with the attacking hunters.

"Damn it all!"

"Keh...Firebolt!!"

Overwhelmed by the fierce sounds of combat at first, Bell was forced into battle when a group of hunters charged him.

However, they thought better of it when the red-cap goblin held the battle-ax aloft at his side and Fels moved to protect the injured harpy, and the enemies backed off entirely once Bell's Swift-Strike Magic was triggered.

"Oh come on...Kinda strong, ain't they? We underestimated 'em."

Meanwhile, shocked members of *Ikelos Familia* were feeling the same way.

Every hunter other than Dix raced into battle, but just as he said, the hunters were losing ground. Aiming for the weakened monsters only served to enrage the Xenos even further, and the monsters' sheer might quickly dismantled the humans' formations.

This was especially true around Lido and Gros. Dix's smile twisted with irritation as his allies fell to the ground one by one.

"No time to hold back...Guess it's time to use it," Dix said. He held his spear in his left hand and thrust out his right arm.

"_____."

The only reason Fels was able to react to this horrid sight in time—

—was due to a wealth of experience that far exceeded the other's.

—But it was already too late.

As Gran and the other hunters took cover as though their lives depended on it, a chill ran through the body of bones that bordered on absolute zero.

The mage's black robes swirled behind the main battle.

"—Get behind me, Bell Cranell! NOW!!"

Bell, eyes wide, was shocked at the disappearance of Fels's usual calm demeanor and obeyed without question.

Holding Lett and Fia close to his chest, Bell dove behind Fels just as the mage extended both arms wide.

A moment later...

"Become lost in an endless nightmare."

The vibrations rose from the man's throat to form a spell.

"Phobetor Daedalus."

A wave of crimson light burst forth from his fingers.

"————————."

A red glow swept over the battlefield.

The ominous light devoured the darkness. There was no explosion, however—not even a shock or vibration. It engulfed everything in range before continuing on, but all it left behind was a hair-raising, malice-filled tone ringing in their ears.

Bell and the two Xenos hiding behind Fels cupped their hands over their ears as they cautiously looked out from behind the robe to investigate. Just then...

"————————————————OOOOOOOOOOOOO OOOOOOOOOOOOOOOOOOOOOOOOOOOOOOOOO!"

Every single monster was thrashing about, completely out of control.

"Wha—?!"

"Lido, Gros!"

"Everyone?! Why...?!"

Bell, the red-cap goblin, and the harpy all looked on in disbelief as the Xenos tried to destroy everything in sight.

The lizardman's eyes were bloodshot, the gargoyle howling like a lunatic. Gobs of drool sprayed from their mouths as they hacked and slashed with swords and claws. Like actual monsters.

All the Xenos had one thing in common: their eyes had taken on the same crimson hue as Dix's.

Metallic echoes surged as cages flipped and stone crumbled underfoot in a deafening frenzy that threatened to rend their eardrums.

It wasn't long before their wild thrashes connected with their own kind. The battle became a free-for-all where ally fought against ally.

"Wh-what could have possibly…?"

The fully armored and healthy Xenos weren't the only ones affected. Even the newly liberated and badly injured monsters joined the fray with just as much vigor. Bell watched it happen, terror written all over his face. Blood poured from their open wounds, but they continued to attack anything in their vicinity. A chorus of screams and howls filled the air.

His hair stood on end at this growing monster massacre.

"A curse…!!" Fels rasped with horror next to Bell and the others, who were still in shock.

Curses.

Like magic that summoned fire or lightning and enchantments that increased physical attributes, they required a trigger spell to be cast. However, their effects were still worthy of being called "curses."

Confusion, restriction of movement, physical pain—there were many types.

The most troubling thing about curses was that they were difficult to block and cure. Only specialized items would do the trick. Even the Advanced Ability Immunity provided no protection.

It went without saying that the monsters were completely defenseless.

Like magic, this technique was unique to humans. There was nothing the Xenos could do except take a direct hit.

"Aww~, everything's as good as over once I cast it…or at least it should be."

Dix watched the monsters' frenzy with glee in his eyes—that is, until he spotted Bell and Fels standing on the other side of the battle.

"Didn't work on some of them—is that robe of yours a magic item, mage?"

"...Well spotted. It protects against curses and anti-Status magic."

Dix shouted across the battlefield, but Fels's response was so quiet that it was unlikely to be heard.

It was the mage's black robe that had protected Bell and the two Xenos behind him from the curse. "Though I'm not sure a curse would do much to this bony body of mine," the mage known as the Fool whispered, glaring back at the smiling goggled man.

"That curse must be the reason their hunts remained undiscovered, and why they withdrew upon discovering *Hermes Familia*...!"

The curse provided the last piece of the puzzle for Fels, connecting all the loose ends.

If anyone who happened to witness their activities got caught up in the curse, they became a monster's next meal even if the hunters didn't get their hands dirty. If, by some miracle, said witness managed to survive long enough to regain their senses, memories from before the curse took effect would be vague at best.

It was also the real reason why they retreated from Asfi's team of adventurers from *Hermes Familia*. Dix was concerned about Perseus's magic items—there was a possibility that she carried something like Fels's black robe or another item that could nullify the curse's effects. He sacrificed that hunt in order to prevent her from learning anything about them.

Bell understood as well.

Dix's curse had the most impact on first sight.

"Phobetor Daedalus."

A curse that mystified targets, confusing them.

Its extremely short trigger spell and wide range made it a powerful, deadly technique.

Anyone exposed to it without protection was instantly drawn into a wild frenzy—and wouldn't live to encounter it again.

Bell couldn't hide the horror in his eyes at a curse that forced its victims to rampage until their bodies gave out.

This was why Dix always seemed so confident.

The reason he had captured so many Xenos. His trump card.

"We're gonna incur some losses, since I had to bust this out, but..."

There were some hunters on the battlefield who were unable to escape from the unannounced curse in time and others who didn't have the magic item necessary to block it. They, too, howled like monsters, slashing at other humans and monsters alike with broken swords in an erratic fit.

Dix gazed out over the afflicted people and monsters and said:

"Eh, oh well—bon appétit, monsters!"

Suddenly, two monsters landed directly in front of Bell.

"?!"

They were Xenos trying to tear each other apart. Another monster's attack had knocked them all the way up to his feet.

The confused creatures scrambled to their feet and jumped at Bell's group.

"AAAAAAaaaaaaaaaAAAaaaAAaaaaAAAAAAaaaaaaa!!"

"Not good!"

The curse now had them in its clutches.

All four dove away from the reckless, unrestrained swipes of claw and fang. One attack slammed into the stone floor with a *bang* and a spray of debris, and the monsters' wild eyes bored into Bell, Fels, Lett, and Fia. The red-cap goblin and the harpy froze in fear at the sight of their terrifying comrades.

As the crazed hunters continued their onslaught despite their serious injuries, the four quickly found themselves at the center of an all-out brawl.

"————?!"

"?!"

Bell couldn't raise a blade to the Xenos, who should be on his side. With blocking and dodging as his only options, the boy was unable to escape a griffin that caught him between jumps. Just before its sharp beak could tear into his flesh, a troll's massive club slammed into them. The pair was launched high into the air.

"Signor Bell?!"

His vision blurred as he careened toward the main battle.

The griffin had taken the brunt of the club and was now writhing in pain and losing its grip. Although Bell managed to escape, he had been separated from Fels and the others. The red-cap goblin's call disappeared into the swirling pandemonium of screams and roars; Bell was completely isolated.

Pushing the griffin off his body to escape, Bell raised his head, and out of nowhere…

"———."

A lizardman stood in front of him, his weapons held high.

—Lido.

Bloodthirsty, terrifying eyes. Scimitar pointed toward the ceiling. The boy recoiled at the terrifying visage.

Bell's mind went blank as he watched the lizardman prepare to slice him in half.

Looking up at the savage expression—murderous intent as plain as day—Bell brought up a knife but could move no farther.

The lizardman brought down the scimitar without waiting another beat.

Time slowed to a crawl. As if in a trance, Bell watched the blade descend, tracing an arc directly at his body. In that moment—

"GEHH!"

A colorless shock wave slammed into the lizardman from the side, sending the monster flying.

"———?!"

Time returned to normal, and Bell spun around to see a mage's right arm and gloved hand extended in his direction.

"Forgive me, Lido…!"

Fels's long-range burst of energy had saved Bell's life. The mage then shouted:

"Stop Hazer, Bell Cranell!!"

"Huh?"

"This type of curse lifts once the caster is defeated! The Xenos will return to normal!!"

Bell turned away from Fels with a start and immediately spotted the man with goggles and a red spear.

Very little distance separated them. Now in the center of battle, Bell was the closest to him. Within striking distance.

Bell glared into the red eyes behind the man's goggles. His whole body burning from within, he jumped to his feet.

For the first time today, the boy who had only been swept along by the course of events showed signs of a fierce fighting spirit.

"Coming at me, Little Rookie? I'm Level Five, you know!"

"...!!"

"That ain't no bluff. Some of those talking monsters were real strong. Doing this as long as I have means surviving more adventures than I can count."

Dix's words were no lie as he watched the boy get to his feet with interest.

Bell's eyes trembled at the intimidating Level, but...

"Curses may be strong, but they come with a price! That man should be dealing with it at this very moment!"

"Aww, damn. Keep your mouth shut."

An aggravated smirk appeared on Dix's face when Fels's voice echoed past them once again.

The main difference between curses and magic was the price the caster had to pay.

Curses required compensation; they inflicted some kind of penalty while they were in effect.

Bell's eyes flashed with determination.

With his black knife in his right hand and his short crimson blade in his left, he charged.

He made a beeline straight through the battlefield.

Weaving past the claws swiping at him, he left the monsters in the dust to engage the man at point-blank range.

"Dix."

"It's fine. You lot finish off that mage."

He jerked his chin at the nearby subordinates, lips curling into a sneer.

They left him, most feared of all the hunters, alone to face the boy closing in at full speed. The man lifted his spear.

"Take him down, Bell Cranell!!"

As the mage's voice echoed across the background, knife and spear collided.

Sparks flew with a high-pitched metallic ring. Bell and Dix crossed blades.

"Hey! I found a survivor!"

"You all right? Answer me!"

The town of Rivira was showered in crystal light.

The small party that had split from *Ganesha Familia*'s main force made their way through what was once the Dungeon's outpost, looking for signs of life. Members of the group called out to each other, rushing in to heal the dwarf they had found buried beneath a pile of debris and an elf lying on the side of the street.

"H-how horrid..."

Modaka discovered several brutally mutilated corpses among the wreckage.

They were nothing more than piles of flesh lying in pools of blood, shredded to the point that their faces were unrecognizable. It was almost as if this massacre was to satisfy a personal grudge.

They had no way of knowing that all these bodies were once adventurers belonging to *Ikelos Familia*.

Modaka's face paled, his hands over his mouth as he surveyed the damage from within the town's smoldering ruins.

"......?"

Focused on the cruel fate that had befallen his fellow adventurers, Modaka happened to catch a glimpse of something far beyond the edge of the cliff from the corner of his eye.

What he saw on the other side of the plains, in the middle of the floor, were monsters emerging from the tunnel connecting to the nineteenth floor at the roots of the Central Tree.

A white ball of fur was sitting astride a four-legged black monster. He was too far away to know for sure, but his instincts told him that they were a hellhound and an al-miraj.

Shaking his head at the bizarre pairing, he saw them make a mad dash for the eastern forest.

"Huh? What was that?" Modaka whispered to himself in confusion—when a new shadow appeared from the tree roots, freezing time for a moment.

"...Oh crap."

That was all he could say.

"Oh crap, oh crap...! Craaaaaaaaap!"

"Oi, what's wrong with you?"

"Run away!! We need to find the commander and get out of here!"

"What are you talking about?"

"This is no time for taming!!"

Other members of *Ganesha Familia* gathered around Modaka, who was on the verge of panic.

Sweat gushing from every pore, he screamed with all his might.

"An Irregular!—A subspecies from hell is here!"

"Great work! Now take control!"

"Only four left!"

Several members of *Ganesha Familia* worked together to corner and restrain a thrashing lamia.

Deep in the eastern forest...

The subjugation team had gained the upper hand against the armed monsters, mainly because most of the creatures had disappeared deeper into the forest, leaving only a few behind. The hooded adventurer's support helped turn the tide, allowing them to suppress the monsters still fighting back.

Taming methods had almost no effect on the armed monsters. Although the sounds of combat still echoed through the leaves, the battle had been reduced to isolated pockets. Only a few of the monsters were still unrestrained. Forest-monster corpses and piles of ash were scattered about the woodland floor. The battlefield had shrunk to one small area.

"Yeesh, all that banging and clashing...gave me one hell of a headache."

"That golden siren intrigues me…It seemed to avoid inflicting fatal wounds."

Aisha lowered her large wooden blade next to Lyu, who was doing the same. Meanwhile, Ilta and the rest of *Ganesha Familia* had the golden siren trapped on a tree branch just overhead.

It was one of the last of the monsters that had fought fang and claw to the end. While the siren's powerful sound waves had kept the adventurers at bay, Lyu's sudden return after parting ways with Bell and subsequent sneak attack had knocked it out of the sky, allowing the adventurers to engage the monsters in hand-to-hand combat.

Strength equivalent to a first-tier adventurer made no difference when outnumbered to this degree. Without the siren's deadly sound waves for support, the other monsters didn't last long and fell almost simultaneously soon afterward.

"……!"

The siren sat perched on the branch, chest heaving up and down as it glared at the adventurers below through one eye.

She was the only monster left that wasn't tied down. Her injured wings were folded against her body. Her face was contorted, dyed red by what appeared to be the blood of her enemies running down her cheeks.

"Finally, the last one…"

Their commander, Shakti, took a deep breath and surveyed the battlefield during a lull in the action.

I doubt we would have struggled to this extent were it not for orders to tame…but that is not for me to say.

It was Ganesha's will, she reminded herself with a nod.

Shakti knew they had to pursue the second group of monsters that had fled into the forest and was about to give the order…

"……?"

She turned around.

She had heard something pushing its way through the under-brush, and her eyes found the source of the sound.

—A hellhound and al-miraj?

Rather than attack, the two monsters rushed by her. In that moment…

"———."

She saw *it.*

And then…

WHAM!

"…Sister?"

A loud *thud* drew the Amazon Ilta's attention away from the monster overhead and back over her shoulder.

She could see the woman she revered as a sister leaning against a thick tree trunk farther back.

All her weight was on the tree as her head and back rested against it.

No, she wasn't leaning.

She had collided with it.

Slip! Suddenly, she shifted.

Coughing up blood, Shakti scraped against the bark as she slid down to the forest floor and landed in a heap.

"Eh…?"

Crick, crick! Ominous cracking sounds came from the tree before it toppled to the ground with a thunderous *bang.*

Lyu, Aisha, the adventurers, and every monster turned to look.

The forest shook around Shakti's helpless body as she lay motionless and facedown on the ground.

"*Sister!*" Ilta screamed. Lyu's eyes went wide, along with everyone else's.

Feeling no need to hide, the presence uprooted trees and plants as it shook the forest, cracking the ground with each step.

Unbeknownst to the adventurers, the siren had taken flight with a sigh of relief the moment it appeared from among the trees.

"Wha—?"

It had fists the size of boulders.

It had a gigantic, towering frame.

It was equipped with thick armor.

It brandished a double-sided ax, a Labrys.

The dark shadow with pitch-black skin glared at the adventurers.

"Damn you!"

Ilta roared with rage as the rest of *Ganesha Familia* readied their weapons and charged forward.

The black shadow that appeared before them—howled.

"Lett, Fia, can you escape from here?"

They were cut off from the Dungeon.

A frenzied brawl unfolded within an immense chamber deep in Knossos, the man-made labyrinth constructed over a baffling number of decades by countless people.

"To rescue Signor Bell?! Given this situation…!"

"No, to the entrance behind us!"

"!"

"Return to the eighteenth floor, reunite with Rei and those who stayed with her. I want you to explain what has happened and bring them all here. You can even bring *Ganesha Familia* at this point!"

Fels knew this was no time to be picky as he shouted out orders left and right.

If adventurers learned of the Xenos's existence, it would turn society on its head, but that was preferable to being wiped out by *Ikelos Familia* here and now.

The two Xenos nodded, understanding his intention.

"Do you remember the route here?"

"Yes!"

"Take this key. It will open all doors."

Fels quickly held out the spherical magic item to the red-cap goblin. The short monster tossed away his enormous ax and turned to face the harpy seated at his side.

"Fia!"

"I can fly…I *will* fly!"

With the oversize fetters still binding her legs together, the harpy opened her wings and forced her body to take flight.

Airborne but unsteady, the red-cap took hold of one of her legs.

The two Xenos climbed high, passing over their crazed brethren before disappearing down the stone stairwell.

"Mage, what have you done?!"

"!"

A voice as rough as a stray dog's growl reached Fels's ears before the mage could see them off.

Ikelos Familia hunters had arrived. Eight men and women who had been spared from Dix's Phobetor Daedalus curse charged in with weapons held high.

"There's something I'd like to know. Why do you follow that man's orders? From what I've seen, he's but a human who leads with an iron fist."

If they all fought as one, their numbers would be too much to overcome. One well-orchestrated attack would be all they needed.

Fels instantly decided to fall back into the chaotic brawl between the Xenos.

"'Cause it's fun as hell, why else? Do what Dix says, and all the money and women we could ever want come to us! Monsters are nothing but toys!"

"...Why did I even ask?"

Fels chose not to respond to that answer with words but with a counterattack instead.

Now the monsters' full-powered swings became obstacles for the enemy to deal with. Whenever one of the hunters somehow managed to make it past the raging monsters or climb over the remaining cages to get in range, Fels blasted them with a shock wave before they got too close.

"Gah!"

"Son of a—!...What is that thing?! Some kind of magic item?!"

"I don't see what's so hard to understand about magic energy being used as a projectile."

"A few monsters do something similar with a Howl," the mage explained.

The utter chaos of the battlefield was Fels's best friend. Although the thrashing monsters did pose a threat, the fact that the enemy couldn't use magic was far more important.

Completing a trigger spell was next to impossible. Even enemies capable of Concurrent Casting would have difficulty finishing a chant. Anyone who left the chaos to stand and cast unaware would be an easy target for Fels's shock wave, which required no time to unleash.

The gloves were magic items designed for attacking: Magic Eaters.

A projectile weapon designed by Fels for the mage's personal use.

"While its inefficiency is a minus…I'm quite jealous of Bell Cranell's Swift-Strike Magic."

Using the Xenos's free-for-all to its fullest potential, the mage felled another marauder.

"If it weren't for those dirty tricks of yours…!" an animal person spat as he closed in on Fels, cursing the mage's black robe among the other magic items that put his opponent on par with or even above Perseus.

"But at this range—!!"

A longsword came slicing in.

Fels snatched it out of the air like a hawk.

"?!"

"These 'dirty tricks' you hunters keep complaining about required several Advanced Abilities to create," Fels replied, easily stopping the blade with a gloved palm despite the hunter's full strength behind it.

The black-robed mage coolly explained to the dumbstruck hunter.

"I happen to be Level Four. Though I've been unable to update since the flesh rotted off my back."

Expressing hatred for a past deity, Fels reached forward and pressed a flat palm against the opponent's stomach.

"Wai—!"

Then—*bang!*

The colorless shock wave exploded directly into his gut and blasted him backward like a cannon.

"Oh, and I was once known as the 'Sage.' I'm quite confident with my ability to use magic energy and Mind," the black-robed mage said with a hint of sarcasm. The intricate designs on Fels's gloves glowed.

Four hunters down. Once the rest were taken care of, Bell would need help. And just when that thought crossed Fels's mind...

The mage barely managed to dodge an attacker from behind.

"That's odd. I happen to be Level Four, too."

"...!"

It was a hulking bald man with a black tattoo on his face—Gran—who sliced off a piece of Fels's black robe with a greatsword. An Amazon, an animal person, and a dwarf had made it through the chaotic battle and were closing in on the mage along with him.

They were the ones who killed Ranieh. *Ikelos Familia*'s main force.

Fully aware of the disadvantage, Fels waved both arms, releasing another shock wave.

A series of shrill explosions and shock waves erupted on the other side of the battlefield.

Bell launched strike after strike at the man in front of him as the heavy vibrations pounded his eardrums.

"Are you really Level Three, boy? Got some quick feet there."

"...!"

The man in goggles spun the two-meder red spear, knocking each hit away with ease.

Simply stated, Bell's attacks hadn't inflicted so much as a scratch anywhere on Dix's body. The man had avoided every single slash of the boy's mad rush.

With the bloody roars of the Xenos behind him, the man in goggles forced the boy back with a series of devastating blows from his spear.

The two separated for a brief moment.

"What that mage said is true. My curse makes my Status drop like a rock."

"......!"

"Can't help that everything feels slow and heavy."

It was as though the man could see doubt in Bell's eyes, wondering if he was really debilitated in any way. So, Dix revealed Phobetor Daedalus's cost outright.

Bell's opponent normally had strength to go head-to-head with first-tier adventurers.

Even if his Status had dropped by a full Level—he was still Level 4.

The boy's face tensed, but he knew the difference in their Statuses already and gripped his knives without fear. Then he launched his attack anew.

"I was just gonna mess around a bit, but it looks like I got no choice. The rumored Rookie lives up to the hype."

But he was getting bored.

The man in goggles smiled.

"Ready for my turn?" he asked lightly.

He was done playing around, and the spearhead suddenly struck down with murderous intent.

"?!"

The incredible impact knocked Ushiwakamaru-Nishiki from Bell's grasp.

As the short crimson blade spun through the air, the wickedly curved crimson spearhead was already back on the offensive.

"Kah!!"

He dodged by a hair.

Bell kept twisting his upper body as strands of his white hair fell away, using his momentum to spin toward Dix with a backhanded Hestia Knife.

"Shifty, aren't you, boy?"

"Gahh!"

However, Dix whirled by him, driving the butt end of his spear into Bell's face on the way.

The boy's strike hit nothing but empty air, and his face burned in pain. The world shook for a second for Bell, but he was quick to regain his bearings. Planting his feet, he turned to face Dix, who was already behind him.

"———?!"

The first thing he saw was the crimson spearhead coming right for his eyes.

Catching a glimpse of the man's evil sneer, Bell used every bit of Strength he possessed to force the Hestia Knife upward and knock the weapon to the side.

"Ha-ha-ha-ha-ha-ha-ha-ha-ha-ha-ha-ha!!"

The spearhead had been deflected, but it rotated at the last moment and sliced into the boy. Dix's laughter accompanied the attack. He had warned Bell; it was indeed his turn on the offensive.

The long spear appeared to curve through the air, striking like a snake with bared fangs. He ramped up his onslaught on the boy, who was forced to defend with only the Hestia Knife and quick, shifty movements. There was no pattern—Bell had no idea where the next attack would come from. What's more, the man combined a few violent kicks with his relentless assault, knocking the boy off balance and making the next attack even harder to predict.

Bell was driven farther back by the man's spear and its unrefined, wild aggression.

"Nice knowing you!!"

The man thrust the spear forward to finish off the stumbling boy.

Bell saw the spearhead coming—and his eyes flashed.

—It worked!

His free left hand swung behind his back, and an instant later, a crimson arc burst forth from a sheath.

It slammed into Dix's spear with incredible force.

"!!"

The red eyes beneath the smoky-quartz goggle lenses opened wide.

It was the spare Ushiwakamaru, accompanied by a technique he had learned from watching the Sword Princess: bait and switch.

Bell remembered the vigorous training sessions alongside an Amazonian girl on top of the city wall just before the War Game and showed an opening when he was at a clear disadvantage.

"Their guard is lowest when the final blow is near."

As his idol's words replayed in his mind, Bell's body became a blur. The first crimson knife allowed him to dodge the spearhead by the slimmest of margins, and he closed in on his floundering opponent.

A spear's weakness was his knife's strength—close range. Bell moved to take full advantage of his weapon.

However…

"——."

Dix, who should have been wide-eyed in surprise, was sneering with confidence.

The man held a battle knife, large enough to be mistaken for a shortsword, behind his back, hidden from Bell's sight.

A gleaming arc flashed from the side opposite the spear, burning an image into the boy's frozen rubellite eyes.

It was as though the man had copied Bell's technique, pulling a blade out from around the waist and swinging toward his shocked opponent's exposed stomach.

It was a perfect counterattack. The battle knife's tip scooped upward.

"!!"

Falling into his own trap, Bell immediately pulled himself into a crouch with all the strength he could muster.

"Oh?"

His line of sight fell just as the strike intended for the boy's stomach was deflected to the chest.

The battle knife's tip came to a halt against his breastplate. The silver armor blocked Dix's weapon with a loud metallic *clang.*

"Ha-ha-ha! Got some good armor there!!"

"Uwh!"

Still recovering from the impact to his chest, Bell was launched back by a front kick.

As rivers of sweat covered his skin, Bell adjusted the breastplate with his right hand, still holding the Hestia Knife in a reverse grip.

Welf…!

The smith had boasted about the dual adamantite mixed into the fifth incarnation of Pyonkichi.

"I poured a lot of money into that ingot metal. You better not break it," the red-haired man had said with a laugh. Bell silently thanked him for the armor from the bottom of his heart.

That armor had protected him from an enemy's killing blow, saving his life.

"Well done, boy. Here comes the next one."

Dix struck again, his lips curled into a grin.

Bell had no choice but to defend against his spear-wielding foe, who had returned his knife to its sheath.

—He's strong.

Dix's skill and tactics would never disappear, no matter how far his Status fell.

Of course not. They had been developed in actual combat, from real experience.

No matter how close Bell came in Status, even if his greatest weapon, his Agility, was comparable, the amount of experience separating the two was insurmountable. In short, hunter Dix Perdix was strong, even without his powerful curse.

Bell became painfully aware of that fact as the spear shaft knocked him to the ground.

The unstoppable approach of burning despair began at his toes and fingertips, much as it had when he was facing Phryne.

"Gah!"

Although Bell managed to roll out of the weapon's trajectory, the crimson spearhead still carved a slice out of his cheek.

A moment later, Bell was back on his feet and trying to gain some distance when…

"Hot…!"

The intense, searing pain in his cheek made his whole body flinch.

"Careful now. One bad hit from this spear…and you'll be dead on the spot," Dix said with a grin, lifting the wickedly twisted, ominous spear up to eye level.

"Custom ordered it from a mage. It's got a curse built in. Whatever it cuts won't heal, not even with potions or magic. As long as the curses are intact, anyway."

"!"

Shock was written all over Bell's face. Another wave of cold sweat ran down his neck at the same time.

No matter how many times Bell wiped the blood away, it wouldn't clot. Dix's claim was true. The blood dripped from his cheek, staining his skin and armor red.

There was no way to recover from even one hit; it truly was a cursed weapon.

Bell gritted his teeth at the crimson magic that exacerbated his wounds.

—Haven't I seen that before?

He glanced down at the gash's reflection in the knife blade.

He was perplexed at the twinge of a memory in the back of his mind.

"No matter how many times you put monsters in their place, they heal up sooner or later. It's way easier if you cut them up so bad they can't move and the wounds never heal."

Bell's eyes flashed as he listened to Dix casually explain his horrifying method.

"Could it be...That barbarian on Daedalus Street...?"

Behind the orphanage. He and Syr had entered an underground tunnel after the children asked them to do a quest.

Bell remembered the large-category monster he fought in the darkness.

"Hey, seriously, boy? You ran into that?!"

Bell watched, dumbfounded, as Dix nearly burst into laughter.

"You bet, we caught that big one. I sliced it up real good with this spear, but...it escaped from my idiotic underlings before we could get it out."

"...!"

"The damn tunnel caved in during the chase and it got away. We kept looking, too. Couldn't exactly let it be."

That large, bloodstained body had had countless bleeding wounds, and yet none showed signs of closing.

Its howls were filled with anger, pain, and suffering.

Bell had been taken aback by the monster's "lament."

Had that barbarian been a Xenos, too…?

"That thing caused us a lot of trouble, so we've been killing all the big ones right away since then, but…So you cleaned it up for us. Thanks for the assist, Little Rookie."

A chill ran through Bell's veins at the grinning, laughing man in front of him, who was far more terrifying than any monster or even the Dungeon itself.

The "evil" Lyu mentioned had to be something like this.

An indescribable sense of cold wrapped around Bell's body.

"Why…"

"Hn?"

"Why do you hurt these monsters…?"

The words came out of Bell's mouth before he knew it.

"Told you I needed money, didn't I?"

"Is that…is that really all…?"

How was he able to continue inflicting so much pain on the Xenos after hearing the lament that Bell had?

Monster howls filling his ears, Bell leaned forward and demanded an answer.

"……"

Dix shut his mouth for a moment as the boy's words hung in the air.

He placed a hand over his goggles…and grinned.

This smile was different from any before it.

"Little Rookie. You have any idea why Daedalus's descendants listen to our crazed ancestor from beyond the grave…? Do you understand why it's gone on for a thousand years? Do you?"

Bell flinched, surprised by the sudden question.

Dix didn't wait for an answer.

"'Cause our *blood* makes us."

"What…?"

"Our *blood* tells us to," he said, pushing the goggles down onto those wide red eyes with all his might.

The man's voice reached a fever pitch.

"It won't shut up! 'Complete this frickin' huge labyrinth,' it says!!"

"———!"

"It won't even let me stop for a breather!! Daedalus's blood forces me back up!!"

It was the first time his voice had any emotion.

Dix ignored Bell's reflexive step back and continued his tirade.

"It's been the same way ever since I was born in this dark, grimy trash heap! The blueprints for Knossos in that notebook work us to death!! No one can escape, not from this cursed bloodline!!"

Dix laughed a laugh brimming over with anger and indignation.

Bell shuddered in fear at the torrent of hatred on display.

—*Cursed bloodline.*

Mad Daedalus's tenacity had continued uninterrupted for nearly one thousand years.

The unyielding obsession the man had possessed, the drive to create a piece that outdid the Dungeon, surpassed the gods themselves.

Was it as Dix said? Had the man's brilliance and insanity been passed down to his offspring through his blood?

"It's bullshit, yeah?! The only one allowed to order me around—is me!"

Bell was caught between what was possible and his own guesses, but there was one thing he knew for sure.

This man in front of him, Dix Perdix…

…possessed a fierce sense of individuality, one strong enough to fight against his cursed blood.

"…I'd love it if this whole thing just disappeared. I ain't joking," Dix remarked coldly, his grin unchanged as if all his built-up anger had been vented successfully. "I hate this labyrinth more than anyone else in the world."

But he couldn't break it.

The blood wouldn't let him. Daedalus's curse was too strong.

It insisted the opposite, to finish the piece.

Dix finally removed his hand from his goggles.

"I used to take it all out on the Dungeon. I hated the labyrinth that drove Daedalus and all my ancestors crazy. I killed monsters, just kill, kill, killed them one after another."

"......!"

"But of course, it wasn't enough."

Then, Dix looked past Bell toward the Xenos still brawling behind the boy.

"How was I ever going to feel satisfied...? That was all I could think about, building this labyrinth. But we found the talking monsters around that time, and the hunts began. Let's see...ah, yeah. Would've been right after those stuck-up bastards Zeus and Hera disappeared."

Dix looked down, chuckling to himself as soon as the words left his mouth.

Chills ran through Bell once again as the man's ominous, guttural laughter sounded in his ears.

"They were no ordinary monsters. They cried and begged for their lives. Imagine that. Monsters born from the same Dungeon that turned Daedalus into a madman, begging for mercy...Ha-ha, still gets me."

"———."

The smile plastered on the man's face when he looked up was so horrid that Bell was lost for words.

"—I found it at last! A desire that could quiet the damn curse!!"

Dix swung the crimson spear forward with his right hand, slicing through the air.

"My first taste of satisfaction came from making those monsters suffer and cry out in despair, treating them like trash! I could slake my thirst and quiet my blood!!"

"Wha—?"

"Just as my ancestors once said, *I purely pursue what I desire*!"

The man didn't stop talking.

"Oh, the rush—pure joy! Finally silencing the blood! Going up against yourself and winning!! No amount of ale or drugs could measure up—it was pure euphoria!!"

Bell saw the man's insanity before him and understood.

In other words, there was no greater meaning to what Dix did to the Xenos, no grand scheme.

Its only purpose was to satisfy his desires and tremendous sadism.

And those fierce desires were strong enough to overcome the curse of his blood.

What the man was after…was to satisfy his insatiable sadistic will, and everything he did was to that end.

This was completely different from Welf's battle with the Crozzo blood in his veins. It was presumptuous to compare the two.

Dix had stopped fighting against his blood altogether—replacing it with a more powerful desire, thus becoming more monstrous than monsters themselves.

"That's why…!!"

He had done what he did to Wiene and the Xenos…

Bell's shoulders trembled as he watched the man drowning in his own pleasure.

"You did all this?"

Dix's expression vanished in the blink of an eye.

"Get over yourself, boy."

"———?!"

"You'll never understand what it's like, having blood-driven impulses run your life."

He charged forward, one-handedly stabbing with his spear over and over as Bell frantically dodged to avoid being run through.

"You'll never understand a guy who can't do anything about a curse burning his eyeball from the inside out!!"

The man funneled all his rage into one arcing sweep. Unable to absorb the blow, Bell was thrown from his feet.

"It was all for the money at first," said Ikelos, surrounded by the blue sky. "Like I told you before, completing Knossos requires money—lots and lots of money. So much money that no amount of treasure brought up from the Dungeon's deep levels can ever hope to cover it."

"……"

"Plus, the risk of losing allies got too high. If you found a way to safely line your pockets, you'd dive at the chance, yeah?"

Ikelos reminisced about when the Xenos were discovered by accident and the black market first got under way.

Hermes's face remained neutral as he listened.

"That's what got Dix started, but...Hee-hee-hee! The guy changed."

"Changed...?"

"Yeah. While he was teaching the monsters to fear pain before bringing them outside...at some point, his eyes started lighting up when he heard them scream and saw them cry."

Ikelos continued by saying that "something" inside him must have woken up.

He then explained that the goal and method of capturing Xenos had switched places.

"I loved it. He looked like a guy going after what he wanted. Those savage eyes, trembling, practically screaming in pleasure...!"

"...That's worse than horrible, Ikelos."

"Hee-hee-hee-hee...!! We gods wouldn't have it any other way, would we? Those brats are a real pain, but I love them all in my own way."

Ikelos's voice faded into the breeze, as though he were cheering for his child to turn the tide against his cursed bloodline.

"Looks like Daedalus's last wish might die with Dix's generation."

"......"

"He's lost all interest in finishing Knossos; that idea's gone to bed."

Ikelos narrowed his eyes.

"Now, he's got what I love—a monster's dream."

Impossible...!

Asfi was overwhelmed at the sight.

Arms and legs lying limp on the ground, red blades of grass dripping tears of blood, glimmering shards of broken weapons scattered about.

Bodies of fallen, barely breathing adventurers were sprawled out below her vantage point in the trees.

They'd been wiped out.

Ganesha Familia's elites, Orario's first-tier adventurers, were all defeated by a single monster.

Much like Shakti, Ilta had been felled by a single blow. It was over for the rest before they knew what hit them.

The enemy had specifically targeted the subjugation team's strongest members, taking them out one by one before moving to overwhelm the ones left standing. The floor shattered with every single-handed swing of its double-bladed Labrys. It felled large trees and stomped out the adventurers' formations with its massive feet.

Its black skin bore no damage whatsoever.

Huff, huff! Intermittent breaths from its powerful snout echoed throughout the quiet forest.

It stood at the center of the battlefield strewn with adventurer bodies laid out like corpses, like a king of calamity.

A black minotaur...?!

She didn't know. She'd never heard of anything like this.

A monster of this magnitude didn't exist anywhere in Asfi's wealth of knowledge.

Her pounding heartbeats shook her whole body from within. She struggled to catch her breath against the powerful rhythm. Desperate not to make any noise, she had to hold her arms and legs to keep from shaking the magic item that kept her invisible.

Pangs of regret tormented her.

She hadn't prioritized information gathering and leaving the battlefield.

Allowing Lyu and Aisha to influence her and letting her sense of justice convince her to provide assistance from the shadows—it was all a mistake.

She should have escaped, and quickly.

Seeing what lay before her, fighting against her uncooperative body, Asfi regretted everything.

"This has gotta be some kind of joke..."

"......"

In addition to the black monster, two people still remained upright in the forest battlefield.

Aisha and Lyu.

They weren't able to join the battle before the one-sided onslaught came to an end. A sense of urgency had overtaken their faces. The two stood, overwhelmed and unable to budge in its presence.

All the other monsters were gone. Almost as if they had known this was going to happen, they had all left the battlefield and disappeared into the east.

……?!

Run away, Asfi silently pleaded.

Get as far away from here as possible! her heart screamed at the other women.

However, the elf and the Amazonian warrior quietly raised their weapons, symbolically rejecting Asfi's plea.

The women were surrounded by the bodies of *Ganesha Familia* members.

However, they were all still breathing.

Unable to abandon these adventurers on the brink of death to their fate, Lyu and Aisha pointed their blades at the black monster.

Asfi gnashed her teeth, feeling powerless.

"………"

Tension filled the forest air.

Lyu sank low, Aisha's wooden blade whistled, and Asfi reached for a holster at her waist amid the stinging unease.

Three hearts beat as one.

"———Ooo."

Then…

The black monster's first step was the signal.

"!!"

Lyu and Aisha took off at a sprint at the same moment an invisible Asfi jumped from her spot in the tree, throwing sharp needles and Burst Oil at the beast.

The monster easily blocked the three needles that appeared from thin air with the gauntlet strapped to its arm. The Burst Oil detonated after an intentional delay a moment later. It wasn't intended to inflict damage. However, the smoke and flames would interfere with their adversary's vision. Lyu and Aisha circled around in different directions, charging in from the left and right.

Caught in a speedy pincer attack, the enemy—aimed for Aisha.

"""" ?!""""

A black shadow broke through the smoke.

The distance between them was reduced to zero with one kick of its mighty leg and a cloud of dirt. The trio shuddered in fear—Lyu, the beast gone from her line of sight, Asfi with her aerial view, and Aisha, the target.

Aisha raised her large wooden sword to defend herself from the Labrys on a collision course with her face

"———————."

Her weapon was utterly destroyed a moment later.

The bones of her fingers cracked on impact. The thick blade shattered in one blow right in front of her face, and a rain of silver shards filled Aisha's vision. While the Amazon had successfully sacrificed the weapon for an opening of her own to attack, she had no way to block the monster's follow-up.

The enemy wildly swung its right hand, smashing into Aisha less than a heartbeat later.

"———Gahh!"

The enemy's palm connected just above Aisha's left arm, pushing her off her feet and launching her backward with a sickening *crack*.

The woman collided with a massive tree trunk, slid down to the ground, and didn't get up.

"Antianeira!"

As if drawn by Lyu's scream, the black shadow wasted no time turning to face her.

"!"

Lyu needed every ounce of her high-speed reflexes to drop to the ground in time to avoid an oncoming sweeping blow that defied the laws of inertia.

The Labrys passed just over her head as the elf practically hugged the forest floor. The wind whipping by in the weapon's wake was powerful enough to shred her cape, tearing off the hood along with it. Lyu's delicate facial features were now exposed.

The elvish warrior wasn't about to let this go unpunished, slashing her wooden sword forward as the enemy passed by—but it was able to dodge her attack with only a single-legged jump.

"......!!"

Its massive frame hit the ground, sending a tremor through the battlefield. Lyu rolled away, shaking off her surprise.

The black monster that appeared directly before her was already locked on to her with the Labrys held high, despite the distance between them.

—Is it going to throw it?!

It did not.

Going against Lyu's expectation, the enemy drove the double-bladed ax directly into the ground at its feet.

The crystals, stone, and vegetation exploded into a wave of projectiles hurtling right for her.

"?!"

Although Lyu managed to get clear of them in time—

"—Geh, agh!"

—she heard several crystals shatter on impact behind her, as well as a pained scream.

"Wha—?"

Lyu glanced over her shoulder and gawked in surprise.

Asfi was sprawled out on the ground behind her.

Lyu understood in an instant.

The enemy's true target hadn't been her, but Perseus and her magic item.

Whether it was by smell or a gut feeling, the monster had detected Asfi's general location and sent a spray of projectiles over a wide area.

Lyu had no way of knowing that she was blocking Asfi's view, delaying her reaction.

"Andromeda..."

The Hades Head had broken under the hail of crystal shards.

No longer invisible, the beautiful young woman had landed on her back. The white cape she always wore was now riddled with holes and stained bloodred. Her silver-rimmed glasses had been knocked from her face and now lay on the ground some distance away.

"……"

Lyu stared at Aisha and Asfi in disbelief. Seeing that neither would be able to rejoin the battle, the elf turned to face forward.

The monster stood before her, a nightmare come to life.

Step, step! The Labrys, splattered with the blood of many adventurers, or perhaps countless monsters, swayed as the beast's advancing footsteps sent tremors through the floor.

Lyu remained silent, lowering her stance and raising her weapon.

She faced down the enemy, gripping her wooden sword with both hands.

The black monster took notice and came to a halt.

Gazing inquisitively into Lyu's stoic, emotionless eyes for a moment, it quietly raised the Labrys into position.

Lyu confronted the monster alone.

"……"

Having lost her hood in the enemy's attack, her elfish beauty was exposed to the forest.

Her will to fight was as strong as ever.

Her eyebrows arching high, she stared down the enemy with the commanding presence and expression of a warrior.

However, the rivers of sweat pouring down her face betrayed her true state of mind.

It has been quite a while…

The feeling of being at death's door.

Lyu hadn't experienced it since she quit being an adventurer and washed her hands of the Dungeon.

There was an absolute line between life and death, one that she had always managed to avoid crossing by the skin of her teeth.

It was before her again, except it was thicker and more distinct than she'd ever felt before.

The brief silence stabbed at her ears.

As her racing heart pounded a warning in her ears, she relaxed her hands around the wooden sword to adjust her grip, then squeezed it tight.

The next moment…

"——OOOOO!!"

"!!"

Lyu and the monster made their moves.

She dropped to all fours to avoid the ax slice that accompanied the battle cry and thrust the wooden blade forward from below.

That strike missed, but she didn't care. Lyu kept her legs moving and picked up speed.

Aisha's battle had taught her that trying to block the enemy's overwhelming strength was not an option. Even the slightest contact had to be avoided at all costs. She ran like the wind, dodging attacks like a blustery storm. And, with the power of a gale, she launched her offensive. Lyu poured her entire being into evasion and counterattacking, utilizing every opportunity to strike the black monster.

Her opponent's ferocious potential always robbed her of the first move, forcing Lyu to read and react at all times.

The monster had skill, and it was adapting to and predicting her attack patterns. It had been the same with a fraction of the armed monsters as well. For Lyu, that was the most intimidating factor of all. Dread threatened to overwhelm her with each enemy strike, but she refused to be afraid. Fear led to defeat and, ultimately, death.

Maintaining low posture in the face of her towering adversary, she tenaciously bombarded its legs.

"—Uoo."

The monster's eyes widened when it realized Lyu's attacks were hitting harder, and each blow's precision and speed was steadily increasing. She could see joy in its expression. This beast was unlike any other she'd ever encountered.

This monster wasn't interested in massacring people but fighting against them.

That thought crossed her mind. And Lyu was certain she knew what that meant to their battle. The difference between a mass murderer and a warrior lay in the latter's insatiable aspiration to reach new heights and desire to taste victory. Lyu's unhidden, elegant features contorted.

And so the battle between an elf, moving fast enough to leave afterimages in her wake, and a monster's seemingly limitless strength was about to come to an end in less than a minute.

Lyu had fought at full strength from the start, with no intention of drawing out the encounter.

Knowing that she was near her limit, the warrior attempted to finish the battle once and for all.

"HYAAA!"

"——!! OOOOOOOOOOOOOOOOOOOO!!"

She thrust from the side. Crouching like a wild beast, Lyu launched herself forward into one of her tried-and-true techniques as the black monster swung the Labrys high above its head.

The massive ax came crashing down far faster than its opponent's mad dash.

"?!"

As the ensuing cyclone carried the wooden blade into the air, the monster's shoulder twitched.

It didn't feel right.

There should have been some slight resistance at the moment of triumph, but the Labrys had cut through sheer air on its way to the ground. There was nothing.

Then, a shadow grew over the monster's body in the momentary lull.

—*You're mine.*

It was Lyu.

She'd leaped into the air from a sprint just before the double-bladed ax came down.

The first part of her strategy had been to keep her opponent focused down. She had manipulated its thought process to set up her own sneak attack.

Lyu played her trump card, an aerial battle.

The moment her enemy was required to adjust from land-based combat to an attack from above, it opened a fatal window.

Lyu's tactics exceeded the monster's strength and skill.

"HAAAAAAAAAAAA!!"

Aiming for her stunned adversary, she drew two shortswords from her waist.

"Twin short swords." She had received them both from a Far Eastern familia that no longer existed.

Lyu sought to carve out the monster's life, blades flashing.

"—Wha…!"

However—it blocked her.

What stopped Lyu's twin-bladed strike in its tracks was a single horn.

The crimson horn grew from its forehead, like a bull's.

It took the twin-bladed attack head-on, staying strong as if it would never break.

From there, the monster used its neck muscles to fling Lyu's vulnerable body through the air with incredible force after absorbing the impact.

"GhAH!"

Crash! Lyu's lean body slammed into a tree, and a boom reverberated through the forest.

Gasping for breath as the air was knocked from her lungs, she saw a black shadow fall over her in an instant as she struggled to stand.

"——!"

The Labrys rose high in front of her eyes, and it was too late to evade.

Lyu gazed up at the massive black shadow, knowing that she would die.

"————————……"

But just before the ax came down…

Her enemy stopped to look in a completely different direction. Wide-eyed, Lyu heard it, too—a monstrous howl from the distance, far deeper in the forest. It was almost as though it was conveying a message.

Falling silent, the black monster lowered its ax and began walking away from Lyu.

Leaving behind the gawking elf, it disappeared into the forest with footsteps that shook the ground.

"…I have been…spared."

Lyu whispered weakly to herself as the creature disappeared from sight.

She stared at her trembling hand, unable to clench a fist, before giving in to her exhaustion and leaning against the tree behind her.

She looked toward the floor's signature blue sky.

Many adventurers lay strewn across the battlefield illuminated by the crystal light penetrating the forest canopy, but she was the only one who moved.

"Do I make you that angry, Little Rookie?"

Dix asked him a question amid the ceaseless frenzy.

"They can talk, that's all. Doesn't change the fact that they're monsters."

"Gh-ah…!"

Bell had taken considerable damage.

While Bell had managed to avoid the cursed spear itself, the man still had an advantage in battle and inflicted a great deal of pain. Since the beginning of the skirmish, Bell had received so many cuts and bruises that it was safe to say he was injured from head to toe.

However, the boy's eyes were still clear, shining like the sun without a cloud in the sky.

"What's wrong with killing them in a pool of their own blood?"

"Ghah?!"

"You've been doing it, too, haven't you? Take out some monsters, get some cash. Ain't that the same thing?"

"GAH…?!"

The boy could barely move, and Dix knocked him back with the shaft of his spear.

Though he could intercept the weapon with his Hestia Knife, Bell couldn't completely protect himself from the long, diagonal slashes. His legs, arms, and face had taken more hits than he could remember.

Dix was just toying with Bell, smacking him around for fun with a smile.

He wanted nothing more than to see the light leave the boy's eyes and watch his spirit break. The words were there to twist the knife for good measure.

"...Even...if...even if that were true...!"

"?"

"Lido, all of those monsters can smile...and laugh...! They can shed tears, just like us...!"

Bell glared at Dix with his rubellite eyes.

"They can...shake hands...!!"

Bell clenched his right fist, remembering the warmth that he once felt in that palm.

"...Boy, you're out of your mind," said Dix, his grin deepening.

With his red eyes sparkling behind his goggles, it was almost as though the man's sadistic spirit had caught fire.

"Now, what to do..."

"UgHA...!"

A solid hit to the top of Bell's shoulder sent him down to one knee.

Dix looked at the boy, who was supporting himself with his left hand as he gasped for breath.

"If I remember right...you had a thing for that vouivre, didn't you?"

Like a switch...

...time came to a screeching halt for Bell once he heard those words.

"—All right then, I'll show you what's what."

A cruel grin grew across the man's face.

"What are you...?"

"Time for a nap."

A powerful kick caught him right beneath the chin, and Bell tumbled across the stone floor.

The chuckling man's presence drifted farther away. Trapped in a swirling, nauseating fog for a moment, the boy bit his lip and fought his way back to his feet. Then he kicked off the stone floor.

Stumbling, Bell ran deeper into the chamber, where Dix had disappeared into the darkness.

What greeted his eyes when he got there were several tunnels fitted with orichalcum doors, as well as a hole in the floor, with exposed metal beneath the stone, that appeared to be an unfinished passage. As the crazed Xenos howls faded far behind him, Bell tore through one of the dim hallways.

A single magic-stone lamp lit the way.

Darkness shifted around him.

Pushing through the blackness that shrouded his path like a veil and nearly tripping over his feet, he made it to the end of the short stone path and heard:

"—Bell!!"

The dragon girl was shackled to chains that hung from the ceiling.

"Wiene!!"

Bell's eyes went wide, and he rested his hand on the stone wall for balance.

There was nothing in this space other than the dried blood speckling the floor.

With her hands chained together, the girl looked as though she was about to be sacrificed to an ancient god. Her legs were fettered, too, and her bruised and battered torso resembled Bell's.

Her silver-blue hair shifting, broken scales flaking off her light-blue skin, Wiene looked up at Bell with tear-filled amber eyes.

It was a long-awaited reunion. They had finally met again.

But this was wrong, completely wrong.

This place, this situation, this physical and mental suffering wasn't what they'd wanted. They would never wish for this.

In that fleeting moment, a flood of countless emotions raged through Bell's heart.

And the one who caused them, the man in goggles, was standing right next to Wiene.

"Pop quiz, Little Rookie."

Dix grabbed a fistful of the vouivre's silver-blue hair with a faint grin on his lips.

"Ahh…!"

Wiene squealed in pain as he jerked her head and chin upward.

Furious, Bell was about to howl at him to let her go…

"What would happen if…I tore the jewel from its head?"

"———."

Bell's felt an icy hand around his heart as Dix brushed the garnet jewel on the girl's forehead:

A Vouivre's Tear.

The reddish stone was said to be worth more than a man's wildest dreams. It was a mystic jewel well worthy of the nickname "Prosperity Stone."

However, the vouivre would turn incredibly violent and vicious the moment it lost the jewel…

"NO!!"

Bell shouted with every fiber of his being.

"N-no, stop! I…*I won't be me anymore…!*"

"Ha-ha! So you know, do you?"

The boy launched into a dead sprint.

His legs, driven by uncontainable rage, carried him toward her.

Toward the chained, frightened, shaking Wiene.

It was far—infinitely far. The distance between them felt endlessly, hopelessly vast.

Shouting Wiene's name, Bell reached for her.

Her teary amber gaze lifted, as if she were reaching out to him.

"Nice knowing you, beastie."

The man ripped off the garnet jewel with a forceful flick of the wrist.

"————————."

For Bell, time skidded to a halt. Colors turned to black and white. The world stopped turning.

A trail of light followed the garnet jewel after its violent removal, tracing an arc from the girl's head.

"Aa———."

As the girl's lips formed a fractured cry, she bent backward and stared blankly at the ceiling.

Her amber irises shrank; her delicate limbs trembled.

"———Ah, agh."

Shudder.

One last convulsion surged through her body like a giant wave before she became eerily still.

The chains binding her rattled as if in fear of what was to come. Then…

A powerful roar burst free from her throat.

"——a, AAAAAAAAAAAAAAAAAAAAAAAAAAAAAA?!"

Bell froze in place, in awe of the incredible sound coming from the girl right in front of him.

The chains rattled and screamed as her body started changing. A large lump appeared in the girl's light-blue-skinned back before a massive wing burst free, following its twin into existence.

But that wasn't all. The girl's arms and legs quivered, swelling with each pulse.

It wasn't stopping. Her transformation was not stopping.

Amid the eerie squelches of flesh, the girl——became a monster.

"……Wie…ne."

Her chains shattered under the strain, pieces of metal falling to the floor.

A cloud of dust filled the shaking chamber like smoke around Bell's broken voice.

"Keh-ha-ha! So that's what happens."

Dix chuckled, clutching the severed garnet jewel as he made a quick exit.

"——aAA."

Bell looked up from his spot, still frozen in place, at the monstrous face looking down at him.

The moment those emotionless amber eyes met the boy's gaze—it howled.

"————————————————————————!!"

And charged.

Two arms took hold of Bell and flung him like a rag doll back against the stone flooring.

As the walls zipped past him in a furious blur, he heard that massive body break through the tunnel as he landed on the main chamber's stone floor.

"Wh-what the hell is that…?" mumbled Gran with his weapon held high, staring in awe at the thing that appeared at the back of the chamber.

"It…couldn't be…Is that Wiene…?!" a voice whispered in disbelief.

Cornered by the attackers and now wearing black tatters, Fels leaned against the wall.

Caring little for their surroundings in their frenzy, the rampaging Xenos kept howling as the new shadow slowly rose to its full height.

"…ah."

Bell, in considerable pain from the hard landing on his back, gazed up at the massive body standing over him and froze once again.

It had to be more than seven meders from head to tail.

Her two legs had fused together to form a giant, snakelike lower body. A pair of ominous ash-colored wings spread outward from a small upper body in an unsettling asymmetry.

Her long, sickle-like dragon claws were sharp once again, and wickedly warped scales covered patches of the creature's body. All that remained of the girl was her silver-blue hair flowing down to the base of the wings and soft light-blue skin.

As for the head on top of its neck, it looked as though a dragon's face had been painted over the girl's; its expression was frozen and its cheeks split. Those hollow eyes were devoid of pupils, white and bloodshot as if to symbolize her savage transformation.

Only a blackened depression remained in the space that the garnet jewel, the third eye, had once occupied.

Finally back on his feet, Bell was lost for words, staring up at Wiene towering three meders over him.

"Ha-ha-ha-ha-ha-ha! Why do you look so surprised, Little Rookie? Everything's exactly how it should be!!"

The man came back into the chamber a moment later, his laughter ringing in Bell's ears.

He was right.

This was a vouivre.

It matched the lamia-esque type of dragon Bell knew from his studies.

A dragon—a monster.

"…A, A, A, AAAAAAAAAAAAAAAAA!"

The dragon monster's long hair fluttered as it unleashed a shrill, earsplitting cry.

The sound made his skin crawl, and Bell could only absentmindedly stare at the creature and try to keep his balance as its dragon tail slammed into the stone floor again and again.

The Wiene he knew was gone.

Her innocent smile, her warmth, her tears were all buried beneath this monstrous visage.

There was no denying it.

This was a monster, through and through.

"Can you look at this and repeat those pretty words, Little Rookie? No, no, Bell Cranell!!"

Bell's face twisted as though it were about to split open.

Dix's words echoed in the boy's mind as though evil itself were speaking to him.

The creature's intimidating frame was nothing like a human's; its ferocious teeth inspired visions of blood; its wild and savage howl rang in his ears.

It was inhuman.

It was abominable.

Revulsion and disgust, the emotions that drove people to fight, were indeed flooding his body.

Dix was not incorrect.

There was nothing wrong with these emotions.

Faced with the dragon monster's true form, Bell was sickened—nauseous.

"…RUUuuuu…uUuuuuuuUUUUUUUUUUUU!"

"Gah!"

The dragon's tail whipped around, striking Bell as he cowered in fear before it.

It was like being nailed with a scaly tree trunk, and the boy skidded across the floor in a trail of dust. The monster's appendage had caught him in the small of his back, shattering the glass vials of his potions on impact. Precious healing liquid leaked from the pouch at his waist.

When he finally came to a stop, Bell was facedown on the floor, coughing up blood and writhing in pain.

"Now do you get it, Bell Cranell?!" Dix hollered at the boy once again.

Bell peeled his bleeding body off the floor as the droplets stained the stone surface red. However, the man's verbal jab was followed by another.

"Look around! What's in front of you?! What's behind you?!"

In front of Bell...

A ferocious dragon with monstrous instincts.

Behind him...

A swarm of crazed monsters, howling like wild dogs.

He was trapped between violent monsters that would never see eye to eye with people.

"The things have nearly killed you! Just now and before!"

The vouivre and the lizardman.

As their bloodcurdling howls sounded in his ears and their bloodthirsty glares stared him down, he had been mere seconds away from death.

He had been on the receiving end of their strength and murderous intent.

"That's what these monsters are! That's what monsters are!" Dix mocked.

The truth in his words was irrefutable.

"Open your eyes, Bell Cranell!! Get your ass on the right side!"

The man's joyous laughter echoed from every corner of the chamber.

Bell's trembling eyes opened wide as the floor darkened with red blood.

"Ha-ha-ha! Really likes it rough, that Dix."

Watching the scene from a distance like Dix, Gran smiled with glee. He chose to watch the drama unfold rather than finish off Fels once and for all.

"Bell Cranell…!" Fels called with agony, desperately trying to stand.

"…RUUUUuuuuu…UUUUUuuuuuuuuuuuuuuuuuuuuuuuuuu…!!"

The crazed monster howls, the vouivre's shrill screeches.

Everything sounded distant to Bell's ears.

His eyes shook. Nothing was in focus. He was drowning in nausea, and his mouth tasted like iron.

Repulsion mixed with the burning pain.

He was surrounded by true monsters.

And Bell—heard a resounding heartbeat.

"Face it, you're only here because you came along for the ride! Own up to it!"

The man's voice battered Bell as his head drooped.

He was right; one thing had just led to another.

He'd found a strange girl, involved his familia, and gotten drawn in.

Everything, every single event had just led to the next.

Were all his choices meaningless?

He had gotten swept up in the course of events, unable to make his own decisions.

So, this was his punishment.

It was time to pay up.

It was time—to give his answer—.

Bell ground his molars, clenched his fists, and willed his body to stand.

"…UuuU…!"

Bell fixed his gaze—

—directly at the massive, rampaging, flailing vouivre.

"…Ruuu…!"

Normally, a charging vouivre had a one-track mind.

They became extremely aggressive in an attempt to recover the stolen Vouivre's Tear.

However, this monster showed no interest in the man holding the garnet jewel, Dix.

"...Bluuuuu..."

It was looking for something more important.

"BELuuuuuuuuuu...!"

She was searching.

Despite her horrific form, she was searching for Bell.

Even as a monster, she longed for the boy.

Bell clenched his fists even tighter and strode forward.

"...i...ene."

Wiping the blood from his mouth, he forced his injured body to advance.

"Wiene...!"

He called her name in an unsteady voice.

"————————————Aaa!"

The vouivre swung its massive tail at the boy as he approached.

As if she were crying out in fear of evil people, in a nightmare where all her friends were killed.

The tail slammed into the boy.

"Hey, hey! You're gonna die if you don't do something!"

Dix's ridiculing laughter filled the air.

Bell climbed back to his feet and approached the vouivre.

"...Wie...ne."

He was hurled backward.

"Wie...ne."

Slammed to the floor.

"Wie...ne...!"

Even still, Bell approached the rampaging vouivre for a third time.

"AAAaaa!"

The monster swiped at the battered and bloodied human before it.

Long, sharp dragon claws flashed. Its left arm came down in a diagonal slash, colliding with Bell's right shoulder.

"——————a."

Bell's body sank under the blow, the heavy weight forcing him down.

But his legs held strong. The stone flooring cracked beneath his boots.

The dragon claws that struck his shoulder, however, stopped.

Even though they dug into his shoulder muscles, they didn't penetrate any farther.

Crick, crick, crick! The claws shook; metallic echoes abounded.

Welf's armor had absorbed the blow, kept the dragon's claws at bay.

"...I'm...fine."

Bell looked up.

At the dragon monster looking down at him from directly above.

"...I'm...fine, see?"

Then, Bell smiled.

Bearing with the pain, his eyes tearing up, he smiled with all his heart.

Like he did when they met.

Just like he did on that day.

"————————————."

The dragon monster roared.

"I'm...right here..."

Ignoring the fresh wave of blood from his mouth, the boy reached up with his right hand and embraced the hand digging into his shoulder.

He wrapped his fingers around her claw, stained with his blood.

"It's okay, Wiene......"

He pulled her rigid, strange body close.

He embraced the cold body and pressed the inhuman face against his chest.

"———."

Dix stood, stunned, watching the scene unfold. Gran swallowed, and Fels was lost for words.

Even the monsters that happened to catch a glimpse of him froze, trembling for a brief moment.

"It's all right..."

He had acknowledged and accepted his own repulsion and disgust, but then he restrained them with a more powerful emotion.

His warm, resounding heartbeat reached the girl who had always wanted to hear it.

Bell had buried his lips in her silver-blue hair, eyes glistening with tears, and whispered to her.

"Ah......"

A clear liquid welled in her pupil-less amber eyes, too.

One drop, two drops, and more. Both eyes were overflowing.

Monsters shouldn't know how to cry, and yet this one knew.

"aa...aaAAAAAAAAAAAAAAAAAAAAAAAAAAAAAAAAAAAAAA!"

The vouivre cried out in fear once again, throwing Bell off.

Her large body thrashed around like a raging storm, and the girl's spirit and the monster's instincts fought for control amid flowing tears and lamentation.

"Wiene...!" Bell yelled from his seat on the floor, his face twisting in pain.

Just as he was about to rush to her side and comfort her once again...

"—Buzzkill."

A red spear attacked from behind.

"?!"

Bell practically threw his body out of its path, whirled around, and stood up to face the spear-wielding man.

Dix glared at Bell with annoyance, eyes narrowing beneath his goggles.

"The hell are you doing, boy? Talk about a letdown. You should've carved that thing up with that knife of yours."

Spraying spit with every word, Dix thrust his spear forward with one hand.

Bell gasped, drawing the Hestia Knife and deflecting the spearhead.

"Told you, didn't I? Monsters are monsters!"

"...!"

"What's the point in getting sappy over them?!"

An enraged Dix yelled from between spear strikes, his weapon a blur.

"What do you owe them? Where's the value in helping these things?!!"

That instant…

"!!"

Bell's eyes ignited from within.

His wide, rubellite irises locked onto the spear's wicked curves. What little strength remained surged through him—and he severed the spearhead.

"Wha—?"

"Anyone is worth saving! Person, monster—it doesn't matter!!"

The cursed spearhead hit the stone floor with considerable backspin and rolled away in a cacophony of high-pitched metallic clangs that faded into the darkness.

His eyes burning with conviction, Bell shouted back at the surprised Dix.

"They want help!!"

That reason was sufficient. The boy readied his divine blade and howled.

"That's more than enough!!"

Those words, and that will, were no one else's but his own.

The boy's answer and sentiments echoed throughout the chamber.

"Bell Cranell, you are…" Fels quietly whispered once the boy's cry reached him.

Something changed among the crazed Xenos at that instant.

For some of them, their shoulders shook; for others, their chests expanded and contracted.

A certain gargoyle's stone eyes opened wide.

Drops fell from a certain lizardman's reptilian eyes.

"—Boy, you're a hypocrite!!" Dix responded to Bell's declaration. His mouth open wide in a savage smile, Dix began his assault anew. "You're saying you'd save anyone, man or beast? You'd save everyone and everything?"

"…!!"

"That's impossible! Even punk-ass kids know that! Makes me wanna puke," the man added with scornful laughter.

Armed with his now curse-less spear and combat knife, he assailed the injured boy with merciless abandon.

"Bell Cranell, you're no rabbit. You're like a bat!! You just flap around and never land anywhere!"

"?!"

Striking Bell across the cheek with those words, the man flung a long leg out in a wide arc. He nailed the boy in the chest, kicking him backward.

"Ugh...!"

"Ahh, so boring...You're just a kid with shit for brains, after all."

Dix stepped forward, smacking his own shoulder with the spear shaft as he approached where Bell lay on the floor.

Voicing his complete and utter disappointment, he twirled the spear.

"Enough of this. Go to hell."

He aimed the beheaded yet still sharp spear point at Bell and brought it straight down.

But just as the spear was about to run him through...

"Thanks—"

A red-scaled tail flashed into view from behind Dix.

"—Bellucchi."

Lido, holding a longsword high above his head, his red eyes filled with bloodlust, brought his weapon down with incredible strength.

"Wh—GAH!"

Dix noticed at the last moment and managed to avoid a direct hit, but blood still splattered from his back.

The goggled man retreated like an injured beast, snarling in disbelief at what he saw.

"Y-you bastard!!"

He had been rescued by the lizardman—Bell looked up at Lido in shock.

Lido's eyes were tinted crimson, proof that he was still under the curse's influence.

However.

"Well, damn, I'm happy. Really happy...I feel strong and have no idea why!"

"...?!"

"Who knew people's words…could make you feel so…hot…!"

The burning determination in his heart had provided a solid foundation to brush aside the curse and reclaim his mind.

Lido clenched his teeth together, nearly cracking them, and grasped the weapon's hilt with all his might. A monstrous smile appeared through his tears.

A dam had broken, sending rivers down his reptilian cheeks.

"Sorry, Bellucchi…and thanks."

After apologizing for everything that had happened and offering words of gratitude, Lido turned to face forward, glaring.

He then unleashed a curse-driven, bloodthirsty monster's roar directly at Dix.

"OOOOOOOOOOOOOOOOOOOOOOOOOOOOOOOO!!"

"!!"

Seeing Lido inspired a second wind for Bell. Drawing every bit of strength from his muscles, he followed the lizardman into battle.

Human and monster viciously slashed at the evil hunter, side by side.

"The hell is this…?! How can you think straight, beast?!" Dix snapped in annoyance. But he also wavered in fear.

In truth, he was at a great disadvantage.

Bell was badly injured from head to toe, and Lido was still feeling the effects of the curse. Although neither could fight at full strength, it was still two against one. Even without his refined sword techniques, the lizardman still possessed the strength of a first-tier adventurer—the potential to match Dix blow for blow was still intact. His Status was considerably weaker while Phobetor Daedalus was active, so Dix couldn't contend with Lido in this state.

On the other hand, if he reclaimed his full power by dismissing the curse, all the crazed Xenos would come back to themselves and immediately turn on Dix and the other hunters.

The man's escape was barred by a foolish hypocrite and one single Irregular.

"Dix?!"

Gran called out in a panic upon seeing his chief losing ground.

His curse was the only advantage that *Ikelos Familia* had at this point. The large man immediately took off toward the back of the chamber, leading a group of hunters to assist their leader.

"———GHAA!"

Just then, a powerful colorless shock wave slammed into the Amazon's defenseless back.

"I won't let you…!"

"Y-you?!"

Gran and the others whipped around when their Amazonian ally slammed face-first into the floor. A mage stood before them, left arm extended and black robe in shambles.

Fuming, the hunters charged Fels all at once. *Whoom, whoom, whoom!* Fels's right arm extended as both hands unleashed shock wave after shock wave.

"Damn it all! You guys, slaughter that mage! The rest of you lot, come with me to help Dix!"

Gran didn't wait for a response, leaving an animal person and a dwarf in front of him like a wall and sprinting off in the other direction. Along the way, he woke up the hunters knocked out thanks to Fels's avalanche of shock waves with kicks and led the group around the crazed monsters still trying to tear one another apart on the battlefield.

However, a heartbeat later…

Shak! Half of Gran's vision went dark as a fleshy sound filled his ears.

"Ga…aah…?"

It took the large man a moment to realize the left half of his face had been gouged out by an attack from the side.

Craning his neck and whispering in confusion, he turned his remaining eye and found a gargoyle, its shoulders rising and falling with every breath.

"A-GAAAAAAAAAAAAAAAAAAA!!"

"Wh-why—GYAHHHHHHHHHHHHHHHHHHHHHHH!"

Xenos that should have been under the curse's power were coming after the hunters in a frenzy.

Gros and the other Xenos who had found a way to resist the curse's effects, as Lido had, were now descending with murderous purpose on Gran and the two hunters desperately trying to finish off Fels.

"SHAAAA!!"

"FHH!!"

"~~~~~~~~~~~~~~~~~~~~~~~~~~~~~~~~~~!"

While the tide of battle turned in the chamber, Bell's and Lido's coordinated attacks were overwhelming Dix.

The lizardman's twin swords swung from the right, and the boy's knife stabbed from the left.

Seamlessly switching sides, the two alternated strikes and attacked in unison as the man blocked with his spear shaft and intercepted with his knife. The screaming of Gran and the other hunters in the background made Dix especially uneasy.

The first beads of sweat appeared on the man's ever-arrogant visage.

Then—he noticed.

"———."

Between Bell's left-handed strikes with the Hestia Knife and the lizardman's sweeping longsword and scimitar—

—defending against three blades simultaneously, there was another sound.

Ring, ring.

"—Boy."

The swirling blades had masked a small chime-like melody.

The sound from Bell's fist was growing louder, loud enough to hear over the vicious battle.

"—Hey!"

White specks of light passed by him, gathering together.

Dix watched the gleam reflected in his goggles—and screamed as loud as he could.

"—What're you doing, BOYYYYYYYYYYYYYYYYYYYYYYY?!"

Argonaut.

And a Concurrent Charge during the heat of battle.

After first acquiring the skill in battle with Lido, Bell was now bringing it to bear while fighting alongside him.

"GURAA!"

"?!"

The brief moment of confusion left Dix open to attack. Lido took advantage of it, thrusting his scimitar forward.

Although the man dodged the blade by the slimmest of margins, he lost his balance as Bell closed the distance in the blink of an eye.

SHWIP! Dix heard Bell's left leg move into point-blank range. The man's face froze.

After a twenty-second charge...

Bell drove his fist forward, roaring.

"AHHHHHHHHHHHHHHHHHHHHHHHHHHHHHHHH!!"

BOOM!

"———GAHHHHHHHHHHHHH!"

A plasma blast like lightning exploded into Dix's armored chest.

The devastating blow sent the man careening into black cages in a far corner of the chamber.

"Hah, gah...!"

Bell grabbed hold of his hand as intense, searing pain rushed through it the moment Dix was knocked away.

Argonaut's charge had shattered weapons in the past, and with much less time. The long charge had ruined Bell's fist.

Blood seeped from the torn skin, and with nearly every bone broken, Bell clenched his teeth as he tried to flex his fingers.

"Ah———."

Meanwhile, the red tint faded from the eyes of Lido and the other Xenos.

"...Wh-what was I..."

"Gros...! Has the curse lifted?"

Fels looked upon the Xenos with relief as they were released from Phobetor Daedalus's control.

Standing above the hunters they had wiped out in their involuntary frenzy, Gros and the other monsters shook their heads back and forth, finally calming down.

"You did it, Bellucchi!"

"……"

No, I didn't.

Lido rejoiced as he came back to himself, but Bell was the only one who knew.

The curse hadn't broken because the caster was defeated.

Dix had dismissed it himself just before impact.

He had no choice but to lift the curse and restore his Status—return to Level 5 to prevent the unavoidable blow from ending the battle, which gave him just enough strength to weather Argonaut's power.

"GaHHH! Agh…That HUUUUUUUUUUUUUUUURTS…!"

Dix cried out in pain from beneath a pile of broken black cage bars. Bell was still on high alert, and Lido realized it wasn't over. The two turned to face him.

Bell had put everything he had into the charged punch and inflicted a great deal of damage, as Dix was in obvious pain. Curled up in a trembling ball, the man was coughing up blood periodically as though the impact had broken every bone in his chest. Colliding into the mountain of cages hadn't helped matters, and he was covered in cuts. Blood poured from the open wounds.

"DAMN……! I'LL TEAR YOUR HEAD OFF…!"

Holding the spear shaft like a cane, Dix pried himself out from the tangle of metal bars, his bloody eyes exposed beneath his cracked goggles, and roared with hatred as he climbed to his feet.

"That's my line."

"?!"

Lido, who had already closed the gap between them, glared at Dix with a ferocious aura and brought his weapon down with a mighty swing.

The man in goggles spun away before it could connect, but Lido mercilessly pursued him.

"You will pay for everything you've done to my kind!!"

"G-get away from me! Back off!"

Dix had no choice but to jump backward, rolling this way and that to evade Lido's vicious strikes. Bell spurred his body forward, fighting through pain and fatigue to save the vouivre who was still suffering in his periphery.

"St-stop! I'll actually die if you keep this up!"

Dix fought tooth and nail, desperately blocking and evading Bell's and Lido's attacks.

His arrogant sneer dissipating, the man retreated, and his stature shrank with each step back.

Slowly, he withdrew into a corner near a row of doors where Wiene was still howling in pain and said:

"Back off now or—"

Dix suddenly looked up and stood tall, a grin growing on his lips.

"—I'll break it!"

The two were about to charge once again when the man held out a single garnet jewel.

"""!"""

Bell and Lido halted mid-swing.

Wiene's Vouivre's Tear. The one and only key that could put an end to her pain.

Dix sneered, taking advantage of their momentary lack of balance by knocking them back with his spear shaft. As he watched them hit the floor, he hoisted the jewel high above his head.

"Is this that important to you? Fine, then. You can have it!"

Then he flung it straight into the hole in the floor, the tunnel still under construction.

"!!"

"KEH!"

Bell's and Lido's eyes shot open an instant before they moved.

Lido caught up to the jewel in the blink of an eye, his physical prowess on display as he flung himself into the hole without any hesitation.

As the lizardman grabbed hold of the jewel from behind, the slower Bell managed to dig in his heels and grab hold of Lido's long tail at the last possible second.

"That worked even better than I hoped!"

Rather than watch the boy desperately try to pull the lizardman up from the edge of the hole, Dix instead pointed his finger at the vouivre.

"Become lost in an endless nightmare."

An ominous wave of red light engulfed Wiene as soon as the short trigger spell was complete.

"—AAAAAAA!"

"What?!"

The vouivre reeled backward, roaring. Fels, Gros, and the other Xenos had been rushing to Bell's aid and saw everything that happened, eyes wide with shock.

"That ought to do it."

Lastly, Dix discarded his broken goggles and exposed the *D* marking the side of his left eye.

As it resonated with the door at his side, the entrance jerked open.

"Go up to the sky."

"———?!"

The rioting vouivre charged through the door and bounded up the seemingly endless stairwell behind it.

"You! What did you do?!"

"My curse can make people see things as long as it doesn't hit too many targets. Bell Cranell, that vouivre is chasing 'you' right now! And that passage connects directly to the surface!"

Dix directed the first half of his statement to Gros before turning his attention to Bell, who had just pulled Lido safely out of the hole.

His lips curled into a grin as he imparted the last piece of information.

"If that monster makes it outside, it won't last long!"

"...?!"

Satisfied with the boy's gasp, Dix used his eye to open another door.

"Dix Perdix!!"

"Oh! Don't mind me, you've got a beast to catch! Hah! Ha-ha-ha-ha-ha-ha-ha!!"

Deftly evading Fels's shock wave, Dix disappeared behind the portal as his laughter echoed through the passage.

"KUH...!"

Gros took to the air, stone wings extended to their full length as he charged forward at breakneck speed. But the door slammed shut just before he could cross the threshold.

With the orichalcum door sealed, pursuing Dix was now physically impossible.

"—Lido, the jewel!"

"Bellucchi?!"

Bell snatched the garnet jewel from Lido's outstretched hand and raced up the steep stairwell after Wiene.

His body burning with scorching heat, he chased after the rampaging vouivre.

"This is bad...Lido, Gros, I leave the rest to you!"

Fearing the exposure of the Xenos, of what would happen if this monster appeared in a city already in disarray, Fels took off in pursuit.

The mage raced after Bell and left the Xenos in charge.

"Lido, Gros!"

Rei, accompanied by the second group of Xenos, arrived at the chamber a moment later.

The red-cap goblin Lett, the harpy Fia, and the others with Rei couldn't hide their surprise upon seeing their freed comrades and the silent, motionless bodies of the hunters.

"—! Rei, do you have a key?!"

"What?"

"The enemy leader has escaped deep into the labyrinth! That one is too dangerous to leave alive!!"

Gros called out from the opposite end of the chamber. Unsure, Rei turned to face the others.

The harpy and red-cap goblin who had led the siren here showed her the magic item.

"Rei, there is only one key. We cannot split up and comb the labyrinth however we wish."

"...Then leave the key for the one yet to arrive."

After a quick exchange with Lett, Gros left the item in the small monster's possession.

After watching him disappear back down the path they came, Rei led the remaining monsters to rendezvous with Lido and Gros.

"Rei, what of the adventurers?"

"We managed to outlast them. As for casualties...I believe there were none. What about this side?"

"As you can see, our comrades have been freed...However, Wiene lost her jewel and has gone berserk. Fels and...that boy are in pursuit."

The new arrivals fell silent upon hearing that Wiene was en route to the surface. The three leaders quickly shared their thoughts.

"Our comrades who were captured are at their limit. They can't move and must rest in a safe place."

"Then we must protect our kin and—"

"We'll chase after Wiene, too."

Gros, Rei, and Lido looked out over their exhausted comrades, the last of their strength spent while under the effects of the curse, before eyeing the door to the stairwell that Wiene and Bell had left through.

The golden siren and ash-stone gargoyle turned toward Lido after his declaration.

"Should we really leave everything to Bellucchi and Fels? Are you fine with just being helped? Going to the surface might cause a huge commotion, but...it's our turn to help Bellucchi and Wiene if they're in trouble. We need to."

Even with the worst possible outcome in sight, it was time for them to put their lives on the line to help the boy and what he held dear.

Gros and Rei stayed silent in the face of Lido's determined gaze.

"...Plus, we'll get to see the surface we've longed for, won't we?"

"You fool. At a desperate time like this..."

"Nevertheless, you are going, yes?"

Gros scolded Lido for his attempt at humor, but Rei grinned beside him, aware of the gargoyle's true feelings.

"I had little hope when I spotted Bell in the forest...Then, once I heard he rescued one of our own...I'm now filled with joy."

Cheeks flushing pink and smiling, the golden siren Rei stumbled her way through the language of the surface dwellers to express what she felt in her heart.

Other Xenos shared their feelings after hearing what their leaders had to say.

Roaring and hollering at the top of their lungs, they voiced their intent to follow.

Keeping his mouth shut, Gros spread his wings after a long pause.

"...Fels is one thing, but I cannot rely on that boy."

He quickly divided the Xenos into a group that would stay and a group that would go based on their injuries. Then, a mighty flap of his wings carried Gros into the air and toward the staircase.

Lido and Rei exchanged smiles before taking off after him.

"So, Gros? Seems there are trustworthy humans after all!"

"...Still no. Worse may yet come to worst..."

"There's just no pleasing you, is there?"

"Gargoyles like Gros are always stubborn as stone."

"Enough!"

Side by side, the three leaders guided the Xenos up the stairwell.

Elsewhere at that moment...

One man had managed to disappear during the massacre of *Ikelos Familia*.

After sliding across the stone floor to avoid the Xenos's attention, he had tumbled down stone steps.

"Diiiix...Where'd you go? Save meee...Damn those monsters... They'll pay..."

He clutched a manufactured ingot in his right hand and a severed crimson spearhead in his left.

The large human had lost the left half of his face, including his eye. Deliriously mumbling to himself, the man crawled deeper into the labyrinth.

Red droplets hit the floor, echoing in the air.

One man made his way through Knossos's dark hallways, his path marked by splotches of blood.

"Agh, burn in hell, ow…!"

His face contorting into a monstrous expression, Dix supported his bleeding body and vented his anger and frustration by kicking at a painstakingly carved statue standing at the end of the hallway.

Dix, able to travel anywhere in Knossos at will thanks to his "Daedalus Eye," had been on the move ever since he escaped the main chamber. Having been forced to read the blueprints drawn in the Daedalus Notebook until it made him sick, he knew these complex hallways like the back of his hand.

Now he was making his way toward the familia's home, the underground base where all sorts of healing items were waiting for him and he could rest.

"All those monsters and that punk-ass boy…! I'll kill them if it's the last thing I do…!"

Apart from him, *Ikelos Familia* had been wiped out. Every Xenos they captured had been taken from them.

Vowing in angry whispers to pay them back tenfold for what they had done after he found a way out of this mess, Dix glared with bloodshot eyes into the darkness.

"……?"

Dix came to a sudden halt.

Something seemed different about the labyrinth he had always called home.

It was as if the air was vibrating, as if the silent tranquility was trying to warn him, as if he'd wandered into the real Dungeon. The magic-stone lamps were few and far between, flickering like candles.

Having passed through several orichalcum doors, Dix had felt safe in the knowledge that he could never be found. But now as he continued his escape, a cold chill ran down his spine.

Impossible, it couldn't be, the doors are shut, there's no way—

A piercing gaze was boring right into his back. As his anxious heartbeat intensified, Dix was running before he knew it.

The pain shooting through his limbs didn't matter. Gasping for breath, he tried to escape the chill threatening to envelop him. However, he couldn't gain ground. That was when he noticed the trail of blood behind him, but hiding it would make no difference. Whatever was sending the chill through the labyrinth stayed close as though it was following his scent.

As soon as Dix closed the next door behind him, he heard a different door open somewhere in the distance. His invisible pursuer's shadow was drawing ever closer, driving him into a corner.

"......?!"

Even though he was following the route etched into his memory, every corner and every wall started looking the same. Fear and panic seeped in as reality and illusion blended together, distorting his senses.

Daedalus's obsession, this chaotic world of an acclaimed architect, showed its true face. This man-made labyrinth, capable of disorienting absolutely anyone, dragged the man into a never-ending nightmare. Was the pursuer coming from behind or approaching from the front? Dix couldn't tell anymore.

His confidence was gone.

The comfort of knowing that, no matter what stood in his way, his curse would allow him to escape had been shattered. That was how much his situation—this ever-approaching *something*—had rattled him. Blaring warning bells dyed his thoughts red.

Dix threw pride and dignity by the wayside and ran.

Then...

"————."

Dix came to a sudden stop.

What he saw directly in front of him, in the middle of a seemingly normal hallway, wouldn't let him continue.

It was a frigid stone passage, so shrouded in darkness that it was impossible to see the other side.

That darkness rippled.

What emerged made Dix's red eyes glaze over.

It was like a dungeon master who had been residing in the deepest halls of the labyrinth, waiting for a sacrifice.

A pitch-black monster—a black bull—parted the darkness and appeared before Dix's eyes.

"...C'mon...You've got to be shitting me."

Dix had made the mistake of getting so caught up in thoughts of hatred and revenge that he had lost the ability to make calm, rational decisions.

Like forgetting that the enemy had a key of their own.

But even more than that, his gravest miscalculation was not learning of this thing's existence.

Huff, huff. Rough breaths bashed against Dix's eardrums.

One step, then another. Stone cracked underfoot as the monster approached, but his feet wouldn't budge.

Foreboding light reflected off the blood-splattered Labrys, clutched in the beast's rocklike left hand.

"Where the hell'd you come from, MONSTEEEERRRRRR———?!"

A dark shadow fell over Dix as the man waved his arms and shrieked in terror.

A heartbeat later—*thud!!*

That was the end.

Unable to activate his curse, the oncoming guillotine claimed his life instantly.

The death of the wretched, violent man couldn't have come soon enough.

The monster walked past the splattered blood and lumps of crushed flesh, continuing on its way.

It was hastening to join its kind.

As if it was starving for a good fight.

"Bell Cranell!"

A long, large staircase stretched upward as far as the eye could see. Just stone steps climbing up and up, seemingly into infinity. Fels had caught up with Bell, black robe flowing, as the boy raced up the equivalent of seventeen floors of Dungeon stairs.

"Your body is in no condition for this. You're beyond exhausted."

"F-Fels..."

Fels warned Bell, reminding him of the considerable damage he had suffered during the battle in the large chamber below.

It was true. Since Bell was unable to move how he wanted, Fels had pulled even with him despite his head start.

"You can keep running, but just wait for a minute."

Fels placed a gloved hand on Bell while the boy gasped for breath.

"*Rod of Asclepius, Asclepius's motherly light. By the power regeneration, all shall be healed.*"

The glove's intricate patterns shone like a magic user's staff as a white magic circle appeared at their feet. It was a perfectly executed Concurrent Casting.

Bell watched in surprise as Fels intoned the spell.

"Dia Panacea."

Different-colored spheres of shining light enveloped Bell. He marveled as the wounds that covered his body disappeared, his broken fist healed, and even his fatigue vanished into thin air.

"What's this…?"

"Healing magic that alleviates all types of injuries and ailments, similar to an elixir."

The high-level magic had completely restored Bell's body.

"Thank you so much, Fels!"

Bell, filled with vitality once again, spoke a few words of gratitude to Fels and picked up speed.

Fels was suddenly trailing behind as the boy hurtled up the stairwell eight steps at a time like a rabbit.

"Seriously…?!"

At the boy's remarkable agility, the words of the gods and goddesses escaped Fels. "I can't keep up…!" The mage moaned as Bell pumped his arms with reckless abandon.

"Wiene…!"

The crack of rock breaking sounded in the distance.

Light shone through from far above, signaling that the monster had reached the surface.

The setting sun drew near the city wall in the west, telling the citizens of Orario that night would be upon them in a few short hours.

Hestia Familia had reached the city's southeast block beneath the still-blue sky and entered Daedalus Street.

"It's no use. There aren't any clues anywhere..."

"It may be aboveground, but this place is more dungeon-like than the real thing."

"M-Master Welf, I haven't the slightest idea what you're talking about..."

While the group made their way through the blackened brick streets, Mikoto scanned their surroundings, Welf scratched his head, and Haruhime began sweating beneath her kimono as each spoke in turn.

"Supporter, looks like asking around is a lost cause. Even rumors that sound promising end up contradicting each other."

"Lilly never thought this would go smoothly, but..."

Hestia and Lilly, who had done their best to gather information from the locals, exchanged looks.

After parting from *Soma Familia*, they had come to Daedalus Street as Zanis had suggested. The group had tried their best to follow even the faintest of monster shadows, but instead they got lost in the slum's complicated, intertwining layout.

Stairwells led up and down, connecting to a jumble of houses and small buildings. Built mostly from bricks, there was no rhyme or reason to the size or height of any of the clustered structures. It was as though the familia were trapped in an optical illusion, an infinite maze of roads and stairs within a bounded city.

"I'm sure Bell feels the same way...but I don't have many good memories of Daedalus Street."

Looking up at the bricks as memories came flooding back, Hestia narrowed her blue eyes.

Turning the corner onto a different road, the group referred to an ariadne sign in a red brick wall to check their location before wandering on.

"—!"

"Hey…What was that?"

Mikoto and Welf were the first to notice something strange.

They turned sharply enough to startle Hestia, and Haruhime's renart ears stood on end a moment later. Lilly gasped a second after that.

The goddess's mind raced, trying to figure out why her followers were suddenly on edge—when a chorus of screams sounded again in the distance.

"!!"

"Let's move!"

"Yes!"

Just as Hestia figured out what was going on, Welf and Mikoto led the rest of *Hestia Familia* in an all-out sprint. The group fought against the flow to reach the epicenter, bumping shoulders with panicked, screaming residents as they went by.

Then, once they rounded another corner—

"Whoa…!"

"A monster?!"

A creature resembling a lamia was running amok.

Even in the Labyrinth City, this was unheard of. One of the buildings adjacent to the wide street was missing a corner, and rubble was strewn on the ground. The monster's scaly light-blue skin was littered with stone fragments, proof that it had already destroyed several walls.

Many citizens had yet to escape from within the thick cloud blanketing the area.

Of course, the only familia or adventurers on the scene was *Hestia Familia*.

"So a monster escaped from the enemy base…? That'd make sense, wouldn't it?"

"…W-wait, please wait. That's…"

The monster on the ground was shuddering as Welf unsheathed his greatsword, while Mikoto raised her long katana, Kotetsu, and spoke in a trembling voice.

She activated her skill, Yatano Black Crow, the instant she heard the uproar. So even though she didn't get a good look at it, she told the group that they had encountered the monster before.

Lilly froze once the monster's face finally appeared from deep within the smoke cloud, whispering its name with her eyes glued on its body.

"...A vouivre."

"———?!"

Welf, Mikoto, Haruhime, and Hestia gasped in unison.

Then they saw it.

An unnatural hole—where the garnet jewel should be—in the forehead.

"It couldn't be...!"

The instant the group understood what had happened to the vouivre in their sight, the monster made a move.

"—————————!"

Unleashing a shrill howl, it charged right at them.

Welf's and Mikoto's reactions were instantaneous, crossing great-sword and katana to make a wall and stop its advance. However...

"Ghwhoooo!"

"Uwah!"

They were knocked aside.

The rampaging vouivre's charge was so powerful that the Level 2 adventurers couldn't hold it back with their blades. Although they did slow the monster down, Welf and Mikoto crashed through the walls of nearby buildings, provoking louder screams from the townspeople.

"Lady Hestia...!"

"Kh...?! Haruhime!"

Hestia, pushed to the side of the street by Lilly, cried out when she saw the renart collapse right in front of the vouivre.

Though she'd been knocked off her feet by tremors in the ground and covered in scrapes and scratches, the trembling Haruhime sat up, eyes open wide as she gazed up at the monster.

"Lady...Wiene...?"

Although they were glowing red, its eyes were amber.

Having spent more time than anyone with the dragon girl, the renart whispered the name.

Tears built up in her green eyes, seeing what had become of her friend.

"AAAAAAAAAAAAAAAAAAAAAAAAA!"

The transformed dragon girl whipped its long body forward as if pursuing an apparition.

Haruhime couldn't move as the dragon whipped its tail, thick as a dwarf's chest, directly at her. "Lady Haruhime!" Mikoto screamed. The rest of the familia called out to her, their voices echoing through the street, when suddenly…

"—Wiene!!"

Bell burst onto the scene like a gust of wind, his legs a blur.

"Bell!!"

Emerging from the hole Wiene had left behind, the boy threw himself onto the dragon's tail and slammed his armored forearm into its side to alter the trajectory. The tail swiped over Haruhime's head, hitting empty air.

The boy heard his familia's cries of surprise and delight as he stood with the renart at his back.

"Master Bell…!"

"Miss Haruhime, please get back!"

Bell winced as though Haruhime's teary-eyed, sorrowful voice had physically cut him, and he yelled back at her.

Mikoto came in to support the girl who couldn't move on her own and dragged her back to the rest of the group.

I prevented the worst from happening, but…!

Bell had followed Wiene's path of destruction through the Labyrinth City after emerging from one of Knossos's hidden entrances and caught up with her in the dungeon town.

However, a great deal of people had already laid eyes on Wiene. His palms broke out in a sweat at the sight of so many onlookers.

Now what? What should I do?

No—the garnet jewel had to be returned to her first. Stopping the rampage took priority.

Wiene was regaining her stance, recovering from the sudden attack as Bell stood tall in front of her.

—That was when it happened.

A gleam of light flashed down from the sky.

"————————."

From behind, over Bell's head…

It appeared from the corner of his eye—a long spear tipped with a golden blade—piercing Wiene's left hand like a lightning bolt.

"a——AAAAAAAAAAAAAAAAAAAAAAAAAAAAAAA!"

The spear's incredible momentum sent her careening hand-first through a nearby building.

Wiene cried out as the spear drove deep into the ground, effectively pinning her to the spot.

The sudden change of events caught Bell off guard, and his mind went blank for an instant.

He forgot to breathe as his brain processed what just happened.

More than likely, someone with incredible Strength had thrown that spear from behind him.

"—So that's what's been causing all the noise, I take it?"

Bell heard it, a voice from far away.

Then——cheers erupted.

"——————————————————————————!!"

"YES, WE'RE SAVED!"

"ADVENTURERS!!"

Those voices, that elation, the excitement.

They all spoke of the ones who had appeared behind Bell.

Hestia and the rest of the familia's silence further implied what had arrived.

Bell heard his heart pounding.

Warning bells blared so hard in his ears that he couldn't see straight.

Dong! Dong!! DONG!! Bell slowly turned around as the increasingly insistent ringing drowned out the world around him.

"……"

The first thing he saw was a blond-haired, golden-eyed knight with a saber in hand.

"It looks as though the residents have not sustained any casualties as of yet."

"What's this? Looks like somebody got here before us?"

"Wait a sec, isn't that…?"

"It's Argonaut!"

"That rabbit-kid again…"

The next people to enter his line of sight were a high elf carrying a long staff; a dwarf with a large battle-ax over his shoulder; twin Amazons wielding Kukri knives and a long, double-bladed sword; and a werewolf equipped with metal boots.

"A vouivre…Think there's any connection with the earlier sighting of that 'winged monster'?"

The last was the one who had thrown the spear, a prum.

Standing atop a cluster of buildings and looking down over Bell and Wiene were Orario's strongest adventurers.

"Braver" Finn Deimne.

"Nine Hell" Riveria Ljos Alf.

"Elgarm" Gareth Landrock.

"Amazon" Tiona Hyrute.

"Jormungand" Tione Hyrute.

"Vanargand" Bete Loga.

And "Sword Princess" Aiz Wallenstein.

After their latest expedition, every single one of the leaders had reached Level 6.

They had pulled even with their rival familia as heroes at the forefront of the Labyrinth City who would be talked about for generations to come.

Orario's strongest familia, *Loki Familia.*

"Is that monster connected with what happened on the eighteenth floor? Those look like shackles, but is there any armor?"

"I cannot be certain about that…but the Guild may have planned for this possibility when ordering all familias to stand by."

"Tsk, a heads-up would've been nice."

For Bell, time froze as the conversation among one of the Amazons, the high elf, and the werewolf passed through his ears.

It didn't make sense. *They were too early.*

This was Labyrinth City's Daedalus Street. Even if they raced here once the commotion started, they would have needed more time. The fact that other adventurers had yet to arrive proved it.

Could it be—they saw it coming?

They had watched the events unfold and analyzed the possibilities when they were ordered to wait on the surface?

Bell locked his trembling gaze on the prum, who was calmly surveying the battlefield from above.

"Captain, what about the monster...?"

"The stone in its forehead is missing. Dispose of it immediately."

There was only one reason why they'd be here.

To *exterminate* any monster that appeared in the city.

The streets were inundated with cheers as though their triumph had rescued the city from the chaos befalling it.

Bell nearly staggered under the sound. The members of *Hestia Familia* turned pale as the noise washed over them.

Those adventurers stood as beacons of hope for the townspeople, having always admired their strength.

But for Bell, they looked like the apocalypse.

"Oh, come on. Why'd Loki's brats have to show up?"

On top of a brick tower, one of the highest points in Daedalus Street...

Ikelos and Hermes were quick to notice the disturbance from their vantage point overlooking the dungeon town, and they watched the events unfold.

"Just when things were getting interesting...Well, that about wraps it up."

"...Sure does."

The two deities watched *Loki Familia*'s second-tier and below adventurers file in behind Aiz down on street level. Ikelos slumped, bored now that Orario's strongest familia would put an end to this.

"Practically all my brats bit the dust…So much for loose ends."

Ikelos turned to Hermes, sarcastically congratulating him with a weak smile. However, Hermes was silent, his cool gaze focused on the boy's face in profile.

—Miss…Aiz.

Amid the burning unease…

Bell looked up, meeting Aiz's gaze as she looked down on him.

The boy's idol was focused solely on him.

Her golden eyes were inquisitive, as if asking, *Why are you there?*

Uh, ahh…

A certain man's words came to life in the back of his mind.

Hypocrite.

Dix scornfully laughing at Bell's foolish decision.

That hollow laughter ringing in his ears asked another question:

"So, what are you going to do now, boy?"

"AAAAAAAAAAAAaa…?!"

The vouivre screamed in pain.

The spear had penetrated deep into the ground, literally pinning the dragon girl down.

Bell's thoughts clouded, and his vision pulsed.

He stood in no-man's-land, directly between the two sides. Forward or backward? Advance or retreat?

Idol and monster, allies and scales, hero and villain, grandfather and girl, apology and repentance, promise and betrayal, genuine and fake, the fork in the road and the choice. *Decide, decide, decide.*

The image burned in his heart: the girl's smile and tears.

Her outstretched hand, her warmth, that promise he made, swearing to protect her…

All his thoughts blended together harmoniously, stirring Bell's heart.

Eternity condensed into a single moment.

Bell.

Bell.

Bell—.

* * *

"OOOOOOOOOOOOOOOOOOOOOOOOOOOooo............?"

The townspeople's cheers began to die down.

Instead, a swirling vortex of confused anger took their place. Lower-ranking adventurers craned their necks to see what was happening, and suspicion similarly darkened their expressions.

An eerie silence had overwhelmed the ruckus in the dungeon town.

"Hah?"

The werewolf frowned at what he saw.

"Hey...What's with that?"

"Little Argonaut...?"

The Amazonian twins were stunned.

"Am I seeing that right?"

"Finn..."

"...What's he got in mind?"

The dwarf, high elf, and prum coldly narrowed their eyes.

"———."

As for the girl the boy idolized, her golden eyes shook with disbelief.

"......!!"

Bell was facing them.

His back was to the monster writhing in pain as he blocked the *people* trying to dispose of it.

As if he was protecting the monster and defending it from the adventurers.

Beads of sweat rolled down his cheeks, his breathing was ragged, and his face was pale as a ghost.

He raised his black knife in a reverse grip, prepared to stand in their way.

Don't be stupid...!

Lilly, Welf, Mikoto, and Haruhime were lost for words.

Hestia's eyes opened as wide as they would go.

* * *

"...!!"

The same was true for the gargoyle Gros, who was watching from a distance.

"What you think you're doing, Bellucchi...?"

Lido and the other Xenos had stayed out of sight by approaching through the backstreets, and now they stood overlooking the standoff. Even Fels, who had reunited with them, was in shock.

"—Hee, HEE-HEE! EEHEE-HEE-HEE-HEE-HEE-HEE-HEE...!"

It was Ikelos.

Watching everything below, his shoulders convulsed with joyous glee.

"Would you look at that, Hermes?! This is hilarious!"

The deity roared with laughter, and his sparkling navy-blue hair swished back and forth.

"I thought they were all cheeky brats nowadays...but it looks like there's still some crazy ones left!"

Standing next to Ikelos, whose body was hunched over with nonstop laughter...

...Hermes's lips silently curved into a distant, almost lonely smile.

"You really are a foolish one..."

The townspeople, adventurers, monster, and deities all focused on one point.

The lone boy who had hurled himself into ruin.

Bell, who had challenged *Loki Familia* to save a monster girl.

CHAPTER
10
THE FOOL
© Suzuhito Yasuda

In Orario's southeast block, one corner of Daedalus Street was wrapped in an eerie silence.

The scene unfolding beneath the blue sky was far from normal.

A vouivre lay halfway through a building wall, pinned to the ground by a spear. Directly in front of it, standing in the middle of the wide street with his weapon raised to protect the monster, was Bell. Hestia and the rest of her familia were huddled up against the side of the road, the townspeople were watching from farther back, and *Loki Familia* was gathered on the rooftops directly behind them.

As plumes of dust billowed up from the brick rubble, the boy stood before the onlookers and their suspicious glares.

"So...what do we do about that?"

Tione's substantial breasts swelled as she sighed at the boy positioning himself to oppose them. Her twin sister, Tiona, was in shock next to her, as Bell, Aiz, and *Loki Familia*'s strongest adventurers stared each other down.

"Wh-what should we do?"

"Just ignore him. No idea what he's thinking, but it doesn't matter. This ends now."

Bete almost sounded bored as he took a step forward.

Just as the remainder of *Loki Familia* prepared to follow the adult werewolf's lead toward the monster—"FIREBOLT!"

"?!"

Boom! A burning thunderbolt tore through the sky with a roaring explosion.

Bete and his allies were moments away from jumping down from the roof, but they all froze in midstep. Startled by the sudden explosion, Daedalus Street's residents covered their ears in fright.

Bell had stuffed the jewel into the pouch at his waist before thrusting his left arm toward the heavens and triggering his Swift-Strike Magic.

It was a threat, a warning to come no closer.

He stood completely still, with sweat running down his skin in rivulets.

"—AAh?"

"?!"

Raw emotion surged from Bete, from *Loki Familia*, and from the residents.

"What's the big idea?" asked countless sets of eyes in unison.

Criticism for the boy protecting the monster wasn't the only thing in their eyes—terrible disdain and hostility were rising as well. He was a mere step away from being ostracized. He could see Aiz's and Tiona's confusion, the wary gazes of the rest of *Loki Familia*, and the shocked faces of his own familia.

The Hestia Knife trembled in his right hand, and the boy's sweat and heartbeat had reached a crescendo.

—This could be the end.

One wrong word here and it was all over.

Bell Cranell would become an enemy of the people.

As for what he said next…

"…Th—"

His parched tongue tangled in knots.

Bell fixed his gaze on the people in front of him and raised his voice.

"…This…this one's mine."

Those words came from his mouth.

"I saw this vouivre first; it's mine…!"

Bete and the others were taken aback, as Bell drove his point home as harshly as he could.

"So hands off…!!"

Backed into a corner at the moment of truth, Bell chose to act like an ill-tempered adventurer.

After claiming the monster's magic stone and all drop items for himself, he brandished the weapon in his right hand at the slack-jawed onlookers, including his own familia.

"————————?!"

"!"

That's when the vouivre, who had been thrashing about, finally ripped the spear from the ground and broke free.

Spewing blood, it bolted away, as if trying to escape both the adventurers and its own pain.

Bell turned his back on the residents and pursued the monster without a moment's delay.

"Ooookay…So what did he mean by that?"

Tiona tilted her head in confusion. Aiz opened her mouth.

"It's against the rules for one adventurer to steal a kill from another…"

"Ahh…vouivres are pretty rare, aren't they?"

"Punk-ass kid…That's only true in the Dungeon. Those rules don't belong out here!"

Aiz's explanation satisfied Tiona, who nodded in agreement, but Bete was on the verge of tearing out his ash-colored fur.

The werewolf wasn't the only one upset that the boy had prioritized his own gain during this state of emergency—other members of Bete's familia and the townspeople were fuming with anger and animosity.

"General…"

"There's no need to let a child have his way. Follow that vouivre."

Tione kept her eyes on the monster and the boy approaching the end of the street as she turned toward Finn, who started issuing a string of orders in a steady voice.

Loki Familia's forces obeyed. Some jumped off the rooftops while others remained above the streets per his instructions, when…

"—OOOOOOOOOOOOOOO!"

"?!"

A monster's ferocious howl echoed through the sky as if to drown them out.

Over twenty monsters carrying weapons appeared on the street a moment later.

"Armed monsters!"

"It looks as though there was a connection to Rivira's destruction, after all..."

Furious footsteps echoed through the backstreets as a lizardman jumped to the forefront and a gargoyle descended into the dungeon-like maze of buildings from above. The two monsters led their allies forward from both land and sky.

Chaos erupted on the street once again—the civilians screamed as adventurers looked on in disbelief. The swarm of monsters gathered in front of *Loki Familia* as if to block their path—offering themselves as decoys—and to prevent their advance.

"Lido, Gros...!"

—Meanwhile, Fels, who had pursued the Xenos in an attempt to stop them, watched helplessly from an alley.

"Please do not stop us, Fels."

"Rei...!"

"We've made our decision. We will help that person and our kin. Should we leave them to their fate now...We lose the right to pursue our desire."

The siren took a bite out of the end of her wing, smearing her face in blood before smiling at Fels and taking flight. The black-robed mage's gloves clenched into fists as her golden feathers fluttered down from the blue sky above.

"Damn...You realize my feelings already move me to help you, do you not?"

Fels left the hiding place, determined to assist the Xenos.

"Finn, your orders?"

Riveria began a counteroffensive with her bow as she addressed Finn.

"...Take as many alive as possible."

"Alive?"

Bete scoffed, but the prum general responded with a nod and said, "Yes. There's something I'd like to know. First off, Tione, lead a group to engage them head-on. Avoid casting powerful magic. It'll damage the city."

"I got you!"

"Understood!"

"Fine, then..."

"Magic users will help protect townspeople as they retreat. Their safety is our top priority. Now go."

"Sir!"

Having received the orders in quick succession, those under his command immediately set off to carry them out.

As Tione, Tiona, and Bete charged forward with the brunt of *Loki Familia*'s forces right behind them, Finn called out to Aiz before she could jump down from the rooftop.

"Aiz, you stay here."

"...?"

"Riveria, prepare a barrier. I know what I said, but I doubt the townspeople will escape right away."

"...Too much renown poses its own problems. I understand, we must be cautious."

"See that it's done. Gareth, I hate to ask, but would you set up a perimeter over there?"

"Hmm? Fine by me...Ye sure they can handle those armed monsters?"

"Yes, those three alone should be enough."

Outright ignoring Aiz's confusion, Finn issued orders to Riveria and Gareth.

They glanced at the civilians, who were hesitant to evacuate now that they felt safe—not to mention excited by the prospect of seeing Orario's strongest familia in action with their own eyes. Riveria sighed to herself as she leaped off the rooftop, already casting her spell.

Gareth hoisted his ax over his shoulder and ran off in the direction Finn had indicated.

"...Finn."

"Oh, sorry, sorry. Aiz, you're our insurance."

*Stare...*Finn apologized right away once he felt Aiz's eyes on him.

He forced a smile as if sensing the aloof, normally quiet Sword Princess's thoughts—her disappointment or perhaps her discontent.

"...Is there...something coming?"

"My thumb is a bit...you know..."

Aiz asked him to elaborate with a docile look on her face while Finn ran his tongue across his thumb.

Now alone with the girl on the rooftop, the prum general lifted his gaze.

The adventurers and monsters were already engaged in combat before him.

The curtain rose over the battle between *Loki Familia* and the Xenos.

The battle commenced as the combatants spread out across the eight-meder-wide street.

The Xenos forces fought with the city's eastern wall at their backs, trying to hold off the adventurers' advance. *Loki Familia* came from the west, closer to Babel Tower, and the two groups collided in the middle of the street.

A troll exchanged blows with a male werewolf; a human girl faced a lamia in combat; a stunningly elegant elf archer fired arrows toward a griffin. Each was armed with their weapon of choice. The battlefield resounded with a nearly constant cacophony of weapon against weapon.

"GAOOOOOOOO!!"

"Lizardman, eh..."

Lido, donning a monstrous visage, clashed with the Amazon Tione.

The former was armed with a longsword and scimitar while the latter wielded a pair of Kukri knives. The two dual-wielding combatants exchanged a flurry of strikes and slashes.

"……?!"

However, Lido soon felt that he was fighting against a storm surge at high tide.

Her long black hair swirled, and her blades blurred in a surging, furious dance. Each high-speed strike was powerful enough to inflict critical damage. Lido blocked them with his full-strength deflections, creating tremendous metallic clangs that overwhelmed his hearing.

The Amazon's dance continued to flow, but she mixed in her own style of martial arts. Her supple wheat-skinned legs lashed out like whips, breaking Lido's prized, solid red scales on contact. What's more, her bare feet didn't have a scratch on them.

As her blades carved through the air like a net, her exceptional hand-to-hand technique used her elbows and legs as well.

When his blades were deflected, the impact sent unbelievably fierce shocks through his gauntlets and into the muscles beneath.

To the lizardman's eyes, to an actual monster, her savage fighting style conjured images of wild beasts; her two Kukri knives were fangs in their own right.

Lido found himself on the defensive almost immediately.

"Interesting…"

Tione narrowed her eyes at the lizardman that was weathering her attacks, managing to avoid the fatal blows grazing past its scales.

Suddenly interested in Lido's swordsmanship, she picked up the pace as if to determine exactly how many skills and tactics the monster possessed.

S-so strong…!

Lido's reptilian yellow eyes trembled.

He had faced many adventurers in combat today and—excluding *Ganesha Familia*'s elite, Shakti, and the man in goggles, Dix—he was confident he could handily dispatch any foot soldier. That was neither an overexaggeration nor a bluff. His confidence came from his many years of consuming other monsters' magic crystals to acquire enhanced-species potential, as well as the time he had spent perfecting his wild fighting style.

Against this opponent, however, he couldn't see the slightest glimmer of victory.

Lido had no choice but to accept the fact that he, a monster, had become the prey before this sharp-eyed Amazon.

—Freya Familia *and* Loki Familia.

—Lido, you must avoid them at all costs.

—They must never become your enemy.

Lido remembered the advice that Fels had imparted deep in the dark Dungeon.

They'd gone far out of their way to avoid the two groups because of the mage's warning, and now Lido knew the true meaning behind Fels's words firsthand.

But—I can't go dying now!

Lido, his eyes alight, skillfully deflected his opponent's strikes and set his sights on a counterattack.

Once he had gained a bit of distance with a few well-placed, deft slashes, he swung the longsword and scimitar forward with all the might his body had to offer.

Of course, Tione knocked the blades away with ease—prompting Lido to lash forward with his tail, and the waist-level appendage connected with incredible force.

"!"

The third strike caught Tione off guard, and the two Kukri knives were knocked from her grasp.

How'd you like that?

The moment Lido slashed the scimitar for the finishing blow—Tione disappeared.

Too fast for his eyes to register, she grabbed hold of Lido's head from the side with her bare hand and slammed him into a nearby wall in one smooth motion.

"—GHAA!"

The blackened brick wall burst on impact, burying Lido in rubble as one eye widened in horror.

"...You're not just any lizardman, are you?"

The one who had flung the lizardman's entire body into a wall with one slender limb said it matter-of-factly as she tightened her grip, cracking his skull under the pressure.

The monster's tail thrashed forward in pain, and Tione jumped back immediately. Now free, Lido pulled his body from the rubble but could barely stand.

"————————————————!!"

"Oh shut up..."

—Near the edge of the street, away from Lido and Tione, Bete covered the wolf ears on top of his head to shield them from a sound wave blasting overhead.

A monstrous-looking siren easily dodged the arrows and other weapons thrown its way while unleashing high-frequency sound waves over a wide area. Bete nearly lost his sense of balance to the powerful onslaught despite the considerable distance between them. Adventurers directly in the line of fire didn't stand a chance and collapsed hand-first to the ground with blood leaking out of their ears.

Menace burning in his eyes, Bete kicked off the ground.

"?!"

The siren Rei flinched as he rocketed toward her from the lower left. As Bete tore through the air like a ravenous wolf hell-bent on devouring the moon, she immediately ceased the attack and banked to evade him.

The two slid past each other in midair, and the siren broke out in a cold sweat as the werewolf's fist brushed against her face in a near miss. At the same time, her opponent seemed to have anticipated this and landed against a nearby building. Whipping his body around in a split second, he sprang off its surface.

Again, he closed the distance like a bullet.

"——————."

Rei, a flying monster, was about to take an attack from the rear. There was no time to gawk.

Bete grinned, his mythril-metal boot flashing in the sunlight as it arced high over his head.

"Crash."

Despite being wingless, Bete slammed his foot into the airborne monster's back.

"?!"

Rei plummeted to the ground like a meteorite.

Unable to breathe or break her fall in any way, she shattered the stone pavement on impact.

It was over in a single blow.

"Why'd you have to go and give that annoying order, Finn…?"

Cursing his instructions to take the monsters alive, Bete walked over to Rei to see if he'd held back enough. His injured allies watched, wanting nothing more than to pay the siren back for what she'd done to them, as he walked over to the small crater where she lay facedown and rolled her over with a careless kick.

The siren's shapely chest shuddered beneath a single layer of battle cloth as she landed flat on her back.

"Ahhn? The hell…?"

Sliding across the stone pavement had wiped away a part of Rei's mask of blood.

She had long, dark golden hair, eyes as blue as the sky, and elegant facial features on par with the elves.

Bete cocked an eyebrow at the form Rei had purposely concealed and grinned.

"Quite the looker for a monster, aren't you?"

Then he lifted his right leg and mercilessly drove it straight into Rei's stomach.

"…ah!"

"But monsters can go to hell."

The siren's lower body lurched upward on the boot heel's impact. With a smile of scorn and anger, he pounded the divide between people and monsters into Rei.

A beautiful yet harsh sun burned into Rei's eyes.

She had yearned to see the surface light for so long, and all it did was illuminate her cruel reality.

"OOOOOOOOOOOOOOOOOOO!!"

"Do any of them know how to shut up?!"

A gargoyle dove for the werewolf with his boot on Rei.

Bete jumped backward, avoiding Gros's rage-filled charge, and shattered the swiping stone claws with a kick before they could rip his head off.

Time stood still for the gargoyle as the stone-claw fragments flew past his eyes, and Bete's metal boot bore down on him with a high roundhouse kick.

"Gwah?!"

"Your kind doesn't belong here."

The brutal werewolf followed up with another kick, telling the gargoyle to hole up in the dreary underground.

"One…and two!"

"?!"

Denied an aerial escape route, the gargoyle desperately fended off the barrage while Tiona disarmed her opponent, a red-cap goblin. The ax was far too big for its tiny wielder, and she sent it skyward with a few skillful swings of her giant, double-bladed sword.

—It's a goblin, but it's about as good as a Level 4, maybe?

Tiona thought to herself, both impressed and bewildered by her most likely enhanced-species red-cap-goblin opponent, as she threw several kicks in a variant of her sister's fighting style.

"Hi-yaaa!"

"GUH!"

In the blink of an eye, Tiona defeated the especially challenging monster.

"I'm not Bete or anything, but it's hard to hold Urga back."

Balancing the double-bladed weapon over her shoulder with one hand, Tiona jogged her way through the clashing adventurers and monsters. "Can't have any fun…" she mumbled to herself in search of prey.

"KIIH!!"

"Heh? An al-miraj~?"

Round red eyes looking right up at her, it had fluffy, cotton-like fur.

It was charging her with one arm held high as if screaming, "This is for my kind!"

The monster resembling a certain boy didn't perk Tiona's interest in the least, and she stuck out her arm to slap it.

"KYU!"

SMACK! An unbelievable sound burst from its cheek as the wide-eyed al-miraj rolled back down the street and slammed into a wall.

The blank-eyed al-miraj—Aruru—lost consciousness with a soft squeak. "Kyuu..."

Her hellhound partner left her there and hid behind a nearby building.

"This is very bad...!"

Fels anxiously whispered, surveying the battle from the roof of a tall apartment building before rushing into action.

One Xenos, then another and another fell to *Loki Familia*. Even the weaker members behind Tiona and the other captains demonstrated considerable strength and outstanding teamwork. Having been in continuous combat since the Dungeon's eighteenth floor didn't help matters as the lamia, troll, and the injured harpy had reached their physical limits.

The writing was on the wall. It had come to this. Grinding bony teeth together beneath the black hood, Fels looked up from the street and scanned the surrounding area.

"The battle is taking place in a corner of Daedalus Street, relatively close to the Coliseum and East Main Street...!"

Catching a glimpse of the amphitheater from between two buildings, Fels's mind was set.

"My apologies, Ouranos...I'm using it!"

Fels withdrew a golden wand from beneath the folds of the cloak and sprinted off to the north.

* * *

"...An earthquake?"

Fwump. The lizardman collapsed to the ground in front of her, and Tione glanced at her feet.

Bete had taken down the gargoyle, and with very few monsters left standing, tremors raced through the earth. They were getting stronger—no, *closer*—and the members of *Loki Familia* were united in their surprise and disbelief for a moment. And then...

The ground split open with incredible force to reveal a mass of shining metal.

"Uwoah?! What is that?!" Tiona cried in amazement, followed by her allies' surprised yells.

"A metallic monster?!"

"A new species?!"

Just as the adventurers said, the thing was made of a silver-like metal.

Its arms and legs were thicker than any large-category monster. The head looked like a small mountain due to the position of its neck and had parts that resembled eyes. A symbol, deeper black than any language could describe, was just above its eyes. Standing over three meders tall and lacking symmetry on either side, the thing might as well have been cobbled together from large chunks of metal. Its crooked body shared some similarities to flame rocks, a type of monster that resided in the Dungeon's deep levels.

"A Golem...It's my own magic item, dispatched into the sewer system after the Monsterphilia incident...!"

Fels monologued on the verge of desperation, announcing the trump card.

The creator could channel magic energy through a wand to control it at a distance, but it was autonomous for the most part. A metallic warrior that carried out simple instructions.

An unquestionably loyal combatant without a soul of its own—an extremely high-quality magic item requiring a level of skill that only Fels, formerly known as the Sage, possessed.

Fels used the wand to order the warrior into battle and assist the Xenos.

"What is this?! One of their friends?!"

"How the hell should I know?!"

Tione and Bete immediately moved to engage the rampaging Golem, attacking at close range.

"—Damn, that's hard!!"

"It's made of adamantite?!"

However, the tips of both Kukri knives snapped on impact, and the shock of his metal boot striking the solid mass reached Bete's foot.

"You're absolutely right…!"

Fels, looking down from high above, would have been smiling with satisfaction had there been the muscles or skin to do so.

The Golem's entire body had been created using adamantite. And not just the standard form but a purer form of adamantite mined from the deep levels. Not even the first-tier adventurers' weapons could easily break it. In terms of money, it would be valued at one billion valis, an ace in the hole that Fels had kept hidden for centuries.

"————!!"

As the mage chuckled with glee far overhead, the Golem effortlessly deflected Tione's and Bete's attacks while advancing toward the other adventurers without so much as a scratch. Its movements might have been clumsy, but the sheer weight and density of adamantite made each wild swing of its arms extremely powerful.

Many adventurers thought better of their attack while others were launched skyward along with their shields. Bete clicked his tongue, when suddenly—

"—Oh-ho-ho! Now that's what I'm talking about!!" Tiona's eyes sparkled; she was grinning from ear to ear.

Fels froze in place, watching as the tide of battle shifted before his eyes.

"Everyone, get out of the way!"

"That idiot…!"

"Hey! Kick all those fallen monsters out of the street!"

Tione's mood turned sour when Tiona appeared, whirling her double-bladed sword over her head like a windmill in both hands, and Bete snapped at her. They were rattled.

The same was true for their allies. "Run away!" "She's coming!" they yelled to one another, desperate to get out of her path.

The townspeople—and *Hestia Familia*, still in the same spot—glanced around in confusion as Finn smiled wanly, Riveria let out a long sigh, and Aiz watched with a hint of envy.

The Golem slowly turned around, suddenly alone on the abandoned street.

The metallic warrior charged her head-on as Tiona flashed an innocent smile at her target—and attacked with her double-bladed weapon.

"Heeereee I gooo———!!"

Then, *SLASH!*

"—————————."

The townspeople, *Hestia Familia*, and the fallen Xenos couldn't help but watch.

The massive blade came down at an angle.

Sparkling metal fragments scattered as the adamantite body collapsed to the ground with a thunderous *bang*.

Still as an eroding statue, Fels stared blankly at the two halves of the cherished Golem.

".................!"

"Huh? The thing's still moving?!"

Crick, crick, crick! Its severed upper body reached outward, startling Tiona as she slashed again.

Light left the Golem's eyes the moment her blade cut through the symbol on its head, and its arm collapsed to the ground. The metallic warrior became silent as the grave.

"Oh! So the head was the weak spot! Finn, I did it!"

"Tiona, you idiot!! The general said to take them alive, didn't he?"

"Ah."

Tione's rebuke struck her sister like a lightning bolt as the younger girl waved. Having given in to her berserker instincts, Tiona froze on the spot.

Her custom-made, double-bladed sword—two massive blades on

either end of the hilt—was huge even by adventurer standards. The hulking weapon glinted in Tiona's grasp.

A few moments passed before the quiet crowd once again erupted with cheers.

"Hah, ha-ha-ha...It's no use, Ouranos. They are the true monsters after all...!"

After coming out of the daze, Fels could only force an empty laugh.

A mixture of awe and fear had taken hold of the mage after seeing *Loki Familia*'s true strength.

And, right then...

"Finn's hunch was right on the money. Sharp as a tack, as always."

"———."

A dwarf's low voice came from behind Fels.

It was Gareth, his battle-ax at the ready.

Finn had reasoned that there must be a tamer—or someone—calling the shots, due to the timing and coordination of the Xenos's appearance, and ordered Gareth to circle behind the strange figure watching over the battle.

"Are you the monster mastermind?"

"......"

"Are you a person or a monster...? Well, taking that robe of yours away should make it clear enough."

The mage froze, unable to come up with a way to escape the first-tier adventurer's overwhelming presence.

Beneath the black robe, Fels remembered the sensation of cold sweat, despite not being able to feel it anymore.

"......!"

With the Xenos's cries of pain and the townspeople's cheers of joy in his ears, Welf tightened his grip on his greatsword.

Hestia Familia hadn't moved from the street side. They hadn't been able to pursue Bell due to the Xenos suddenly appearing in their way, but above all else, they'd been in awe of *Loki Familia*'s teamwork and skill in battle.

The young smith's vision was filled with badly injured Xenos, bleeding as they crawled across the ground. Welf couldn't take it anymore and stepped out from their hiding place.

"You mustn't, Mr. Welf!"

Lilly jumped out right behind him, grabbing ahold of his waist.

"Let go, Li'l E!! At this rate, they'll all—"

"We can't! Mr. Bell's situation is still unresolved, but should any of us protect them as well, *Hestia Familia* will be…!"

Lilly was also fighting against fear.

Fear of what would happen to their soon-to-be-denounced familia and fear of the first-tier adventurers' unparalleled power, scarier than any of the monsters.

Welf bit his lip, seeing Lilly tremble as she warned of persecution and retribution.

"…It's fine. Go to it, Welf."

"Lady Hestia?!"

"Just say your goddess told you to. Followers can't go against their deity's wishes, can they? Deities are always after entertainment…If it looks like my whim, people shouldn't be too hard on you."

Lilly couldn't ignore her goddess's words and compassion for Wiene's comrades. Letting go of Welf's jacket, she thrust her hand into her item pouch as though determined to assist their cause.

"…I shall attempt to weigh the adventurers down with my magic. Use that opportunity to reach the Xenos."

"Miss Mikoto…"

"Lady Haruhime, would you lend me your Level Boost? To be blunt, I doubt my ability to restrain top-tier adventurers for long…"

"…But of course!"

Mikoto stepped up to Welf's side, sheathing her katana. Haruhime gave her a firm nod.

Everyone sweated as the tension escalated, and Mikoto and Haruhime were just about to hide behind the nearest building so that the renart's spell wouldn't be overheard, when suddenly—

A rumbling howl filled the air.

* * *

"______"

Aiz, Finn, Riveria, Tiona, Tione, Bete, and Gareth—each stopped what they were doing on the battlefield and immediately turned toward it.

Welf, Mikoto, and the rest of *Hestia Familia* froze at the sight of the trembling sky.

"What...was that...?"

The cheering crowd was suddenly silent.

The combatants of *Loki Familia* had come to a sudden halt, but even the noncombatant Haruhime stood completely still, her fox tail twitching, her instincts telling her to flee in terror. Hestia, a deity, was stunned.

Then...*thud...thud...*

The heavy, threatening echoes and shuddering earth heralded the arrival of a newcomer.

No one needed to see it to know those were footsteps. They were approaching, steadily, from behind the wall that the vouivre had broken through on its arrival.

Every set of eyes focused on the wall, still shrouded in smoke.

Many monsters were still lying facedown in the street, and all other sound disappeared from the battlefield.

Moments later...

A shadow appeared in the smoke, crushing rubble underfoot as its form took shape.

"—What the...?" one of the adventurers whispered.

It had skin so black it could have been born from the deepest, darkest bowels of the Dungeon. Over two meders tall with muscles built like boulders, it was equipped with adventurer's armor.

A nigh-indestructible breastplate, shoulder armor, gauntlets, waist plates, and greaves.

The full set of plate armor couldn't cover the entire body and almost resembled light armor on its massive frame. Holding an enormous Labrys aloft with one hand, the new arrival had another massive ax strapped to its shoulder armor. Each weapon's blades were dyed red with the blood of its victims.

Both of the horns on its head were crimson.

The sight called to mind the words *raging bull.*

A creature absent from the Guild's files and unfamiliar even to *Loki Familia*—an "unknown" monster stood before them.

The ever-calm Finn unfolded his arms and stepped forward, suddenly anxious.

His thumb convulsed, sending spasms down his arm.

"———."

Huff, huff. The monster rotated its thick neck in their direction, and its ragged breathing sounded in their ears.

The instant it saw the adventurers and the fallen monsters—

—it roared with all its might.

"oOOOOOOOOOOOOOOOOOOOOOOOOOOOOOO
OOOOOOOOOOOOOOOOOOOOOOOOOOOOOOO!!"

A dreadnought Howl obliterated the silence.

The residents of Daedalus Street tumbled to the ground one by one, their eyes rolled up in shock after the dust-raising roar.

"———a."

"Supporter! Haruhime!"

A pale Lilly and Haruhime weren't far behind the townspeople, knees buckling until they were sitting on the street.

Welf, Mikoto, and many members of *Loki Familia* were blown back, fighting tooth and nail to remain standing as Hestia screamed.

A Howl, far stronger than normal.

A monster's intimidating song that bound living creatures with primitive fear.

Those unworthy to meet the challenge were immediately rendered motionless—the roar restrained its victims.

Welf and Mikoto dropped to their knees. They both stared into the palms of their quivering hands; even their higher Levels couldn't save them from its effects. There were many within *Loki Familia*'s ranks who were on the verge of losing their will to fight, jamming their swords into the ground for support to keep on their feet.

"......!!"

With only the worthy remaining on the battlefield, the monster charged.

The rocketing, massive black shadow's first target was Tione.

"!"

Tione glared at the monster descending upon her like a night-colored storm surge.

Raising her two Kukri knives, she planted her feet to meet the attack with her own.

"Get out of there, Tione!!"

The air whistling past the Labrys drowned out Finn's desperate call as the silver blade streaked straight down—into the ground one meder in front of Tione's feet.

There was an explosion and shock wave, followed by sudden weightlessness.

Awe flashed through Tione's eyes.

Her feet left the ground, robbing her of any chance to evade as swirling dust and stone debris blinded her. The monster immediately descended upon her, its left arm homing in on her.

Tione crossed the Kukri knives at the last moment to defend herself, but the two blades could do nothing in the face of that massive palm.

They shattered.

"——GHaHH?!"

The blow broke through her defense and collided with the left side of her body—strikingly similar to Aisha's fate—and sent Tione hurtling into the corner of a nearby house.

"Tione?!"

It all happened in the blink of an eye. However, the scene was more than enough to rob the adventurers of their will and sense of time.

The monster stood tall, roaring at the other adventurers before Tiona's scream could reach their ears.

"UOOOOOOOOOOOOOOOOOOOOOOOO!!"

As it stepped forward with a ground-shattering stomp, the monster swung its clenched left fist in a wide semicircle with the force of a hurricane. Every single adventurer standing over a Xenos was swept up in the blast and launched backward, just like Tione.

Bones broken and coughing up blood, the adventurers collided with their allies who happened to be out of range, screaming at the top of their lungs.

"UWAHHHHHHHHHHHHH!"

As the men's screams rose into the sky, *Loki Familia* lost more than half of their forces in one devastating fell swoop.

"You'll pay for that—!!"

"Cruz, move it! Outta my way!"

Tiona charged forward, double-bladed sword held high with Bete right behind her, jeering with all his might.

First-tier adventurers collided with the raging bull as other adventurers dragged those affected by the Howl and the injured to safety.

The double-bladed sword couldn't power through the Labrys's solid strike. A wide-eyed Tiona managed to absorb the heavy blow and fight it off, immediately opening a window for Bete to come in low and attack its legs.

The monster was knocked off balance. Two Level 6 adventurers worked in tandem to drive it back.

"Elfie, get all the unconscious people to safety! Now!!"

"S-sir!"

Finn called down to the pale, cowering magic users at the back of the formation. Startled at their general's direct order, the women quickly moved to the bodies sprawled out nearby to speed up the evacuation.

"Finn, shall we support them with magic?!"

"No. That would only draw the enemy's attention toward the bystanders around us. Your barrier is powerful, but it won't hold up against a direct hit."

Riveria looked up from her position at street level as Finn told her to hold off until the evacuation was complete.

With a magic circle spreading at her feet, the high elf shifted her completed spell to standby mode as she frowned at the front lines, frustrated.

"A black minotaur…?"

"I don't think so…Looks more like a black rhino subspecies to me."

Aiz kept her eyes on the rampaging monster that was paying little attention to Tiona's and Bete's wave upon wave of attacks. Finn noticed the girl looked anxious to join the fight, following her gaze and theorizing that the creature was an Irregular from the deep levels.

That, and that it was an enhanced species like the rest of the armed monsters.

"…A-Asterios…"

The fallen Xenos looked up from the ground to face the black shadow.

Badly injured, Lido whispered the name of their final comrade.

"…Damn show-off."

—Elsewhere, amid a pile of brick rubble…

Tione emerged from the debris and, coughing up bloody saliva, smoothly pulled back the bangs that hid her eyes from view.

Then her eyes flared to life.

"So you think you're hot shit, bovine bastard?"

Completely ignoring her broken ribs, she exploded with anger.

Tiona and the others didn't have time to react to her snarling howl, barely recognizable as a person's voice, before Tione raced back into battle, unarmed.

Clearing Tiona and Bete in a single bound, she hurtled toward the raging bull with her left fist held high, challenging the beast one-on-one.

The monster shifted to meet her head-on, pulling its own left fist back and setting its feet.

"GRRAAAAAAAAAAAAAAAAAAAA!!"

"OOOOOOOOOOOOOOOOOOOOOOOO!!"

Tiona slammed a punch directly into the enemy's clenched, metal-like fist.

The resulting bloodcurdling collision made bystanders want to cover their ears.

The tremendous impact drove the monster's fist straight back and snapped every bone in Tiona's hand.

She clenched her fleshy, broken, bleeding blob of a hand tight and threw another punch.

"?!"

Taking a hit to its solid midsection for the first time, the raging bull staggered backward.

"I'll make mincemeat outta you!!"

Tione didn't stop.

Consumed by a fiery rage that became her strength and fueled her onslaught, she unleashed a rush of punches and kicks onto her enemy's large body. Heel, elbow, knee, fist. As her long black hair trailed behind like a snake, her furious dance of physical blows shook the monster's metal-like frame from head to toe.

"—UoHoOOOOOOOOOOOOOOOOOOOOOOOOO!!"

The black bull didn't flinch, taking each blow head-on and responding in kind.

"Wh-what are you doing, Tione?!"

"Shut the hell up!!"

Tiona called out despite being knocked back, but Tione would have nothing of it and yelled at her furiously.

Bete and Tiona looked at her with fatigue.

"No use. She's pissed..."

Her true self had been exposed—Tione was even more of a berserker than her younger sister.

Her offensive continued to escalate no matter how much of her skin was torn up on contact with her enemy's towering, solid body or how many of her leg bones cracked in the process. Evading the occasional counterattack, she had every intention of obliterating the enemy in her sights.

Living up to the sea serpent of her title, her hair whipped back and forth as she fought with extreme ferocity.

"SHII!!"

Then, after weaving past her enemy's massive arm, Tione put all her strength into a left-footed kick that caught the bull square in the face.

It was a shattering blow, even for monsters from the deep levels.

Tione, who had launched the hit in the air, glared up at her opponent only to go wide-eyed in disbelief.

Even with her foot buried deep in its jawbone, the black minotaur was still standing.

Damn, this, thing——.

She had no answer.

An adventurer could never attain this amount of resilience, this toughness no matter how hard they trained. Not only was its defense powerful enough to break Tione's foot on impact but its two legs were still firmly planted on the ground.

The black raging bull grabbed Tione's left leg, still wedged in its face, and flung her.

"?!"

Tiona threw down her double-bladed sword and dove to catch her sister just before she careened into a wall. However, that didn't prevent the ensuing explosion from the building.

"The heck's gotten into you?!"

"Keep your nose out of it!! I told you to shut the hell up, didn't I?!"

The two went through the wall together, pulverizing it as they argued back and forth. Meanwhile, Bete moved in to engage the monster one-on-one. The werewolf unleashed a barrage of kicks no less potent than Tione's, while the bull howled and countered with the Labrys. The two went back and forth, alternating offense and defense until Tiona and Tione rejoined the battle, their argument escalating to the point of exchanging insults.

The double-bladed sword and the Labrys violently collided, the metal boots redirected attacks, and a frenzy of physical blows connected with the creature's armor.

Neither adventurers nor monster surrendered a step. The rest of *Loki Familia* watched in awe, and then they saw it.

"Th-that's a grin..."

The ferocious smile on the monster's face.

Its large white teeth had appeared from beneath a split in its cheeks. No doubt, the raging bull was having the time of its life.

Taking on three first-tier adventurers at once and absorbing countless hits did nothing to deter the colossal fighting spirit pulsing through its body.

The black bull swung its head and loosed a ferocious roar.

Is it just me, or does this feel like...?

Tiona's skin broke out in goose bumps as she weathered the roar and brought her double-bladed weapon down for another strike.

This sensation, I've felt it before...!!

Clicking her tongue in frustration at the ineffectiveness of her attacks, Tione dove out of the Labrys's path.

This creature, it's almost...!!

Bete felt as though he were fighting against an extremely small floor boss. His metal boots were a blur.

This excessive strength.

It was the same as something else, a distant shadow lurking in their memories.

The young adventurers were reminded of a certain man.

"......"

Ottar watched the battle unfolding in the dungeon town from the highest floor in Babel Tower.

"Do you recognize that minotaur?"

One rectangular wall was constructed entirely out of glass. Standing before it, watching the entire scene at once from Orario's highest point, Freya addressed her attendant, who was fixated on Daedalus Street.

"That...No, then again...Impossible."

Ottar's face remained stoic as he faced forward, fumbling around to find the right words to respond to his goddess.

Stepping beside the warrior and taking a sip from the wineglass in her hand, Freya looked away from *Loki Familia*'s battle.

Even at this great distance, the deity's silver eyes could see a blur of color and a shimmering, transparent streak.

It was the vouivre, weaving a path of destruction through the dungeon town, and the boy, hot on its tail in pursuit.

"Helen."

"My Lady."

A girl standing nearby straightened her posture at the goddess's call, but Freya kept her back to her as she continued.

"Any word from Alfregg and the party I sent to the Dungeon?"

"They have yet to return."

"I see…Could you catch up to the charging vouivre if you departed now?"

"…I do not believe that I would make it in time."

Taking her follower's honest opinion in stride, Freya ordered, "That's fine. Go."

As the girl made a bow and exited the room, Freya whispered quietly under her breath:

"To think monsters like this existed."

Marveling at this world's unpredictability, the silver-haired goddess smiled from ear to ear.

"—Like I've been telling you, my brats have been catching those monsters."

Gareth narrowed his eyes as a god's confession dissolved into the sky.

"They were after money in the black market, but the darn things escaped, as you can see."

"And you're expectin' me to believe that?"

"If my word isn't enough, I'll tell you right where to go in the sewers beneath Daedalus Street. You'll see the cages where these monsters were kept."

Ikelos had appeared on the rooftop with Gareth and Fels mere moments ago when the dwarf was distracted by the black bull's entrance. Then, he suddenly began explaining his involvement in the situation.

"So, how about letting Black Cloak here go, eh?"

"……"

"The poor sap's got nothing to do with my brats. Just got caught up in all this, is all."

Ikelos pointed his finger a few times at the black-robed figure, who was still as a statue, facing away.

While he wasn't lying, he was also not telling the truth. After decades of training under Loki, Gareth could see through Ikelos's faint grin and decided to press for an answer to what had been on his mind from the start.

"And why are you tellin' me here and now?"

"Because I lost...Had to do what the winner wanted."

Right after he said that...

The black-robed figure jumped from the rooftop, slipping away during a lull in the conversation.

Gareth sighed as he saw his quarry disappear over the edge but made no efforts to pursue.

"...I'll be askin' fer details later. For now, ye're comin' with me."

"Yeah, sure. Just be gentle, okay?"

Ignoring Ikelos's words and his grin, Gareth grabbed hold of the deity's collar.

As the battle escalated out of the corner of his eye, the dwarf knew that time was of the essence and paid no attention to the screaming god as he bounded through the air.

"Looks like he's on his way."

"...You have my thanks, God Hermes."

—Hiding in a backstreet, Fels watched Gareth disappear from the rooftop above and turned to thank Hermes, standing before him.

Not only had Hermes been observing the battle from his vantage point on top of the brick tower, he had also witnessed Gareth's approach behind Fels and convinced Ikelos to intervene with a one-sided negotiation. Knowing that the mage functioned as Ouranos's right hand, he had saved Fels by offering up the deity instead.

"What can I say? The way things are now, we're gonna need your power to get through this, Sage."

"...I go by Fels now, God Hermes."

The black-robed mage sounded bashful, but the dandy god simply shrugged.

But Hermes knew that there was no time for small talk and got right to the point.

"All right then, Fels. As a way to thank me for saving your life, I've a favor to ask…Bell is alone right now. Please help him."

"But…were I to leave now, the Xenos…"

"Thanks to that black minotaur, things should work out okay, don't you think? And from what I've seen, Braver wants to capture them alive. Worse shouldn't come to worst today."

Hermes carefully crafted his argument.

A few moments passed in heavy silence, and then the deity narrowed his eyes behind the brim of his hat.

"I have a lot of things I'd like to sweep under the rug as well, you know? I'm sure Ouranos's right arm understands."

"……"

"This won't make amends for the past but…could you find it in your heart to do this for me?"

Hermes leaned in close to whisper beside the silent mage's hood.

Fels took a few moments to think before extending a hand toward Hermes.

Then several black spheres, smaller than an oculus, fell from the black glove into the palm of his outstretched hand.

"These are for an emergency. Break them to use them."

"…Understood. I am Hermes and swear by my name. Lulune."

Hermes handed the spheres to a chienthrope girl who appeared from deeper down the alley.

Watching her disappear, Fels set out in accordance with Hermes's will.

"Bell and the vouivre were headed south. I bet they're out of Daedalus Street, probably somewhere in the Pleasure Quarter reconstruction project by now."

"Acknowledged."

After Hermes had imparted what he saw from on top of the tower, Fels sped down a path leading southeast.

The battle raged on.

Combat between first-tier adventurers and the black minotaur had reached a fever pitch. One step forward, one step back. Offense and defense switched sides every second in an epic back-and-forth while the other adventurers gawked. However, numbers were on the adventurers' side. Once Tiona and Bete ignored Tione's raging fury and showed some semblance of teamwork, the monster was forced to give ground.

Just as the tides of combat appeared to be flowing in their favor…

The monster's next action turned the entire battle on its head.

"WOOOOOOO!"

As yet another blow connected with its armor, the black minotaur reached behind its right shoulder.

Those five meaty fingers wrapped around the elongated metal ax hilt.

—Dual Axes?

Faced with the prospect of an abrupt change in battle style, the three watched the black minotaur's every move with nervous eyes.

"————."

The first one to recognize the danger wasn't in *Loki Familia*'s ranks—it was Welf.

"—We're getting out of here, now!!"

"Eh?!"

"Just move it!!"

Shaking off the last effects of the Howl, Welf willed his body forward, picking up Lilly's unconscious body and grabbing hold of Hestia's hand. With Mikoto carrying Haruhime in her arms close behind, Welf ran headlong in the other direction, toward where Riveria stood with her staff held high in front of *Loki Familia*'s forces.

"!!"

Arm and shoulder muscles pulsing, the monster swung the blood-stained ax down with its right hand.

The instant it connected with Tiona's double-bladed sword—thunder struck.

"""""?!"""""

A flash of light engulfed Tiona along with her weapon, and Tione and Bete on either side of her were also swept up in the shock wave.

Crackle! An electrical current danced across the blade in front of the dumbstruck trio.

The blood coating it was blasted away, and the weapon's true beautiful golden hue came to light.

Tiona, Tione, Bete, and the rest of *Loki Familia* all recognized in that moment the weapon for what it was.

The blood-splattered ax—was a magic weapon.

Finn's face contorted, Aiz watched in amazement, and Riveria readied her staff with incredible speed thanks to her abilities as a magic user. Welf, who had prioritized his own familia, gritted his teeth while the rest of *Loki Familia*, still on the battlefield, froze with fear.

"OOO———"

Still reeling from the unexpected electrical shock, the three momentarily numbed adventurers watched as the hulking black shadow's right arm swung the ax yet again.

The weapon rose high into the sky. The beast prepared for another volley to blow all of them away.

Finn called out, and Riveria triggered her magic at nearly the same instant.

"Riveria, the barrier!!"

Just as the last member of *Hestia Familia* dove into the magic circle…

Riveria's magic—an enormous dome barrier—took shape.

"—ooOOOOOOOOOOOOOOOOOOOOOOOOOOOOOOO!!"

The Howl tore through the air along with the shock wave.

"—Damn you!"

Bete forced his tingling foot high into the air and brought it straight down onto the magic weapon. Brutal lightning bolts burst forth the instant his metal boot touched the black minotaur's weapon.

Blinding yellow light drowned out their surroundings. Each bolt raced forward like one of a hydra's many heads, with electrified fangs that tore up the street and turned the vicinity into a swirling whirlpool of destruction. Being so close to the blast, it went without saying that not only Tiona, Tione, and Bete but adventurers still out on the street had no chance to evade. They were all caught up in the barrage.

The bolts advanced all the way to Riveria's barrier. *Ka-boom!* An immense shower of sparks flared on impact. The barricade of green light shielded the unconscious townspeople, the young magic users, Finn, Aiz, and Welf without so much as a quiver.

As their ears recovered from the blast, they all waited for the smoke to clear…only to see an utter ruin before their eyes. Every house and building that once lined the street had been razed, the stone pavement was carved up as if by dragon claws, and the burned, smoldering bodies of adventurers were scattered throughout.

It looked as though the apocalypse had arrived, but they all were still breathing by some miracle.

"S-so tingly…! I'm paralyzed~!"

"Damn it…! Why couldn't you take the whole thing, you damn werewolf!!"

"Want me to smash your head in, damn Amazon…?"

Just before the explosion, Bete had put his body on the line to block the blast at close range by sticking out his metal boot—the mythril absorbed the electricity—and greatly reducing its power. But of course, he couldn't block the entirety of a discharge on that scale.

After hurtling through the air and rolling across the debris, the three badly burned first-tier adventurers were on their knees on a corner of the street. They were the only ones still moving, but they exchanged harsh words despite their injuries.

Although they managed to get through the blast in one piece, sparks traced their bodies like flashing thorns, and none of the three could move from the spot.

"…"

Apart from where the monsters lay on the eastern side, not even a shadow remained of the buildings on the central road where the minotaur was standing. Everything to the west was completely unrecognizable.

Finn narrowed his eyes as he took in the destruction, glancing over the mountains of rubble and the monster staring up at him.

"Forget about taking them alive."

Golden hair shifting on his head, the prum general opened his mouth to speak.

He said from his spot, alone on the rooftop:

"Do it, Aiz."

Suddenly, *thump!*

"______"

With the unmistakable sound of boots on stone, the blond-haired, golden-eyed knight landed behind the monster's back.

"Understood."

A soft chant left her lips at the same moment she withdrew her silver saber.

"Awaken, Tempest."

Her beautiful voice sounded on the breeze.

The extremely short trigger spell activated her magic.

"—VUOOOO!"

Its back vulnerable, the minotaur immediately turned to swing with the magic weapon in its right hand.

The blond-haired, golden-eyed knight saw the electrified blade coming toward her and quietly whispered:

"Airiel."

Wind blew.

The moment it enveloped her body, she slashed forward with blinding speed.

Her blade—pierced the enemy's arm.

"_______________________."

Time stopped for *Hestia Familia*, the Xenos, and the black minotaur.

The wind-lined blade sent the magic weapon spinning along with most of the monster's right arm. It twirled through the air until it slammed blade-first into a broken piece of stone pavement with the handle sticking straight up.

Electrical energy pulsed through the ground underfoot as the gigantic monster reared back.

"——————————?!"

As the minotaur screamed into the sky, blood gushed from what was left of the creature's upper arm; everything from halfway above the elbow was gone.

Protected by the wind currents around her body, Aiz avoided the fountain of blood entirely. Every drop of blood was blown away.

Her Magic was called "Airiel."

A wind enchantment that enhanced the user's weapon and physical attributes.

As they didn't belong to her familia, that was all that Welf, Mikoto, and even Hestia understood.

—Aiz Wallenstein.

The only being other than adventurers not to be affected by the Howl, Hestia was taken by the girl's majestic appearance in that moment.

The Sword Princess. Aiz Wallenstein.

A prominent adventurer in both name and reality. Orario's strongest female knight.

Bell's idol.

Engulfed by wind, blond hair flowing in the breeze, she had the air of a fairy straight out of a hero's tale, and she was so beautiful that Hestia had to accept her as worthy of the boy's admiration.

The only one unfazed by the monster's Howl shaking the battlefield, the girl whipped her sword through the air.

"——OOOOOOOOOOOOOOOOOOOOOO!"

The minotaur, eyes wide open, swung the Labrys down in a counterattack.

It was a blow that had permanently removed many adventurers from battle. The monster's mobile guillotine.

And Aiz knocked it away with a single flick of her thin saber.

There was no time to take pride in her successful ambush that claimed her enemy's arm, nor could she let her guard down.

She stared down the flabbergasted monster, her golden eyes narrowing.

"Here I come."

She attacked at full strength, sword and wind combining into their own melody.

"~~~~~~~~~~~~~~~~~~~~~~~~~~~~AAH!"

It was a series of unrelenting, merciless strikes.

Aiz carved into her opponent's towering body, slashing from countless angles seemingly all at once.

Diagonal over the shoulder, upward arcing, spinning, down from overhead—the now one-armed minotaur had no hope of blocking them all. Gashes opened in the beast's incredibly tough black skin; lines appeared in the thick armor covering its body with every movement.

Facing a bladed storm, the minotaur stepped back for the first time.

"You know, Aiz's magic is sooo unfair!"

"You've only just noticed, bonehead...?"

She moved faster than Bete, hit harder than Tiona, and struck more often than Tione.

The Amazonian girl, unable to join the fight, watched in anguish. Next to her, a werewolf clicked his tongue in frustration at one of the main reasons the girl had become known as the Sword Princess: the power granted to her by the wind.

The monster stopped trying to defend itself and went on the attack. Aiz charged to meet it, their blades clashing with incredible force.

Saber crossed ax. There were no sparks in the air, only deafening wind. The currents pounding against the unyielding minotaur were far more powerful than normal, allowing Aiz's unholy technique to land three strikes in the time it took for her opponent to swing once.

She picked up speed.

Her face devoid of emotion, Aiz saw only the minotaur while blocking out everything else.

Her precise strikes escalated, as if she were pushing herself to a higher plane, progressing further than ever before.

Blood spewed from her enemy's large body with every howl of wind and every flash of silver.

"Th-that's..."

Although already taken, Hestia watched in shock, her face twitching as she gulped.

Mikoto was much the same, pale as a ghost and voice quivering.

"That's...the War Princess."

She'd heard the term somewhere before.

"War Princess."

A monster slayer wearing a girl's skin. The one standing atop a mountain of dead beasts. Fearless, ever prowling the deepest bowels of the Dungeon without tiring.

Welf, and even the other members of *Loki Familia*, beheld the incredible girl with a mixture of awe and fear as she danced amid the fountains of blood, though her wind protected her from the spray.

The wind screeched louder still over the battlefield.

"!"

The large body staggered. The enemy was off balance.

Wounded yet again, the minotaur had shown weakness. Aiz took the opening, determined.

Kicking off the ground with enough speed to turn the stone pavement into gravel behind her, Aiz put all her strength into a diagonal, over-the-shoulder blow to finish it off once and for all.

"——OO!!"

"?!"

However, the enemy's next move took Aiz by surprise.

Realizing that there wasn't enough time to counter with the Labrys, the minotaur swung its head instead—its mighty horns. The crimson projections deflected Aiz's wind-coated saber strike on contact.

With a suddenly vulnerable girl in its sights, the minotaur stuck its foot into the ground and swung the Labrys with all its might.

"?!"

Wind howled.

The beast's sheer strength tore apart the gale protecting the silver blade.

Blown back by the overwhelming force, Aiz's feet carved up the stone pavement before she finally came to a stop and examined her saber.

It was trembling, the wind enchantment completely obliterated.

Aiz's hand had gone numb after absorbing the devastating impact and could no longer maintain a strong grip on the hilt. While her face was still aloof, her golden eyes opened a little wider before looking up at what stood before her.

Huff! Huff! The blood-covered minotaur gasping for breath was smiling.

Even now, the beast was ferocious, gruff, and fearless.

Aiz's eyebrows furrowed, her eyes wide.

"Awaken, Tempest."

Airiel's currents engulfed her tingly arm once again, forcibly tightening her grip with the power of wind.

The minotaur howled at its powerful, unyielding adversary, swinging its ax directly into the charging Aiz's path.

Their blades collided as the battle started anew, the resulting clash knocking *Hestia Familia* and other onlookers backward, when suddenly…

"NGAH!"

"GOOH?!"

Just as Aiz appeared to have gained the upper hand, the battle was interrupted.

It was Gareth, equipped with heavy armor. Finally returning to the battlefield, the dwarf had dropped off Ikelos on top of a nearby building after a constant stream of complaints from the deity ("Brats these days, I swear…"), and then he had jumped down behind the minotaur and sliced the beast's back with his massive battle-ax.

"Aiz, pincer attack."

"…! But Gareth, I—"

"Ye're puttin' us all at risk, actin' like that. Tone down that ego—don'cha agree, Finn?"

A long spear answered Gareth's question by hurtling toward the monster.

"......?!"

"That I do. Then again, I might not be needed with you here, Gareth."

Having retrieved his spear, Finn had thrown it again, and he shrugged as it pierced the minotaur's shoulder. Whether he had sensed an issue with Aiz or not, he had temporarily set aside his duties as commander to join the battle himself.

Under his stern gaze, Aiz reluctantly nodded. Three seasoned first-tier adventurers surrounded the minotaur.

The monster put up a fight despite being seriously wounded, but it wasn't long before...*thud!*

"......!"

The battered, bruised, and bloody frame fell to one knee.

"Asterios...!"

Lido grimaced at the sight of the minotaur kneeling before the adventurers and their silver saber, massive battle-ax, and spear.

And so the last of his kind had been rendered unable to fight. He sensed the other Xenos like Gros and Rei shifting nearby as he glared at those adventurers' backs—when from out of nowhere, three black spheres were thrown into the middle of the street.

"!"

They broke open on contact with the pavement, spewing a stream of black smoke.

Lido's, Gros's, and Rei's eyes flashed with immediate recognition.

Fels's magic items.

"!"

"Smoke screen...!"

"This smoke, it's spreadin' out fast!!"

Aiz, Finn, and Gareth were stunned to see the swirling, intertwining smoke not only rushing toward them but threatening to engulf the entire battlefield.

A few seconds ahead of the first-tier adventurers, Lido and his two comrades exchanged knowing glances, gathered the last of their strength, and all moved as one.

"——————————————!!"

The gargoyle roared.

Other Xenos began to stir as the cry reached them, the minotaur immediately looking skyward.

While the tremendous roar was still ringing in their ears, the siren took to the air and unleashed a powerful, ever-expanding sound wave.

""""?!""""

The threatening wall of sound targeted only the first-tier adventurers. The three of them froze in place, bracing against the attack coming from behind.

Visual and aural senses.

They might have been first-tier adventurers, but a momentary lapse was inevitable without sight and sound.

——*! The minotaur's aura is...!*

Gone.

Limited by the smoke obscuring their vision, her ears under assault, Aiz couldn't believe it when the monster's presence seemed to disappear into the darkness.

"I've seen that...!"

—Meanwhile, Hestia's memory flared to life as she watched the black smoke inundate the street, hiding Aiz and the other adventurers from view.

On the moonlit night when she had met Fels for the first time, only a few days prior, this same smoke had come pouring from the black-robed figure's sleeves before the mage brought her to Ouranos. Another black sphere landed right in front of Hestia's group only a moment later, engulfing the area in a black fog.

"!"

Unable to hear Finn's or Gareth's voices due to the deafening sound waves, Aiz decided to use Airiel on her own.

The torrents of air surrounding her increased in velocity and cleared a space around her in a few moments.

Once the coiling, almost animal-like fog retreated far enough to see, it was true. The minotaur had vanished without a trace.

—Don't hold this against me!

Then…

The instant Aiz and the other adventurers emerged from the fog and into Lido's line of sight, he swelled up his chest like a balloon and released it all at once. Aiz, Gareth, and Finn had been distracted by the missing minotaur and swiftly turned to face this new threat, but they were too late.

An inferno came streaming out of Lido's mouth.

"A fire-breathin' lizardman…?!"

Aiz ignored Gareth's flabbergasted remark and enveloped them with a protective wall of wind. However, they weren't Lido's target.

The lizardman swept his head to the side along with the inferno, igniting a wide area.

"?!"

Aiz's wind alone wasn't enough to protect the residential buildings on either side of the street from the flames.

This being the slums, many flammable objects immediately caught fire. Wooden materials and magic-stone products ignited, turning the whole block into a hellscape right before their eyes.

"GROOOOOOOOOOOOOO!"

The siren and lizardman ceased their attacks and took off running the moment the gargoyle's voice echoed through the din.

The other monsters were already barreling through the backstreets; the Xenos were in full retreat.

"……!"

"…We're shorthanded as it is. Cruz and the others take priority."

Finn looked defeated as he ordered Aiz to stay put just as she was about to give chase. The three of them included, very few adventurers could still move.

"What is transpiring out there…?!"

Riveria stood motionless, making sure the barrier protecting the townspeople remained firmly in place.

She couldn't dismiss the magic due to the smoky black fog

obscuring her vision and keeping her from comprehending the situation—and her concern it might be poisonous. The people she was tasked to protect had become her fetters.

Without someone to orchestrate their movements after Finn joined the front line, *Loki Familia* had lost the offensive advantage.

The adventurers were quick to regroup once Finn retook command. Gareth went to Tiona, Tione, and Bete before collecting Ikelos and bringing them all to safety. Aiz also took part in the rescue effort. To contain the fire, uninjured magic users joined Riveria in freezing the area with ice magic and summoning streams of water to douse the flames. Even *Hestia Familia*, who was unable to side with either the Xenos or *Loki Familia*, pitched in.

The damage was contained to a single block within ten minutes thanks to the powerful magic users' efforts. The fire had been completely extinguished.

Pillars of black smoke rose above the stone street, now a charred, barren wasteland of rubble.

"Finn, what happened to that minotaur...?"

"...It's underground."

Aiz walked somberly through the middle of the street toward Finn, who was looking at the ground.

The paving stones had broken open from underneath to form a passageway to the area below.

"What's this...?"

"The hole that metallic giant left behind. That monster probably passed through here to enter the sewers."

Aiz looked with surprise at the hole where Fels's golem had emerged.

Indeed, there was a trail of blood leading into the darkness beneath the charred opening. The black monster had disappeared into this gap during the commotion.

"...Should we pursue?"

"Yes, please do...but considering how well they pulled off the escape, I think it's safe to say these armed monsters are quite intelligent. Please don't go after them alone."

Finn sighed as he answered Aiz's question, noticing that the minotaur's severed arm had also disappeared.

A little more time passed before other adventurers and Guild employees arrived on the scene in a flurry.

As people still suffering from the Howl received medical attention all around him, Finn looked up at the sky and reflected on his blunder.

"That was a mistake...This failure is on me."

The vicious monster howls, explosive echoes, and, above all, the stories of the townspeople fleeing from the labyrinthine district plunged the relatively calm Orario back into chaos.

As Royman and the rest of the Guild's upper management blanched and issued orders to every familia left and right, adventurers descended upon Daedalus Street in the city's third district, the southeast block.

"Keh...!"

The setting sun had nearly reached the city wall, burning one side of the boy's face.

Bell was running.

He was in hot pursuit of the vouivre destroying everything in its path.

"Wiene!"

Bell's scream didn't reach the wailing dragon girl as she plowed forward.

Breaking through walls and racing up stairwells, the vouivre and Bell burst out of the dungeon-like district, leaving the slum behind.

"Eep...! EEEEEEEEEEEEEEEEEEEEKK!"

"Hey, you—adventurer! Over here! It's over here!"

A group of demi-humans shrieked and scattered in all directions once they caught sight of the furious monster.

Leaving Daedalus Street meant that they were now careening through busier city roads, creating a ruckus and terrified cries.

Women dressed like courtesans called out to adventurers one after another.

Bell grew more anxious by the moment.

"Wiene, stop!"

"AAAAAAAaaa!"

He'd jumped onto her many times while passing through the dungeon town; he'd held on to her only to get bucked off by her undulating snakelike body. His hands were already cut up and bloodied from trying to hold on to her sharp dragon scales. Calling out to the girl had proven useless, making the task of returning the garnet jewel next to impossible.

Bell had clung to her dainty upper body, and her relentless convulsions had flung him around like a rag doll until he was dislodged by a collision with a street sign and rolled across the ground once again. Witnesses screamed, fearing for his life.

The curse should have lifted by now...!

The ominous red tint was gone from Wiene's eyes.

Dix's curse should have been broken. But even so, the dragon girl's rampage persisted.

Bell, blood flowing down his face, glanced at the messy puncture wound in Wiene's left hand.

—The spear that had pierced her.

As unfortunate as it was, there was a high possibility that Finn's spear attack had been exceptionally traumatic.

It was a reminder of Dix's spear, his scornful laughter, his wickedness.

The curse of his existence wouldn't go away.

"There it is! Right there!!"

"?!"

Unable to stop Wiene, adventurers started appearing one by one.

They were hesitant at first, seeing a crazed vouivre, a rare large-category monster like a lamia, charging toward them. However, they raised their weapons, determined not to let it come any closer.

Their longbow strings creaked with arrows at the ready; their fingers clasped around javelins; the jewels of their staffs glinted.

Bell screamed, enough to hurt his throat, at the adventurers lining the road and standing in their path.

"STOP—!"

However, Bell's cry was drowned out by the adventurers' shouts as they attacked.

A javelin plunged into the dragon's tail; an arrow pierced her shoulder; fire magic hit head-on. Countless broken scales fell from her body.

"————————————!"

A shrill howl came from Wiene.

Writhing in pain from the adventurers' merciless assault, she sped up in a desperate attempt to escape from the threat.

She bowled over the adventurers in her path.

"......!!"

Bell clenched his teeth so hard they nearly snapped.

As even more adversaries gathered in the vouivre's path, Bell cast aside the discord and doubt in his mind and thrust his right arm in their direction.

"Firebolt!!"

A round of Swift-Strike Magic raced toward the adventurers preparing to attack.

"The hell?!"

"?!"

"WHOOOOOOOOOOOOOAAA!"

At their feet, off their armor, into their bodies.

An electrified inferno ignited, knocking them onto their backs in an explosion of sparks.

Hot on Wiene's tail, Bell rounded on those who should be his allies, the adventurers.

"Little Rookie, you bastard!"

Red-faced adventurers roared at Bell as his burning lightning bolts interfered with their attacks.

Lower-class, upper-class adventurers, even their familia didn't matter. They all seethed at the lone newbie getting in their way.

Wide-eyed women and children peeked out from the higher

floors of buildings lining the street, bearing witness to his barbaric actions.

Was he crazy? Did he want the drop item that much? What was he thinking, at a time like this? Each one of his fellow adventurers' criticisms cut deep into his heart and made his hands quiver, but Bell continued casting his magic nonetheless. Protecting the vouivre, chasing her down.

The endless pursuit soon reached a new arena, the Pleasure Quarter reconstruction zone.

Formerly *Ishtar Familia*'s territory, it had been heavily damaged during the attack from *Freya Familia* that drove the former owners out of business. Many buildings still bore the scars of that day, and piles of debris were still rampant even for the Pleasure Quarter. Citizens had been forbidden to set foot in the area. Brothels stood in shambles; scattered barrels and ash covered the streets. A master-less Belit Babili overlooked a lonely, empty castle town.

The two barreled their way through the web of debris that filled the street.

A group of adventurers had circled ahead, waiting for Bell and Wiene directly in their path.

"......?"

Zing! Bell immediately knew something was off.

...They're not attacking?

Weapons held at rest, even the sounds of their pursuers had vanished.

The adventurers just stood to block Wiene's path or perhaps intimidatingly fire off their weapons, but the onslaught had stopped as far as Bell could see.

Almost like they'd given up...

—No, that wasn't it.

A cold chill zipped down the boy's spine the instant he revoked his own reassuring hypothesis.

They're leading her...!

All color left Bell's face a moment later.

"Wiene, don't go that way!"

She was being drawn into a trap.

Nothing else mattered to Bell once he realized it, and he screamed at the top of his lungs.

A human alongside a dwarf with a massive shield at the ready appeared in their path. The vouivre veered away, racing down a different passage to avoid the people blockade. Bell reached out to grab her tail, but an arrow crossed just in front of him, denying him the opportunity.

It came from an animal person on top of a nearby roof as if to say, "Don't get in the way."

"……?"

Then Bell's wish was proven to be in vain.

The dim backstreet suddenly opened into a wide area that was illuminated by the setting sun.

It was like a bowl, a clearing surrounded by a ring of rubble.

The vouivre broke through an iron gate, shattering the bars with astonishing force before the ground disappeared beneath her, and she fell all the way to the bottom.

The stone pavement crumbled with a series of crashes until she came to a stop at the very center. Countless adventurers stood on the rim looking down at her from all directions.

The adventurers had conspired together—across familias.

Bell's heart pounded even louder at the sight of so many magic users prepared to release the spells they had on standby.

He dove into the clearing without missing a step.

"Little Rookie! Stand down!"

"You crazy or something?! You'll die!"

Adventurers shouted angry warnings at the boy the moment he landed.

"Doesn't matter! Just do iiit!"

A man who seemed to have lost himself in the chaos shouted from somewhere around the rim, and his voice set everything in motion.

Innumerable flashes of magical energy erupted in a volley of simultaneous spells.

"————————."

The fusillade descended directly toward the center of the clearing.

Wiene's eyes shrank, her face briefly illuminated before the light engulfed her.

"AAAAAAAAAAAAAAAAAAAAAAAAAAAAAAAAAAAAA!"

Magic explosions drowned out the monster's shriek.

Wiene disappeared amid the roaring wind.

"———!"

Bell raced forward.

Streaking flames, electrical discharges, and icy wind rocked his body back and forth as he made a break for the middle of the clearing.

No matter how much his skin was scorched, his hair sizzled, or his body burned with frost, Bell rushed to reach the girl at the eye of the swirling vortex of magic energy.

A wordless scream burst from his lungs.

Time slowed to a nauseating crawl.

Trapped in this world without time, Bell reached out.

There, amid the flickering magic energy, was a scale-less dragon monster staring up at the sky.

Smoke was rising from all over its body; its faint silver-blue hair swished back and forth as its ash-colored extremities started rotting away.

Catching a glimpse of the approaching boy, she looked at him with vacant eyes as her lips formed one word:

Bell.

"!!!!"

Bell thrust his hand forward with all his strength and was just about to reach her, when suddenly—

A crimson spearhead plunged through her chest.

"———."

The missile had been thrown from behind Bell.

It was a cursed blade with a deep-seated grudge.

"HAH! Hya-ha-ha-ha! AH-HA-HA-HA-HA-HA-HA-HA! Got it! I finished it off!"

A large man hooted with the scornful laughter of the insane.

Half his face missing, the stocky human's cackling set time in motion again.

The skewered girl's body started to tilt ever so slightly in front of Bell's eyes.

"—Wiene!"

Just as the crying boy's scream rang out—the ground gave way.

"What's that?!"

"It's caving in!"

The clearing crumbled at the center, the focal point of the magic volley.

The stones disappeared from beneath his feet, and he fell right along with her.

Bell grabbed hold of the girl falling into darkness and embraced her.

Adventurers and magic users shielded their faces with their arms, motionlessly observing the scene below.

A cave-in.

Swelling clouds of dust in the air.

A gaping hole had opened in the center of the bowl, making the area resemble a man-made inverse anthill. *Crumble! Crack!* A few stone fragments collapsed into the hole as if only just realizing what had happened.

Designed by Daedalus himself, secret underground passageways crisscrossed beneath the Pleasure Quarter. One of these underground tunnels passed under the bowl, meaning the space beneath the clearing was hollow to begin with. Unable to withstand the cascade of magic, the stone pavement had collapsed in on itself.

A few adventurers cleared their throats, filling the silence.

The boy and the vouivre had fallen deep into the hole and disappeared without a trace.

"Ha-ha-ha-ha-ha-ha-ha-ha!"

There was a large human among them, laughing like a madman.

It was *Ikelos Familia*'s Gran. The last surviving hunter had used a key to return to the surface via Knossos's stairwell and, lost in his own rage, hurled Dix's spearhead at Wiene.

"Did you see that, Dix?! I killed the beast, killed it dead! Me, all me——!"

"!!"

A gargoyle claw plummeted from the sky and crushed the deranged man.

Gros had witnessed the shining beacon from the air after escaping from *Loki Familia* and led the winged monsters in a dash to the clearing. That was when he saw it.

The gargoyle, having ended the hunter's life for sure this time, stood amid the adventurers' screams and gawked at the hole where Bell and Wiene had fallen, trembling.

"——OOOOOOOOOOOOOOOOOOOOO!!"

"A flying monster?! What's it so upset about?!"

"Dammit, let's get out of here!"

The Xenos went wild.

With the last vestiges of strength in their badly injured bodies, they rushed after the screaming adventurers in full retreat.

All so that the boy and girl could spend their last moments together uninterrupted.

A steady stream of sand and rubble poured down around them like an hourglass counting down the remaining time.

The stone and debris of a dark underground tunnel surrounded them.

A red sky looked down on Bell embracing the girl's limp body from a hole over their heads.

"Wiene...Wiene?!"

Eyes glistening with tears, he took hold of the cursed spearhead lodged in her chest.

The curse was already eating into her flesh. Pulling the wickedly curved blade from the girl's body, Bell cast it aside with a dry *clang*.

The light-blue body twitched.

Bell withdrew the garnet jewel from his pouch and pressed it into the limp girl's forehead.

Although a faint flicker passed through the reddish stone, the girl in his arms didn't move.

In fact—*thud!*

The long dragon tail was turning to ash.

"...?!"

Deep inside the spear wound in her chest...

The bloody purple crystal just visible inside the opening was cracked.

Outer portions of her body turned to ash, falling away as the crack expanded.

"No...Don't!!"

Bell kept yelling, bawling like a child.

Don't, don't do this—don't go. He repeated the same words over and over again.

An endless stream of tears fell from his eyes, squeezed shut, and dripped onto her cheeks as she lay weakly in his embrace.

"...Be...ll?"

"!"

Bell's eyes flew open the instant he heard her weak whispers, barely more than breaths.

Wiene was awake. The light had returned to her amber eyes, peeking out from behind her cracked eyelids.

Her cheeks were still solid and elongated.

She gazed up at Bell, so feebly she seemed about to expire at any moment.

"Wiene......!"

"...Be...ll...I'm...so sorry."

She apologized in a hoarse voice, fixated on Bell's bleeding face.

As the sound of crumbling ash grew louder in his ears, Bell shook his head over and over.

He laughed through his tears with a smile that could hardly pass as genuine.

"I'm fine, just fine, so...don't worry about me, just...!! Please, Wiene—!"

—Don't disappear.

Bell tightened his grip on her shoulder, pleading with all his heart.

Trembling, Wiene pressed her cheek against the boy's chest, smiling as if all was right with the world while tears welled up in her amber eyes.

Fsh...a faint sound came from her chest as her dragon abdomen crumbled to the floor.

"...I...had a dream."

"You did...?"

Only Wiene's humanlike torso remained as she gazed up into Bell's wide eyes.

"No one...would save me...It was so scary."

She was turning to ash in his arms.

The last moments of her life ticking away, Wiene lifted a quivering hand.

"But, you know?"

It softly brushed against his cheek, crumbling on contact.

Her voice barely audible between sobs, Wiene continued.

"This time...someone came...Someone saved me."

Bell's eyes opened as wide as they would go.

"I'm so happy..."

She closed her eyes, and a single transparent tear ran down her cheek.

Her lips parted, but a single dream, one tiny desire, held her close.

In that moment, the exceptional girl was whole.

Her body was dissolving.

The girl's form was becoming unrecognizable.

"Thank you," she said to the shocked boy.

As she cried, a smile bloomed on her lips.

Then...

"Bell...I love you."

* * *

She was gone.

She had crumbled.

Ash flowed through Bell's fingers.

Her warmth had vanished.

"———."

Time stood still as unyielding tears silently slid down Bell's cheeks.

The motes of ash drifted gently around him, glimmering in the light and fading as his memories of her did the same.

Their meeting.

The fear.

The sadness.

Bewilderment.

Touch.

Gratitude.

Name.

Joy.

Smile.

Embrace.

Tears.

Amid the ash falling from his chest, only the beautiful reddish jewel remained intact.

"Agh, aaggghhhhhhhhhhhhh—"

His heart was breaking.

A hole had opened in his core.

His throat quivered, but just before a wail could follow...

"O untrodden domain, O forbidden wall. Today on this day, I turn my back on the laws of heaven—"

The words of a spell echoed.

"?!"

Tears flew from his cheeks as Bell whirled around to look over his shoulder. It was the black-robed mage.

"Rod of Asclepius, Goblet of Salus. O ye who is beyond the power of healing—I ask you to wait."

A white magic circle expanded by the moment. The twinkling magic energy surpassed the realms of human comprehension.

Bell watched with wide eyes as Fels continued to chant in a loud voice.

"Lord's judgment, lightning of conviction. Shall I be burned, rejecting your providence—"

The white magic energy illuminating the underground tunnel burst through the hole overhead, forming a white pillar that reached to the heavens.

Everyone in Orario, both monsters and people, spotted the beam piercing the twilight.

"That light—Fels?!"

"......?!"

Rei and Gros had successfully driven off the adventurers and were now carrying a badly injured Lido over their shoulders. The lizardman whispered in disbelief as all three stared at the bright light coming out from the cracks in the pavement under their feet.

"Lady Hestia!!"

"A deity being sent home...? No, it's not!"

Hestia was checking up on her familia's condition when Welf got her attention by pointing to the pillar of light.

"Finn..."

"From the Pleasure Quarter...Bell Cranell—no, the vouivre?"

Loki Familia's adventurers stared up at the heavens as well.

"Using that now, are you, Fels...?"

A wizened deity closed his eyes.

"That light, how many times have I seen it now?"

A silver-haired Goddess of Beauty smiled from her vantage point at the top of the giant tower.

"Somethin' big's goin' down..."

So said a goddess with cinnabar-red hair, sitting cross-legged on a rooftop.

"A miracle if I've ever seen one."

A god narrowed his eyes beneath his traveler's hat.

"—*I shall journey to the realm of the dead myself.*"

The song's tempo increased.

As the magic circle glowed even brighter, Bell's face and the black robe disappeared in the white light.

"*Gates of Charon, over the river of time. Lend your ears, O Lord. Listen to this deranged melody.*"

It was a reverberating, majestic tune. A divine harmony.

And a sinful deed that went against the laws of the earth.

"*Never-ending tears, lamenting wails. The price has already been paid.*"

It was taboo magic conjured with an extremely long chant.

It could overturn predetermined fate, a secret technique capable of defying an irreversible, absolute truth.

"*O path of light. I ask you to sacrifice the given past and cast light on this foolish desire.*"

Resurrection magic granted to only the Sage of old.

"*Yes, I will not turn away.*"

The conjuring was complete, the magic energy at its peak.

And a request was made in exchange for all of Fels's Mind.

"Dia Orpheus."

The pillar of light began to flake apart.

In its place, millions upon millions of light fractals overwhelmed the underground tunnel.

Sparkling white jewels fell like snow. Bell's wide eyes glittered with the reflections as a high-pitched tone filled the air, and the pieces began spiraling into a single point.

Lastly, soft blue light from beneath the magic circle swirled into Bell's chest.

The light pillar shattered a moment later with the sound of breaking glass.

Bell reflexively shut his eyes to protect them against the blinding flash that turned the world white for an instant, shuddering as weight and warmth returned to his chest.

Slowly, cautiously, Bell opened his eyes as if in prayer...only to see the dragon girl, eyes closed and curled up against his chest.

"Aa———."

A small cry escaped him as his vision blurred and he placed a hand on her cheek.

Cold. And yet warm. He felt a soft beat. She was breathing.

She had four supple, humanlike limbs. Gone were the dragon wings, and the piles of ash on the floor were noticeably smaller than before.

The reddish jewel embedded in her forehead started to glow, spotlighting Bell's eyes.

"...That...was my first success."

Plop! A dull *thud* sounded soon after.

The black-robed mage fell to a seat on the floor behind Bell, every ounce of energy and willpower spent.

"Eight hundred years, has it been...? How I loathed this pointless magic, this useless hope that took up one of my Status slots all this time..."

Bell met the mage's gaze, certain he could feel a smile coming from beneath the hood.

Fels looked up, staring into empty space.

"But yes...there was a point."

Tears flowed from Bell's eyes as he watched Fels struggle to form the words.

The boy then turned his attention to the girl, feeling the warmth in her cheek once again—and embraced her with all his strength.

A single, transparent tear trickled out from between the girl's closed eyelids.

The sun sank into the west.

The white pillar piercing the heavens had vanished without a trace.

The world had been momentarily cast in white light, but it was now silent. Twilight returned to Orario, leaving behind only confused townspeople and the excited whispers of deities.

In a corner of the slum in the white tower's shadow…

Finn was receiving an update underneath the evening light.

"Sorry, Finn…A water main broke halfway through…and we had to give up the chase."

"The winged monsters that appeared in the Pleasure Quarter also vanished into the sewers beneath the broken courtyard…There's no trace of them."

"I see…What of Bell Cranell? The vouivre?"

"He is still missing. However, on the spot where he fell along with the vouivre…we discovered traces of blood among a great deal of what appeared to be monster ashes."

Finn said nothing, running his tongue along the base of his thumb as he listened to Aiz and Riveria's report.

Out of the corner of his eye, he took note of Aiz's reaction to Riveria's information and added, "All right, thank you," with a nod. The prum general dismissed the two women and cast his gaze back over the battlefield.

"So they got away in the end…"

He whispered while surveying the damaged and burned cityscape.

At long last, he started issuing new orders to *Loki Familia*, which had been busy helping the other adventurers attending to the wounded and rescuing people from the rubble.

"……"

Aiz watched him in silence before gazing at her own hand, then silently raised her head toward the sky.

The red sun was about to sink below the city.

Bell quietly stared ahead, hidden deep in the shadows where the evening light could never reach.

"Wiene, Wiene…!"

"Th-thank goodness…!"

They had arrived at the entrance to a drainage canal located deeper inside the city's sewer network.

Concealed behind a trapdoor, this tunnel was surprisingly large and resembled an area beneath a bridge. Bell had a feeling he'd been here before, but he couldn't place it at the moment.

Bell, Fels, Wiene, and all the Xenos who had been able to make it this far had hidden in this drainage canal, which was still beyond the adventurers' range.

Lido, Gros, and Rei, as well as a lamia and a troll, were all huddled around Wiene in front of Bell. Although she had yet to wake up, the Xenos were trembling and crying tears of joy to see that their comrade was safe and sleeping soundly.

"...Fels."

"What troubles you, Bell Cranell?"

Bell wanted to pose a question to the mage, who was standing outside the ring of the Xenos just like him.

"Are they all that's left of the Xenos who came up to the surface...?"

"No, there are Xenos who have yet to regroup. You might not be aware, but many of them were separated during the retreat from *Loki Familia* and are still hiding in the city, or..."

Fels's words hung in the air, and Bell closed his mouth.

Bell could count the Xenos survivors in front of him on his fingers. He was concerned for the safety of all the monsters who had rushed into the battle to buy time for Wiene and himself.

Lost in his train of thought, Bell focused again on the Xenos surrounding Wiene.

"Bell Cranell..."

Still exhausted from the earlier spell, Fels spoke in a meek voice while leaning against the wall.

"May I ask as to why you seem upset?"

Fels stepped forward immediately, pressing for the boy's thoughts as he looked upon the Xenos with a heavy heart.

"......"

"The Xenos were saved thanks to your efforts. That is no lie. The same is true for Wiene. You have my gratitude as well."

"I..."

"Regret your decision, do you?"

You regret the actions you chose to take?

That was the question, but implied rather than spoken.

Bell immediately started to shake his head, but then stopped and stared at the ground as he answered.

"That man…The adventurer who wore goggles said something to me."

The tyrannical hunter who had captured and tortured the Xenos.

Bell repeated Dix's words.

"That…I'm a hypocrite."

"……"

The goggled man had declared and laughed scornfully at him.

He claimed that Bell's decision was nothing more than pretty words, an absurd dream, a fabrication.

Nothing more than a "bat" flapping back and forth, unable to make up its mind.

—He was correct.

Bell was desperate not to get driven out by the people but lent the monsters a helping hand.

He'd become the target of *Loki Familia*'s hostility.

He'd attacked other adventurers with his magic.

Bell remembered everything.

He had betrayed so many during his single-minded effort to save the girl.

He'd stood opposite his idol, driven away his allies.

He'd even turned his back on his desire to be a hero according to his grandfather's teachings. He had been that close to leaving it all behind.

A monumental feeling of powerlessness had been waiting for him at the end of it all.

For without assistance from Fels, the other Xenos, Lyu, and so many others, he would never have been able to rescue Wiene.

He was unable to protect or save anyone—a hypocrite.

That man's laughter resounded deep in his ears once again.

"……"

Fels listened to the boy's answer as he hunched over.

Stepping away from the wall, the mage turned toward Bell.

"Bell Cranell, this is nothing more than a theory…However, I see it like this: Only those criticized for hypocrisy possess the necessary qualities to become a hero."

Bell's eyes flew open, and he looked up.

"Please continue to worry, feel anguish, and doubt as you make decisions, like today."

"Fels…"

"Heroes have to make decisions that are sometimes cruel, heartless, and go unforgiven…but they are also the most noble."

Bell couldn't help but feel that Fels was smiling deep within the darkness underneath the hood.

"Because your answer—just like the heroes' of old—was not wrong, no matter how scorned or criticized it might be."

Fels's words touched his very soul. Bell had no response and could not answer.

It took everything he had to manage the emotions coursing through his heart.

"Allow me to speak as one who has lost flesh and skin. I, a mage composed of nothing but bones and regret, say this to you."

The long-lived, black-robed skeleton got to the point at last.

"Be a fool, Bell Cranell."

"……"

"You are the one who must do so. What you possess seems foolish to us…However, I'm absolutely sure it is irreplaceable in the eyes of the gods."

Fels stepped aside, allowing Bell to see the monsters again.

"Bell, thank you, thank you so much…!"

"Sorry, Bellucchi…And thanks!"

"…Thank you. You have…my gratitude."

Bell's vision blurred at the sentiment of these monsters who could never see eye to eye with people.

He took one look at the sleeping dragon girl, and his throat trembled.

"There were many who showed compassion and shared an

unusual bond with the Xenos just like you...However, none of them were able to care for and save them, as you have just done.

"Thank you."

Bell looked back down at his feet upon hearing those appreciative words.

The boy's back was toward the setting sun, and the last of its rays dyed the sky red as they caressed the boy's cheek.

You don't have to be proud.

You can doubt yourself.

But never ever regret.

Because lives saved by foolish hypocrisy are surely right before you.

—He felt as though the red rays had borrowed his grandfather's voice to tell him so.

EPILOGUE THE DECISION'S COST

He walked through city streets illuminated by the western sun.

The sky was still red. Bell had parted ways with the Xenos and was now en route to Daedalus Street.

Although it pained him to leave before Wiene woke up, he left her in their hands.

The public would be more than just suspicious should anyone see him together with her. Fels joined Lido's group to help the Xenos who were now scattered about the surface.

Bell walked with his head down, so as to not draw attention.

He'd arrived on one of the mazelike district's main streets where *Hestia Familia* and *Loki Familia* were most likely still around. He couldn't just run home and let the whole thing blow over.

Bell had to see with his own eyes exactly what had happened, what his decisions had caused.

No one had shouted at him on his way through the city streets—but the situation changed the moment he set foot back here.

"......?!"

Guild employees rushed about; injured people sprawled out on the ground. Several broken walls also looked familiar. People in the area started to notice the pale boy taking in the sights as he passed through.

Townspeople, adventurers, and Guild employees glared daggers in his direction.

He was the boy who had prioritized his own greed, protected a monster, and pursued it himself for money, and they silently criticized him with a vengeance.

"Yo, Bell Cranell. You get that dragon's jewel?"

"Why would you do it...? And *Loki Familia* was fighting so hard for us."

"Some adventurer you are...Little Rookie, my ass!"

Although it wasn't long before people he'd never met began to take out their anger on him.

They didn't hide their merciless contempt for the boy as he trudged through the street.

Hostility, hatred, and despair.

Never having been faced with these dark human emotions before, Bell's breath caught in his throat.

The name of the "Little Rookie," renowned ever since his victory in the War Game, had fallen from grace.

Fame and high hopes could be lost with a single action. They were two sides to the same coin. One side meant trust; the other, disappointment.

Bell had betrayed them all. The coin would never flip.

As he encountered the anger of those hurt by his actions, Bell felt his trembling hands turn cold as he endured and pressed on.

Then…

"——."

Bell came to a halt when he arrived at the street.

The stone pavement was split and broken everywhere. Mountains of debris occupied spaces where houses once stood. There were charred remnants of the battle. The devastation told him one thing—this was what his decision had cost.

"Bell…"

Hestia stood off to the side of the road. Welf and Mikoto were with her. Lilly and Haruhime looked physically ill. It made Bell's heart ache.

"……"

Aiz was a short distance away. She was staring in his direction with the rest of *Loki Familia* looming behind her. While some were busy at work, there were others who clearly wanted to give him a piece of their minds. Bell swallowed hard.

"……!"

Then, several Guild employees came into view, along with what was the main battleground.

Amid all the venomous glares, one of the women caught sight of him and immediately rushed over.

She had swishing brown hair, emerald-green eyes behind her glasses, and pointed half-elf ears.

"Miss...Eina..."

Eina came to a stop right in front of the dazed boy.

Her piercing gaze was accompanied by a deep frown, a severe expression that he'd never seen on her before.

No one dared approach.

Everyone around stood completely still; the silence seemed deafening to Bell's ears.

Eina slowly opened her mouth.

"You put numerous people in danger for self-centered reasons. You even attacked other adventurers——Is this true?"

—It's not.

He wanted to say so.

The last thing he wanted was for her of all people to get the wrong idea.

Unfortunately, he couldn't say anything for Wiene's sake—for all the Xenos.

Bell hung his head and answered.

"...Yes."

A moment later—*SLAP!*

A dry impact accompanied the pain in his cheek.

Eyes wide with shock, he looked up. Eina stood with her right hand out and tears in her eyes—she was angry.

"I don't believe you...!"

Then tears spilled from her emerald eyes.

"I could never...believe you...!"

Crying, Eina wrapped her arms around Bell.

She had seen through his lie, and she was angry that he was hiding the truth, pained by his unwillingness to talk to her.

Bell was speechless as Eina hung off him and hiccupped between sobs.

—Lend a weeping lady your shoulder, hold her.

His grandfather's teachings echoed in the back of his mind, and both of Bell's arms rose to the middle of Eina's back...before falling limp at his sides.

—Gramps, I...

I don't know what to do.

It was his fault that Eina, whom he practically saw as his older sister, was weeping. The people around them forgot themselves watching the miserable scene.

Hestia and her familia quietly observed them.

With both of Eina's arms wrapped around his shoulders, Bell raised his head toward the sky.

The darkening red reflected off his eyes.

It was early morning.

The sun still had yet to rise, and the sky was a light-gray hue.

The rain that had fallen through the night had finally lifted. Amid a light morning fog, the northernmost gate of Orario's city wall opened.

"So my days in Orario have come to a close...but I never thought you'd be the one to see me off, Ganesha."

"It is because...I am Ganesha."

Ikelos stood before the open gate, just about to walk out as Ganesha and his followers stood witness. The wheat-skinned deity's navy-blue hair swished to the side as he flashed a grin at the masked god and said, "You know, that's not an answer."

Loki Familia had brought Ikelos before the Guild, where he admitted to his familia's involvement in black-market dealings. He had also confirmed that they had been capturing monsters behind the Guild's back.

It was determined that his familia's activities had caused the monster surface breach that had sent the city into chaos, and he was therefore permanently exiled from the city two days after the incident as punishment.

With all his followers gone and his familia's assets confiscated, the deity was expelled with nothing but the clothes on his back.

"Well, sure beats being sent back up to heaven."

"The Guild certainly considered that, and I hear there was much debate."

"I know, I know. They needed a scapegoat to make a scene, right? After all my familia did, can't really blame them…"

Ganesha was silent beneath his mask as he watched Ikelos accept his fate with a grin.

The Guild had granted townspeople entry into the North Gate to witness the send-off and, despite the early morning hour, a large crowd of people and deities had gathered. They were all here to see Ikelos leave with their own eyes.

"But you know…my only regret is that I lost my front-row seat. Just when things were starting to get good."

Ikelos looked back inside the gate, taking in Orario for the last time.

"I'm jealous, Hermes."

"—To sum it all up, things are starting to settle down."

Hermes casually opened his arms toward the elderly deity and brought his report to a close.

Beneath Guild Headquarters, in the Chamber of Prayers, Ouranos at his altar and Hermes were conducting a secret meeting amid the light of four torches in the darkness.

"I've got my children out combing the city, but they can't find too many people upset with the Guild. That's probably all thanks to Ikelos taking the blame and responsibility."

Ikelos and his followers were being held accountable for allowing monsters to escape onto the surface and putting the city in danger. There was no one else to blame, so all the criticism was concentrated on him. The Guild had managed to alleviate the situation for now by sentencing the culprit. The fact that this incident was no longer considered a "monster surface breach" also benefited their cause.

The deity played his role as a scapegoat, agreeing to permanent exile.

"The public is still not aware that sentient monsters exist. But then again, Rivira's residents saw armed monsters, and there's the connection between the eighteenth floor and Daedalus Street...It's only a matter of time before people figure out there's a way into the Dungeon outside of Babel."

However, only a few familias and the Guild knew about Knossos.

"I leave the rest up to you," Hermes remarked offhandedly. "From what I've seen, this incident already seems to be going away, so there's no problem."

Ouranos opened his mouth to speak to the dandy deity, who was trying to wrap it all up with a nice bow.

"However, it is not over."

"I know," Hermes said with a nod before him.

"The Xenos who escaped from *Loki Familia*...As none of them can return to the Dungeon, they live in constant fear of adventurer search parties. Their lives are on the line."

"Kind of ironic, finally getting to see the surface like they always wanted but having to go back into the Dungeon to survive. Problem is, the Guild's higher-ups have not only kept Babel off-limits but they've sealed off Daedalus Street as well. Not to mention Loki's children are standing watch all over. They have no way to get home."

"It's only a matter of time until the Xenos are captured, along with Fels for protecting them..."

With the world against them, Hermes ventured, "How about bringing Loki into the fold? Slim as our chances are."

The god slumped when Ouranos responded with perfectly composed silence. He widened his narrow eyes, his aura changing instantaneously.

"Ouranos, you are the pillar of strength holding up the Guild and the city itself. If you pray for peace and order to continue within Orario's walls, you must symbolize those very things."

"......"

"Even if there are undertakings you'd like to keep hidden, anything that would dirty your reputation..."

"...I'm aware."

Hermes's continuous chattering finally elicited a response from Ouranos.

The dandy deity smiled the instant he heard that answer.

"—So then, Ouranos, why not put me in charge of keeping further incidents under control?"

"...What is your thinking, Hermes?"

"What's with that tone? I just want to get in your good graces. Think of it as a reward for working as your pawn."

That was Hermes's request.

"I can't allow that boy—Bell Cranell—to up and disappear. I've bet everything on him, Ouranos."

Public opinion had shifted drastically, and many now hated the young adventurer.

Hermes declared his intent to prevent the boy from being destroyed and exiting center stage.

"Why do you favor the boy so?"

Without offering any of his personal feelings toward the boy, Ouranos decided to ask the deity directly.

Hermes grinned.

"Because he's a parting gift from Zeus, maybe?"

Crackle! A sudden burst of sparks from the torches illuminated Ouranos's wide eyes.

The elderly god remained silent and slowly closed his eyes.

"May I have your cooperation this time, Ouranos?"

The elderly deity remained silent in the face of the dandy god's dark smile, accepting of all things good and evil—and nodded.

A bluish night sky looked down over a pile of rubble on the outskirts of town.

A single monster had concealed itself in the shadows, breathing ever so quietly.

The black minotaur, missing an arm.

The blood, still flowing from open wounds, had dyed its black fur a rusty crimson. *Drip, drip.* The Labrys protruded from the blood-splattered ground at the bleeding minotaur's side. The monster's incredible vitality was the only thing keeping it alive.

"......"

The tranquility was so complete, the thrill of battle felt like a distant dream. The monster slowly shifted its gaze to the hole in the crumbling ceiling overhead.

The sky on the surface. It could see innumerable pinpricks of starlight that didn't exist in the Dungeon.

A waning quarter moon appeared from behind wispy, flowing clouds.

It was shining white tonight.

Gone was the golden glow, replaced by cold light.

The monster gazed at the white crescent as though searching for something it had yet to find.

【BELL • CRANELL】
BELONGS TO: *HESTIA FAMILIA*
RACE: HUMAN
JOB: ADVENTURER
DUNGEON RANGE: TWENTIETH FLOOR
WEAPON: HESTIA KNIFE
CURRENT FUNDS: 81,200 VALIS

STATUS

Lv. 3

STRENGTH: D 577 DEFENSE: D 508 DEXTERITY: D 582
AGILITY: A 807 MAGIC: D 531 LUCK: H IMMUNITY: H

《MAGIC》

【FIREBOLT】
- SWIFT-STRIKE MAGIC

《SKILL》

【LIARIS FREESE】
- RAPID GROWTH
- CONTINUED DESIRE RESULTS IN CONTINUED GROWTH
- STRONGER DESIRE RESULTS IN STRONGER GROWTH

【ARGONAUT】
- CHARGES AUTOMATICALLY WITH ACTIVE ACTION

《DAEDALUS ORB》

- A KEY USED INSIDE THE ARTIFICIAL LABYRINTH KNOSSOS TO OPEN THE ORICHALCUM DOORS.
- CREATED FROM MYTHRIL AND THE EYES OF THE FAMOUS ARCHITECT DAEDALUS'S DESCENDANTS. THE FOLLOWING GENERATION CRAFTED THE ORBS BY CARVING OUT THE EYES OF THEIR DECEASED FOREBEARS.
- THE EYE HAS A "D" MARK ON THE SURFACE. ONE SUCH ORB WAS IN THE POUCH LYU GAVE TO BELL.
- IT'S UNKNOWN HOW THE ORB CAME TO BE IN HER POSSESSION. PERHAPS LYU STOLE IT FROM SOMEONE...?

Afterword

The other day, I had an opportunity to talk with Tsuyoshi Nanajyou, a fellow author and coworker of mine at GA Bunko, about a certain strategy RPG.

"Book nine's cover artwork, the one that just went on sale—she looks a lot like Tiki, don't you think?"

"…I didn't notice that before, but yes, she does~."

I know everything. The look in Mr. Nanajyou's eyes was terrifying.

There's quite a bit that I would like to write here.

I could talk about how the plot became so difficult to work with that I nearly threw my pen across the room, the problems that introducing so many new characters caused, how much it took established characters out of the spotlight, how I couldn't establish the presence I wanted for the minotaur heroine, how I became nauseous thinking of 800 years' worth of failures, my history with Mr. Nanajyou and Tiki, and how he told me at the last moment.

I faced many problems writing this volume, but I feel like what happened at the end is what saved me. Thank you, Tiki. Sorry for always using the Aum Staff.

With that out of the way, this is the tenth book. I hope it was worth the wait.

While I'm both shocked and honored to reach such a milestone, I'm most grateful for being able to write what I want. I will continue to challenge the rules of the fantasy genre as well as myself to continuously produce interesting content.

Changing topics, I would like to say that while making books nine and ten into two halves of the same story was damaging enough, the original plan was to have characters from book five of the side story, slated for simultaneous release, involved with the plot as well. "The reason this character had this item was because…" That would have been fleshed out in the side story, but it would have taken too much away from this book. I believe readers who have not read the side story would have taken a very serious issue with this, so I've made the decision to proceed with the main story in a way that readers won't have to read both series to enjoy. Please don't worry.

And now to stop with the apologies.

To my supervisor at GA Bunko, Mr. Kotaki; to Mr. Suzuhito Yasuda, who once again came through with beautiful illustrations for this volume; and to everyone who lent their support, please allow me to express my gratitude here. This series couldn't have reached ten volumes without all your help and support. It is thanks to you and, of course, to my readers above all else. Thank you so much for your constant encouragement.

I would also like to say thank you to Mr. Ponkan ⑧, for creating the limited-edition cover illustrations at release and to Mr. Kunieda for bringing this world to life in comic form. I'm extremely grateful for your work.

Nothing would make me happier than to meet again in the next volume. I'll take my leave until then.

Fujino Omori